A Cry in the Night

By Alison Bruce

A Cry in the Night
Cambridge Blue
The Siren
The Calling
The Silence

A Cry in the Night

A Gary Goodhew Mystery

ALISON BRUCE

WITNESS
IMPULSE
An Imprint of HarperCollinsPublishers

Previously published in the UK under the title *The Backs* by Constable, an imprint of Constable & Robinson Ltd, 2013.

First U.S. edition published under the title *The Backs* by SohoConstable, an imprint of Soho Press Inc., 2013.

EPub Edition NOVEMBER 2014 ISBN: 9780062314079

Print Edition ISBN: 9780062314086

10 9 8 7 6 5 4 3 2 1

Iakona,
Aloha Aku No, Aloha Mai No,
Alekona x

Acknowledgements

Thank you to Krystyna Green, Peter Lavery, Sophie Brewer, Saskia Angenent, Jo Stansall and the entire team at Constable & Robinson; I am very grateful for the support you have given the Goodhew series and I love the new cover designs . . . especially this one!

And to my agent Broo Doherty, I truly appreciate all the support and advice you have given me, as always. Thank you so much, Broo.

And also thank you to my lovely sister Stella, to Genevieve Pease, Jane Martin, Claire Tombs, Sue Gully, Gary Goodhew, Justin and Chris Lansdowne, Charlotte Hockin, Ayo Onatade, Cath Staincliffe, Kelly Kelday, Kirsty Forsyth, Cressi Downing, Jon and Gabrielle Breakfield, Jayne-Marie Barker, Edith Welter and Joyce Reeves, James Linsell-Clark, Christine Bartram, Dave Sivers, David Prestidge, Lisa Hall, Barbara and Graeme Key, Jim and Anne Cross, Brenda Mead. And thanks to the Goodhew series I'm delighted to be back in touch with old friends Beris Cumming, Emily Merrick and Ali DiMaggio.

Special thanks: to Steve Mosby and Richard Reynolds for their generosity. To the Royal Literary Fund for their support and also the privilege of being appointed as an RLF Fellow. To Dr William Holstein for specialist advice and entertaining emails, and to Kimberly Jackson for creating a jaunty but sinister three-word phrase. To Miles Orchard: I wrote you a sentence; it's to make you smile, Chadwick!

Thanks to everyone who's emailed me about the books, Goodhew and my music choices. I'm on Twitter@Alison_ Bruce and can also be contacted via my website, www.alisonbruce.com. Once again the readers I've met libraries, bookshops and reading groups have made it a very special year. Thank you all.

Finally, and most importantly, I have to say a big thank you to Jacen, Natalie, Lana and Dean, my fantastic family who make home a happy and creative place to be xxxx

Prologue

GUILT.

When Genevieve Barnes was eight years old, her uncle had dropped dead in front of her. No cry of pain, clutching at the chest or desperate gasps for breath. One moment he was laughing with her mother and the next collapsing to the floor with so little resistance that afterwards she imagined that she'd seen him deflate slightly on impact.

His eyes rolled up into his head, and for one second his gaze seemed to sweep over her. Then he was gone.

His death had been as unexpected and almost as instant as it was possible to be, yet she relived his last minutes over and over. Imagining she knew about CPR. Thinking she should have known enough to spot a warning sign sometime earlier in the day. Rerunning the entire scenario and thinking of a hundred different ways of changing the outcome.

From then on she developed a new awareness of the world around her. She carried her little burden of guilt quietly and learnt first aid at school, then later trained in nursing, and after that as a paramedic.

Now, at thirty-four, she had already faced the challenge of saving lives more times than she could count. She understood that sometimes it would be impossible, but even that realization still hadn't shaken off the shadow of helplessness and unjustified guilt that had followed her since that day in her childhood.

Guilt had become the architect of so many of her subsequent decisions.

Except, ironically, on the one day in each year when she thought of her uncle again as the real person, rather than just a watermark in the vaguest corner of her memory.

His name was Eric, and there had been no greater passions in his life than his twin loves of DIY and real ale. Genevieve still didn't understand how anyone could be so enamoured with bookshelves and tiling, but the rugged charm of real-ale pubs and Cambridge's annual beer festival did appeal.

And so, each year, like today, she'd arrange to meet her husband in the beer tent, pick the three most obscurely named beers, and enjoy a half pint of each. *Cheers, Eric.*

Genevieve cut through the back streets, and then the back alleys of other back streets. As she came closer to Jesus Green there would be others, like her, heading for an after-work drink, and an almost equal number coming away. The bursts of heavy rain wouldn't deter many; it certainly wasn't going to put her off.

The sun had broken through, drying big patches of pavement, but leaving anything in the shade untouched. The surrounding buildings were affected similarly, the grey and cream of rain-sodden brickwork having darkened to the colours of pewter and damp sand. The sun was hitting them again, restoring them to their natural shades. Even the air now smelt clean, and Genevieve slowed down a little to enjoy its warmth.

She crossed Alpha Road and turned down the narrow track running behind the houses on Searle Street. This short-cut saved her from walking the long way to Carlyle Road. The garden fences here were too high to look over but she could still see the upper-floor windows, many of them children's bedrooms with a toy on the windowsill or a bunk-bed just visible through the glass. A skinny tortoiseshell cat watched her from the top of one fence.

She stopped to stroke it. It pushed its head into the palm of Genevieve's hand, then jumped down and nudged against her ankles until it was ready to walk on.

Genevieve bent down and the animal immediately flopped on to her side and then rolled over. 'Are you still a kitten?' Genevieve asked out loud.

Her voice sounded out of place here in the silence of the alley-way. Suddenly it felt as though every house around her stood empty, and that she'd slipped into a completely abandoned corner of town. The only sound came from the distant main road, but the noise of passing cars had all but evaporated by the time it reached her.

She made herself talk to the cat again, 'Good girl, good girl.'

The animal tried wrapping its front paws around Genevieve's fingers but, although she continued to pet her, Genevieve's attention had moved away. The cat stood up again, disappointed. Genevieve straightened, too, listening hard.

She tried to rewind what she thought she'd heard: a yelp, defi-nitely a yelp. Human, not canine. She wasn't sure which direction it had come from, or how close.

'Hello?' She made sure she uttered it with confidence but noticed that her voice sounded small and thin in any case.

She felt for her mobile in her pocket. She could phone Jimmy but, even if he could hear his phone inside the rowdy beer tent, what would he do? Most likely tell her to walk away, tell her she'd overheard nothing more sinister than a couple of shagging teenagers.

She stayed still and replayed the sound in her head once more. It had been small. Small but desperate. It had sounded female, she thought.

How would she feel if that had been a cry for help? What if the shagging was actually rape? Or the woman had fallen, and lay injured? Genevieve's own working day was filled with such incidents, and often worse.

'Hello!' She said it with more force this time, and not as a question but more as a demand for a reply. No response came back.

The yelp hadn't been loud, so she guessed it must've come from one of the gardens nearby. Probably just ahead of her and to the right.

She pushed at the nearest gate but it was locked. The second swung open by four or five inches before snagging on the uneven concrete underneath. She pushed it harder, and it gave a little. She squeezed through, shoulder first, and found herself in a small back yard, plain and tidy apart from four old tea chests piled beside the three-foot wall separating this property from the garden with the locked gate. The wall was the same height on both sides, so she could check out three gardens at once.

Both the neighbouring yards turned out to be empty apart from a bird feeder in one and a rotary drier in the other.

She patted her mobile again, glad she hadn't bothered Jimmy with her over-anxiousness. She'd scanned the beer festival programme and now decided that her first half had better be *Wild Goose* – unless one called *Looking for Trouble* had since been added to the list.

She smiled, and was still smiling, as one of the back gates, two houses along and on the other side of the alley opened.

The gate was newly constructed from untreated wood panels, and it fitted badly. As it opened, a gap appeared between the hinges and, from the angle at which she stood Genevieve could see more clearly through that than through the gate itself. She saw a young woman beyond, half-sitting, half-slumped against a fence post. Genevieve swiftly pulled the mobile from her pocket just as a man stepped through the gateway. He wore a dark woollen overcoat and his hands were thrust deep into his pockets.

He didn't speak, just stared at her.

'I'm a paramedic, what's happened there?'

He took a step forward and she wondered if he'd been hurt too. 'Help her,' he breathed. He reached out to the nearby fence for support. 'Help her,' he repeated.

Genevieve pushed past him and headed into the back garden. She'd already dialled 999 and it was connecting by the time she knelt beside the young woman. She held the phone between her ear and shoulder while feeling for a pulse. 'Ambulance,' she said, 'and police.'

She gave their location: 'The back of Searle Street, the alleyway that joins Alpha Road and Carlyle Road. I don't know the house number.' She began to manoeuvre the woman on to her back, still speaking as she worked. 'Early twenties, female. There's a faint pulse. I'm putting down the phone now, trying resus.'

The woman lay at the edge of a paved area, the weight of her body forcing a large clump of Spanish bluebells to splay out around her. Genevieve slid her hand from behind the woman's back, expecting the damp there to be from sodden leaves. Instead she recognized blood, diluted from the wet foliage, glistening on her palms in semi-transparent smears.

She wiped her hand clean on her thigh and pinched the woman's nose, leaning forward to breathe regularly into her mouth. It was then, like previously, she heard a strange noise, not a yelp this time but a harsher grating sound – followed by a grunt.

She looked into the other woman's face, stupidly intent on carrying on even though she knew that the grunt had emerged from herself, and that at any moment the pain would follow.

The other woman's lips were pale, and without Genevieve she'd be gone in a minute. It was Genevieve who was hurting now.

She felt her strength fading and she slumped forward, the world contracting to encompass her left hand lying limply amid the flattened bluebell leaves. She spoke again, hoping her voice was loud enough to reach the phone. 'I've been hurt.' The words seemed just clear enough. 'Help me,' she breathed, then realized that helping them to catch him might be all she could achieve here. Only one other item came within her shrinking field of vision. 'There's something, a card on the ground, it's . . .'

And her fingers twitched, as if there was a point in reaching out for it.

There was none.

She was dying, and the other woman would be dead too.

The thought hit Genevieve hard, in a final moment of clarity: the revelation that her entire life had been driven by her obsessional avoidance of guilt. What had that achieved today except leaving Jimmy to face bereavement? She should have thought of the pair of them first and stayed away. She should have learnt that guilt is just an evil little gremlin masquerading as something virtuous. It had needed flushing down the toilet like the toxic little shit it truly was.

Some lessons in life are learnt the really hard way.

And some lessons are learnt too late.

Chapter One

11 August

THE CALL HAD come in at 11.47 p.m. A car burning out on the Gogs.

Burnt-out cars belonged to Thursday, Friday and Saturday nights, or summer holidays, not Sundays. Usually it would be something easier to steal than this one, typically a mid-size saloon in the last few years of its life, and too often taken by kids who didn't understand the dangers lurking on the apparently flat and straight Fen roads.

PC Sue Gully had attended too many of those incidents but, then, so had they all.

The ones that crashed them, and survived well enough to walk away, often burnt out the car in the process; the ones that didn't crash often torched the vehicle in any case.

But this clearly wasn't like that.

The vehicle itself was about a hundred yards behind her and, since she was facing towards Cambridge, she should have been able to recognize the amber smudges of the city's lights tinting the sky. Instead she faced the oncoming traffic, diverting it back up the Babraham Road, the headlights dazzling her as they approached. Then, as each vehicle turned, she saw the occupants' faces staring beyond her, oval with curiosity. And momentarily she would see the burning car reflected in their window glass, looking only about the size of an incinerating match. The next car swung round, and she caught sight of someone else in the window's reflection.

She didn't turn to look, but waited until he was almost at her elbow and had addressed her first. 'So, what do you know, Sue?'

She glanced at him finally. As far as she knew, DC Goodhew had no reason to be there, but equally she wasn't surprised to see him. 'About the same as you, I suspect. Less, actually, since you've been up there. You wouldn't know what's happening, would you?'

'It's a car on the central reservation. But it doesn't look like it crashed first.'

'Gary, that's not exactly illuminating. It's a Lotus Evora.'

Goodhew half nodded, half shrugged, as though that name vaguely rang a bell.

'Someone's pride and joy. Not an easy steal, so the assessors will be looking closely at it if he tries to claim.'

'He?'

'Yeah, they have the name of the owner, but no trace of him yet.' She'd heard it over the radio, so was a little surprised Goodhew hadn't as well.

'He's not inside the car, then?'

Gully shook her head, 'Obviously not one hundred per cent sure at this stage, but they don't think so.'

Two fire engines were already on the scene, therefore soon it would be just a smoking and blackened shell, but the intensity of such an inferno could soon turn a human being to ash. Forensics would be testing the debris, just to be certain.

'What's his name?'

'You're not even on duty, *are* you?' She gave him a wry smile. 'Paul Marshall, thirty-eight. Married with two kids and a big detached house out in Linton.'

'Heading home then?'

'Unlike you, clearly. Rubbernecking an RTA isn't your thing, Gary, so why are you here?'

'Curious about something else,' he muttered. And, although he'd answered her question, the tone of his voice told her that something had just distracted him. He stood in the inside lane of the road, gazing at the burning car.

'Curious about what?'

There was a long pause before he answered. 'Nothing . . . just a different case. Nothing, really.' His response was monotone, not actually ignoring her, but intended to push the conversation aside. He was asking for space to think.

She took the hint but, following his gaze, tried to read his mind.

The Gog Magog Downs were a series of low chalk hills that would have been unremarkable in another landscape but here, lying alongside the resolute flatness of Cambridgeshire, they became surprisingly dramatic.

Daniel Defoe had referred to them as mountains. Legend suggested they might be sleeping giants, and long dead university students had been warned to stay away.

Goodhew stared at the dying blaze, then moved about thirty yards closer, towards the grassy strip that ran under the central crash barrier. Further along, this strip widened and the out-of-town carriageway took a higher route up the hill, with a band of trees and shrubs between it and the two lanes that guided traffic back into the city. He climbed the barrier, looking up at the wreck from this new angle, then clambered back down and stared in the other direction, across the adjoining farm land. After a few seconds, he moved further towards the fire site again.

Yes, Gully was already trying to read his mind, but of course she failed; nothing new, then. And she had no idea why he'd now turned on his mobile phone's torch, before easing himself through the hedge and into the field beyond.

The sky was never totally dark at this time of year but, without the light from the flames, everything below the level of the horizon was black. For the first few steps, Goodhew was illuminated by the pulsing blue light of the nearest fire engine. A little further on and she could pick out his location only by the light from his phone, dancing like a firefly.

At the top of the slope the two figures nearest to the blue lights had stopped, also watching his progress. One turned and headed down the hill towards Gully, after a few yards solidifying into the familiar shape of PC Kelly Wilkes. She waited until she was up close before asking, 'Where's he going?' The flash of light hadn't travelled very far, but it was now only a pin-prick.

'I don't know, but he seemed pretty distracted.'

'By what?'

Gully shrugged. 'If it was something I said, then I missed it.' They stood side-by-side and waited. The road behind them remained empty but, as she turned to check it, Gully ran her gaze over the nearest clumps of trees too. 'Does it feel to you like we're being watched, Kell?'

'No, but it would do if I was Goodhew. What *is* he up to?'

A slow, single beat of silence followed, then, as if in reply, their radios responded simultaneously: *One oblique one.*

They both understood instantly, but Wilkes said it anyway. 'Shit, he's found a body.'

GOODHEW HAD STUDIED maths right through until taking his degree, but it was during his mid-teens that he'd loved it the most. Later, as some of the theories became more abstract, he'd found it less appealing. He liked geometry and the truth and certainty of simpler numbers, the way seemingly random answers could turn out to be linked by the same formula, or a complex quadratic equation unravelled to reveal x as just a straightforward integer. Some people thought that those maths lessons had no bearing on the *real* world, but his present job was full of all those constants, variables and unknowns – and the pressures that squashed the shape of people's lives from order into chaos.

And it was a subconscious distillation of all those things that had led him to suspect that there was more than just the burning vehicle at play here. This didn't have the hallmarks of a theft gone wrong, or an insurance scam. The car hadn't been quietly dumped and burnt out in any kind of remote location; instead they'd chosen just about the highest point visible on the Gogs. No, this was the place of beacons and the old semaphore line. It was all about communication.

The crash barrier and ridge between the carriageways was the only place to stand which would give him a better view of the area than the location of the car itself. He quickly realized, though, that on the Cambridge-bound side there was too much surrounding vegetation to allow a clear view of the Lotus.

The possibilities were narrowing now.

He crossed back over the barrier and moved closer to the car, staring into the darkness and using the repetitive flash of the emergency lights to check the trees and hedgerows for a viewing point. It took several seconds before he saw it. About twenty feet before the car itself there was a dip in the hedge, a six-foot-long section where it looked as though the trimmer blade cutting it had slipped and accidentally scooped away the upper eighteen inches. Beyond it was a field, and beyond that a thick line of trees marking the boundary between the farmer's land and the perimeter of the Gog Magog Golf Club.

Goodhew drew an invisible line from the car, through the dip in the hedge, and found the silhouetted outline of a treetop that was a few feet taller than its neighbours. The end of his straight line lay just to its left.

DC Kincaide was within earshot but Goodhew said nothing, because explaining why he wanted to check out the best view of the burning car would have taken longer than simply walking over to it. He used the light from his mobile to pick the right spot, then plunged his way through the hedge. The field had recently been ploughed and Goodhew headed across the deep furrows, taking the most direct route he could, but still aware that he was drifting off course. He paused before getting too close to the trees, and it took him several seconds to locate the single tall tree, then he edged forward again, adjusting and readjusting until he was standing right on a direct line with the Lotus and the dip in the hedge. It was only a few steps from there to move under the edge of the canopy.

And during those few steps Goodhew glimpsed a flash of paleness in the grass. He knelt close to it, but didn't touch. A mobile phone case. Cream leather. Feminine. Expensive.

He remained kneeling, then snapped a photo of it before peering deeper in amongst the trees. Half-word, half-groan: 'Oh.'

The man was sitting upright, tied to a tree, his legs taped together in front of him, his hands secured behind his knees. Goodhew moved closer. Thick wire held the man to the tree, wrapped round in three places: waist, chest and neck. He'd suffered extensive head injuries and at some point during his ordeal the man had fought back. As a result, the wire had dug into him, blood seeping out in a heavy band around his throat, and the patches at his armpits were too dark to be sweat alone.

Dead, obviously and utterly. His face twisted in agony, even in death. Goodhew felt for a pulse in any case, and a remnant of body heat sank through his fingertips.

Goodhew kept very still; perhaps he'd already disturbed the crime scene, so it was vital nothing should be made worse. Clearly he needed some assistance. A boundary must be set up, a SOCO, the works. However, someone else needed to organize it, because, until they arrived with floodlights and a police photographer, he wasn't intending to move.

He could see Kincaide's figure standing close to the Lotus; Wilkes was up there too, and Gully would still be manning the roadblock, probably choking with boredom by now. He could have just shouted across but, instead, he phoned DI Marks, explained the situation, then waited within hand-holding distance of the corpse.

The first few minutes he spent on the Internet, then he used the rest of the time just to think. When Marks arrived, Goodhew passed him his phone with the Google image filling the screen. It was simply a head-and-shoulders shot but enough to give the impression of a solid man, a sporty type with a strong jawline and unweathered skin. Indoor sports maybe, or a gym membership, or maybe both? In the photograph his hair looked blow-dried, his face freshly shaven, and he could have modelled men's grooming products.

Goodhew double-checked, but really there wasn't any doubt. 'The dead man is the Lotus's owner, Paul Marshall.'

Chapter Two

22 August

JANE OSBORNE WAITED until Ady had left for work, then retrieved a packet of Nice 'n' Easy from behind the detergent box in the cupboard next to the washing machine. The shade was *palest blonde;* it was a lot to expect from just one application when she'd been *darkest brown* for the last six months. It didn't matter even if it came out orange, because the important thing was change. *Radical* change.

Her rucksack was ready, stashed out of sight of course, but she didn't even need to open it to make a mental list of the things she required, and tick them off against its contents.

While she waited for the new hair colour to take, she changed her clothes, dragging a pair of black Converse trainers, some combat trousers and a vest top out from under her heaviest winter coat. She let her dress slip from her shoulders and stepped out of it, then, illogically, folded it gently and laid it on top of the coat.

She slammed the drawer shut; there was no way now she was going to stop and think this through again. She'd thought it through plenty. And hers wasn't a life that had any space for sentimentality.

By 10 a.m. she was towelling her hair dry; it was definitely blonder, but not blonde enough. She'd do it again later, with more peroxide. She tied it into a ponytail then held it over a carrier bag and hacked it off just a couple of inches below the rubber band. She then knotted the carrier bag and stuffed it into her hip pocket, swung her rucksack over her shoulder, and closed the front door behind her as she left Ady's flat for the final time.

She hurried to the end of the road, then moved on through the next estate, until she'd gone far enough to be confident that none of her neighbours would recognize her while she waited for a bus. She jumped off in the city centre, dumping the carrier bag of hair in the first litter bin she came across. Another two streets and she found a barber's offering haircuts for £9.50. Her budget had been ten quid.

His name was Frankie and, once she'd told him what she wanted, he spent the next twenty minutes both asking and answering his own questions: 'Me? I'm the third generation of the Rona family in Bradford. All barbers, except my brother.'

Snip, snip.

'My brother? Thought he'd become a chef, but ended up as a optician. Brothers, eh?'

And so on, until Jane's hair was shorn to a number two on the sides and a couple of inches of blonde on top. The colour was patchy but she'd sort that out later. She swung the rucksack over her shoulder and shouted 'Cheers' to Frankie and left the barber's shop conscious that she'd used *Cheers* instead of *Thank you*, *goodbye.* It was a small point but confirmed to her that it wasn't just her physical appearance that had changed overnight.

She hurried back to the bus stop and handed over the fare for the one-and-a-half-mile journey to Thornbury. She sat upstairs at the back, pretending to doze but quietly checking each bus stop for the unlikely bad luck of seeing someone she knew.

Armley Branch Road was the second to last stop on this route. She roused herself, then rang the bell and hurried down the stairs.

She was the only person alighting there, and the driver didn't open the doors immediately. He looked at her accusingly through his rear-view mirror, bushy dark eyebrows and bags under his eyes. 'You paid for Thornbury.'

'Yeah, and I fell asleep. If you knew which stop I wanted, why didn't you wake me? Now I'm screwed.'

'Not my job. You'll have to pay the extra.'

'I don't have any fuckin' money, do I? You've had it all.'

His disembodied eyes blinked. He hadn't told her not to swear, so she guessed he was remembering the way she'd delved in her pockets, scraping together the last few coppers to make up the fare. She sensed the discomfort of the passengers seated behind her. 'You're going to walk back?' His voice remained impassive.

'What choice do I have?'

He sighed and finally turned towards her, leaning out of his seat to look at her face to face. 'The next stop's the end, then I come back, so if you stay on, then I can drop you at Thornbury.'

She shook her head. 'If the inspector's waiting to get on, then I'll have to get off there. And we'll both be in the shit.'

She liked watching him think; he was so easy to read. 'Get off, then, and I'll pick you up on the way back. Twenty minutes.'

'You're a star. A complete star.' The doors opened and she stepped out on to the pavement. She beamed up at him, 'You've saved my life.'

She crossed to the bus stop on the opposite side then waited until the double-decker disappeared around the next bend, a couple of faces still watching her from the rear window until the last moment. Maybe she could've risked staying on until the final stop, but this was better – especially if Ady managed to trace her progress this far. Overall, she doubted that he'd even bother.

On foot, she followed the bus route into Leeds city centre, pausing only as she caught sight of her reflection in the dark window of an empty shop. Her make-up was wrong, still signifying old Jane. She needed paler foundation and black eyeliner and mascara, darker lipstick also. Hairspray too, or maybe one of those rock-hard styling mousses that would keep her hair in aggressively rigid tufts.

She remembered that there was a branch of Boots the Chemist inside Leeds railway station. Perfect. *Buy one, get four free.*

Her visit to the make-up shelves was swift. She stood with her back to the security camera, picking up one item with her right hand whilst her left pocketed the one she really wanted. One, two, three, four – *done.* She spent marginally longer in the hair-care section, wanting to be sure of not being shadowed before she approached the till to pay. She chose a travel-size tube of Boots' own maximum-hold hair gel for £1.99, then paid, by breaking into the first of her £20 notes.

She made it less than ten paces outside before a dull-haired woman in a plum overcoat stepped in front of her. 'You have items . . .' she began.

Jane glanced down at the woman's shoes: square-toed courts and she didn't look like a runner. Jane stepped back, then spun through one-eighty, straight into the arms of a depressingly fit-looking security guard. He grabbed her wrist in one hand and her rucksack with the other, pulling it from her shoulder with a decisive tug. It was as if he knew that she wasn't going to think about bolting without it. It held the start of her new life. She knew what would come next, and, suddenly staying home with Ade didn't seem so unappealing.

Chapter Three

THE PHONE CALL from DS Tierney of Leeds CID was answered by DI Marks at a little after 2 p.m. Tierney sounded harassed: 'Got a woman in custody, mid-twenties, picked up for shoplifting. No previous, but we got a match on her prints. Flags up that we need to contact you lot.'

'What's her name and why do we want her?'

'Calls herself Jane Franklin.'

Marks felt the back of his neck prickle. The first name was correct.

Tierney tutted then rattled on, 'It doesn't even say why you want her, and it's old – like seven years old.'

Marks nodded to himself. 'Can you email her photograph to me?'

'Look, I don't want her in here. We're talking twenty quid's worth of cosmetics, so I want her charged and released.'

'No.'

'We've got her home address, and she won't do a runner for only that much.'

Marks leant his elbows on the desk, the handset close to his mouth. 'DS Tierney, I said "no". Forget the photograph. You have a fingerprint match. I need to speak to her in relation to a murder investigation and if you let her go anywhere whatsoever, you will soon appreciate the real meaning of stress. Is that clear?'

Tierney muttered an apology.

Marks continued, 'Has she called anyone yet?'

'Doesn't want to. Just tells us to piss off.'

'But you have her home address?'

'A flat in Allerton, Bradford . . . was living there with an Adrian Cole. She said they've split up and he wouldn't miss her.'

'We'll have someone there by midnight.' So Jane wasn't cooperating, and she had no incentive to stay in the area. How was that not a flight risk? 'Don't lose her,' he warned, ending the call. He then leant back in his chair and stared up at the ceiling. The paint was uneven and grey with age. 'Oh, hell,' he sighed. He closed his eyes and felt pretty much like the ceiling looked.

Seven years was a while ago in some ways, but not so many in others. Finding Jane was good news. Seeing her in person would be harder.

Marks blew out a long slow breath, and went to find Sergeant Sheen.

Finding was the wrong word, Sheen would be at or within touching distance of his desk, surrounded by notes and files, and shelves heavy with even more of the same. Sheen's 'office' occupied an open-ended cul-de-sac on the second floor. It had a good view of Parker's Piece and was overlooked by no one else.

Sheen sat with the *Cambridge News* open in front of him. He glanced up at Marks, and pushed the paper to one side. 'It is work-related, you know,' he said slowly in his Suffolk drawl. Several blocks of text had been outlined or highlighted.

Sheen had been at Parkside for his entire career and now, with retirement on the middle horizon, it seemed to Marks that the Sheen technique of colour-coding and cross-referencing had been honed to an art. No one else knew three decades' worth of Cambridge people and crimes like Sheen did.

'D'you have a minute, Tom?'

Sheen nodded, nudging the spare chair towards him. 'Unusual to see you up here.'

Marks ignored the chair. 'Jane Osborne's turned up.'

'Has she now? Where?'

'Caught shoplifting in Leeds. We'll get her back down here before we talk to her.'

'Poor kid.' Sheen paused respectfully for a moment. 'And how can I help? I doubt many people know that case like you do.'

Marks gave a grunt, not minding which way Sheen interpreted it. 'I am curious about anything else you've picked up since the case was closed.'

Sheen's instant reaction was to swivel his chair so he could look directly up at the top shelf on the wall behind his desk. He then reached for a fat green lever arch about two-thirds of the way along. 'Big file that one. Maybe you should sit down.'

This time the DI took Sheen up on his suggestion. 'You know Greg Jackson's still in the area?'

'Of course I know . . . probably me that told you.' Sheen underlined this by smacking the green file on to the desktop, where several loose sheets of papers quivered and backed up by a couple of inches. 'He's a local boy, wasn't going anywhere else once he was released.' He slid his hand inside the file and parted its contents at the first page of the third and largest section. 'The Osborne murder takes up a big chunk of this one.' He flicked through a few pages at a time. 'Not much since, to be honest. The mother left town, the dad's still here – and so is the son. But there's one clipping you need to see.'

Sheen found the relevant page and spun the file round to face Marks, who nodded as he recognized the headline, *Exhibit Destroyed*. 'Yes, I remember. The press jumped on it.'

'They thought it might be a publicity stunt.' Sheen pursed his lips. 'I'm ignoring your own feelings on the case when I say this, but I later discovered he'd smashed that item on the day he heard about Jackson's parole.'

'No, I hadn't heard that.' Marks sat very straight as he attempted to remain detached. He pictured Gerry Osborne, hatchet in hand, destroying his own centrepiece sculpture. Did it help to know the catalyst for that? Probably not. 'Why does it matter now?'

'On its own, it don't—'

Sheen allowed another long pause, Marks silently corrected Sheen's grammar, took a breath and waited for the rest of the sentence.

'But at least two times I've heard that Jackson's been seen talking to Gerry Osborne. That breaks Jackson's parole conditions, so Osborne only needs to make a complaint and Jackson's gone. If Osborne was really so upset about Jackson coming out, why doesn't he try to get him sent straight back in?'

Marks didn't comment, but instead spun the file back towards Sheen. 'And that's it?'

'Pretty much. Ask me about the case and I have it in spades, but more recently everyone connected with Jane Osborne has stayed well out of sight. Except Jackson, of course.' Sheen placed his hand flat on top of the open pages. 'You know I would've told you if there'd been anything? I do know how you feel about this one.'

Marks just nodded.

'So what really brought you?' Sheen kept talking. 'Seems to me you're bogging yourself down with what you're going to tell her once she gets here. I don't envy you that conversation, you know.'

'Thanks a lot.' Marks almost managed a smile. In truth he wasn't totally sure why he'd come to see Sheen, but maybe he just needed to share the news of Jane's arrest with the only other person at Parkside who knew the case almost as well as he did. Marks stood up. 'Anyhow, I thought you'd like to know.' He shook Sheen's hand, then turned to leave.

'It wasn't your fault, you know.' Sheen said it quietly, almost to himself.

Marks turned slowly. 'The chain of evidence was compromised.'

'And you were only one link of that chain. There was no official blame.'

'That's not the point.'

'Go up and collect her yourself. You'll feel better once you've spoken to her.'

'Wouldn't be appropriate.'

Sheen snorted. 'You know who you *should* send?'

'Is the name DC Goodhew about to emerge from your mouth, Tom?' One look at Sheen told him he didn't need to wait for an answer. 'Why Goodhew?'

Sheen patted the file again with his flattened hand. 'Since he discovered that Jackson's case was on your mind, he's been up here reading that file on several occasions. He's smart, sneaks up here when I'm off duty, and doesn't leave a single trace.' Sheen tapped the side of his nose. 'But I had a feeling someone had been at my desk, so I stayed late one night and watched for him. Besides, who else would it be?'

Who else indeed?

Chapter Four

THE WORLD HAD slowed and warped in the last few hours.

Jane wasn't altogether surprised.

The holding cell was a small cube of nothingness. She lay on the bench and just stared up at the ceiling. Bland and blank was what she needed right now. Walls that felt clammy to the touch, a ceiling marked with unidentified stains, and a floor that had been hit many times with enough vomit to leave the air permanently sour.

Those particles of other people's rancid lives would never totally leave a place like this. She imagined those particles, nicotine-stained grey and hovering like a band of dirty smog only inches above her face.

Apparently she would be collected before midnight and then taken back to Cambridge. That gave her several hours in which to think.

Cambridge.

She pointed a finger into the non-existent smog and stirred it gently. First in a circle, then as a figure of eight. She considered the pattern and retracted her hand as she realized that there had been a pattern at play in her life too.

She hadn't seen it until now. But then, until this morning, it had only involved two occurrences. It was this third time that made it obvious what she should have noticed previously.

She turned her head to one side and stared straight into the centre of a lopsided pentacle that some previous occupant had gouged into the stodgy gloss covering of the beige-painted wall. Patterns were everywhere when you looked for them.

She wondered why she hadn't recognized that first tremor of restlessness as more than just the need to change her address again. It was more than just a change of address, of course; it was a swapping of lives, a morph from current Jane to next Jane.

Usually it crept up on her suddenly, an overpowering sense of needing to run from her current situation, something instinctual that whispered to her and told her it was time to move. She would then plan her next exit, involving a few items in a bag, a change of appearance and a change of abode. Then the quiet closing of a door, the closing of a chapter, and goodbye to yet another version of herself. *Time to go.*

But in these last few weeks a different emotion had called out to her.

Anger.

Not anger at anyone or anything. Just anger for anger's sake, and that should have provided the warning. She had simply woken one morning with a knot of it trying to fight its way out of her gut.

Ade didn't stand a chance, of course. His attempts at understanding merely made her livid. A week later and it was his indifference that incensed her.

The mug that slid off the draining board and failed to smash was thrown at the door with enough force to sending it bouncing back to shatter on a corner of the cooker. The terracotta pot sitting on one side of the back step was kicked down on to the patio, just for the hell of it, and whether Ade had noticed it or not, Jane knew there were other items she'd trashed over those weeks – just for the hell of it too. Just to spite him, and for no real reason except having woken up and found herself in the thrall of a mood for self-destruction.

She'd gone through the motions, just like the other times, copying that pattern of changing her identity, but without the true urge to move on. Instead she'd been rushing somewhere, anywhere, losing traction, slipping ever faster . . . until she crashed.

The arrest.

The worst collision possible: the current Jane brought face to face with the first Jane. It had had an inevitability, she saw that now. There had been a point of no return, like Donald Campbell skimming Coniston Water, riding it one moment then gone in the next.

The first time round she had seen the smog drifting in on her, yet had been stupid enough to believe herself safe and in control.

If I told you to put your fingers in the fire, you wouldn't do it, would you?

Of course not. But if I thought I knew the secret for stretching my hand into the flame and not getting burnt, maybe I would, just to show you I was capable of rising to your challenge and comprehensively shutting you up.

She'd stood defiantly in the flames then, while feeling nothing and refusing to see her life blistering and the scars forming. Anger could deceive like that until the moment it was extinguished. That's the moment when she'd run the first time.

And, for the same reason, the second time too.

The lock on the door was being opened even now, and all she wanted to do was run yet again, but this time she guessed she'd never get the chance.

TWO OFFICERS HAD come for her, one male, one female and both of them just a little older than Jane herself. Only the woman was in uniform, and unless the bloke was someone random, like a junior doctor or a cub reporter, she guessed he was the senior of the pair.

He spoke first, introducing them both, but Jane blanked out their names and avoided eye contact too, deliberately not engaging.

They led her into the underground car park and then headed for their car. The woman held open the rear door immediately behind the driver's seat. Jane stepped in and slid right over to the other side of the car. If she sat behind the front passenger, then the only person able to observe her properly would be the driver, and he'd be too busy watching the road.

The door closed behind her and through the window she could see only their mid-sections. She watched them talking and the police-woman offering him the car keys. He must have said no because she dropped them into her other palm. He glanced at his watch, a plain-faced analogue. It reflected the light from the overhead panels, and for the first time Jane realized that she didn't even know whether there would still be daylight outside. It would take three hours to get to Cambridge, give or take, but that didn't really matter when she didn't know when she was leaving here or likely to arrive.

She'd become adrift from time, unanchored, and in some way that consoled her. Perhaps she could stay like that on every level: returning to Cambridge without having to attach herself to her own history, family or personal responsibilities. But that would only work if she could be in and out quickly.

The detective was sitting in the passenger seat in front of her now, while the PC was negotiating the narrow gaps between the bumper-scuffed concrete walls leading to the exit.

Jane spoke, but to neither in particular. 'Who do I need to see?'

It was the detective who answered. 'Detective Inspector Marks will be talking to you initially.'

Initially.

'Then who?'

He twisted in his seat and studied her for a moment or two before replying. 'I don't know, actually. Maybe only DI Marks.'

'And what does he want?'

'You've been missing since you were fifteen.'

She half-closed her eyelids, setting her jaw so that she barely moved her lips as she spoke. 'There has to be more than that.'

He said nothing in reply, just watched her further and waited for her response.

She allowed her jaw to jut a little more stubbornly and turned her gaze to the rain-splattered window. She then counted the street lights as, one by one, they flitted in and out of her life. She'd never see them again. Or recognize them again. She was disconnected. Anonymous. Unanchored. She would allow herself to be steered to Cambridge, then drift right back out again.

Not a problem.

Chapter Five

ON LEAVING CAMBRIDGE, Sue had said she'd do the first half of the journey and leave Goodhew to drive the, other eighty miles. But it seemed to DC Goodhew that, once she got her hands on a steering wheel, Gully was reluctant to let it go. That suited him fine; in fact, never having to drive at all suited him pretty well. It gave him time to think.

She'd shown the same reluctance to hand over the keys when it came to the return journey, too. Sue was an efficient driver and they'd cleared the first hundred miles already, even though the roads were swamped with both traffic and the kind of driving rain that fills the windscreen before the maxed-out wipers have the chance to make their next sweep.

They'd both been watching the road ahead, and neither of them had said much, mostly because they were both very aware of Jane Osborne's presence in the rear seat.

Up until that afternoon he'd only seen photos of their passenger, showing a dark brunette scowling out at him. She had scowled again at Goodhew when he first addressed her today. She didn't suit her short blonde hair, her dark eyes glaring out from beneath straight-across eyebrows, her forehead broken by a pair of vertical frown lines. They served only to accentuate the dark unhappiness that seemed to be written into her features.

DS Tierney had dealt with the handover quickly but by the time the paperwork was complete, Goodhew had come to realize that Jane Osborne scowled at everyone.

She'd settled into the back of their car, choosing to sit behind Goodhew and settling low into the seat. She then kept her face turned to the window, hiding behind a mask of total disinterest. For such a small space, she'd made a pretty good job of putting distance between herself and them. There had since been a couple of bursts of reluctant conversation but mostly silence.

Goodhew had deliberately twisted the second rear-view mirror around so that he could see her clearly. But she leaned closer to the door and turned her head away, staring out the window, so it became almost impossible for him to see anything but part of her cheek and her exposed right ear. It was pierced at least six or seven times, with two studs at the lobe and a short run of identical small gold sleepers around the helix. He shifted his gaze on to the wing mirror so that each time they passed under a street light he had a fleeting view of her expression. Or lack of.

Without warning she spoke. 'Do my family know I'm coming back?'

Gully answered, as Goodhew turned, 'They know we've located you, nothing more.'

'We can arrange for someone to meet you at Parkside,' he added.

Jane turned away from the window and glared at him instead. 'A happy reunion with Mum and Dad?'

He hesitated, knowing they'd divorced and her mum had moved out of Cambridge. He wasn't sure if Jane even knew. 'If that's what you'd like.'

'Right. When I ran off, it was because I'd had enough of them all to last me a lifetime. Nothing's changed. In case you haven't worked it out, people don't change.'

'Some do.' It took him a few more seconds to put the dates together: if they hadn't divorced by the time she'd run, they must have been fairly close to doing so.

'Bollocks.' She turned her head back to the window. 'The police should've just let me go.'

'And then you'd have run away again?'

'Why not? No one gets banged up just for a bit of eye make-up.' She turned her head back to the window, ending the conversation just like that.

Goodhew went back to watching her in the wing mirror. People who chose not to communicate could achieve it in a variety of ways. One involved talking too much, bouncing around and over a subject and filling the room with chatter. Also the look-you-in-the-eye lie could be effective, and the head-hanging withdrawal often worked too. Everything about her said *Back off*. It was written right through her, as though she had carefully considered every aspect of her outward appearance and engineered each one to send out the same message. Maybe that's what was needed when you ran away from home at fifteen. Or maybe, if the world had already had that much of an isolating effect, running away might seem like the sensible option.

The rain was now pounding his window, the wing mirror, her window and everything in between. He doubted she realized that he was watching, though he couldn't see her that clearly anyhow.

It was her constant watchfulness that intrigued him, that and the question of how much she actually knew.

It had been just over seven years since her sister Becca had died. And just a few months since the man responsible for that death had been released from prison. It was possible that Jane already knew of either event or both, but equally possible that she'd missed each brief fanfare in the press, firstly regarding the attack itself and then the trial that followed.

Goodhew had one particular reason for having researched the case, because last year's imminent release of Greg Jackson had weighed heavily on DI Marks. Rumours persisted that Marks had made an error with crucial evidence, a mistake which had led to Jackson being convicted merely on an assault charge – or, in the words of the less sympathetic, *he got away with murder.* It had seemed to Goodhew that answers were rarely that clear-cut, so he'd dug around for the details. And somehow Marks knew that Goodhew knew.

How long he'd known was a mystery, but once Marks needed to use that information, he'd laid it on the desk between them like the proverbial smoking gun. 'I want you to go and collect her, but don't tell her about Becca unless she already knows. And then, if – and *only* if – she asks questions, I want you to answer them.'

Goodhew had said nothing more at the time, but he understood why Marks wanted to speak to her back in Cambridge, and how long the journey would seem if she'd been full of questions and been fobbed off with three hours of *I'm sorry, I don't know.* What Goodhew didn't understand was Jane Osborne's reaction. If she had known everything that had happened since, why hadn't she come home? If she knew nothing, why wasn't she questioning this journey now?

They were just into the third hour of their journey when they came to a halt on the approach to a roundabout. Alongside stood a sign directing them straight on for Cambridge. The board was green and white, with four-inch letters taking the full glare of a floodlight that shone up on it from the verge. The rain had now stopped and he stole another glance at Jane via the wing mirror. The light was reflecting straight on to her face. She was staring up at the signboard too, and for a split second he saw a flicker of emotion pass across her face.

Pain definitely, yet mixed with something else. But that expression had been so fleeting that he couldn't pinpoint it.

He turned and looked directly over his shoulder at her. The customary defiance was back now but, before she could stop herself, she'd already responded to the question she'd registered in his face. 'Cambridge?' she said. 'That fucking place!'

Chapter Six

THE MEETING WAS to be at 11.30 a.m. Jimmy Barnes arrived at the Michaelhouse Café thirty-five minutes beforehand. It would have been so easy for him to have been here even before sunrise. He was an habitual early riser but today he'd woken at least two hours too soon. The usual fear of what the new day would bring had, for once, been overridden by an unfamiliar sensation of guilt.

Guilt because he was keeping a secret from his wife.

He pushed aside the urge to wake her up and tell her. Tell her what? That an unknown friend of a friend might be able to help. Even starting such a conversation was too fraught with issues, the route from *Good morning* to *I'm meeting her at eleven* held too many opportunities for stepping on shaky or, more likely, collapsing ground.

He let his wife sleep on until the alarm went off, telling himself that she'd never suspect anything was different as long as he stayed quiet at breakfast and left for work at the usual time. What was there to see in his expression but more of the same anxiety that they reflected back and forth between them.

Back and forth.

The tag on the tea bag swung gently from side to side as the darkening colour plumed and spread within the cup. Jimmy had ordered pastries along with the tea even though he wasn't hungry, having bought them to sit there uneaten and justify his occupation of a table as the café filled. He'd chosen to sit up on the balcony, looking down on the entrance, and for almost half an hour he watched people arrive. They were mainly tourists taking a break in the sightseeing for some refreshment, and then leaving their bags at the table and walking across to photograph the Michael-house chapel and its famous east window.

At 11.10 he spotted her. She barely glanced around the room but headed straight towards the stairs, as if the upper level was the only place he could possibly be. The man accompanying her looked about forty years her junior, and he dropped behind to follow her up the narrow spiral staircase. They had the same slim build, but he was several inches taller and, despite his casual appearance, Jimmy couldn't dispel the feeling that he was looking at a man who was constantly on the alert.

Jimmy stood up as they approached his table, and he could see his own hand trembling as he offered it. He wanted to smile and ask how they were, but it felt wrong to start with a lie. He'd gone past the point of being able to even pretend to empathize with anyone else's well-being, or to share even the tiniest of pleasantries without his internal voice screaming at him that it didn't matter. *It really didn't matter.*

This was a state of emergency now, the throwing of everything over the side just to try and stay afloat. Social niceties had gone overboard several months ago. And there were days when he wanted to stop, to wait until he hit the bottom, to then have the stern hand of responsibility send out doctors and bailiffs, and maybe a removal van or two, making the decision to change the route of his life anyone else's but his own.

That's why his hand shook. Hers, of course, didn't. 'Good to see you again,' she said and stepped aside to introduce her companion. 'This is Gary Goodhew.'

THERE ARE PLACES to meet, places to avoid and a multitude of shades between the two. It appeared to Goodhew that his grandmother divided her time between the high-end and the very shady. She also seemed to be pretty much an expert at matching location, companion and agenda. Michaelhouse Café struck him as an unusual choice. *There's someone I'd like you to meet,* she'd texted. He hadn't bothered to ask more; if she wanted him to know beforehand then she would have told him in the first place. He knew from experience that on the rare occasions his grandmother introduced him to someone, it usually involved a suggestion of extra-curricular investigation work. Without exception he had refused. However, that thought didn't gel with a meeting held in such a busy and public place.

She had met him at the entrance. 'His name is James Barnes, always known as Jimmy, though. Name ring a bell?'

'I don't think so.' He shook his head, though somewhere he felt a recollection stir.

'All I ask is that you listen to him.'

'Why do you do this to me?'

'He's a friend of a friend.'

Great. Since there seemed to be a maximum of two degrees of separation between his grandmother and most of the residents of Cambridge, it wasn't much of a reason. 'I warn you I'm going to say no.'

'That's fine,' she said, leading the way into the café. 'But listen first, then say no.'

He followed her up the stairs and although there were no free tables, and several of them were occupied by lone men, it was still easy to spot Jimmy Barnes. He was a big man, early forties, broad-shouldered and, judging by the way he made the café furniture look like it had come from a primary school, stood at least three inches over six feet tall. He had the pallor of someone who'd woken hung-over and had been struggling with an uncooperative head and stomach ever since. He probably realized he wouldn't start to recover until he'd got the crap out of his system. Goodhew doubted, however, that alcohol was Jimmy Barnes's problem. The man had spotted Goodhew's grandmother from the first moment she'd walked towards the stairs, and was now watching her keenly.

Barnes wiped his palm quickly on the thigh of his trousers before they shook hands. The man's skin remained damp and, although his grasp was firm enough, Goodhew detected a slight hesitancy. Maybe nerves?

Goodhew took a seat to one side of Barnes but, rather than joining them, his grandmother draped her jacket over the back of the nearest available chair and headed back towards the stairs. He was about to speak when Barnes drew himself closer and whispered, 'I know you're a policeman and I'm not asking for anything but advice. Well, that's not true, I want help. But most of all I don't want to be ignored. Do you understand?'

'Go on.'

'It's my wife.'

And before Jimmy Barnes said another word the familiarity of the surname finally took shape. 'Genevieve Barnes?' Goodhew asked sharply.

Jimmy nodded. 'Your grandmother told you, then?'

'No. I've just heard the name recently.' He wasn't about to admit to knowing the case closely, even though copies of all the documents he'd read on it were currently sitting in a drawer at home. Nor could he ignore the fact that the previous evening had been spent fetching Jane Osborne back to Cambridge. The timing was interesting. 'She was injured whilst treating a stab victim?'

'That's right. I was due to meet her at the beer festival, and she cut through all the back streets when she headed through town. Not just the back streets, but back alleys too.' He glanced sharply at Goodhew, as though expecting interruption. 'That was just her. She liked spotting things she hadn't seen before: unusual buildings or a beautiful garden hidden behind a fence. But they queried that explanation in court, like she had made a gross misjudgement or something. As though in some small way she'd brought it on herself.' He pressed both index fingers to the gap between his eyebrows and pressed them hard against his brow. He drew them apart slowly, his eyes closed, as if concentrating on his breathing. 'I was so angry,' he muttered to himself.

Goodhew waited until Jimmy's eyes reopened. 'Then what?'

'Gen found a girl lying injured . . . young woman I'm supposed to say. Gen was a paramedic, so of course she went to help. Luckily she phoned for an ambulance. Because by the time it arrived she'd been attacked too. It was her own phone call that saved her life – how ironic is that?' Jimmy's voice had risen noticeably and all the other occupants of the balcony now had the opportunity to consider the irony, too.

This had been a stupid place to meet.

Goodhew leant closer, speaking quietly, and hoping Jimmy would follow suit. 'I know Rebecca Osborne was the woman that died.'

'So you know they arrested her boyfriend?'

'Greg Jackson.'

Jimmy's gaze darted away. 'Gen lost a huge quantity of blood. The knife was rammed in so hard it broke two of her ribs. Yet, from first bending over the Osborne girl's body until Gen herself woke in hospital, she remembers nothing. I thought that would be a blessing, because surely there would be less trauma from an attack you can't even remember?'

Goodhew shrugged. 'There's also the trauma of not knowing what happened.'

'I see that now.' Jimmy had thick straight hair that could easily have been styled to make him look like a seventies ad for Grecian 2000. He pushed it back from his face, then pressed his hand to the back of his neck, again shutting his eyes as he continued. 'That day was terrible. I'd already spoken to her when she was on the way to meet me, so when she didn't show, of course I phoned her. Each time the call I made went to voicemail, Gen was almost two hours late by the time I received a call from the police. I rushed to the hospital but she was in theatre and no one seemed to know whether or not she would survive.' His eyes snapped open. 'Of course, I prayed desperately for her to pull through. But I was stupid enough to think that, if she survived, we'd be able to just go back to normal.'

'But it's not that simple, is it?' Goodhew said quietly.

It was a small and obvious statement but enough for Jimmy to relax a little. His gaze again settled on Goodhew and this time his eyes focused properly, as he dropped his hands into his lap. When he spoke, his voice sounded more natural. 'I've been holding on, waiting for everything to improve – or at least settle down.' His expression softened further. 'I don't mean I've been holding on instead of leaving her. Gen and I are in it for good. I mean I've been holding on waiting for it to get better, but instead things are only worse.'

'How?'

'Gen couldn't return to work. She tried, as soon as she was physically well enough, but just imagine it. A paramedic turns up daily at situations other people hope they'll never have to face . . . loved ones collapsing in the street, road accidents, assaults. She and her partner Derrick had been called out to a suspected accidental overdose. They arrived at the house, found the front door was ajar, and Derrick went on in. Gen couldn't step over the threshold. She just froze. He called back to her, told her it was safe, that he needed her help with the patient. But she couldn't move. Derrick then brought the kid out and they treated him on the doorstep, kept quiet about it too, but it wasn't the only time it happened, so eventually she left.'

'And now? Does she still work?'

'Yes, part time at Addenbrooke's. She has to work, as she can't stand being on her own anywhere, even at home. She now can't walk down a quiet street, says she feels it closing in on her . . . starts feeling convinced that she's being watched. We were still having good days together, fantastic days sometimes, even though we always seemed to pay for them with huge lows descending afterwards. We were coping, that's the point. Then we heard how Greg Jackson was up for parole.'

The years between the attack and now must have ticked by so slowly at times, and yet Goodhew could see how the release of Jackson would feel as though it came upon them in an instant.

'Gen *sees* him all the time. She looks up and he's there, watching her – by the bus stop, at the end of our road, in the supermarket.

It's becoming impossible. Our real life has disappeared, left us behind. It's just over there,' he glanced to the right, 'where we can't reach it but can still see what might have been. I realize I need to find something more I can actually *do* about this.'

'And this is why you've contacted me? If Jackson's been making contact in any way, you can report it. Harassing your wife will break the conditions of his parole.'

'I want you to help.'

'No, you just need to contact the police. I don't understand why you think I can do anything.'

Jimmy took a deep breath. 'I can't contact them. I don't believe her.'

'Because she's making it up, or you think she's imagining it?'

'I don't know. Really, I don't. She claims she saw him three times in the first couple of weeks after his release. Initially I thought maybe she'd made a mistake, or I put it down to one of those unfortunate coincidences like going on a first date and running into your ex. But by the third time . . .'

'Did you suggest she should report it?'

'Of course, but she suddenly became upset – hysterical really, I suppose. She kept repeating that it was *too late* and I *wouldn't understand*. I tried to make her tell me but in the end we had this massive row and I stormed out. When I came back home she was very subdued, she'd clearly been crying a lot and I suppose she'd just burnt herself out. She'd convinced herself that Jackson was coming for her, and that he held her responsible for his conviction.'

'Hers wasn't the only evidence.'

'No, but she was the only witness to put him there at the scene. We later heard that the only other piece of evidence that could have carried more weight never made it to court. Gen says he came out of the gateway as she went in. So he knew Rebecca Osborne was critically injured. He didn't just stand there while Gen was being attacked, did he? It's obvious to anybody that he was guilty.'

'But not to your wife.'

'I'm not going to the police with an accusation of harassment against that man. It would probably take them only five minutes to prove she's making it up, and then they'd want to know why. Gen went through plenty in court, so do you think I'd let her throw it all away by having her convince the police that she may have made a mistake? I'd be opening the door to her taking the biggest downhill slide possible. There can't be any doubt over Jackson, because Gen would be vilified.'

Jimmy was making sense, but Goodhew still failed to see where he himself might fit in.

'If only I had the money, I'd hire someone to watch her.' Jimmy grunted. 'Except that still wouldn't be right. She needs some kind of resolution. D'you know her only reason for thinking Jackson is innocent?'

Goodhew shook his head, but Jimmy hesitated, almost as though he had trouble bringing himself to continue.

'Jackson's expression was *wrong*.' Jimmy strummed his fingers on the table and looked at him, clearly agitated.

Goodhew sat a little straighter. 'That's it?'

'That's it. I understand the trauma, her fear of being alone, even the fear that the man she's sent to prison might come after her. Then I think, if she really believes he's innocent, why isn't she scared of the real killer? What the fuck is the *wrong* expression? That's the reason she says she can't move on.

'Look, I'm not walking out on her because she's developing mental health issues – if she is – but the idea that she has been festering for so long over something so trivial . . .' abruptly he pressed his lips together and scowled. 'I don't know what I'm asking you . . . Maybe you could find a detail that's been missed? Something that will make sense of a *wrong* expression?' Jimmy pushed his chair back and hurried to his feet. 'Now I've said it out loud again, I can hear how stupid it sounds. Forget it, I'm sorry.'

Goodhew didn't try to stop him. He'd already promised himself that he'd turn down anything pushed in front of him, so watching the man trudging out of the Michaelhouse Café should have been the very end of it. But the whole meeting had left him thinking, something he was still engaged in when his grandmother rejoined him.

'An interesting man,' she remarked as she placed a tray of tea things on the table between them.

'Seems perpetually uncomfortable. What does he do for a living?'

'He works in the purchasing department at the Council offices. He's been there since leaving school, secondary education. He married Genevieve when she was twenty-four, after they'd dated for five years. No children, small mortgage, no debts.'

'How do you know all this?'

'It doesn't matter, the point is, I do.' She filled up both cups. 'I doubt he's ever courted the limelight, so I don't think he's crying out for help for any other reason than he truly needs it.'

That made Goodhew smile. 'I hope that's not emotional blackmail. You *know* I'm not getting involved.'

She smiled too. 'I forgot.'

'But you're right about the limelight. He's not the adventurous type, not a risk-taker or a narcissist, yet he's come here to tell it all to a complete stranger. And in such a public place . . .' he glanced at his grandmother. 'Is that why you picked here as our meeting point?'

'In part.'

'And the other part?'

'Are you going to look into it?'

'Into what? A wrong expression?'

'Come on, that's the part that intrigues you.'

'It's obvious there's nothing I can do.'

His grandmother pointed over at the chapel. 'Look at the east window.'

He knew it well: five tall panels with Christ in the centre one, surrounded by saints, angels and martyrs. Above the main five panels were eleven smaller ones depicting doves, stars and still more angels.

'Do you remember what you once told me?'

The glass containing the second angel from the right had been installed incorrectly, in a mirror image of the way it should be. He'd noticed that on his first visit.

He nodded.

'I don't know anyone else who has ever spotted it, Gary, and even though I know you won't agree to help Jimmy Barnes, you won't be able to stop yourself from noticing if the smallest detail there is out of place either.'

Chapter Seven

JANE'S DRAMA TEACHER used to shout *Own it!* in reaction to any half-hearted attempt at acting. Of course the kids, Jane included, mimicked this expression without mercy, shouting it out whenever a classmate in any other lesson hesitated with their answer. There had been times since when she'd remembered this and wondered whether hiding the truth had always been her destiny.

In life, Jane lied frequently: some days she felt she was good at it, at other times she was doubtful, but most of the time she did it without thinking. Tonight she'd need to concentrate, working hard to keep her expression blank, revealing nothing and reminding herself that being believed was all down to *owning* her forthcoming performance. DI Marks needed to believe the news of her sister's death had come as a shock.

In the end it wasn't so hard to achieve.

As she stepped from the police car, it was the change in location that hit her first. The Cambridgeshire air was dry and warm; they'd driven through all of that rain and come out the other side as they entered the north of the county. She glanced up at the cloudless night sky and remembered how different the solar system looked here compared to anywhere else she'd ever visited. The stars here seemed better spaced, as though the dome of the atmosphere was somehow grander and had lifted them up and away from each other.

The police station was directly in front of her, ugly as ever, while behind her – on the other side of Warkworth Terrace – stood well-kept townhouses, the kind with fat front doors reached by a short flight of stone steps and basements that begged to be stared into as you walked along the pavement.

The familiarity of it startled her. She had expected to feel like a total stranger but all this was etched somewhere in the back of her mind.

DI Marks too.

She'd only ever seen him on the news giving updates on the case but, now that he faced her, she recognized that shrewd expression and the neat precision of his words. He'd aged, how-ever. Who wouldn't, doing that job? His black hair was streaked with grey and he was thinner than she remembered. But it was him all right. It made her wonder how her own father might have changed. She'd promised herself she wouldn't think of him again, and maybe that was unrealistic, but she'd kept this bargain with herself for a long time now.

DI Marks had escorted her to the room where she now sat, some kind of interview room but with less starkness than usual. A female officer was with him, but she seemed mute: a pair of eyes and ears, nothing more. There was a table with a single plastic chair on each side, but there were also four easy chairs grouped around a coffee table, and a box of toddler toys in the corner.

'This is a room for bad news, right?' she asked. The comment had been involuntary.

'Sometimes, unfortunately,' Marks replied.

She realized she'd now given him a cue – an opening through which to drop his bombshell. He directed her to sit in one of the soft chairs, whereupon the black vinyl huffed wearily. And that's when he explained that her sister had been murdered.

She knew already, of course, but she'd only cried when she'd been on her own. She'd never spoken about it, never had the opportunity to ask questions, only to try to find answers within the news reports. And that wasn't the same.

She'd meanwhile stopped listening to him. Instead she stared into her lap and caught sight of her own chest rising and falling in exaggerated breaths. Becca had died seven years and three months ago. Jane thought she'd done all her crying, yet here she was still fighting tears. She drew in a deep breath, and for a second her head cleared.

DI Marks was still speaking. 'I'm very sorry.' He had now said it twice; perhaps he assumed she hadn't heard the first time.

Those were, she realized, the very first words of condolence anyone had offered her. 'Thank you,' she breathed. Acknowledging them meant she'd accepted them. The tears then broke loose, erupting as though they'd only ever been buried in the shallowest of graves. She heard her own pain too, voiced along with sobs that sounded primitive but disembodied, out of her control. She realized she was shouting 'No, no, no' between the sobbing.

The silent policewoman pushed a box of tissues into her hands. Jane pushed them away. Right then she didn't want to stop to even think about what she'd done. She'd missed her sister's funeral. Never been to visit the grave. That bastard had gone to prison, but she'd always known he wasn't the killer. How had she thought it OK to let a guilty man go unpunished? How much respect had that shown to Becca?

'Am I free to go?' she asked.

Marks nodded. 'You are, but I need an address.'

'I don't know what I'm doing about that yet.'

'I still need an address.'

'I see.' She nodded, but didn't have an answer.

'A friend perhaps? It would be better for you to have some support.'

'I'll go back north tomorrow.' Lies always found her when she needed them. 'Back to my boyfriend. Please can I phone him? I can sort it out.'

She could tell he doubted her; he thought for a few seconds, then let it go. 'No one will pursue the shoplifting charge on this occasion. I would appreciate receiving an address from you, when you can. I'll now leave you with PC Wilkes; she'll get you in touch with victim support.' He shook her hand and left her. Then the silent policewoman spoke for the first time: 'Where are you going right now?'

'What time is it?'

'Just after three a.m. You might find a hotel but you'll never get into a B and B at this hour. I finish at six, so I could leave you in here until then. Would you like me to fetch you a sandwich?'

'No. I'm just going to clear off, but thanks. I've got friends who won't mind. I can get a taxi there.'

'OK, if you're sure.'

Sometimes people believed lies just because it suited them.

Ten minutes later she exited through the front door of the police station, hoisted her rucksack on to one shoulder, and set off across Parker's Piece. The sky had stayed clear, and although it was still night time, it didn't seem all that dark. If the building itself hadn't been in the way, she would have paused a moment to turn to the north-east and look for the faint glow that shone from beyond that horizon. Apparently it was Norway, though she couldn't remember if she'd once been told that or just invented it. Anyhow, it was what she always chose to believe. The idea of standing in the night time of one country while looking at daylight in another still fascinated her. She'd often watched skies like that from her bedroom window because, even as a kid, her instincts had been telling her to get as far away as possible.

That wasn't how she felt now, though. She didn't feel any danger walking through the city streets at night; in her mind a sleeping Cambridge was a benign Cambridge. She took her time, stopping frequently, moving aimlessly, telling herself that this really would be the final time she visited. It was only as she reached Magdalene Bridge that she realized she'd been instinctively heading towards her childhood home ever since leaving Parkside station. Again she stopped, staring at the red of the traffic lights positioned at the junction ahead. She felt the pull of seeing the house again and the pull of walking away, too.

But tonight had confirmed that leaving somewhere behind was a whole lot more complicated than just walking away.

She now pictured the house, standing a half storey above street level, the low mottled wall at the front of it holding in the shrubbery by means of six or seven layers of Cambridge brick. Too many rooms now for whichever parent had kept it after the divorce. She reckoned she'd know which it was just by observing it from the pavement outside. Even in the dark. Her father would change as little as possible, adhering to the stitch-in-time theory, constantly tinkering but never renewing. Her mother, on the other hand, never settled with anything for long.

Jane crossed at the traffic lights, passing the Folk Museum and Kettle's Yard, then following the road as it sloped up Castle Street and next into the narrower curve of St Peter's Street. Ten years ago this could have been her attempting a post-curfew sneak back from a nightclub. She turned the corner from St Peter's Street into Pound Hill, the area still suffering the same identity crisis as it had then. A patchy approach to development here had resulted in an uneasy standoff between functional seventies cubes, a few grander houses, and buildings like the Castle End Mission which remained as testament to a bad-old-days version of the same city.

It was turning this corner that made her heart first start to thump. Again she assured herself it would look the same. Her strides suddenly quickened. From arriving back at the periphery of Cambridge, and through all the hours since, she'd been looking out specially for things that hadn't changed. She didn't know why she'd done that: she'd moved on, so surely everything else would have done so, too.

Just a few yards ahead of her now, she picked out the familiar gambrel roofline of one of the neighbouring properties silhouetted against the blue-black sky. Her gaze shifted further along but, instead of seeing her old home peering over next door's hedging, she saw just a mass of shrubbery. Her parents' small front garden was dwarfed by it, and the only part of their house still visible from this angle was one upstairs window and a small section of shallow roof above it.

A branch of a tree extended out at head height and, although she knew the location of the steps to the front door, the gap between the surrounding foliage revealed only blackness. She retreated to the other side of the road to wait for the clearer light of dawn.

Chapter Eight

'JANE?'

She'd had enough of just staring at the house and thinking, by then. She remained in the same spot but was getting restless now.

'Jane.'

He was off to her left, approaching the house from the opposite direction to the one she had come. She let him shout her name one more time before turning.

'What do you want?'

Her father's face was perpetually red, as though he'd been holding his breath and forcing the blood into his head. He was now slightly out of breath and a deeper shade than usual.

'To see you, obviously. We didn't know where to find you.'

Wasn't that the whole point? 'I told the police I didn't want to see anyone.'

'Campbell spotted you sitting out here and he phoned me.'

That bloody curtain-twitcher had been dobbing her in it since childhood. She wondered how she'd missed having the feeling of the old boy's eyes on the back of her neck. Maybe that's what happened when you spent too long looking in the wrong direction.

'So you don't live there now? I would have thought you'd have paid through the nose to hang on to it.'

'You know about the divorce, then?'

'And Becca. The police told me.'

A brief frown came and went. 'I did live there. I bought her out, then she wouldn't leave,' he said.

She guessed he didn't want to get into an argument within the first few minutes of seeing her again, but she had no reason to feel the same way. 'And you just let her?' she snorted.

'I didn't want to have to fight her, not after we lost your sister . . . and you.'

He'd never been an expert at smiling: eyes down, thinking, frowning, working were basically his thing. Her mother always remarked that he hid behind his beard. Other times she said he hid behind his sculptures, or his unkempt appearance, or his ability to disengage from any conversation. Jane had always considered him easy to read and, long before adolescence had ruined her bond with him, she had been able to spot the way his expression always softened when they spoke. He took a step towards her and she caught the whiff of sweat and dust. She recoiled swiftly, keeping a sensible gap between them.

'What is she doing in there, wrecking it for you? Look at the state of the place.'

'I sleep at the studio. I don't mind.'

Jane scowled at the house. 'Who else is living in there?'

'No one now.'

'She's got that whole fucking house to herself? That's bollocks. She's not cut out for living alone.'

'Do you need to swear?'

'Does it really matter? Really? Does it?'

He didn't reply to that. Which meant it didn't, but he'd be letting himself down just to say so. 'Jane, your mother moved away. The house is empty now. I wanted to keep it, but I realized I didn't want to be in it. I rented it out for a while. Now it needs too much work, so I'm selling it.'

Jane frowned at the house. 'When?'

'Right now. It's been on the market since May.'

May? The month of change.

'No one wants it at the asking price, and I can't afford to sell it for much less. Can't afford to have it standing empty for much longer, either. Forget the state of the economy, it's done nothing compared to the destructive force of your mother.'

He wasn't looking at her now, just staring across at his house and looking equally empty. Jane didn't have room for sympathy, but she knew the creak of a door opening when she heard it. She didn't say anything for almost a minute, running a fast double-check on her logic.

She picked up her rucksack, and he glanced back at her then, and she knew she had his full attention. He didn't seem able to find any words, and she guessed he was scratching around for something fatherly to say that didn't instantly sound insincere.

'Would you let me live there?'

The creases in his forehead deepened. 'No.'

'Why not?'

'I don't want to move back there.'

'I don't want you to.' She eyed him carefully. 'I just want a few weeks to sort myself out. All I had lined up was a fortnight on a mate's sofa. I want a few weeks here instead.'

'My God, you have a nerve. Then what? You just bugger off again?'

'I don't know – that's the point.'

'You only came back because the police brought you?'

'Yeah, and it's been different here to what I expected. At first I couldn't think about anything except leaving, but now I think it would be good to spend some time at the house.'

'The central heating's knackered.'

'It's August.'

His stance changed: he positioned himself squarely and bowed his head slightly. Becca used to call it his charging-bull expression. It appeared just before he mowed his way through whatever obstacle stood in front of him.

'I don't know why I even mentioned the heating. I just don't want you at the house. You don't have any right to ask.'

'Don't I?' She gave him a hard smile. 'Thanks for telling me.' She took a couple of steps backwards, then turned sharply away from him and started walking down Pound Hill towards North-ampton Street.

'Jane?'

She didn't acknowledge him. He called out again but no foot-steps came after her. Was it any surprise he'd never managed to find her across all those years, when following her down the hill was too fucking much?

She'd rounded the bend and was about fifty yards short of the Punter pub when she heard him shout.

'You win.'

She didn't slow.

'Damn you, Jane. Have the house.'

Chapter Nine

Jane returned with the keys just before 10 a.m. There were three in the bunch; front, side and back doors. She needed to duck under branches as she climbed the stone steps up to the house itself. The steps were smooth with age, though in places patterned with bursts of pale-green lichen. The paint on the front door was crumbling, so that dark blue flakes lay amongst the leaves scattered in the open porch. Some had gathered along the narrow gap between the door itself and the threshold, pinned there as if something was dragging at them from the other side. They were last autumn's leaves, blown in during the dry winter. It made her wonder whether the estate agent had been inside at all.

Somehow it felt wrong to open the main door, so, even though the key was in her hand, she swapped it for the longer brass key next to it and headed for the side door. That entrance led into a four-foot-six hallway, then through another doorway into the kitchen. From there she would be able to silently observe the house, to watch it while it slept.

The side door opened easily. The air smelt earthy, a residue perhaps of all the times wellington boots and winter footwear had been removed and left to dry beneath the row of brass coat hooks.

The only movable item in the kitchen was a red-and-white striped mug with a missing handle and paint drips down one side. That sat on the draining board, and she put her rucksack down next to it. The stainless-steel sink was bone dry, the single spout tap over it encrusted with limescale, and an arc left by one last wipe-down lay across the surface in a milky smear.

Her shoes made a light padding sound on the solid floor as she crossed the kitchen gently, still not ready to cause any kind of stir. To the left of the doorway lay two rooms, with the entrance hall, staircase and another room to the right. She glanced along the hall towards the front door; from this side the paintwork looked white and intact. There was, of course, nothing sucking at those dead leaves from the inside, just a benign heap of junk mail and free newspapers on the thinning carpet. Like the exterior of the front door, it too had once been dark blue. Where it met the skirting she could see the original colour, and how the weave had resembled chunky corduroy.

Everywhere else the carpet had turned a dusty air-force blue, hers being amongst the footsteps that had caused that. Becca banging her way up the stairs, chaotic and shouting for help; Dan clattering down, heading for a date or a sports fixture, and leaving doors wide open behind him. She wondered what mark she'd left on the memory of this house. She remembered spending a lot of her time being quiet and serious and listening to everyone else. Maybe she'd never left a mark here and that's how she'd found it so easy to slip unnoticed through all the intervening years.

The atmosphere began to feel oppressive, so she coughed loudly and said, 'Upstairs then,' just to break the silence.

The cat that lived in one of the houses behind theirs had been a bad-tempered tom. According to his red collar and heart-shaped name tag, his name was Twinkle and, although he was clearly someone's much loved pet, his only skills seemed to be territorial. Jane paced around the upstairs rooms now like that cat would have done. She felt the need to enter each in turn, walk about them slowly, remind herself of the view from each window, then close the door carefully behind her as she left.

She had already made the decision to confine her living space to her old bedroom, the bathroom and the kitchen. But walking through the empty rooms felt like a rite. With each door she opened, she braced herself for experiencing further unexpected emotions. But instead the emptiness inside translated into blankness, nothingness, a silent vacuum. This place felt like a dusty Tussauds' exhibit, the props and figures gone, and the deserted set exposed as something flimsy, meaningless and without any context.

She left her own room until last. The wallpaper was almost as she remembered it, cream adorned with blue stripes and sprays of sweet pea. She had thought the decor childish at the time, but now, strangely, it seemed far too mature for her: a room she would only grow into in twenty years or so, or maybe only in a different lifetime. She'd always doubted she'd make it to thirty, never mind almost fifty. She opened the window and the fresh air squeezed past her, pushing its way all round the room. She left it to chase out the staleness and retreated downstairs to the back room that her mother had called the playroom. There was a patio door leading into a short garden, but primarily this had been the room where the three kids, a TV set and a bunch of toys had been left to socialize. And, sure enough, they'd all developed a great relationship with that TV set.

The air felt damper here than it had upstairs, but just as still and forgotten, devoid of molecules of perspiration or exhalation and anything human that was more recent than the ever-present debris of dead skin cells and fallen hairs.

She had no desire to look into either the attic or the cellar, and her father had muttered to her that all the contents left behind were stored in the outhouse.

A painted, iron patio chair lay on its side in the grass. She brought that in first, then continued towards the brick-built shed beyond. It had a black painted door that looked like it had been made from four planks with a 'Z" of timber to hold it in place. *Not locked, just full of crap*, according to her dad.

He hadn't been wrong on either point.

She salvaged one saucepan, one dessert spoon, an old sun-lounger and a dustbin sack filled with pairs of old curtains. She piled them into her arms and, at the last moment, added a rusty shaving mirror and a jam jar containing an assortment of ballpoint pens.

She dumped all of this just inside the playroom, then slipped out to buy enough groceries to last for the next couple of days. Once she returned, she changed her mind about sleeping upstairs and arranged the 'bed' and metal chair alongside one another, facing the patio doors but at enough of an angle that her own reflection wouldn't stare back at her. In the end she didn't use either but sat down on a folded curtain, with her back to the solid wall, and watched absolutely nothing happening out in the garden.

Sometime later she closed the curtains, and later still, when she realized she was too restless to sleep, she scooped up the pile of post and newspapers and dumped them on the playroom floor. She sat back down on the curtain, cross-legged this time, and began at the top of the heap, with what looked like the latest freebie newspaper. As she flicked through the first few pages, familiar place names jumped out from meaningless columns of text, stories of minor crimes or complaints from parents struggling through road works while making the school run. These were people who had probably never existed in Cambridge at the time she did, or only in previous incarnations. She'd been away long enough for students to turn into parents, and for most of last decade's burning ambitions to be scuffed into nothingness by the intervening years.

She dumped the newspapers in one heap and, for no particular reason, started a junk-mail pile next to it. She glanced at each item in turn, learning that Cambridge now had the best opportunities for solar panels in East Anglia, the most exciting furniture store in the south, and at least three award-winning restaurants capable of dolloping their top cuisine into plastic tubs and delivering it to her own doorstep. Both the newspapers and the leaflets ran on a weekly loop, their headlines so bland that after the first few front pages each had less impact than the two-for-one pizza offer announced on the sidebar next to it. How many takeaway menus did one house ever need?

Occasionally an envelope lay amidst the other papers. The first few were white with printed labels and postage paid by someone running a stack of envelopes through a franking machine. A couple more had cellophane windows and advertised their sender with a logo printed on the front. Jane didn't feel so bereft of a life that she needed to investigate correspondence from Bar-claycard to feel part of the human race, yet she did reach for the first handwritten envelope with perhaps a little too much keen-ness. It was pale lemon in colour, and the front read *The Osborne Family* – which probably explained why it had slipped through the postal-redirection service. Whatever her father had registered with the Post Office, it wouldn't have included the word *Family*. The writing was shaky, its uneven strokes trying to recreate a once beautiful hand. *Aunt Gwen!* The name flashed into her head, just a name – and the memory of her mother's aunt once sighted at a family wedding. A rarity, in fact, like the sighting of a barred warbler; a name you knew but a face you wouldn't recognize in your own back yard.

It contained some kind of greetings card, and Jane slid it from the envelope. The front carried an uninspired photograph of a bunch of daffodils. *Happy Easter.* Months old now and from a rel-ative disconnected by almost a decade. *To Gerry, Mary and family.*

Jane stood it on the floor, and glanced at it every few minutes as she worked through the rest of the pile.

She didn't consider herself as having one of those addictive personalities. Yes, she'd tried cigarettes, risked £1 each week on the lottery and enjoyed a couple of bottles of beer at the week-end, but she changed her behaviour often too. Dependence scared her: it felt like avoidable baggage. Now she could understand why alcoholics needed to not drink at all, not even a sip, because, after all these years, she could still taste her childhood and it was too intoxicating to ignore.

It surrounded her: the cracks, dents and scars in this old house that were suddenly so familiar, and the unfurling of other random, inconsequential memories that they unlocked. Familiar shouts from the other end of the house. The smell of bolognaise catching the bottom of the pan. Waking early to the strimmer clipping off the top of the grass in their tiny lawn.

It hadn't all been bad, after all.

Under the carpet the varnished floorboards were dappled with darker knot holes. Did the largest of them still look like an eye? Would the third tread on the stairs still creak at the right-hand end, and had there ever been a secret compartment behind the rectangular repair made to the landing ceiling?

Something inside her gave way. It tremored and then it burst.

Instinctively she scrambled towards her own room, stumbling up the stairs and grabbing at the door handle. *Running to ground.* A tangle of truths and doubts hit her all at once. *She hadn't been wrong. Coming home had been the mistake. Not the leaving. Not her anger. Now she had to stay and face them all. Because coming home was necessary.*

She clutched the handle, with her forehead pressed to the paint-work of the door, simultaneously wanting it open but not letting herself enter the bedroom that had acted like her comfort blanket for so many years. Neither her hand nor her head won the contest; the cold smoothness of the gloss itself was enough. Her nose and lips pressed against it . . . and she fell back twenty years, to jars of white spirit and her mother picking loose black bristles from the drying paint. Her father masking windows, then scraping streaks of dried emulsion from the glass where stray drips had still found their mark. The smell of decorating: wallpaper paste and sugar soap. The sheer newness that advertised they were building something fresh, that they hadn't yet watched it for so long that they'd missed the moment when it began to decay.

Damn them all – all those she had burnt up with hating. And damn them even more for reminding her that it hadn't only ever been that way.

She'd cried once already during the last twenty-four hours, but the unfamiliarity of crying still surprised her. She kept her face pressed to the paintwork and continued pulling the handle towards her, as though the stupidity of the tears could stay a secret between her and the door. This body-racking sobbing surprised her more than anything; it continued until her body ached and she had huddled there long enough for the paintwork to feel as warm as the skin of another human being.

Chapter Ten

PC SUE GULLY stepped through the doorway, holding two mugs.

Goodhew's battered swivel chair still had enough life in its gas lift to bounce a little as he leant back in it. 'The real McCoy?'

'Yep . . . well, posh instant, but it's in real china.' She passed Goodhew his coffee then pulled a second chair up to one side of his desk. 'It was actually your turn to make it.'

'I know – which means you're after something.'

She grinned. 'You know me.'

He opened the top-left desk drawer and passed her an unopened packet of Jaffa Cakes. 'Why can't you eat chocolate digestives, like any normal person?'

'I'm cultured.'

He pretended to think that over. 'No,' he said finally, 'that's definitely not it.'

She opened the packet and offered it to him. 'Just one.'

She made a tower of three biscuits in front of her then sipped her coffee.

'I can see from your face that the Jaffa Cakes weren't your only objective. What's up?'

'Why does there have to be a subtext?'

'There doesn't, but today there clearly is. Getting dodgy biscuits out of me is usually a bigger victory. Something more than chocolate's on your mind.'

She narrowed her eyes in mock annoyance. 'Fact is, Gary, I've spent the last couple of weeks trying to work out why you were out on the Gogs that night.'

'We were in the car together for hours the other night, but you didn't ask me then.'

'I was still trying to work it out. So do you know how pissed off I am at having to give in and ask? You're either going to refuse to tell me or the answer will be so obvious that I'll be kicking myself for the rest of the week.'

Goodhew shook his head, then smiled. 'Three weeks ago we had several calls from motorists on that road. They reported seeing a young woman all alone walking in the dark towards Cambridge. We had four similar calls, but no one bothered to stop. We sent out a car but there was then no sign of her. If you add all the calls together, she may have been drunk, or on drugs, or beaten up or thrown from a vehicle.'

'No one stopped?'

'You know . . .' And he knew she did. They'd seen it so many times, the well-intentioned who couldn't bring themselves to intervene. Scared of being wrong, looking foolish, or sometimes scared for their own safety. Scared of opening a door that held even the smallest chance of derailing normality. 'She was in her early twenties, with long messy blonde hair, wearing a skimpy dress . . .'

'Your description?'

'No, the callers'. The dress was light-coloured, stained maybe with mud, maybe not. Carrying her shoes. Obviously crying. Staggering too.'

'Maybe someone did stop in the end. Was anyone reported missing, locally?'

'No. I've also checked nationally. Nothing.'

'So maybe someone stopped, gave her a lift into town, then left her to sleep it off.'

Goodhew shrugged.

'Look, Gary, there's no crime reported. You can't afford to spend time on this.'

'Unless it's my own.'

She flopped back in the chair, folded her arms and fixed him with an angry stare, genuine this time. 'So you drive up there a couple of weeks later to see if you can work out who she was?' Gully didn't wait for a reply. 'Why? Because you can't stand the idea that you'll miss something one day, and then you won't be able to hack the guilt.'

'No one would choose to be walking up there at that time of night, not barefoot.'

'So, she had a fight with her boyfriend, he drove off, left her to walk. Then felt sorry, came back. End of. You know I'm right.'

'I know you're *probably* right.'

'And why aren't you working on the Paul Marshall murder?'

'Officially because I'm giving evidence in eleven cases this month. That means it's court, paperwork and minor cases for the next few weeks. Unofficially I think it's because I was off duty when I found the body. Marks doesn't want some defence lawyer having to cross-examine me as a witness and then again as a police officer. If one appearance was discredited, the other would be, too.'

Gully gave a wry smile. 'Like when they try to make you give reasons for being up there in the first place?'

'Exactly.'

He could see that Gully's irritation had now completely passed. Nothing seemed to make her as happy as verbal sparring, sarcasm and a box of spongy biscuits. As if to prove the point, she tapped another from the packet, dunked it in her coffee and said, 'The words *Serves you right* are on the tip of my tongue, but I'm not going to waste my breath on them.'

The phone on his desk rang just then. He answered quickly and heard the caller take a sharp breath. It sounded like a woman.

'Can I help you?'

'This is Jane Osborne. Can I talk to you?'

'In person?'

'Please.' She hesitated. 'I'm downstairs now, but out the front. I'd prefer not to come in. D'you mind?'

'There's a bench on Parker's Piece, straight across the road from the station . . . see it? Is it free?'

'Yes.'

'I'll be down in five minutes.'

'Thank you.' The phone cut off so abruptly that he was left with the impression that it had been heading back to the cradle even as she spoke.

Gully raised one eyebrow.

'Jane Osborne,' he explained. 'There's obviously something on her mind.'

'Do me a favour? Let Marks know.'

She left the room then and, after she'd gone, he continued staring at the empty doorway until he heard a door further along the corridor close behind her. He went over to look out the window.

Jane Osborne was already sitting there.

The bench she occupied was the typical design of three scrolled cast-iron uprights supporting horizontal wooden slats held together by chunky nuts and bolts. Identical, in fact, to all the others positioned at regular intervals around the perimeter of Parker's Piece. They'd been installed years before, but while the others were generally used as a pleasant place to sit and wait, or relax, or read even, this one had become an informal police-station waiting room. The place people chose to stand when they waited for news but needed fresh air or a cigarette. The place where people congregated to bitch about the police or show their support for a friend or relative who'd been dragged in. The ground all around this bench was scuffed bare, the grass having receded into a semi-circle and the mud decorated with cigarette ends and beer-bottle lids. It was the one bench that was only ever used by people who needed to be at the station but also had reasons not to go inside.

Jane sat in the middle, her back towards him, but if her expression matched what he could assess of her body language, it said *Find somewhere else to sit.*

It was no surprise then that she still had the bench all to herself as he crossed the road to join her. The scowl remained, and it was clear that she'd been crying, but she looked up at him with a strange bemusement. 'I'm out of the habit of talking to anyone.' She didn't smile. 'Apparently it's *"obvious I have trust issues".*'

Goodhew didn't know who Jane might be quoting, but the words still stung her enough to make her eyes blaze and the statement sound defiant.

'OK if I sit?'

She shrugged and moved a foot over to her left. 'Obviously the words of an ex-boyfriend,' she added, as though his silent query had been voiced. 'Said plenty of other stuff too, and I always thought he was talking complete shit, just throwing all that at me because I didn't want to do it often enough.' She gave a short laugh, a disconnected *ha*. Her expression darkened again and this time her gaze drifted further afield, settling somewhere only she could see while she collected her thoughts. 'I need to get my head straight about my family. I want to speak to my mum before I make up my mind about leaving again. You offered to contact my parents last night, so can you just call her for me?'

'You can't ask your dad?'

'No.' Another humourless snort of a laugh. 'Even if he knew, he probably wouldn't tell me.'

'Your brother?'

'I phoned, and apparently she *"buggered off"*. My family's screwed, all through my life it's been screwed . . . and once I realized, I left.'

'But now you want to get in touch with them?'

'Just her. I spoke to my dad in the end. I'm staying at the house we lived in, and that's enough. I don't know that I want to talk to him any more than that.' She folded her arms across her chest and chewed on her bottom lip for a couple of seconds. 'I thought I'd just want to get back out of Cambridge straight away.' Her sentences began sounding increasingly clipped. 'But coming back has stirred up something. That's a bit of a revelation. I didn't expect to feel . . .' she shook her head, 'anything at all.'

'So you want me to get hold of your mother?'

'Yes.'

'And that's it?'

Again the scowl. 'If I could do it myself, I would. I don't *want* to be here having to ask you.' She stood abruptly, sliding her flattened hands into her back pockets and chewing a couple of times on non-existent gum.

Goodhew nodded. 'OK, how do I get hold of you?'

She glanced around, then back at him. She seemed more edgy now, as if fighting a desire to bolt. He wouldn't have been surprised if she'd backed away then, told him to *Fuck off and don't bother*.

Instead she dipped into her front pocket, then passed him a receipt with a mobile number scrawled on the back. 'Or at the house. Just don't leave any messages with my dad, because he doesn't live there.'

Goodhew stood and refolded the slip of paper. 'I won't,' he promised. 'And if you happen to get in touch with her first, please let me know.'

'Sure.' Her voice held a tiny note of hesitation, like a comma instead of a full stop at the end.

'Jane . . . ?'

'I left the house this morning, walked down Pound Hill towards that pub, the old Town and Gown.'

'The Punter?'

'Yeah, whatever.' She waved away his words, impatience pulling her back closer to him. 'He was on the opposite side – just standing there. Saw me when I was about halfway down the road. He knows I'm back already, so maybe he wants me to know he's here too.'

'Who?'

'Greg Jackson.'

'Did he try to speak to you?'

Jane shook her head. 'No, he just stood there and stared at me until I'd gone past. Maybe it's nothing to worry about.' She took a couple of steps away. 'I really don't like you people, but I thought you should know. Greg's never been someone you can predict.'

Chapter Eleven

GOODHEW ENTERED THROUGH the front door of Parkside station to see Gully waiting on the other side of the foyer, propping the door open with her shoulder. A Post-it note was held between the tips of her two forefingers. She waved it at him to indicate it was his, then stuck it to the light switch before finally releasing the door and letting it shut in her wake.

The note read, *See Marks NOW, he's not happy. ITYS.* Goodhew had almost reached his boss's office when he clicked what that meant. *I told you so.*

Marks stepped out into the corridor. 'Something funny, Goodhew? No, I didn't think so.' Marks liked using rhetorical questions, especially when he was angry. He had a dark look in his eyes and Goodhew was confident that question hadn't been the last one. His superior returned to his desk and, once seated, half-swivelled his chair so that the wall-length window was to his left.

'Jane Osborne. I happen to look outside and there she is, chatting to one of my DCs. Don't tell me it was social?' Marks rarely raised his voice; in this instance he barely sounded annoyed, but this was the tone he used that felt most dangerous.

'Of course not,' Goodhew replied.

'Why don't I know about this?'

'She phoned in and I first wanted to find out what she wanted. I was going to let you know.'

'Because you're such an expert at letting me know, aren't you, Goodhew?' Marks's eyes darted from Goodhew, to the view of Parker's Piece, and back again. 'This isn't the time to perpetuate that habit.' He nodded at the nearest chair.

'Jane has asked whether we'd be able to locate her mother. She doesn't want to ask her father – probably didn't want to ask us either.'

'Making us the lesser of two evils? What else?'

'Just her parting shot: she saw Greg Jackson. He was near her house and she thought we might want to know. She says he didn't try to speak to her, but was definitely watching her.'

'I see.' Marks's focus slipped long as he thought for a moment. He remained motionless apart from the fast, light tapping of his index finger on the arm of his chair. Then he drew himself back. 'To change the subject,' he said, as if the words were a memo to self, heavy pen, double underlined. 'You realize why you haven't been put on the Paul Marshall case?'

'I think so.'

Surprisingly that answer didn't prompt Marks to offer Goodhew any further clarification. 'As ever, my team is under-resourced and it's become an issue for me. I need more bodies on that case and you're one of them. But I need you to be cautious.'

Goodhew nodded.

Marks nevertheless asked him if he understood.

'Yes, sir,' he replied.

'Good. Catch up with Kincaide. He has more statements to take, so accompany him for today and tomorrow, and he'll update you.'

Marks leant forward in his chair as if about to stand, but he didn't actually rise. It was the signal for Goodhew to leave.

'There's one more thing, sir? Mary Osborne – is it OK if I find her for Jane?'

'As a department we certainly should do so, moral obligation and so on. But you . . . ?' His index finger tapped a few more times.

'Like you said, the department's stretched. It shouldn't take me long and I won't let it impact on the Marshall case.'

'You sound like my daughter negotiating a lift home. Part logic, part dogged determination. Unfortunately for me, you and Emily are proficient at both. Sadly, it doesn't mean either of you behave sensibly.' Marks waved him away. 'Let me know once you're done.'

Chapter Twelve

CATCH UP WITH *Kincaide*. Goodhew and Kincaide's working relationship functioned best when they stayed apart, on two separate lines of inquiry, and only exchanged information under close supervision from Marks himself. Perhaps the situation wasn't quite that bad, but it was close.

Goodhew had expected the usual sour greeting and reluctant cooperation, but Kincaide had looked up brightly as soon as he entered the room. 'You can grab that desk, Gary.' Kincaide had pointed to the desk which abutted his own. He'd then reached across and tugged some folders back to his own side. 'Sorry, didn't realize I'd spread out so much.' He had glanced down at the papers in front of him and tugged a small sheaf of pages free from the rest and held them towards Goodhew. 'Here's some notes to get you started. I'll pass you the rest in a few minutes.'

Goodhew had managed to thank him and possibly smile. But now, half an hour later, he still felt bemused. The desk was clean, relatively new and within sight of a window. He opened and closed its drawers, switched on the equally well-cleaned computer. Even the chair looked new, but he was careful not to be too quick to put his full weight down on it – just in case. The mood continued to be accommodating although Goodhew struggled to stop his forehead puckering with suspicion. However, Kincaide remained too absorbed by the information on his PC to notice. Every few seconds he tapped some keys, read further, tapped, then jotted notes on the pad next to the keyboard.

A series of 10×8 photographs of Paul Marshall were pinned to the noticeboard that occupied most of the wall space alongside their two desks. Eight of them were shots taken either from the scene or at the time of the post-mortem examination. Another five were enlargements of snapshots taken during the last year and a half. One showed Marshall with his car, the rest individual. The man had stayed in shape, and it looked as though he'd preferred to wear T-shirts one size too tight just to prove the point. His haircut, clothes and even expression were reminiscent of a school leaver starting work the first day in his new job, all boyish and optimistic. Twenty-plus years seemed a long time to hold on to that sentiment.

The most recent 'live' photo was dated 6 March and had been taken at a party. Marshall posed under a *Happy Birthday* banner with the curving edge of a lilac balloon sneaking into one corner of the picture. Part of the upright of a character was visible; if it was a number it was probably a '1'.

'Daughter's birthday?'

Kincaide looked up. 'Yeah, twelfth. He had two girls, Molly and Evie. Evie's only eight.' His eyes moved on to the other shots, and Goodhew waited for the inevitable comment. Judging by these shots, it would be somewhere between *Purple's not his colour* and *He probably had it coming*.

Kincaide shook his head as he turned back to his work. 'Poor bugger,' he sighed.

Weird.

'Where is everyone?'

'On another door-to-door round his estate, following up more work contacts. Or friends . . . even acquaintances will do.' Kincaide raised an eyebrow. 'Yes, it is reaching that point.'

Goodhew had seen minimum details on this case: in a rare victory over himself, he'd beaten his own urge to know more than the information appearing in the press. And, thanks to that self-control, he'd now have to start from close to zero. Paul Marshall, a plumber. Married to Carmel. Grew up locally, lived locally. Two children. Flash car. It was barely enough to merit a photo caption.

'Who did he work for?'

'Self-employed.'

'Debt?'

'No.' Kincaide nodded towards the other pages in the sheaf he'd handed to Goodhew. 'Some of it's there. Ask me when you've read it.'

Goodhew picked up the top one: *Autopsy Summary.*

Apart from the cause of death being listed as *cardiac arrest due to hypovolemia*, the other injuries received were listed with little interpretation. Few clues about which had come first, or weapons, angles and degrees of force involved.

The injuries were listed in order, travelling up the body from Paul Marshall's feet to his head. Goodhew read through it all, picturing a non-specific human form, like a flesh-toned C3PO, which his mind's eye marked up consecutively with each new wound described.

Minor bruising and scratches covered much of the surface area of Marshall's skin. Deeper bruising around the face, hands and ribs. Fractures to three fingers, the left knee and left eye socket.

First-degree burns to the upper part of Marshall's right shoulder, lower back, right cheek and ear. Second-degree burns in the genital area, the type the pathologist had described as *superficial partial thickness*.

Goodhew winced. No doubt the word 'superficial' was technically correct but it hardly seemed appropriate.

The wire that had secured Marshall to the tree had caused extensive damage, cutting into the soft tissue of his stomach but going deeper and leaving deep gashes at the armpits. It had been the wire around his neck that had caused the final, fatal wound.

He mentally put the injuries in a rough chronological order. Marshall had been incapacitated, moved, tied, tortured and killed. He'd weighed just over eleven stone eight pounds. Not heavy for a man, but no featherweight either, and he'd been healthy and fit, too. Maybe he'd been surprised but, even so, Goodhew doubted this attack had been swift or easy.

Of course, the full report would include all the technical stuff, but this was the way it looked to him.

At the bottom of the page was a handwritten note: *Toxicology to follow*. Clipped to the front sheet was a batch of photographs. He separated them from the sheet and spread them out across his desk. Each shot showed a close-up of injuries to a particular area of the victim's body.

'Have you seen these?' he asked.

Kincaide glanced across, then quickly looked away. 'Yes.'

'Why did they send them ahead of the full report?'

'Marks says it is relevant to the psychology of the perpetrator. Let's face it, this one's extreme.'

Goodhew's attention fell on to a close-up of Marshall's right hand. 'Have you seen this?' He held it out to Kincaide, who didn't bother to look up again.

'Are you trying to flash that burnt penis photo?'

'No, look.' Goodhew rattled the photo a couple of times until the noise forced Kincaide to look over. 'What's that?' Goodhew pointed to the knuckles, then passed the image across the desk. 'It's a mess, but look at the gap between the knuckle damage. See?'

'The bruising?'

'Yeah, but look, the discoloration's different. I think it's older.'

Kincaide held it a little more into the light. 'It's possible,' he conceded. 'I'll email back right now and make sure they cover it in the full report.' He turned back to his PC and began typing.

'Thanks,' Goodhew muttered. Now he was convinced Kincaide's behaviour was really, really weird.

Goodhew flicked through the remaining sheets of paper and realized they amounted to a briefing document, about a dozen pages in all, outlining the victim's last known movements, summarizing his finances, medical history and the course of the investigation to date. Then he read the report through twice. The first time he took in the key facts, committing them to memory. The second time he allowed his thoughts to wander between the words, between the lines, and the only time he wrote on the sheet of A4 next to him was to remind himself of the questions he needed to ask.

'How was his marriage?'

'His wife claims it was good. Maybe it was.'

'But you don't think so?'

'Sadly, I'm not the greatest believer in happy marriages, I thought you'd have clocked that by now. Jan and I . . .' Kincaide stopped mid-sentence and shrugged.

It was a cue, but Goodhew ignored it. 'So are there any suspicions of either Paul Marshall or his wife having an affair?'

'No. We've looked. A lover's pissed-off husband would have been my first guess, too, or even the wife's lover clearing the field.'

'Burning the car is revenge for something . . .'

'And there's nothing like love to generate that much hate.' Kincaide paused to reflect on what he'd just said, nodded to himself, then snapped his attention back to the conversation. 'Unless, of course, Carmel Marshall's after the life policy. But there's nothing whatsoever that points to her involvement in his death so far.'

'Main lines of inquiry?'

'Usual. Fair amount of his business stayed off the books, so we can't see everything we might like to from the accounts alone. We've run his car and van through the ANPR database, phone records, card payments . . .'

'Internet?'

'One PC, two laptops and internet via his mobile all being audited as we speak.'

'And the mobile phone case near the body?'

'His, apparently.'

'Really? It looked like a woman's.'

'That's what I thought but the manufacturer calls it a— hang on.' Kincaide stopped speaking as he located and opened an email. 'A unisex design with a feminine bias,' he read. Kincaide then snorted, but the predictable *in the closet* comment didn't follow. 'I need to get home now, so is there anything else you need before I go?'

There probably was, but at that moment Goodhew's mind remained blank. 'No, we're good, thanks.'

And, for several minutes after Kincaide had left, he continued to dwell on their conversation. *We're good.* He never used that expression. But he'd just said it to Kincaide. Goodhew went for some coffee to distract himself from the urge to check for a hidden camera. Perhaps Kincaide wasn't playing a practical joke, but something here was out of whack.

PCs Sue Gully and Kelly Wilkes were at the coffee machine, drinks already in hand. Kelly saw him first and nudged Gully. She turned to face Goodhew. 'Did you meet him?'

'Who?'

Mischievous grin. 'The all-new Kincaide.'

He looked from one to the other and realized that he'd just stumbled on the current topic of their conversation. 'Yes. What's happened to him?'

'No idea, but all this week he'd been odd,' Kelly replied. 'If you were meeting him for the first time, you'd even think he was a decent bloke.'

'Polite? Cooperative?'

They both nodded. 'Not even the usual snideyness,' Kelly remarked.

'Or ignorance,' Sue added. 'Yep, it's creepy. What did you call it earlier?'

'Jaunty but sinister.'

Goodhew was sure that Kincaide would be quietly pleased if he'd known of their consternation. Or perhaps only the old Kincaide . . . Had Kincaide's recent words and responses been made by anyone else in the department, the three of them would not have been at all fazed. Yet here they were – trebly bemused.

Goodhew's thoughts drifted, reflecting that normal behaviour attached to the wrong person could generate such a reaction. Who would have called the police after spotting a casually clothed, lone *male* walking the Gogs?

Even at night?

No one.

Or a drunk girl wearing a skimpy dress and high heels stumbling through the city centre at 1 a.m.? The answer remained the same. Goodhew took his coffee back to his desk. For the moment, Paul Marshall and Michael Kincaide could both wait.

He'd emailed himself a list of four names and their corresponding phone numbers: Barry Tolhurst, Melody Chukwu, Rod Skinner and David Searle. He began at the top of the list.

The call was picked up by an answer phone. As soon as Goodhew identified himself, the real-life Barry Tolhurst cut in with a clipped recitation of his own name then, with barely a pause, 'Is this about that young woman?'

'Yes, it is. I'd like to ask you a few further questions about her appearance.'

'Of course, if I can help . . . As I told you, she was blonde, early twenties at most. I picked her out in my headlights when I was still some way back. She stumbled at one point, then stopped to remove her shoes. Her dress was a pale colour that caught the light, so must have been one of those fabrics with a sheen to it. Her shoes were patent, a beige-y colour, not much darker than her hair really. Ridiculously high, I thought – no wonder she had to take them off.'

'Did you see her face?'

'Briefly. I slowed a bit and she turned her head towards me.'

'Did you speak to her at all?'

A hesitation.

'Mr Tolhurst?'

'I lowered the window and I asked her if she was all right. I don't know what I would have done if she'd said "no" . . . given her a lift maybe.'

'What did she say?'

'Nothing. She just stared at me, shook her head, then kept walking. I assumed I'd scared her, so I drove on. I thought of doubling back at the next roundabout but, when I got there, I just didn't.'

'Can you describe her any further than that? Height? Build? Anything?'

'Above average height, I'd say – not towering but maybe five foot seven. She would have hit six foot in those heels, though. Lithe, too, looked womanly.' He pulled himself up short. 'Sorry, inappropriate way to describe her, perhaps, but I had this stupid feeling, the moment I opened the window, that having her in the car with me would have looked inappropriate, too. I'm an estimator for a drainage company, no one would really care what I do.'

'And her face?'

'Big eyes, make-up smudged like she'd been crying. Reminded me of Twiggy . . . or that *Clockwork Orange* eye. Her legs were bare, streaked with mud, and her hands looked dirty too. So I guessed she'd fallen over. Long hair, kind of Scandinavian-looking . . . I couldn't describe her any more than that.'

Melody Chukwu and Rod Skinner were less forthcoming. They'd rung out of civil duty, nothing more: Melody in case the girl had been in an accident, Skinner in case she actually caused one. Tall, blonde and in a mess: these remained the common denominator.

'David Searle?'

The voice at the other end had a long-time smoker's rasp. 'He's out, I'm Mrs Searle.'

Goodhew introduced himself, then continued, 'I'm ringing regarding your husband's report of a "distressed woman" beside the A1307 on 28 July . . .'

'Woman? She looked only about seventeen, too young to be out alone like that. I was driving, and I told him to ring. I insisted.' She coughed and her lungs rattled. 'She was asking for trouble, but how would we both have felt if something bad had happened to the girl?'

'But you didn't stop?'

'We were keen to get home and anyway we weren't the only ones driving up there. So did you find her?'

'Not yet. I'm hoping that you or your husband may be able to remember something that might help us identify her.'

She fell silent for several seconds, and Goodhew waited, listening to the tobacco tin opening and the almost silent ritual of rolling her next cigarette. 'She obviously got herself home in one piece, or else you'd know who she was by now. My husband thinks there's a murderer on every corner, so, no, we didn't stop. And, from my experience, nothing much happens in real life to girls like that.'

'Like what?'

'Daughters who go unsupervised turn into women who need watching.'

'I'm sorry?'

'Typical man, you are. Let's just say she looked like the type who was used to being out alone at night.'

'Can you describe her for me?'

She ignored the question. Or perhaps, in her own eyes, she didn't. 'Ten-a-penny trollops.' Pause. Puff. 'Go in any newsagent's and they're there, glossy women with wholesome faces and fake smiles. Making men think that there are women out there who really love sex. They've become the modern role models, you know.' Puff. 'When did the quest for women's equality become twisted into a game of who has most notches on her bedpost? When?'

Goodhew sagged into his chair and waited until the rolling of the next cigarette temporarily silenced the ranting. No wonder this woman's husband had gone out.

'Not that many years ago a decent man wouldn't have tattooed hands. That meant he could cover up the tattoos when he went job hunting. Larry says the army used to burn them off squaddies' hands before discharge, so they could look OK at any interview in a shirt and tie.'

He'd obviously missed the start of this particular outpouring. 'She had a tattoo?'

'Tattoos are for men and, in my opinion, women with tattoos make themselves look like whores.'

'And this woman had one?'

'Across her foot and up her ankle.'

'And you could see this without slowing?'

'I slowed down a little.' She sniffed, and that made her cough. 'I always notice tattoos, because they disgust me. It was just one of those flimsy daisy trails, but I noticed it all right.'

SOMETIMES FINDING A person with the right specialist knowledge could be tricky, but locating an attractive young woman with a pretty tattoo? That was a relatively easy dilemma. Goodhew next phoned Bryn, who might not have the exact answer but would have many, *many* ideas about where to look. He promised him an all-he-could-eat takeaway meal, and found him already waiting on the doorstep by the time Goodhew returned to his flat.

'It's being delivered,' he assured Bryn as they climbed the stairs to his grandfather's former library.

'Fantastic. I had a sub and a Mars Bar this afternoon, but apart from that I haven't eaten since lunch.' Bryn was a couple of inches shorter than Gary, and undoubtedly more solid, though never close to being actually overweight, no matter what he ate.

Goodhew left Bryn in the room and carried on up to his flat under the roof. When he returned with some beer, he found his friend happily selecting tracks on the jukebox. 'Couldn't you swap this machine for one that plays CDs? There would be more choice then.'

Goodhew handed Bryn a bottle but didn't even bother to reply.

'Or maybe a picture of a jukebox and an iPod. Seriously, was it an heirloom or something?'

'No. I bought it when I was eighteen. And if it's so crap, why do you keep fiddling with it?'

Bryn patted the glass front. 'I love it, but I just don't understand why you'd keep this thing when you could sell it and buy a car.'

Bryn was capable of many variations of the same conversation. What he clearly wasn't capable of was accepting that Goodhew did without a car through personal choice. 'You'll change your mind one day, Gary.'

'And talking about changing your mind, are you still thinking about a tattoo?'

'I was, then I wasn't, now I am again.' Bryn leant back against the jukebox and the record jumped. 'That was a rubbish change of subject, by the way.'

'Well, I've got a tattoo question for you – and I still don't want a car. And how can you keep changing *your* mind about something as permanent as a tattoo?'

Bryn swigged his beer then held the bottle in front of him, probably positioning it so it looked as though Gary was trapped in the bottle with his head sticking out. If there was a mirror in the room Bryn would have drawn a smiley face on it by now. 'I checked out half a dozen tattooists, and it turns out the tattoo shop round the corner from the garage is the one I like best. I went in one lunchtime but, when I saw the photos of everyone else's tattoos, I couldn't decide what to go for.'

'But now you have?'

'No, I haven't and that's the problem. There's this girl working in there . . .'

Goodhew fought to stop his eyes from rolling.

'Don't pull that face, Gary. I think she might be *the one*.'

Goodhew blinked. 'The one?'

'Yes, the one that's next.' Bryn grinned. 'Anyway, I was thinking of a tattoo and she has a few – a whole graveyard scene across one shoulder for a start – so she's not going to be impressed with my virgin skin.'

'And she's worth getting tattooed for?'

'I really had no idea I found tattoos on women so sexy, and I was planning on getting one anyway.'

'But then you weren't.'

Bryn waved Goodhew's point aside. 'I love women, right? So I'm going to have a hula girl from here to here – ' he drew invisible top and bottom lines near the top of his arm and just above his elbow. 'Last year's Hawaiian calendar had some hula girls. Do you still have it somewhere?'

Goodhew waved his hand in the vague direction of the bookcase in the corner of the room. 'Probably somewhere over there.' If he had kept it at all, it would most likely be with a collection of Hawaiian photos kept in the lower cupboard. 'Just take it if it's useful.'

'There are plenty of women who appreciate the female form, Gary, so what a great ice breaker, eh?'

'Amazing,' he replied flatly.

Bryn put the bottle down and sighed. 'What's your question, then?'

'I'm looking for a woman who has a daisy tattoo running across her foot and up her ankle. I have no idea whether she had it done locally, but that's my only starting point.'

'So what's your question?'

'How can I find her, from that particular tattoo?'

'Is that her only one?'

'The only one I know of.'

'But you know what she looks like?'

'Tall and blonde, late teens or maybe a little older, which means that even if she's had the tattoo done when she was under age, there are good odds that it was within the last couple of years.' As Goodhew explained all this he realized how little chance there was of finding her this way.

Bryn was more to the point. 'That's impossible.'

It was true, for even if he found the right tattooist, the odds of them actually knowing her name or address were slimmer than slim. Goodhew wondered how he'd initially jumped at information that was now such an obvious dead end.

Bryn tugged open the bookcase door. 'Of course, if you had all of Cambridge gathered in one room, it would be easier. You could inspect their ankles, then let most of them go again.'

The sound of the doorbell chimed up to them. Goodhew grabbed his wallet, hurried down to the front door, and returned with two carrier bags, bulging with takeaway cartons. By the time he'd made it back upstairs, Bryn was sitting on the floor in front of the bookcase, flipping through the calendar he had mentioned.

Halfway back up the stairs, Goodhew had been overtaken by a familiar restlessness. 'I need to go out,' he explained, as he handed Bryn the food.

'I thought you were hungry?'

Not now. Goodhew shook his head. 'Leave me the balti. I'll have it when I get back. Let yourself out after you've eaten.'

'Really? And I've found some pictures.'

'Pictures?'

'Hula girls?'

'It's fine, Bryn, take whatever you want.' Goodhew could feel himself being drawn away. 'I'm sorry, but it's something I just don't want to leave until tomorrow.'

Chapter Thirteen

DAISY TATTOO. IT sounded like a stripper's name or maybe a bur-
lesque act. During the previous hour it had inadvertently become
Goodhew's name for the woman on the Gogs. It was a bad thing
to do, turning her into a fictional persona which, in the worst case,
could taint his impression of the real woman and make her even
harder to find.

This thought had occurred to him halfway up the stairs, just as
he'd started to wonder why Bryn was expending so much effort on
a mere drawing of a woman, rather than the real thing. It had been
swiftly followed by a much more important thought: *Jane's need to
find her mother was real, so why wasn't he chasing that instead?* He'd
checked his watch – 8.30 p.m. – and decided it was still early enough
to do something, and he knew he'd lie awake later if he didn't.

He'd hurried on up to his sitting room, which nestled in the
loft space. He had left his laptop on the sofa and he sat down next
to it, pen and paper ready, as it booted up.

Originally he'd occupied only the rooftop flat here in his
grandparents' former home but, after discovering that he had

inherited the whole building, he'd then moved his jukebox and a few items of furniture into his grandfather's library, and hadn't yet considered expanding into any of the other rooms. He guessed he wasn't ready yet to see them changed.

He'd already slid his hand into the magazine rack and retrieved a slim Seagate external drive from his hollowed-out hardback of *The Maltese Falcon*. Over the years he'd bought several copies, and all but one had met the same fate. He now plugged the drive into the laptop. It contained details of anything workwise that he thought to be of special interest: photos he'd taken, documents he'd copied, notes, ideas and contact details – in short, information he wanted but would not officially be allowed to keep.

There he'd found the phone numbers and addresses of Jane's father and brother, saved them directly to his mobile, and headed downstairs again, calling out goodbye to Bryn as he reached the street door.

Jane's father lived in Newnham Road, close to Goodhew's own grandmother, Daniel lived in Castle Street, closer to Jane. The two properties were about a mile away, but in different directions. Goodhew had doubted there'd be time to visit both without risking complaint that he was disturbing them too late at night.

When he rang Gerry Osborne's mobile, the call had been answered swiftly.

'Mr Osborne?'

'How did you get my number?' Gerry Osborne's voice had been immediately familiar. The man had participated in TV interviews, as a sculptor, sometime before his daughter's death, and again several years afterwards, and stayed silent in between. One sentence from him was enough for Goodhew to picture him standing there bearlike and glowering.

As Goodhew identified himself, Osborne's tone seemed to improve.

Minutely.

'I have a couple of questions, so I'd like to drop in and see you. There's no need to worry, though.'

'Yes, I realize that. From my previous experience, terrible news comes with no warning, just a sudden knock at the door.'

'I can be with you in about fifteen minutes.'

'I'm visiting my son.'

'And I can see you there? He's still on Castle Street?'

And, shortly afterwards, Goodhew waited outside the narrow Edwardian terrace houses, as the fuzzy outline of a child fiddled with a set of keys on the other side of the frosted glass. A larger figure soon loomed behind and the door was opened by a woman in her early thirties. She reminded Goodhew of an advert for something healthy, like spring water or mountain bikes or apple shampoo.

The little girl at her side was a scaled-down version of the same. 'Are you the policeman?' the child asked.

'Yes, I am.'

She looked disappointed. 'Oh.'

Her mother scooped her up and turned her round to face the stairs. 'Go on up, Reba. I'll be right there.' She turned back to Goodhew and smiled. 'She was expecting at least a uniform. And a police dog would have made her day.'

'How old is she?'

'Five-and-a-half.' She rolled the four words into one as though she'd said this a thousand times. 'I'm Roz, by the way. Come on in. The men are out in the workshop.'

The polished wood flooring had been laid with the boards running towards the back of the house. Although narrow, the property turned out to be deceptively long. As she led him through the hallway, it looked as though they were heading down one of the lanes at a bowling alley.

'Gerry's been here a lot since Jane returned. She doesn't want to see him, but I think he wants to stay close. It's sweet.' She opened the back door and, on the other side of a small courtyard garden, he saw a single-storey workshop similar in age to the original structure of the house. 'There you go.'

Based on this particular father-and-son pairing, family resemblances seemed less of a trait on the male side of the Osborne clan. Dan shared his father's height and his stubborn jawline, but that was about it.

A large sculpture dominated the interior of the workshop. It appeared to be made of stone, metal and leather, but Goodhew couldn't even begin to guess whether it was now finished or not. Gerry sat on a tatty kitchen chair beside it. The rest of the set of chairs were in the room, but Goodhew wasn't offered a seat. Dan hesitated near the door. 'Do you want me to go?'

'No need. Either of you may be able to help. We need an address for your mother,' he turned from Dan to Gerry, 'your ex-wife.'

Gerry's expression darkened and he rose from the chair. 'Why?'

'We need to contact her.'

'For what reason?'

Jane Osborne had not asked him to either admit or deny that this request had come at her instigation. On balance, however, Goodhew preferred discretion. 'Your daughter's return highlighted the fact that Mary Osborne's details were no longer up to date. It's merely routine.'

'That's bollocks. It's Jane, isn't it? She's asked you to find her mother.'

So much for trying discretion.

Gerry Osborne's face was tanned like a gardener's, but, behind the deep brown, he visibly reddened. 'Having that woman back in Cambridge is the last thing we need.'

'Dad . . .'

'No, Dan, your sister is deluding herself . . . and you.' He glowered at Goodhew, his right hand making a fist as he spoke. He clenched it tightly, until it trembled, 'You people . . .' His words trailed away.

Dan stepped slightly closer. 'We are still angry over the failure to secure a murder conviction against Greg Jackson.' Dan sounded angry, too, but clearly kept his feelings on a tighter rein. 'His release has been hard for all of us, especially Dad.'

'Thank you, Dan, but I am here in the room and capable of speaking for myself.' The older man's eye colour was either an extremely dark shade of brown or his pupils were dilated to their maximum. 'Detective Goodhew, I appreciate you coming in person, which either demonstrates the existence of some degree of respect or a cynical ploy by your senior officer. Either way I am not prepared to share information with you about *that* woman.'

'Jane would like to contact her mother, to let her know that she is safe and well.'

'She's had years to do that. Why come back and then immediately screw it up by letting Mary back in?'

'Surely that's her choice to make?'

'And mine to stop it from happening.'

After Gerry stopped speaking, Goodhew let the silence lengthen and become heavy. It was Dan who spoke again first. 'She's in France.'

'Do you have an address?'

'No, but we've had a couple of postcards, and they both have the same postmark. Would you like to see them?'

The same heavy silence returned as soon as he'd gone. It was less comfortable, and this time it was Goodhew who broke it. 'Greg Jackson spoke to you recently?'

Gerry set his jaw and folded his arms across his chest. For a few seconds Goodhew thought he wasn't going to get a response. Then Gerry dipped his head in the briefest of nods. 'He came to see me, yes.'

'What did he say?'

'Why?'

'I'm curious.'

'Good, then stay curious. He came to tell me he'd never killed Becca.' Gerry took a couple of steps back, with lips now tightly shut. For a while, his chest rose and fell with heavy breathing. 'What a fool,' he then continued. 'Does he think I don't know him? I was full of bile towards that man long, long before he murdered my daughter.'

Dan returned, postcards in hand. Gerry glared at him. 'I really hoped you'd have the sense to come back in and say you'd lost them.'

Dan looked down at the cards, as he spoke. 'Sorry, Dad, but she's still my mum. I don't want to get in touch with her, but I understand why Jane does.'

Gerry Osborne thrust his hand towards Goodhew, an abrupt and unexpected move. 'I appreciate your time.' His grip was hard.

'Thank you for seeing me,' Goodhew replied. Gerry then left without another word to either of them. The moment the door closed, Dan held out the two postcards. They were typical Brit-goes-to-Paris tourist fare: one an aerial view of the Arc de Triomphe, and the other a night shot of the Eiffel Towel emblazoned with firework-style writing that read *Bonjour de Paris*. Goodhew turned them over.

'They're both postmarked *Limoges*,' Dan explained.

'Yes, I see that. The dates are hard to read, though. When did they arrive?'

'This one' – he tapped the Arc de Triomphe – 'came last year, and the other one about a year before.'

'And any before that?'

'About one each year, I guess, but I wouldn't know where to find them right now. Assuming we still have them, that is.'

Goodhew started reading. The actual correspondence space on each card was typically small, and Mary Osborne seemed to have had difficulty reducing the size of her handwriting to fit. The loops on her letters remained disproportionately large, so that the smaller characters – such as a, *c* and *e* – were almost lost amid the tangle created by the *l*s, *t*s and gs.

> *Don't forget to visit Becca. Just so you know, I think of all our kids. Time it was your turn – Mary.*

And the other read:

> *All's fine here. I think of Cambridge from time to time, but know I did the right thing when I left. Sorry if you still hate me – Mary.*

THEY'D BEEN SENT to the house on Pound Hill without any addressee's name but they had clearly been meant for Gerry. 'Why do you have them here?'

Dan had stepped back to give Goodhew space to read. He was now leaning against the wall, with one hand resting on the Car-Hits-Cow sculpture. 'Dad rented out the house after she left, and had the post redirected here until he worked out what he was going to do next.'

His fingers drifted across a seam on the sculpture, where the metal joined the leather.

Despite its basic outhouse appearance, the room was dry and the ceiling high, with glazed panels fitted in the roof for natural light. 'Does he do this work in here?' As soon as Goodhew said it, he registered the absence of any tools.

'No, his current home address is his studio . . . or, to put it another way, he dosses in a corner of his workshop. We just store this item here.'

'Does it have a name?'

'That's your polite way of saying *What is it*, right?' Dan waved an upturned palm in front of the piece. 'This thing is the infamous *Singular Fascination*.'

It took Goodhew a second before he realized. 'The same one he smashed?'

'I brought the bits back here. At first he wasn't interested, but he repaired it eventually.' Dan pointed to a scuff and a dent in the metal. 'Of course, some of the damage was tricky, and in a couple of places Dad chose not to replace the parts. Since its whole dynamic had arisen from us losing Becca and from his divorce, I suppose it was fitting that his later reaction to Jackson getting paroled has left its mark too.'

Goodhew tilted his head slightly. He'd seen art critics do the same and wondered whether this slightly new angle of view would help at all. It didn't.

'You don't have to "get it".'

'No?'

'Think of it like the catwalk where the fashion models wear apparently extreme designs. Those designs showcase the designer; they are a calling card for the inspiration, the *Zeitgeist* of the creator, and it's from there the high-street collections are born.'

'So some form of this object ends up being a commercial product?'

'From this particular exhibition, Dad received several commissions: a sculpture for a company headquarters, work for private collectors, even the design installations at a London casino. You'd be surprised.'

Goodhew was inclined to agree about that. He stared at the sculpture for a few more seconds. 'You work for him, don't you?'

'Only since Becca. I'm surprised that's on record.'

'I guessed, actually. I noticed how your tone changes when you talk about his work.'

'I was writing copy for a staff magazine in town, and offered to help my dad in my spare time. I started with the correspondence and accounts. Eventually he needed more assistance, so I decided to "make the leap", as they say. The biggest risk in that was wondering whether we'd be able to work together.'

'And you can, I guess?'

'My father's spent more time in the eye of the media than most, therefore talking about him openly with complete strangers is part of my job. I know he appreciates my perspective.' Dan thought for a moment. 'If you find my mum, would you let me know? I think I should speak to her.'

'Despite your father's point of view?'

Dan patted the sculpture forcefully, then moved away. 'I was hugely into sport when I was a teenager: rugby, cricket and rowing at various times. But sport isn't on Dad's radar, so he didn't want to know. He's pretty egocentric. I don't think he would try to stop us from contacting her, but he would probably take it personally if we did. Mum's gone from his life now, and he's never been good at seeing any viewpoint apart from his own. I won't be telling him, either, if you do manage to track her down.'

'Your sister wants to contact your mother, yet she won't see her father?'

'Her choice.' Just the two blunt words but, for a moment, Dan's expression sparked with far more complexity than that, as though a flash of intangible memory was reflected on his face.

'Have you seen Jane yet?'

'We have met up a couple of times, briefly.' Goodhew realized it was the first time he'd seen Dan smile. 'It's strange,' Dan continued. 'We've both changed, and sometimes it feels as though I'm talking to a complete stranger, then at other times I have moments when I could almost forget everything else that has happened in between.' He paused, thoughtfully. 'She hasn't met Reba yet.'

'You didn't give her any help in finding her mother, though. She told me that.'

Dan's smile remained, though it dimmed. 'I argue with my father but in general I agree with him, too. I suppose I find it hard to let him know that.'

'And, despite this, you still want to speak to your mother?'

'Yes. I'll tell her to stay away from Jane.'

Chapter Fourteen

UNIVERSITY GROCERS HAD been the local shop of Jane's childhood, a home of sweets, magazines and ice cream in the summer. Beyond lay the bridge into the city centre, making the small shop even more tempting.

Today its draw was Heinz tomato soup, bread, eggs, milk and a copy of the *Cambridge News*. She glanced over towards Magdalene Bridge, but the upwards slope towards the house appealed to her more.

He'd been standing at the bottom of the hill again.

She'd checked the street outside before leaving the house, and spotted him. He'd been on the opposite side of the road to the Punter, making a poor attempt to stand discreetly in the rear gate of Westminster College. Perhaps the act of loitering outside a centre of theological study had made him squirm; it had certainly had that effect on her in the past.

She'd watched him for a few minutes as he leant with one shoulder up against the wall, rhythmically elbowing the brickwork. Next he had pushed away, walked a few purposeful strides, then returned to the same spot. Whenever his feet were still, another part of his body wasn't. And this level of distraction was more than enough to allow her to slip out through the side gate and skirt around the back of her house.

After almost ten years of running and hiding, she reckoned she'd become proficient at it, but by the time she'd reached University Grocers she felt angry with him and furious with herself. Now she strode the quickest route home, head down, with her clenched hands anchored by shopping bags. And there he was, in the same spot, staring down the hill at her and talking or maybe just mouthing words.

She raised her chin. 'I can't hear you,' she shouted.

His weight shifted and he made a couple of small steps forward.

Neither of them spoke until the distance between them had closed to less than ten feet. 'What's your problem?' she asked.

'Guess.'

She curled one corner of her mouth into a smile. Deliberate and taunting. 'I'm sorry, when I said *"What's your problem?"* I meant, realize you've got one and take it somewhere else.'

His hands moved up to rest on his hips. His feet were planted wide. *Little man trying to look big.* 'I want to know what you're hiding,' he said.

She felt her own expression lock down, become impenetrable. 'So you stand outside my house, trying to intimidate me?'

'I'm waiting to talk to you.'

'No, you're trying to scare me. Won't happen, Gregory.' She paused to let the sound of his unabbreviated Christian name cause him maximum irritation. 'I know you, remember?'

'And I know you. You've always despised me. I bet you threw a fucking party when I went down, didn't you?' He stepped closer and circled his index finger close to her face. 'See, I've learnt plenty since I've been *away*.' He smiled, one as forced as hers had been. 'A change in breathing, the smallest flush of pleasure, you can't hide it all, Janie. You can pretend you were at the other end of the country and never saw a newspaper, but you knew I'd gone to prison. I can see it in your face. But I'm telling you, I didn't attack your sister and I never touched Genevieve Barnes. So *you* tell me, who did, eh?'

Here they stood, in the middle of the street, and yet she felt cornered. Just like the first time she'd ever faced up to a bully and been smacked so hard she'd felt her little-girl spirit hit the ground first. Only, then, she'd been unprepared and there had been many years in between. 'I don't know anything.'

He reached out and grabbed her arm, his grip firm but not painful. Not yet. She saw his other hand flatten, palm upwards.

'Why don't you just slap me? That's what you want, isn't it?'

She didn't fight the pressure on her biceps, his thumb now digging into the bone, the tendons jumping aside with a small popping sensation. She focused on his face, watched his slow self-questioning of whether she was bluffing, whether she wanted him to strike her – and why. Her arm was throbbing, the nerves sending light-headed signals to the brain, but she held still. Would he really risk forfeiting his probation over her?

The answer never arrived.

From somewhere to her right, Campbell's reedy tones reached them. 'I'm going to call the police, you know.'

Jackson's grip loosened to merely painful and he turned his head towards the other man. 'I don't think you should.' His voice took on a hoarse quality as he shouted. He continued to stare, and Jane noticed his lips twitching and recognized the shapes of numbers being counted. Was he counting down to something, or just cooling off?

She didn't even need to look at Campbell. He had to be at his upstairs window to be so outspoken, leaning out by a daring six inches, yet careful not to disturb his row of model E-Types on the window ledge.

'You've been warned,' he bleated, and then pulled the window shut.

'He won't phone the police,' she whispered. 'He'll call my dad.'

'I don't give a shit.' But Jackson released her then. 'Fuck you,' he hissed, still hoarse.

'Sorry.' She stepped away, kept her head up and showed no sign of hurry. 'You may have fucked my mother, and fucked my sister, but I'll pass.' Another couple of steps backwards, then she turned and followed the straightest line possible towards her door.

No footsteps followed. None walked away either.

She felt his eyes on her as she placed her shopping by her feet and unlocked the door. The key trembled, skating several times round the metal plate before slipping home. The tips of her fingers throbbed Burgundy red and white bloodless bars scored her palms from carrying the plastic bags for so long. Now her hand was starting to shake in earnest.

His hoarseness reached her. 'I haven't finished. Don't forget that.'

She hauled the bags over the threshold, then straightened and paused in the open doorway, long enough for him to witness her hatred.

'I'm not giving up, Jane. Someone. Has. To. Pay.'

Chapter Fifteen

ONCE INSIDE, JANE sank to the floor, with her back to the door. There she waited – for Jackson, for Campbell, or even for her father. The dusty nothingness of the hallway soothed her; no one would lie on such a floor through choice. She was that *no one* for a minute, then: invisible, invincible even. The evils of her life could pass her by. Like a game of tag, shouting 'home', and being safe until the moment came to run again.

Run or *home*, therefore, but not both.

Her mind drifted like this for a while, then circled and regrouped.

Later there came a knock at the door: a sharp treble rap. She kept very still until she sensed they'd moved away, then carefully slid the bottom bolt into place. Even her father, with his own key, couldn't come in through that door now.

She moved from room to room, securing every possible entry point. Then finally she smiled.

Home.

She drew a long slow breath.

Her home. She turned the words over in her mind. Accepting them. Letting the implications open up to her. She'd stopped running now. She felt it without understanding why it had happened; all she knew was that these two trains of thought had been shunting each other back and forth. Pulling her away. Pulling her back. But now, without complaint, the two of them had fallen still and silent.

The memory of Cambridge returned: the familiarity of this house, the mess of her life that she somehow knew could only be re-anchored here. Self-preservation had propelled her away; maybe it was the same instinct that wouldn't let her do it again. It didn't matter why. She'd finally stopped running, and in that moment came the certainty that she would never run again.

Jane unpacked the shopping and soon after took a bowl of soup and mug of coffee into the playroom. Tomorrow she'd check her bank account, see what was left. Buy food with it. And some other basics.

She ought to make a list. There was a pencil in the kitchen.

She wrote on the back of an old envelope: *Item 1 – buy a notepad and pen.* Joke.

She wasn't really a list person but she then jotted down the basics.

Tins and dried food.

Toilet rolls and Tampax.

Tea and coffee.

Emulsion and brushes.

Speak to Dad or just refuse to move?

She contemplated this last point, doodling a pyramid of regular bricks. And, as for the paint . . . adding emulsion to the list had been nothing more than a wry observation of her present surroundings. But why shouldn't she do something about it? She ran her hand along the wall where it met the skirting board. The paper was heavy, already layered with paint. Another coat would at least freshen it. She tapped it with her fingertips and heard the hollow tip-tap of paper that had separated from plaster.

She lifted the edge with her nail, worked her finger under for a better grip, then tore the paper from the wall. In places it came away in fat panels, crisp with age; in others she removed it, inch by inch, with the rounded tip of her only spoon. There was no plan until, with just a single panel remaining, she knew she had to stop.

Sleep came swiftly and, as it overtook her, she truly believed that nothing was going to wake her again before mid-morning.

Chapter Sixteen

THE RAIN BROUGHT her back to the surface. It drove in at an angle that hit the patio doors with a sharp rattle that made it sound like hail. On other mornings the daylight slid up between the curtain rings and threw bright triangles on the ceiling. Right now there wasn't even enough light outside for her to know where the top of the curtains met the wall. She guessed at 2 a.m., then checked her phone. It was 4.30. She felt tired but another five or six hours' sleep still seemed viable.

She dozed . . . off and on.

The downpour continued unabated for another couple of hours then, within the space of five minutes, subsided to a drizzle. She imagined the weatherman pointing to the front of higher air pressure, and the isobar completing its invisible fly-past. The post-rain silence would have been complete if it hadn't been broken by constant dripping. Amplified dripping at that. This dogged plunk-plunk-plunk was about as soothing as a cold finger tapping her in the forehead.

She burrowed further under the covers and finally succeeded in blocking it out. Except, like a catchy melody that wouldn't let her go, she could hear it even when she couldn't. She knew it was still there, and at 7.24 a.m. she gave up and pulled back the curtains. Only then did she find that the leaky guttering at the rear of the house was trickling silently. She opened the patio doors: everything outside was sodden but equally soundless.

She listened carefully, then slowly turned back to face the room; the dripping had been inside the house all along. Years before her family had owned this house, the cellar entrance had led from the scullery. Walls had been moved, purposes of rooms changed, but no one ever moves a cellar. No one had ever blocked it off either, and that narrow, half-height door in the corner had mostly gone unnoticed. Unless the cellar happened to flood.

She now stood ankle-deep in wallpaper debris, deciding she needed to add everything from dustbin sacks to cutlery to her original shopping list. It was tempting to add wellies and a bucket, and simply leave the leak until later. She resolved to take a peek; perhaps there would be some way to muffle the sound and ignore the problem. *Who are you kidding?* She pulled on her trainers and switched her mobile phone over to torch mode. She had no intention of doing anything less than fixing the noise. She then grabbed her trusty spoon and unhooked the gate-style latch that held the cellar door shut.

The cellar wasn't a full storey deep, but the stone steps leading down were shallow, and there were as many as in a normal staircase. They were worn away in the centre, so Jane found it hard to keep her footing. Cellar steps always seemed like this: the least used but most worn. She stumbled on the last couple, and was thankful when she stepped on to solid flagstone rather than into water.

As far as she was aware, there had only been one very serious flood. That was back in the early nineties, when a burst water main had overwhelmed the natural advantage of living on a hill. Even so, this cellar had always been prone to dampness. It smelt damp now and she had no doubt that there would still be sections of brickwork around the walls that were silky green with it. She shone her torch and found them, the patches seeming too vivid to belong here in the dark.

She found the dripping too, moisture falling from the saturated moss and wet bricks in the furthest corner. It kept hitting the base of an upturned enamel bucket. She smiled to herself, because she knew that bucket. According to her long dead great-gran, it had boiled countless nappies – they'd been simmered on the oven top and prodded with a stick. Gran had never been much of a cook, but the bucket would be handy.

From wall to wall, she doubted it was more than fifteen feet across, but Jane crossed the cellar slowly, making sure her trainer found a good grip before stepping forward. It seemed unusual to leave a bucket upside down . . . unless it was there to sit on or use like a footrest or a table. With her next step she wobbled again, but took another two quick strides and made it safely to the other side. She looked back towards the stairs, and at the weak light coming down from the ground floor. Who was she kidding? No one would decide to spend time down here.

Then another thought occurred to her. She tapped the bucket with her toe, but it didn't move. She pushed firmly and it moved sideways without much difficulty, but she could tell that something was definitely hidden underneath. She squatted, balancing on the balls of her feet. One hand trained the mobile phone's light on the point where the rim of the bucket met the floor, the other gradually tipped it. She silently prayed that nothing would scuttle towards her or, worse still, over her fingers. She saw some earth first, then a few fragments of stone. She lifted the bucket fully and the pile underneath it collapsed. The light found just mud and rock, and Gran's old bucket. She grabbed it by the handle, and had hurried halfway back up the steps before she froze.

Above her, someone was banging at the front door. Her gaze drifted in the direction of the front door, then back down the cellar steps. It took her several seconds of listening to the incessant rapping before she could collect her thoughts and decide exactly what she must do.

She locked the cellar door, left the bucket in the kitchen, then slipped out to the tool shed and returned with an axe.

Chapter Seventeen

As THE RAIN fell on Cambridge, Goodhew had heard nothing. He'd been swimming his regular one hundred lengths of front crawl, oblivious to the world outside. This activity had been a deliberate choice, aimed at shutting down his thoughts. This pattern of snatching two or three hours' rest per night was a familiar and recurrent one, and the previous night had proved another sleepless one. This was one of those days when swimming would help refresh his mind.

His clear head lasted just until he reached his desk. Kincaide was already seated at his, and DI Marks was heading for the door.

'Ah, Goodhew, perfect. Apologies for the early start.' He glanced at his watch. 'You have time to grab a coffee, if you bring it in with you. I'm going straight down.'

As soon as he left, Goodhew turned to Kincaide. 'I thought the briefing was scheduled for eleven?'

'He changed it. I sent you a text.' Kincaide's expression remained accommodating.

Goodhew shrugged. 'Same room?'

Kincaide nodded.

'Good, I'll see you there.'

Goodhew waited until he was on the stairs to check his phone. There was no text.

He poked his head round a doorway on the first floor and found Gully writing up a report, leaning in towards her monitor and frowning.

'Morning, Gary.'

'Hi, Sue. Listen, I need to be quick.'

'So do I. And the faster I try to write these things up, the slower I seem to be. Now I'm becoming word blind.'

'Sue? Do you speak French?'

'*Oh, oui, mais comme une écolière.* Which won't help with my paperwork.'

'I heard the word "oui". It seems Jane Osborne's mother moved to France, possibly to Limoges. I've already emailed the police, so could you just phone for me, find out who will be dealing with it, and try to persuade them to hurry it up?'

'Why the rush?'

'There isn't.'

'Liar.'

'OK. Greg Jackson's been seen hanging around Pound Hill. Mary Osborne had a relationship with him, so I wanted to speak with her.'

'*And* reunite her with Jane?'

'Of course.' He pressed a slip of paper into her hand. 'All the details are there. Will you phone?' He backed towards the door.

She shrugged then nodded. '*Oui.*'

GOODHEW MANAGED TO slip into the briefing without being last through the door. Kincaide, DCs Young and Charles, and a handful of other officers were all present. Just nine of them, including Goodhew. A few moments later, Marks followed him into the room, beginning to address the officers even before he'd extracted his notes from the black document wallet he carried.

'Paul Marshall's full autopsy results reveal several new factors. We already know, of course, that he was the subject of a violent assault. Once the car was alight the assailant would have been aware of the increased risk of discovery, and *if* his intention was to kill, then it is reasonable to assume that would have occurred very soon after the car began burning.'

He paused deliberately, swinging his gaze across the faces of his team. Goodhew glanced around too, and noted the collective look of uncertainty that was reflecting back towards his boss. Although Marks's expression betrayed nothing, Goodhew thought he seemed pleased. The DI slid his hand back into the document wallet and retrieved a length of wire. 'This is the same type of wire used in the assault. It is known as twist wire or, rather appropriately in this case, tying wire. It is sold by most builders' merchants, common as muck and untraceable in all but the broadest sense. Goodhew? Come over here, please.'

Goodhew went over and turned to face the room.

'Hold your hands like this.'

He copied the position that Marks demonstrated, crossed at the wrists but at the angle where the fingers of each hand could reach to wrap round the opposite forearm. The way Marshall's had been.

'The most effective way to secure it is using pliers.' Marks dipped back into the document wallet. 'Here we are.' Goodhew held his hands still while Marks twisted the length of wire in place. 'Marshall's legs were bound with duct tape, but this wire was also used to secure Marshall to that tree – at the waist, chest and neck. Well, Goodhew?'

'Yes, sir?'

'Is that uncomfortably tight?'

'No.'

'Can you get free?'

'I don't think so. No.' Goodhew twisted and pulled against the wire. 'Definitely not.'

'Marshall was bound even more tightly than this. Therefore he had no chance of escape. If Goodhew here kept struggling it would dig into him more deeply. This wire would cause soft tissue damage, and eventually it would rupture the skin. At some point in Marshall's torture, the wire did just that. He struggled enough for it to sever the blood vessels in his neck. Collapsed his windpipe.'

Marks reached forward to free Goodhew's hands.

Kincaide spoke up. 'So if the assailant wanted information, Marshall may have died before he could provide it?'

'Precisely. This bears hallmarks of a rage-driven attack, but the perpetrator was prepared, focused and had planned it extremely carefully.' Marks finally removed the twist wire and waved Goodhew back to his seat. 'The reason for my demonstration must by now be crystal clear to all of you. Keep your wits about you. The man responsible for this crime is capable of disabling a fit adult male. He achieved this with blows delivered to the head and kidneys, followed by a kick which shattered Marshall's kneecap. Questions?'

No one ventured to say anything. Goodhew meanwhile scribbled the word *Revenge?* on a clean sheet of his notepad.

Marks continued, 'There seem to be discrepancies between Paul Marshall's appointments diary and the appointments he actually kept. For example, he booked two full days – 27 and 28 July – to complete a job that actually involved only a couple of hours' work.'

'Sounds like our plumber,' Clark muttered. A ripple of agreement fluttered through the room.

'Trading Standards have never received a complaint about his work or practices, but if he was trading irresponsibly we need to know.' Marks had a habit: without warning he would fall silent and still, jaw taut, then only his dark eyes would move, flicking a beady gaze around the room. Like a bird of prey in a room full of juicy voles. They all held their breath and, as always, Goodhew felt tempted to shout *boo!* But he never had, and knew he never would.

It was only when Marks finally exhaled that the room also found the collective urge to breathe. 'Right then, toxicology.' Marks shuffled through the papers and slipped a new sheet to the front. 'Our Mr Marshall was a busy man: steroid use and cocaine. Some damage to the liver and kidneys and the telltale nasal septum decay, obviously all due to the coke. Which, not forgetting the Lotus, amounts to him having expensive tastes. He paid for the car in cash, so no doubt he did the same with the drugs. I want to know whether this money was siphoned from his business receipts, who he paid, where he hid it, and what else he purchased.'

Goodhew wrote down *Thrill-seeker. Vain.*

'The location of the body was very specific, clearly the theatre involved in burning the car was a reason for choosing that spot, but as one of the highest points in the area, and therefore more conspicuous, it did increase the risk of being observed. What, then, was the significance of the Gogs?' Marks looked up. 'Any thoughts?'

Goodhew's pen hovered over his pad. 'Who's the psychologist on this one?'

'Dr Bhagat.'

'What does she say?'

'Thinks there will be a reason why it had to be the Gogs. In her opinion the killer will have a specific and highly personal motive for the attack, and therefore is someone with a strong connection to Marshall or to some aspect of his life.'

'But nothing's shown up so far,' Kincaide said thoughtfully. He twisted round in his chair to speak to Young. 'How far did you get with Marshall's PC and laptops?'

'Consistent usage mostly, with no sign that anything has been wiped. But we have all the email contacts, online purchases, downloads, viewing history. They all need going through in more detail, because nothing's shown up as yet.'

Marks cleared his throat. 'I have received that list, thank you.' He paused just long enough for all attention to be facing the front again. 'According to Paul Marshall's wife, and his appointments diary, his business was thriving. He employed no one else, but he subbed out some work from time to time. So, finally,' Marks picked up the document wallet again and this time produced a single sheet of paper, 'we have drug usage and large cash purchases by a family man with a legitimate business. It's obvious to me that there is more to Marshall than there might seem.' Marks began reading out items from the list: the leads, the lines of inquiry – and who he'd assigned to each. Goodhew listened carefully, memorizing all the pairings of names with the tasks. Finally Marks announced, 'Goodhew?'

'Sir?'

'Phone bills, both work and home. Unusual calls, calling patterns, premium-rate numbers and so on.'

Goodhew wrote these instructions on his notepad, then stared at the page for a moment.

'You look like you have a question?'

'Yes, I may need to cross-check, for example, against bank statements, internet usage and so on.'

Marks dropped the wire and pliers back into the document wallet and zipped it closed. 'You possess initiative, Goodhew, so I expect you to employ it. That goes for *all* of you.'

Goodhew drew a careful circle around the words *check phones*, then made the briefest eye contact with his boss. Marks glanced at Goodhew, then at what he had written, before his attention moved on. Goodhew closed the notebook. It didn't matter what he'd been assigned; he already knew where he needed to look.

SUE GULLY WAS still working in the office when Goodhew returned. Kelly Wilkes had joined her. They sat facing away from the door and angled away from each other. Their desks were positioned on the inside curve of a horseshoe, so if they both scooted their chairs back at the same moment, they would collide.

Kelly could touch-type, and her fingers skimmed the keys with a neat economy that gave the appearance of less productivity involved than Sue's determined two-fingered, one-thumbed tap-tap-tap. Kelly now pressed the return key, and paused. 'I bet he's seeing someone.' She continued typing.

Sue was typing up notes, so maybe she'd heard, maybe she hadn't. Goodhew opened his mouth to speak just as she reached the bottom of the page. 'Like a counsellor?' she suggested. Another long pause, another field filled, and a new screen. 'Or another woman?'

Goodhew dived in. 'Can I guess?'

Kelly started. 'You made me jump.'

Sue twizzled her chair to face him. 'Have *you* worked him out yet?'

'Kincaide? No.'

'Nobody changes overnight like that. Anyway,' she swung back and snatched a Post-it note from one side of her monitor, 'here's Mary Osborne's address.'

'Your schoolgirl French did the trick, then?'

'Not a problem.'

Kelly turned too. 'I was in the room, Gary, and she didn't use a word of it. She did say "You really have a lovely accent" a couple of times, though.'

'Even their addresses have lovely names,' Sue remarked.

'Crap. Probably named after some crusty politician.'

Goodhew studied the address: *9 Rue Élie Berthet, 87000 Limoges*. He hadn't thought that Sue would have been simply wasting her time, but he still felt surprised. *Surprised at what, though?* That Mary Osborne had been so easy to find, yet none of her family had bothered trying? *No, not that.*

'Gary?' Sue spoke his name through gritted teeth.

He looked up at her, surprised. 'What?'

'I said, what did he write?'

'Who?'

'Élie Berthet. You just said "he was a novelist".'

'He is, but I don't think I said so.'

Kelly nodded. 'You did, actually.'

'Sorry. Is there a phone number with this?'

'No, nothing for that address, apparently. What's up?'

'I don't know, but I feel like I should ring her first. Perhaps she doesn't want to be found.'

Kelly stopped him. 'No, she made an appeal for Jane to come home. I remember it was in the papers before Becca's funeral, then again later. And Jane also wants contact now. I don't see an issue.'

He felt as though he should agree, but instead continued to hesitate. 'It's been weird how Jackson cropped up, then Jane Osborne . . .'

'Jackson didn't "crop up", he was paroled. Months later, Jane Osborne is arrested. They both come from Cambridge, they both end up back here, so what's the big deal?'

Judging by Sue and Kelly's expressions there wasn't one. But they hadn't met with Jimmy Barnes. Only Goodhew knew that Jackson was watching both Jane *and* Genevieve. 'I should tell Marks.'

'No, just keep him informed about the case you are supposed to be on.' Sue scowled. 'Don't start pressing his Greg Jackson buttons while his head's in the Marshall case. He's up to here already.' She demonstrated by slicing the air under her chin, then swung her hand out to grab the phone as it gave the first bleat of a ring.

He folded the Post-it note in half, then in half again, and turned to go.

'Gary,' Kelly hissed. She held up her *Wait* finger, then pointed it at Sue.

'I'm on my way.' Sue covered the mouthpiece. 'Can you come to Pound Hill?'

I really shouldn't. But he nodded.

'OK. Goodhew's coming with me.' She hung up and grabbed her keys. 'Looks like our little friend's got herself in trouble.'

Chapter Eighteen

GULLY COMPLETED THE journey to Pound Hill in less time than it took for her to relay to him the details of the phone call. The bare fact was simple: Jane had been seen entering her home and now wouldn't respond to repeated calls at the front door.

'So who called it in?' Gary asked her.

'A bloke called Campbell.'

'First name or last?'

So Goodhew hadn't yet had the pleasure of meeting Mr Campbell – lucky sod. 'Both, apparently. He practically has a hot-line to Parkside. Reports problems several times a month: danger-ous driving, dangerous parking, probably even dangerous litter. It came up in Jane's notes that we picked her up from Leeds, so that's why this call came my way.'

'Campbell Campbell?'

'Yep.'

As they pulled on to double yellows on Pound Hill, a face loomed in the window of the flats across the road. It vanished again and several seconds later a man in his late fifties appeared in the doorway. He hurried towards them, bustling and impatient. By the time Goodhew and Gully were out of the vehicle, his list of concerns had been primed.

'Mr Campbell?' Gully lit the fuse, and it was a short one.

'I moved in here while Gerry's parents still had the place. Decent people. Even Gerry, for all his faults, is decent too. But the children, that's where it went wrong. And I don't know what that girl thinks she's playing at.'

'Jane Osborne?'

'Jane-bloody-Osborne. I phoned her father soon as I saw her.'

'Today?'

'No, just after she turned up again. But I haven't phoned Gerry this time. God knows, he doesn't need to go through any more.'

Campbell was a short man, beige clothes, brown shoes, badly dyed hair. His head nodded as he spoke, not up and down exactly, more like a forehead-first butting motion. 'You need to get yourself inside that house quickly.'

'I need more details from you, Mr Campbell. DC Goodhew is already checking the property from the outside. When did you last see Jane Osborne?'

'This morning. She'd been out shopping and she hasn't left again since. I don't understand why you let him do it.'

Gully double-blinked; had she missed something? 'I'm sorry, who is "he"?'

'Well, my dear, if you release a man like that and don't keep watch on him, you're nothing more than a bunch of fools. I mean Jackson.'

'Greg Jackson?'

'Of course you had to let him out again, after the pig's ear made of the first murder investigation. I'm not afraid to testify, though.

I would have stood up first time if I could have – if I'd known anything at all.'

'So,' Gully readied her notepad, 'you saw Jane Osborne return home at approximately what time?'

'Eleven-ish.'

'Have you seen her since?'

'I knocked at the house.'

'What time?'

'The first time, probably within the hour. Then again about an hour after that.'

'So you knocked twice. Or more than that?'

'I kept trying. I never left it longer than an hour in between.'

'And did you hear or see anything there?'

'She was inside, all right.'

'But she didn't reply?'

'No. But I held open the letterbox and listened, and someone was definitely moving around.'

Gully could see Jane's point of view. She wouldn't have felt like opening the door to Campbell either.

'If I wasn't the age I am, I'd have those locks open straight away – not go pussyfooting around it like your young detective there.'

Goodhew was currently about thirty feet away, examining the property's exterior. If Campbell decided to employ any more animal references, Gully had a feeling that 'monkey up a drain-pipe' might be about to come into play.

'So, what specifically makes you feel she may have come to any harm?'

'Jackson was right at her door, banging at it. Before that, they'd been out here in the street. That girl's always been a bolshie little cow, but even she looked shaken up.'

'Did you overhear any of their conversation?'

'I leant out my window and threatened him . . . said I'd call the police if he didn't clear off.'

'And Jane was out here at that point?'

'Yes, but this was hours ago. Jackson started banging on her door after that. I saw him heading round the back. Who knows where he went from there.'

'So, you didn't actually see him enter the property?'

'I never said I did. But he could have done.'

'Mr Campbell—' she began, but he interrupted her.

'Living across the road from an empty house is a responsibility I take very seriously. When I phoned, I explained I was concerned for a neighbour.'

'Who may have gone out.'

Campbell tipped his head in acknowledgement. 'Doubtful. Let's go and see what your man has to say.' He turned towards the house itself. It seemed Goodhew had given up on the idea of scaling the outside wall and was talking into his mobile as he now approached them.

He finished the call and slipped his phone back into the pocket of his jeans. 'Locked down from the inside.'

Campbell glanced back at Gully. She kept her eyes fixed on Goodhew, but if she had bothered to meet his gaze, she could picture, in precise detail, the I-told-you-so smile and slight raise of his eyebrows disappearing behind his fringe. He touched her arm. 'Whenever it's something that concerns this street, mine is the voice of experience.'

They both ignored him. Goodhew carried on addressing Gully. 'I phoned Jane but there's no reply, so I've called the station. They're contacting her dad and brother, and sending a van round so we can gain access.'

'Not a locksmith?'

'No. We'll need to break the door down.'

'Gerry won't be happy about that. You should really wait for him and his key. I offered to hold one, but he said it wouldn't be necessary. He'll wish he'd taken me up on it, won't he?'

'A key won't help us if the doors are bolted.'

Gully sighed a little too loudly. 'Gary, did her phone go straight to voicemail?'

'It rang first.'

'Text her.'

Goodhew shrugged. 'It's worth a try.'

In the distance a police siren began to wail. Further along the road, several people were standing outside their houses, pretending to talk but watching, waiting for the possibility of a main event.

'Tell her they're about to break in if she doesn't come out.' Goodhew spelt out a few more words, then hit the 'send' button.

Gully waited for the phone to buzz with a reply, or to see the screen light indicate an incoming call. Nothing happened, and a few minutes later it was the arrival of the second patrol car that provided the only sound and light.

'Did you warn her they'll force entry?'

'You're assuming she's in a condition to even read texts. We should have an ambulance on standby.'

Gully focused on the front door, as if doing her best to scowl it open. But if Jane was on the other side, scowling to keep it shut, then Gully wouldn't stand a chance. Goodhew and 'comb-over' Campbell might well be imagining Jane lying in a pool of blood but, personally, Gully didn't buy it.

She reached over and tugged Goodhew's phone from out of his fingers. She quickly sent Jane a new message, then handed it back.

'Do you realize you text faster than you type?' Goodhew observed.

'Yes. It's annoying.'

'So what did you put?'

'You could just read it.'

'No need.' He moved suddenly, and behind the obscured glass in the front door she saw a flash of movement. 'Just tell me.'

She repeated her message quietly, so that Campbell wouldn't hear. Goodhew nodded and she turned back to face Campbell. 'Sir, I'll contact you if we need a statement.'

His eager expression followed Goodhew as the young police officer headed up the front steps. Gully placed herself between the neighbour and the house itself. 'Thank you for your help, Mr Campbell. We'll take it from here.'

'No reason I can't stand out on my own street now, is there?' He sniffed and raised his chin so he could look down his nose at her, a smile of superiority touching his lips. Any second now he'd add 'I know my rights'.

The front door cracked open by a few inches and a narrow panel of daylight slipped through the gap, finding Jane's face. Gully knew that neither Jane nor Goodhew needed an audience for their exchange.

Gully smiled patiently. 'On second thoughts,' she added firmly, 'I'll take that statement now.'

Campbell's smile faltered.

'Your flat or at Parkside, whichever you prefer.'

GOODHEW HAD HEARD her put the security chain in place, then watched the door begin to open. Daylight made her squint and she raised her hand to shield her eyes as they adjusted.

'Have you really found my mum?'

'She's in France. In Limoges.'

Jane managed the smallest of smiles. 'That's funny. She hates France.'

'Can I come in?'

She looked beyond him, across the street towards Campbell and Gully. 'What do *they* want?'

'Campbell called us; he was worried when he couldn't get a reply from you.'

'Right. That nosy old git has been spying on us ever since we were kids.'

'So you knew he was knocking?'

She stepped back from the door, and he could still see her but she'd partially faded into the shadows. She watched him, her gaze unwavering, till he wondered whether she was about to close the door again. 'I don't know, but I knew someone was,' she replied.

'Jane, I really need to speak to you properly. It would be easier if we could talk inside.'

She ignored him. 'Have you spoken to her?'

'Not yet. I only have an address but not her phone number. The French police will let her know you're safe. They'll pass on your number, if you like.'

'And I can have her address?'

'Absolutely.'

She closed the door. For a few seconds there was silence, then he heard her remove the chain. She opened it again but fully now, and he saw her clearly for the first time. She was filthy, apart from her palms and fingers which were rosy pink as though they'd just been washed. Her nails were still ingrained with dirt, and dark marks disfigured her clothes. A tell-tale rusty stain covered the knee of her jeans. Blood. She blinked at him, staring as if she was trying to adjust to a whole lot more than just the daylight.

'Are you by yourself, Jane?'

She nodded.

'Do you reckon Campbell there was the only one who knocked?'

'I don't know.' Her gaze drifted to the door. 'I don't think so.'

'Did you let anyone in?'

'Like who?'

'Jackson.'

She blinked slowly and as she reopened her eyes her gaze was fixed on him. 'I don't have anything to say to Jackson. He can hang around outside as much as he likes. I don't know anything at all that would interest him.'

Goodhew could see the head of the stairs and along the ground floor as far as the doorway at the end of the hall. Not even the dust seemed to have been disturbed.

'You have blood on your jeans.'

She looked down at her leg. 'I didn't realize. I guess I cut myself.'

'And what was on your hands before you washed them?'

'You have my mum's address, then?'

'Sure. But you know I need to look around the house, don't you, Jane? Tell me what's been happening here.'

'I've made a mistake. I thought . . .' Her voice trailed off as she lifted a hand to gesture towards the rear of the property. For several seconds she tried to find the words, but couldn't.

'Can you show me?'

She led him along the hallway, where the door to the final room was ajar. As she pushed it open, the arc in which it travelled was the only patch of carpet that remained clear. Stripped wallpaper debris covered all the rest of the floor.

'First –' she drew in a deep breath and finally some of the colour returned to her face – 'can I explain?'

'Go ahead.'

'I thought that maybe I wouldn't move on again after all – that I'd stay on here in Cambridge. I hadn't made my mind up, then came that knocking on the front door. It could've been Jackson, Campbell or even Dad, but definitely no one I wanted to speak to. Suddenly I thought *Fuck it, I'm not running. No one's going to make me.* No big deal, right?'

Goodhew shrugged. 'Depends, I guess.'

'Well, for me it was huge.' He saw her inherent stubbornness rise, but the exhaustion evident on her face remained overwhelming. 'I decided that it was time to face up to anything that needs it. And I got this idea – a stupid idea – that there was something down there.' She pointed to what looked like a cupboard door in the corner. 'It's a cellar.'

'Show me.'

'Is there a light on your phone? Mine's nearly flat.'

She held his mobile in front of them as she led the way into the basement. The stairs felt greasy underfoot and the stale air smelt of wet earth.

She stopped as soon as she'd reached the bottom, raised the phone and directed its light down on to the floor. He could see the room clearly for the first time. As they'd descended, he'd seen what looked like an uneven floor surface, but now he realized there were three large flagstones standing like tombstones up against the opposite wall. A corresponding-sized rectangle of broken ground lay in front of him and the harsh light picked out a pile of brick chunks and rubble that had been pulled free.

'I only had the axe, so I used it to lift the flagstones and hook out the rubble. I thought it would be easier to dig out than this.'

The exposed area measured about eighteen inches across and four feet long. The proportions weren't lost on him. 'Why start digging in the first place?'

'The stones wobbled when I walked on them . . . and water seeped up. The floor wasn't like that before.'

'But there could be any number of reasons. Who knows how many repairs have happened here since you left?'

'Very few I'd say. This isn't exactly makeover mansion, you know.'

She had a point.

'You said you'd made a mistake?'

She lowered the phone till its light beam picked out her trainers. The laces had been knotted, but the one on the right foot had come loose. A small patch that should have been clean white sock peeked out at him. It was as filthy as the rest of her clothes. 'You thought there was a body there, didn't you?'

'What else would it be?'

'Like I said, it could be anything.'

'I couldn't think.'

He realized her mistake then; the untidy laces, the bloody knees and the relentless digging told him more. 'Did you think it was your mum?' he asked gently.

'It seemed to make sense. Two and two making five, I suppose.' She slapped the phone back into his hand. He followed her back up towards the sea of stripped paper. 'Selfish cow, swanning around France while I'm up to my knees in all this crap.' A smile flickered at the corner of her mouth, then vanished.

'You're not nearly as tough as you'd like us to believe, are you, Jane?'

'Tough enough to get by.'

'A survivor, then?'

'That's right. Now what?'

'We'll speak to your father about the cellar. I'm sure there *will* be an explanation.'

'And if not?'

'I guess we'll excavate.'

'Good.' Jane shoved her hands into her pockets and tried to looked determined. 'I really think you should.'

Chapter Nineteen

28 JULY. THE day the woman had been sighted on the Gogs. The date had jumped out at Goodhew, seeming as familiar as a birthday or the date of New Year's Eve.

Goodhew's diversion to Pound Hill had cost valuable time on the Paul Marshall case and, of course, he'd known that when he agreed to go. But he couldn't also afford time to wait around for the first senior officer to now arrive at the Osborne house, especially if they then decided to hang on to him for the rest of the day.

Gully had tossed him the car keys. 'You'll be quicker if you drive back.'

'I'll swap this one for an unmarked and leave it in the car park.'

'Drop the keys at the front desk. Get going, though. You'll be toast if Marks gets this one, and finds you here.'

Whatever happened, he'd known that Marks would already be on the warpath, so had been thankful to make it out to Lin-ton without a *get-back-here-and-explain-why-the-hell-you-were-with-Jane-Osborne* phone call from his boss.

Now he stood on the doorstep of Paul Marshall's home. The house was modern, with white gables, rose bushes and matching net curtains. The grass was weedless, the windows spotless, and the doorbell undoubtedly working.

House Number One, Perfectsville.

Carmel Marshall was barefoot as she opened the door. She wore a striped T-shirt over jeans, ruffled but damp hair touching her shoulders. She managed a smile but the strain on her face kept it in check. 'I thought DC Kincaide would come.'

Goodhew hadn't realized she'd been expecting anyone at all before half an hour ago, when he'd arranged to see her. He introduced himself, adding, 'And I'm sure DC Kincaide will be in touch with you later.'

She moved away towards the back of the house, leaving him to follow. As she walked, she pinned back her fair hair, with two clips on each side. The action lifted her T-shirt above her waist, exposing a faded tan line across her lower back. She led the way to the kitchen and pointed him towards a small corner table with two chairs.

'Will here do?'

'Yes, of course. Are your children here, Mrs Marshall?'

'With my parents today. Coffee?'

'Please.'

She brought milk and sugar to the table, while the kettle boiled, then emptied and rinsed a large cafetière. Everything she did seemed deliberate, in an uneasy relationship between thought and action. She came back with two mugs and the pot of coffee, placed them on the table, then spent several seconds turning items round so that the ear-of-corn motif faced the front on each one. 'I seem to be having a couple of days of emotional calm now, but I have been extremely upset, just in case you were wondering. For the first few days I just couldn't stop.' She sat down, shunting her chair around a little until she faced him squarely. 'In fact, I've never cried like that before. It acted like a cocoon and I was curled up in the centre of it screaming my brains out.' She raised an eyebrow. 'Not what my kids needed, really. Cue Mum and Dad.'

She poured coffee into the two mugs. 'Have you ever cried like that?' she asked.

'No, never.'

'It was beyond my control at first. Then, later, when I was exhausted and knew I could stop, I made myself cry some more – just to avoid dealing with everything. I could see what was coming: an endless stream of questions and decisions, police, insurance, the children, neighbours.'

Goodhew sipped his coffee, watching her carefully. 'You must miss him.'

'Must I?' She stared straight into Goodhew's face, challenging him to answer.

'Well, do you?'

'I'm undecided. You see, once I stopped crying and started facing up to my new life as a widow . . . newly single woman, or whatever I am . . . I started thinking. I don't know why someone would have done that to Paul, so I reasoned that there's a side to him that he kept secret.'

She paused as if for affirmation, so Goodhew nodded to just show he understood.

'But I figure I still knew him as well as anyone, and there are a few details . . . I don't want to hold back on something that might be important. Money's the first thing. We didn't have an issue with it. He'd never owe anyone money, never lend it either. Paul worked hard, but indulged himself too. Too much sometimes, but always with our own money.' She paused, then corrected herself, 'His own money.'

'Do you work?'

'Not at the moment. I'd just qualified as a teacher when I met him. Then I gave it up when I became pregnant.'

'Molly and Evie, they're twelve and eight? Didn't you ever want to return to work?'

Her gaze dropped to her lap, then focused on Goodhew again. 'He liked me at home.'

'And the money was his?'

'Everything was his – me and the girls included.' She gave a wry smile. 'Funny thing is, I knew he was controlling, but I couldn't see how far from normal it all was until he died. Now, suddenly, everything is up to me. My choice. So I keep thinking about what he'd done that had pissed someone off that much. DC Kincaide asked me if either of us was having an affair, and I said no.' She frowned and tapped the tips of her first two fingers against her lips. 'I really don't think he was, but there *was* something.'

'You refer to the money as being his, but did you know where it all went?'

'More than he realized, actually. I kept the books on the business and, yes, there were times when we received cash for jobs and didn't declare it. Mostly small amounts, though: a few hundred here and there.'

'That's not everyone's idea of insignificant, you know.'

'Not mine either, but he spent sixty thousand on that car. It's like he wasn't always in the real world. I knew he had a chunk of money from selling a rental flat we owned, but it wasn't that level of money, so that's when I realized he had to be hoarding it somewhere. A few weeks later I found five thousand pounds in a watertight container, at the bottom of our cold water tank. He was a plumber so it was an obvious place for me to look. I didn't want it, just wanted to know him better.'

'So you weren't planning to leave him?'

'No, I think our marriage was good. We all keep secrets, but do they make us bad people?'

Goodhew didn't answer. He'd come back to that question in his own time. 'When was this?'

'A year ago.' She shrugged. 'Give or take.'

'Then what?'

'I checked again a few times, then one day it had gone. Gradually he built it up again until it hit almost five thousand pounds. This was about a month ago, then it vanished again.'

'Perhaps he was being blackmailed?'

'You don't know Paul.'

'Meaning?'

'Just, no, it wouldn't have happened.'

'OK.' If Carmel Marshall had an answer, she wasn't going to share it. Most likely she didn't, but either way it wasn't worth pressing for right now. 'Can you be more specific with the date on which the most recent stash of money went?'

'Yes, easily. Paul worked over a weekend, a rush job in London, he said. He left on the Friday, and I went up into the loft on the Saturday morning. That would have been . . .'

She began counting back the dates but Goodhew answered easily, '27 July.'

'That's right. How did you know?'

'It's in his appointments diary. He booked a full weekend for that rush job and invoiced only a couple of hours. You spotted that, right?'

'Sure.' She reached for the coffee cups, and picked up the cafetière, as if ready for him to leave. 'He said he'd invoice the rest later.'

'And you believed him?'

'I liked to think he didn't lie to me.'

'Really? I thought everyone kept secrets.'

She took the crockery over to the sink, making no attempt to reply.

'Mrs Marshall, where do you think he went?'

Still no reply. Goodhew changed tack. 'Did you know he used cocaine?'

She began rinsing the mugs. 'Before the police told me?' She picked up the tea towel and only turned to face him as she was drying them. 'Yes, I knew he'd dabbled. But I could always tell when he'd used it. We did it together a few times when we were first dating.' Carmel stopped speaking abruptly, as though she was still in mid-sentence. If she had planned to say more, she'd clearly just decided against it. 'I'm tired.'

'I'm sorry, I just have a couple more questions. Also you will need to make a statement covering our conversation today. I can type it up and bring it back for you to sign. You clearly wanted to tell Kincaide about the money today?'

She nodded.

'Was there anything else?'

'No.' She took a deep breath. 'Because the money was gone before he died, it puzzled me, but I didn't think about any connection to his murder. That's why I didn't mention it earlier.'

A lie. The words rang hollow compared to everything else she'd already said. She turned away from his gaze and stared out at the rear garden. She'd been smart enough to find the money in the first place, and Goodhew guessed she'd been desperate to know how it was being used. Yet she'd kept quiet until she'd given up in frustration.

'I understand your confusion, Mrs Marshall.'

'I'm not confused.' She turned to him sharply, her expression defensive. 'I'm merely adjusting. Who wouldn't be?'

Goodhew didn't respond, waiting to see if deliberate silence would prompt her to say more. Instead she crossed to the hallway and waited there for him to follow. They were at the open front door before she finally spoke. 'I loved him for a long time, despite his shortcomings.'

'But not recently? Is that what you mean?'

'I can't see recently very clearly at the moment. So I don't know the truth of it. But I will grieve, Detective, when I know what I'm grieving for.'

'Then tell me where he may have been that weekend.'

There were only inches between them, not the width of a kitchen, and that made the question harder to escape. Finally she gave up. 'Point Clear, Essex. He had a small cabin cruiser moored out on the estuary. He told me he'd sold it, but I don't think he did.'

'It hasn't come up in our background checks.'

She shook her head. 'Why would it? He paid cash for the mooring and Marshall's not an uncommon name.'

'So what else do you know about it?'

'It was blue and white. No name on it, just a number.'

'That's it?'

She reached past him and opened the door wide, and for the second time he heard her lie. 'Yes, it is.'

Chapter Twenty

GOODHEW RETURNED TO Parkside and spent the next few hours digging for information. Then phoning and hassling in order to dig up some more. He tried to blot out the frequent updates that kept coming in from Pound Hill, though he listened closely when DC Young announced that they'd started using ground-penetration radar, and would use the resulting data to decide whether to excavate.

Maybe this was a good day for unearthing.

By the end of the afternoon he had collated enough information to fill an A4 envelope. He hoped it would be enough to convince Marks, so he picked it up and headed out.

POUND HILL HAD by now passed the tipping point of more bystanders than residents, and amongst all those gathered Goodhew could pick out reporters, a medical officer and new arrivals from the forensic team. A man holding a clipboard and a grey moulded plastic case of gadgets stood close to Marks's car.

Marks was in the driver's seat, making notes as he ended a call on his phone. Goodhew opened the passenger door. 'Mind if I have a word, sir?'

'Get in, then.' Marks continued to make notes. 'Wait.' Then, when he'd finished, he closed his pad. 'Go.'

'I've been to see Carmel Marshall.'

'I heard.'

'Paul Marshall had a boat moored in the Point Clear Estuary. I'd like to take a look.'

'Goodhew, I heard about the boat, too. You and Kincaide have been acting like a man and his shadow all day. It's not productive. But, unlike you, Kincaide has no burning desire to dash off to Essex. And I have no burning desire to send you there unless you can explain properly.'

'Well, it might be nothing.'

'Goodhew, just level with me.'

'Paul Marshall took off for a couple of nights, on 26 and 27 July. He'd told his wife that he was away working on a property in London, but she caught sight of an invoice that he'd raised for just a few hours' labour, so she was suspicious that he had been doing something else.'

'Such as?'

'Either she wasn't sure or was avoiding facing up to it.'

'Go on.'

'I contacted the customer in question, a company called Flat-Great. They have property in Cambridge and also Highgate, London, and have always used Marshall. He hadn't done the work for them over the weekend at all, only nipped down on the Thursday afternoon, completed enough to keep them happy, then went back there during the following week to finish the job.'

'Leaving his weekend free.'

'Exactly. Then I ran through the ANPR check on the move-ments of his Lotus over that weekend. Three hits: one on Trump-ington Road, one on the M11 and the third as he travelled cross-country from Bishops Stortford.'

'The route to Point Clear, but from Cambridge, not from his home.'

'Yes, and there were no card transactions or phone calls made throughout that weekend. The last time he refuelled was the Tues-day afternoon, which was 23 July. He usually filled up completely when it reached quarter-full, but on that occasion he only added about fifteen litres. Assuming he was topping it up and the tank was then completely full at that point, then the car could have covered a range of about four hundred miles. Point Clear is about seventy-five miles away, so he would not have needed to make another fuel stop during that weekend.'

'And why do I need to know what he *didn't* do?'

'Because the alternator packed up on his van on the Thursday morning, so he used the Lotus to get to Highgate and back. He obviously hadn't thought about topping up the tank again.'

'And driving to London would have eaten through the fuel. So where did he stop?'

'A Gulf garage, Pump Hill Service Station, St Osyth. He put in forty pounds' worth of petrol, paid cash.'

Goodhew finally opened the envelope and slid out a bundle of documents. A print-out of a low-resolution photograph of the garage forecourt lay on top. The date and time appeared in the corner: 26-07-2013 18:41:20:00. There were two rows of pumps and at the back of the centre aisle, despite the poor quality, the Evora's number plate was easily identifiable.

'We have shots taken at five-second intervals for the full six minutes the car was there.'

Marks immediately pointed to the passenger side of the windscreen, where the blurred face of a woman was visible. The image was almost like a child's drawing, two big dark eyes and a painted mouth. A block of yellow hair. In a photo like this, 79-mm-high black-on-white digits were a whole lot easier to read than facial features.

'And is there a clearer shot of her?'

'Not really.' Goodhew shook his head. 'But look at this.' He pointed to the bottom of the shot, where the top of a man's head was just coming into view. 'That's Marshall himself. Now watch.'

He flipped over the top sheet to reveal each consecutive shot in turn. Marshall, his back to the camera, striding towards his car. Then his arm extending. Surprise on her face.

In the next shot his arm was fully outstretched with his forefinger pointing directly towards her.

The next was the same, but now he was at the car itself, still pointing at her as he returned to the driver's side. She had folded at the waist, her face lowered to her knees. Recommended crash position, except her hands weren't clasped behind her head but somewhere in front of her seat. It was impossible to see more. Goodhew had been trying to from the moment he'd taken it from the printer. He wasn't sure why he felt so uneasy just looking at it.

The final group of shots showed the Evora driving off from the forecourt and the girl's head still pressed to her knees. The last image only caught a partial shot of the passenger door, the back of her head, and Marshall's left hand clutching her hair right down at the roots.

'God bless digital security cameras,' Marks muttered. 'So what do you know about her?'

Goodhew picked the clearest of the photos, the one where her eyes were wide and lips forming an 'O' of surprise. 'Do you remember some reports of a girl up on the Gogs?'

'Those sightings that led nowhere?'

'Yes, sir.'

'If there's a connection, Goodhew, I'll need to see how strong it is.'

'Technically it's circumstantial.'

'Marvellous.'

'But it has reasonably probability.'

Marks looked distinctly unimpressed. 'Sell it to me, Gary.'

'OK, the day Marshall came back from Point Clear was Sunday 28 July. We know he had a passenger with him on the way there, and that he'd started his journey from Cambridge. It is reasonable to think that she got into the car in Cambridge itself, and it's therefore highly likely that she needed to get back there at the end of the weekend.'

'All possible,' Marks conceded.

'However, something happens, a fight or something, and he throws her out of the car, abandoning her to walk home over the Gogs.'

'And, judging by these photos, he's clearly prone to violence. Although there's no history of anything like that at home.'

'Which could just mean that he was never exposed.'

'Even if enhancing these pictures was possible, I think that establishing a positive ID would be a long shot. It is clear, however, that she has the same hair colour and build and is of a similar age to the woman I've been looking for.'

'The woman *you've* been looking for? What happened to "There's no evidence of a crime, therefore don't spend any more time on this one"?' Goodhew recognized the rhetorical question and stayed quiet. 'Carry on.'

'There isn't much else, except that it explains the location of Paul Marshall's body. Think about it, if he did something nasty to her and then dumped her there, doesn't that make it the perfect spot to return the favour?'

'And the Marshall attack had revenge written all over it? Hmmm.' Marks closed his eyes in thought. 'We can't get far with that line of inquiry without first knowing who she is. But we can't ignore it either.'

'The local police are currently trying to locate details of his boat – someone in a pub or restaurant might remember the pair of them. I could start there.' Goodhew paused, knowing that sometimes heart-on-the-sleeve honesty was the most productive way forward. 'I'd really like to. I think it's important and I'd like to see it through.'

Chapter Twenty-one

POINT CLEAR VILLAGE stood in the parish of St Osyth, apparently famed for witch persecutions and having the lowest rainfall in the country. Goodhew knew nothing about either the witches or the supposedly dry climate. The rain had begun about ten miles south of Cambridge and seemed only to intensify once he hit the outskirts of the village. There was a lake near the centre of St Osyth, where a moored ski-boat jiggled about in the water, buffeted by both the wind and a heavy downpour.

A PC Beales from Clacton had left a message saying that he'd wait outside the grocer's on Point Clear Road. That had sounded vague, but the small shop turned out to be one of the more noticeable landmarks on the long straight road. Goodhew pulled alongside the patrol car and wound down his window. Beales did the same, and Goodhew shouted across the gap between them: 'Shall I follow you?'

'Leave yours here and we'll go in this one.'

'I don't know how long I'll need to be.'

'You can have as long as you want.' Beales was probably a similar age to Goodhew, but his expression still brimmed with the excitement that came with new experience. 'And I'm a better person to row you out there than anyone else you'll find at this time of day.'

Goodhew nodded and lifted his rucksack across to the other vehicle.

'Thanks.'

'No problem. Bet you didn't bring a life jacket, either? But don't worry about it, I have two with me.'

Goodhew hadn't even considered the logistics of reaching Marshall's boat. He'd imagined it being tied to some kind of jetty, so that he would be able to reach it on foot and step aboard from something solid.

'It's out in the channel leading up to St Osyth Creek, moored out in the middle but easy to reach.'

'How did you find it?'

'I checked all the names of people who'd paid for moorings. I went to school with Artie Hallam's grandson, so I know Artie's been dead for a good ten years. As soon as I saw his name on the list, I guessed.'

'That's a lot of local knowledge.'

'Not really. Everyone knew Hallam because he was your standard waster and bastard – only the brewery would have missed him. And maybe his widow.' Beales pulled a face that implied he felt doubtful even about that. 'Anyhow, I went to see her and learnt she'd sold it to a man who wanted it as a surprise for his girlfriend.'

'When was this?'

'Old Mrs Hallam didn't have a name or date but said it was right after Artie's death in '98.'

The light was fading quickly, mostly due to the rain. Beales turned down a lane which was flanked on one side by the perimeter fence of a holiday camp and on the other by a ribbon of exposed houses. The road then deteriorated into a crumbling concrete track, but Beales seemed to know the potholes well and wove deftly around them, barely slowing.

'I arranged for a dinghy to be left at the Point Clear ferry station. With any luck it'll have a motor, so I was joking about the rowing.'

'How long have you been in the force?'

' 'Bout two years. Before that I was a lifeguard in the summer, and volunteer lifeboat crew all year round. So you probably won't drown but if the worst does happen to you, I'll know what paperwork needs filling in.'

Goodhew looked away and smiled to himself. The constable was good company and, when he thought about it, he actually preferred Gully's company to no company at all; though even a year ago he probably would have felt differently.

Beales reached the end of the track and pointed out a wooden walkway that stretched from the hard standing to the water's edge. 'Grab your kit, then.'

'That's a ferry station?' It looked as though the full service here might consist of a man in a cable sweater with a coracle under one arm.

Goodhew opened the door, realizing the temperature had dropped further and the rain felt sharper. His jacket was waterproof, but felt flimsy against such weather. Cambridge stood forty-five miles from the nearest coast, far enough that he never needed to consider the rough weather that rode in from the North Sea. Beales opened the boot and flung Goodhew a thick coat and a life jacket. 'It'll be much colder once we're out there.'

'Oh good.'

'Better get on with it, then.' Beales stepped on to the walkway. 'Stay on the boards, otherwise it's nothing but mud between here and the water.' Goodhew followed and within minutes they were on board and bobbing on the water, as Beales coaxed life into the small outboard. 'So what's in your rucksack?'

'A couple of torches, a camera, a SOCO suit – evidence bags just in case.'

'Just the one suit, I suppose?'

'I'm afraid so.' Goodhew totally understood Beales's disappointment, but equally he wanted to inspect the inside of the boat without distraction. Now they were moving he had a better view of the estuary. Pleasure craft of varying sizes and budgets were moored along the centre of a crescent-shaped stretch of river. Some were tied to a jetty there but the rest occupied random spots, like marks on a scatter diagram. 'Which one belonged to Marshall?'

Beales pointed upstream towards the far limit of the moorings, about half a mile away. 'Third from the end, with the dark-blue stripe.'

From where he sat, Goodhew could only pick this out as a boat-shaped smudge bisected by a dark band. They spent the rest of the short journey in silence, both leaning forward to watch the cabin cruiser's shape sharpen and solidify. It looked about twenty feet in length, with a small deck area at the front and a lower deck at the back. The cabin area had one low but wide double window on each of three sides. The dark curtains appeared tightly closed across the two windows that were visible as they approached.

Beales pulled alongside and tethered the two boats together. 'If you want to suit up here, it should be steady enough.'

Goodhew nodded and was about to unpack the white suit, but then he rezipped the rucksack. He raised his voice, shouting to Beales, 'I'll do it once I'm on board, otherwise I reckon I'll be risking too much contamination going across from here.'

'What are you expecting to find?'

Goodhew shrugged and removed the life jacket and the thickest coat. 'Possibly nothing, but the clean suit is just in case.' A few seconds later, on board Marshall's boat, he pulled on the coveralls, his thoughts still on that last exchange: would he really be going to these lengths *just in case*? No. He stared at the closed door next to the wheelhouse. He was expecting to find *something*; he just didn't know what.

GOODHEW SET UP the first torch at the back of the boat, shining directly towards the cabin area. The other he carried, training it on the floor, checking that there was nothing to note, before stepping forward. He ran the beam around the whole of the rear deck.

The open area was sparse: the only fittings, apart from the steering equipment, were two vinyl chairs and a tiny side table, all wall mounted. He guessed that the vessel was around thirty years old, fairly well maintained from the outside but not at all the high-end toy that he'd expected.

The cabin door and the steering wheel were both of wood varnished in a thick orange-tone lacquer. He wasn't surprised to see a lock on the door, even though no key had been recovered. It had probably been melted into the sub frame of the Evora, and if he found something here now, they'd need to check the wreckage of the car more closely.

He slipped his hand into his rucksack and located a rubber-handled screwdriver and the smallest of his three lock-picking sets. He opened the small pack of bump keys and found the right type to fit the lock. He gave it several sharp taps with the screwdriver handle. It opened smoothly and he pushed the door gently.

Despite his face mask, he knew at once that the air smelt bad – not in a distinctive or identifiable way, just bad. He shone the light inside, and the interior looked like a squat. The far end was occupied by a bed, wide enough to be a double at the foot but narrowing a little towards the head as it followed the lines of the hull. The half of the cabin in which he stood housed a short sofa on each side, with a narrow aisle running between them. The upholstery and carpets were both gun-metal grey, and the heap of bedding at the far end was a mix of yet more grey and dark blue. He photographed the scene before he touched anything, then activated the voice recorder on his mobile phone and placed it on the floor by his feet.

His precise remit had been simply to identify the craft, determine whether it had been recently used and check for anything suspicious. It was that last part of his instructions which had been Goodhew's green light to come fully equipped. He knew this hadn't been Marks's *exact* intention, but it was also Marks who had urged him to use his initiative. And his rucksack here was brimming with it.

Like, for instance, the orange glasses and the small UV torch that he'd zipped into one of the side pockets. He first turned off the cabin's main light. The torch on the rear deck still shone so he reached behind and shut himself inside the cabin. He then began with the floor in front of him, kneeling to shine the UV light on to the long thin strip of carpet tiles. The floor glowed back at him like an upended panoramic image of fireworks night: speckles, shadows, glitter and white glowing streaks.

The smell rose again. He felt his throat constrict and his torch beam shuddered for a second. He steadied his hand before he began speaking. 'The floor area is heavily stained. Small dark circles indicating blood droplets, and another area – maximum measurements approximately ten centimetres by seven – indicating pooling. Several fluorescing stains point to the presence of powder residue and bodily fluids.'

He kept to the same spot but ducked lower and shone the torch over the furthest section of carpet, directing the beam of light under the twin sofas. More marks glowed back at him. 'Several objects are concealed under the seating; there appears to be a bowl, a mug and several fabric items. I am further away this time, but all these items indicate possible DNA evidence.' He straightened and swung the torch across the upper side of the sofas. 'The visible surface of the seating shows powder and some minor marks. At this point I am making the decision not to step further into the area. A small proportion of the duvet is visible, and it also shows staining.'

Goodhew drew a long breath and tried to pin down the strange smell that had first hit him. It was harder to notice now that he'd been in the room for a few minutes. He shut his eyes in order to focus on it, but instead, and for the first time, he noticed the bobbing of the boat. He shook his head, deciding he'd seen enough. He switched torches to use the standard beam again. In this light his surroundings just looked shabby.

He bent over to grab his mobile phone and caught a sliver of that same smell. He turned slowly to his left and it became a little stronger. Sweat? Yes, sweat and who knew what else – but, now it had been identified, there was no mistaking it.

When he was just inches from the door, he killed the standard torch and flicked back to the UV light.

Above the door itself a heavy-duty ring had been bolted to a wooden block up near the low ceiling. Below it he could see shapes fluorescing back at him. Sweat stains that had been sucked into the dry grain of the wooden door. Indicating a woman's proportions, and reminding him of a watermark.

The sweat stains left by contact with her upper arms, her shoulder blades and her buttocks marked from near the top of the door to the area of its wooden surface level with Goodhew's waist.

He stepped out on to the rear deck and extinguished the torch. The rain was reduced to a light spray and he drew in several deep breaths of the damp air.

Then he locked the door behind him and climbed back into the dinghy alongside Beales. The constable eyed him warily. 'What did you find?'

Goodhew felt around in the hull of the boat until he located the extra coat and the life jacket. 'This boat needs taking to a secure location. Can you arrange that?'

Beales nodded, then kept staring at Goodhew all the time he had radio contact with the shore. 'They said they'll bring it in before dawn.'

'Good.'

Beales looked uncertain, 'What happens now?'

'We wait.'

'You're kidding?'

'We're not leaving it unattended. Call them back if you need to.'

Beales did, and in less than an hour they saw the lights of another boat heading across the estuary. By now, Goodhew had already spoken at length with Marks, and had received the simple instruction to return to Cambridge at once. He didn't argue.

Beales had been listening quietly to the phone call. Goodhew hadn't minded, but was thankful when Beales didn't press him for more news as they waited. It was only when Goodhew was dropped back at his own car that Beales spoke. 'You looked shaken when you got off that boat, but now you seem absolutely fine. I don't understand how you do that.'

How do you cope with dead bodies? That was the usual question.

A shrug and a non-committal answer was the usual response.

But Beales wasn't asking out of mawkish curiosity.

Goodhew smiled sadly. 'I don't. And I don't believe others who say they just switch off from it. Why would becoming desensitized be such a good thing, anyway? I'm sure it gets to us all eventually.' He shook his head, 'Sorry, I don't suppose that's what you wanted to hear. I genuinely don't know the answer.'

Beales shrugged. 'Kind of a relief to hear it put like that. It makes sense.'

Goodhew drove back towards Cambridge with Beales' final words lodged in his head. *It makes sense.* It was another thirty miles before Marks's words displaced them. *Get back to Cambridge as soon as you can.* He remembered the exact tone of his boss's voice. Without a doubt something back there had changed.

Chapter Twenty-two

GOODHEW CHECKED THE time: 12.30 a.m. He sent the text in any case. 'Are you awake?'

The reply arrived in less than thirty seconds. 'Of course.'

'Can I come round?'

'I'll be home in about twenty minutes. Put the kettle on if you arrive before me.'

His grandmother's flat came into view just as he saw a taxi stop outside it. She stepped out but stood chatting to the driver until Goodhew had reached them. They then waved goodbye to one another and the driver gave Goodhew a thumbs-up as he pulled away.

'That's John Warrell,' she explained.

'Who?'

'He went to school with your dad. John always drives me whenever I pop up to the city.'

'You've been to London tonight?'

'Gary . . .' She shook her head and led him inside. He couldn't see her face but guessed she was smiling.

'What?'

'Ever heard the expression "You need to get out more"? London's only sixty miles away and I don't just sit indoors in the evening.'

'I never thought you did.'

'Well, then.' She opened the door into the kitchen. 'Tea?'

'Coffee, thanks.'

'Backgammon?'

'I'd better not. Apparently Marks expects me to be "fresh and well-slept" in the morning.'

'He said that?'

'Left me a note. I've been in Essex for most of the day and when I arrived back at Parkside there was a Post-it on my monitor. I thought he wanted me back because something had kicked off.'

'But nothing has?'

'I don't know the very latest on the Marshall case, but the boat I located in Point Clear needs full forensic investigation.' He screwed up his face.

'Unpleasant?'

'It smelt bad. I feel as though that got inside me somehow.'

'You mean there were fumes?'

He shook his head. 'Not fumes, but damp mixed with human smells.' He lifted his coffee from her hands. 'Thanks.' Tiny milky bubbles pirouetted on the surface. 'Primarily sweat, I think.' He stopped short of sipping the drink and held it down near his right knee so that its aroma couldn't reach him. 'Do you know that feeling when you can't see or hear – or in this case smell – something well enough to identify it, but at the same time you feel that all you want to do is back away?'

'Surely you just mean instinct?'

'No.' His tone sounded sharper than he expected, so he repeated the word more softly. 'No, not instinct. Some kind of association.'

'So a memory?'

'I suppose.' He looked down at the coffee. The liquid was almost still now and an innocuous wisp of steam drifted from it. 'It smelt sour in there. I can't pin it down, but the smell is still inside my head.' He gave up then. 'Who knows.'

His grandmother shrugged and changed the subject. 'I ran into Bryn yesterday. Actually, I had a feeling he was looking for me, because he knows I love the coffee in Savino's, and I was barely through the door when he appeared. We chatted for nearly an hour.'

'Not girlfriend advice?'

'Yes, *he's* actually worried that *she's* blowing hot and cold.'

Goodhew waved the idea away. 'He'll change his mind by next week.' He couldn't get himself excited about Bryn's love life, even if only to indulge his grandmother.

'Maybe, but I think it would do him good to get dumped for a change. And what's this tattoo he's having done?'

'I don't know. Didn't he tell you?'

'He said he didn't want to say until it was actually done. But he also said you gave him the picture . . . and I'm just nosy.'

'Oh, yes, I forgot about that. From last year's Hawaiian calendar, I think. He was after a picture of a hula girl.'

'Cool. Have you ever thought about a tattoo?'

'No, never.' He felt tempted to ask his grandmother the same question but then a lyric from a 45 on his jukebox popped into his head. *She had a picture of a cowboy tattooed on her spine, said Phoenix, Arizona 1949.*

So he decided to keep quiet, just in case.

And, in the silence that followed, his thoughts drifted across town. 'I haven't heard yet if they decided to excavate the Osbornes' cellar.'

She straightened. 'I heard it on the radio in John's taxi. I assumed you already knew because you always seem to . . .'

'All I've done is think about that boat. Marks told me nothing.'

'The road's cordoned off. There's no announcement expected before morning, but the reporter referred to an increased police presence.'

'So there's something,' Goodhew concluded quietly. And, despite Marks's instructions and Goodhew's best intentions, the idea of being *well-slept* tomorrow vanished in the blink of an eye.

Chapter Twenty-three

HE GUESSED IT was about a mile from his grandmother's to the Osborne house. The main road was the most direct route, even on foot. It was out of sight of the river but followed the same arc as the Cam as it curved north towards the site of the original Cambridge Castle, and passing the Punter pub at the bottom of Pound Hill.

After five minutes' walking he approached the junction with Silver Street. A police car crossed at the lights and headed in the opposite direction. The driver didn't notice him and Goodhew realized he had no desire to speak to anyone either. Street lamps lit all the roads, but even without them the night was clear and bright. It was easy enough to pick out the creamy surface of the footpath that ran parallel to Queens Road and the Backs.

He crossed the road and stepped over the single, low-level railing, striding most of the final half mile without seeing anyone at all. One hundred yards from Jane's house and all that changed. Three orange and white road-closed barriers blocked the street from halfway up the hill onwards, and the sign hanging over the middle one read 'Access Only'. The section of road on his side of the blockade was filled with residents' cars, while the other side was cluttered with official vehicles.

Two were ambulances, which seemed optimistic for an excavation.

Marks had recently changed cars again and his latest, a two-year-old black Honda, was parked near the top of the slope. Goodhew showed his badge to the nearest PC. 'I'm looking for DI Marks.'

'You can't see it from here, but there's a mobile unit parked just round the corner, across from the house. Last time I saw him, he was there.'

The unit was a mobile site office that Cambridgeshire Constabulary had kitted out as a mobile information centre and often trailered to school events and fetes. Marks had pulled down the blinds on all but the window facing the Osborne house. He was standing inside, his head turned away from the door as he concentrated on his radio. He caught sight of Goodhew and waved him inside.

'There's a bunch of you expected on duty first thing, so if you're staying now, don't expect to slack off when the others turn up. OK?'

Goodhew nodded. 'Nice office, by the way.'

Marks picked up a pamphlet that had fallen to the floor. 'Fancy a career in policing?'

'I think that's the leaflet my careers teacher handed out.'

Marks shoved it back in the rack. 'You make me feel old sometimes, Gary.'

The furniture consisted of a standard-height table and three low and totally incompatible chairs. Marks perched on the edge of the table. 'First regarding the cabin cruiser: forensics are working on it but they've warned it'll be a slow one. The senior SOCO asked me to pass on his thanks for, quote, *not fucking it up*, unquote.'

'Carmel Marshall must know more about it than she lets on.'

'Undoubtedly, but she'll keep for a little longer.' Marks tipped his head in the direction of the window. 'This business is more pressing. By the time the radar survey results came back, we had enough data to conclude that there's something buried down there. Then we lost most of the afternoon while structural engineers worked out whether it would be safe to dig.'

'But then it went ahead?'

'Yes.' Marks glanced at his watch. 'OK, if you're staying I'll explain. There's a team of four down there but, because of the confined space, they're working only two at a time. The ground-penetration data gave some tricky results because the hole was refilled with the original soil mixed with several buckets of hardcore, probably carried in from the garden. This messes with the readings, but they now know the deepest point of the trench and they're getting close.'

'And there's still the possibility of a body?'

'Before the dig, I sent down the cadaver dog, and she came up with nothing. But she's just gone in again and this time she's detected some human remains. Space is getting tight for a complete body, but there's *something* there. And that's why I'm pleased you're here.' Marks spoke the last sentence with a hint of satisfaction. 'I want a complete chronology of everyone who's lived here, who rented it, who lodged here, even anyone who ever dropped in to use the loo.'

'Between which dates?'

'This dig has come about because of Jane Osborne's observations, so go back to the year when she ran away.'

'2003?'

'Yes, from then until now. Once something more substantial is unearthed, we'll be able to narrow it down further. Anyone who has lived at that property at any point is a potential witness, so the more names and dates the better, as far as I'm concerned.'

His mobile sitting beside him on the tabletop started to ring, and Marks looked down at the caller display. 'Here we go,' he muttered before snatching it up and pressing it to his ear. 'Yes?'

EVERY SEARCH CAME with its own challenges, and although the excavation of this cellar had lasted only a few hours, the confined space and airlessness had produced the same jaded expressions as characterized a far longer dig. Finding a body was hardly a cause for celebration, yet Marks could understand the sense of achievement and relief that came at the moment a search like this suddenly bore fruit.

The call Marks had taken had come from George, a SOCO who looked like a hobbit and had the complexion of a man who rarely made it out into the daylight. Everything about him was like a geeky fifteen-year-old, except the obvious fact that he was now getting closer to forty than thirty. George's pride in his work edged towards the macabre: a total fascination with the scene itself and virtually no interest in any part of any case surrounding it. Marks knew that even when George had taken a break from the excavation, he would have stood on the cellar steps and watched, unwilling to miss the crucial moment of revelation.

Job satisfaction was a good thing, but, as Marks followed George down into the cellar, he had to admit that in this case such zeal was a tiny bit disconcerting.

The room had been rigged with bright LED lighting, which gave off no heat, and the stark and shadowless space felt unnaturally clammy. All things considered, the excavation had been extremely swift; it could often take a full two days to uncover a buried body. In his peripheral vision he could see George moving restlessly, and could imagine his bony fingers working deftly through the rubble.

Marks was careful to avoid looking down at the corpse until he stood right next to the grave. He wanted to concentrate on just that and nothing else.

At first glance there was surprisingly little to see. The earth had been removed in layers and, apart from a few protruding glimpses of bone, all the rest had yet to be excavated.

George squatted at the edge of the pit and pointed towards a small section of skull. 'That's the right parietal bone, close to the sutures where it joins the occipital and temporal bones. If you imagined the head being positioned with the left eyebrow, cheek and jawbone resting on the floor, that's the angle I'm talking about.' He indicated a series of points within the trench, tracing a pattern that loosely resembled the constellation of Pisces. 'There is some brickwork down here that probably came from an older structure. The body itself is actually positioned in a narrow channel, which explains why it is lying on one side, with its legs bent back like that.'

'The position looks very unnatural?'

'Dead is dead, I guess,' George shrugged. 'It's not as though comfort was of any importance. But you're right, squeezing a body into that confined space would have involved quite a bit of physical manipulation.' He eyed the narrow channel thoughtfully. 'Stamping on it might have worked. And, as far as we can tell from the bones we have uncovered, the body was naked when it was buried. It's possible that part of the incentive for removing the clothes was to try to fit the body into this space.'

Stripping a body was also a good way of delaying identification. A few years underground could strip the skeleton whilst leaving any synthetic clothing barely out of shape. 'I don't suppose there are any clues to the identity yet?'

'Do you know how much of the skeleton is fully excavated so far? Two intermediate and three distal phalanges.'

This time Marks gave up. 'Parts of the skull I could just about manage, so which bits of the body are we talking about now?'

'Fingers!' George beamed. 'Finger *tips* to be precise.' He held up his hand and would have given a joint-by-joint explanation, but Marks interrupted him.

'How long till it's fully exposed?'

'Hard to say, but we won't be holding back.' For a man who hadn't slept much, George had far too much of a sparkle in his eye.

'I'm going to speak to the owner of the house and his family, but as soon as you have measurements or uncover any items that may aid identification, I want to know straight away. Is that clear?'

'Absolutely, and we'll continue to photograph the process every step of the way. In fact . . .' George reached into the neck of his T-shirt and, for the first time, Marks saw that he wore three differ-ent-coloured lanyards, each hung with a matching-coloured flash drive. George chose the green one. 'They're all the same, but the green one is for other people to borrow. Green equals the memory stick that's "to go" – well, that's how I remember it.'

'What's on it?'

'All the photos so far. Two prints and an enlargement, as my dad would say. More like a keyring and a modern photo book these days.'

George laughed. Marks didn't.

The psyche of some criminals was scary, but sometimes with his colleagues he suspected it was worse.

Chapter Twenty-Four

'MR OSBORNE, I am just trying to establish dates.'

Gerry Osborne sat in a winged armchair, the only item of traditional furniture in his son's sitting room. It looked so out of place that Goodhew guessed it had been forced on Dan and his wife with the same charging-bull mentality that was blackening Osborne's expression at this very minute. An empty tumbler and a half-full bottle of whisky stood on the floor next to Osborne's right foot.

Goodhew took up position on the nearest seat, a bucket armchair stiffly upholstered in oatmeal and chocolate linen. He tried again: 'I am not implying that you are involved in any kind of scandal. I simply need to establish some facts.'

Osborne snorted. 'You are a fool if you think that I would willingly open myself up to police questioning a second time. I'm not a naive member of the public now, am I? One minute you are "establishing facts" and the next I'll be taken in for questioning and find that every public comment I've ever made is out there with the twittering judge, jury and executioners of the public domain.' He sank further back into the armchair, which was appearing more throne-like by the second. His expression managed to be both aggressive and unreadable.

'You and Jane are very alike, you know.'

If anything, this mention of his daughter seemed to deepen his angry glare. He shook his head. 'Becca looked like me. Jane's just like her mother.'

From Goodhew's own observation, he thought the exact opposite was true.

'You and Jane have the same personality. I didn't know her before she left Cambridge, of course, but, over time, I bet she's been scowling just as much as you have. She has the same two lines in the middle of her forehead, the down-turned mouth and the thousand-yard stare. That's why she's looking even more like you as time passes.'

'You know well enough I've barely seen her.'

'And why is that?'

'I don't know, but you can stop trying to antagonize me by pretending Jane and I have some special empathy with one another. If I had avoided the large part of the last decade, in the way that she has, I might believe that we had a little more in common.'

'You're making quite a few assumptions about how easy she's had it. From my experience of meeting runaways, they don't leave home because they're happy there, and it's rarely straightforward for them to find happiness afterwards.'

'You're an arrogant little shit. You know nothing about Jane.'

Goodhew was very careful now to keep his tone and expression neutral. 'I know the anger and resentment you are feeling towards her is pretty much the same as the anger and resentment she feels towards her mother.'

'My feelings are none of your fucking business.'

Goodhew didn't respond. 'We are arranging for your ex-wife to come back to England as soon as possible, but in the meantime Jane needs support. And when her mother does arrive, if they can't patch things up, she'll probably need even more support.'

'And, what, you now think you're a shrink and a social worker?'

'No, I'm a policeman,' Goodhew replied quietly. 'But until you can answer the questions I need answered, I will continue to tackle the subjects that seem to be causing you to obstruct me.'

'I am not obstructing you.' The two lines in Osborne's forehead had creased to cleavage-like proportions and a film of sweat glossed the skin above them. He was a physical man, a man whose thoughts and emotions were used to being expressed through the persistent banging and cracking of hammers, rifflers and chisels. Goodhew understood this, but it didn't mean he was prepared to give in to it.

'So, let's start with the date that you and your wife stopped living together.'

Osborne folded his hands in front of him. 'There is no particular date. There are many. There are the weeks I spent in my workshop, the weeks she spent "finding herself", the days when I walked out the front door and some other man walked in through the back.'

'Who broached the subject of a divorce?'

'She did, of course.' He looked down at his hands, then turned them over and stared at his palms as if something small was cradled there. After a moment he again glanced up at Goodhew from under those heavy brows. 'I said "of course".' This was the first time that Goodhew had heard any softness in the man's tone. 'And it's "of course" because giving up has never been in my nature – but it always was in hers. When I work, I aim to create pieces that will outlive me. I realize how arrogant that sounds, but it's the truth. Mary thought in terms of everything being disposable – consumerism for the sake of.'

Osborne reached down and scooped up the glass and the bottle with one hand. He filled the glass close to halfway and glanced up to see whether Goodhew would make a comment. When he said nothing, one corner of Osborne's mouth hinted at a smile. 'There was a time when Mary and I seemed in phase. Way back, that is, when we first met. We opened each other's eyes to new ideas. By the end of our marriage, I decided she was the most selfish person I'd ever known.'

He then went on to their early relationship, Mary's mercurial charm and his own devotion. Then the rifts and dysfunction that followed, as he gained recognition as a sculptor.

As Osborne spoke further and finally opened up, so his body language changed. Quite abruptly he switched into another voice: Gerry Osborne, sculptor, creative visionary, passionate commentator on Cambridge art. He sat taller, his expression lightened and everything about him became animated. The transformation was startling. Keyser Söze would have been proud.

When he finally sat back in the chair, he was smiling. 'Mary was a self-absorbed woman, selfish to the point of neglect towards all of us. People were drawn to her and I, too, could never quite shake my addiction, even when I could've cheerfully wrapped these hands around her throat.' He splayed the fingers of one hand.

Goodhew still said nothing, just waited as Osborne drained his glass.

They could always get official dates of occupancy from council tax records and rental agreements, and probably with more accuracy than from Osborne's memory alone. But that wasn't the whole point; Goodhew wanted this opportunity to understand the household better and if that included watching Osborne getting drunk, then so be it.

By now the man was staring right through him. 'So, what else do you want from me?'

'You were giving me those dates.'

'Was I, now?'

'If you want to try baiting me, that's up to you. But there's a body in your basement and these questions aren't going to go away.'

Osborne tutted. 'Don't get so uptight. I'll tell you what I can remember, up to the date Mary took it from me. And then from when I bought it back. And up to the time I handed it to the letting agent. You see, I'm not at all obstructive.'

Abruptly, he rose from his chair and made a consciously coordinated move to the door. It was already ajar but he pushed it wider then leant heavily against the frame. 'Dan, we need you in here.' Osborne leant further into the hallway. 'Dan!' He returned to Goodhew. 'Give him thirty seconds.'

Dan arrived as Osborne was halfway back across the room, probably about to yell into the hallway again. Dan's face was a mask of exhaustion. 'What's up?'

Instead of speaking to his son, Osborne addressed Goodhew. 'Dan will have the details of the tenants. I tried not to get involved.'

Dan nodded. 'I'll be able to find details of either tenants or, failing that, the letting agent. I don't know how to say this tactfully, so I'll just say it. We never had the best quality people living there, because of the state of the place. Some tenants sublet, and they shouldn't have done, but there you go. We don't have those details, of course, so you'd need to ask the official tenants themselves.'

'How soon can you pull the information together?' Goodhew asked.

Dan glanced at his father, who nodded. 'I'll get straight on it,' Dan replied. He looked as though he wanted to leave the room immediately, but hesitated. 'The body . . . do you know who it is yet?'

Goodhew shook his head. 'I'm sorry.'

'You must know whether it's a man or a woman. That would be a start, surely?'

'I'm sure there will have been some preliminary findings, but for now all we can confirm is that the body has been there for some time, certainly six months, possibly years.'

'Hence the need for records?'

'That's correct.'

Dan still seemed anxious to leave, but couldn't quite tear himself away. 'I need to ask this. Could it be Greg Jackson? I mean, could it be someone Jackson has killed?'

Osborne didn't react, though clearly he'd been harbouring the same thought.

'We will need to establish everyone's whereabouts and precise connection with the property, including Mr Jackson's, but beyond that . . .'

'Mr?' Osborne laughed. 'Even at your incompetent worst, you police must know exactly where he was between his arrest and getting parole? And whether that body was buried during that time. Or is even that a leap too far? And when Mary turns up, you'll be treating her, too, with the respect she doesn't deserve, I suppose?'

Dan stepped towards Goodhew and then turned so that he partially blocked his father's line of sight. 'I'm sorry, Detective, but Dad knows he's not great at handling drink. He usually keeps away from it, but he's also not great with anything that "impinges on his personal life" – his words, not mine.'

Goodhew followed Dan to the front door. 'Drink aside, has your father always been this volatile?'

Dan smiled, a one-corner-of-the-mouth effort that made him look just like his father. 'Mum's always gone for the bad boys, so I imagine so. Though I don't think Dad would appreciate any comparison being made with Jackson.'

'I'm curious about that. How did your mum take it when Jackson moved on to Becca?'

'Ask Mum that yourself. But in my opinion? She didn't give a toss about him by that point, but she was bitter about it in any case. She'd been abandoned by Jane, and then betrayed by Becca. That bitterness was only swept away by Becca's death. And what could she do but start again after that mess?'

'So that was the trigger for her leaving?'

'Without a doubt. Maybe if Jane had come home . . . But, as it was, Mum now had the money from the house, and nothing else to stay here for.'

'Not you and your family?'

He smiled coldly and frowned for several seconds, before speaking.

'With me on Team Gerry? I don't think so. If there's one thing both my parents know, it's how to hold a grudge.'

Chapter Twenty-five

THE FRONTAGE OF Café 1900 featured a small canopy shading a single window on each side of a modest front door. A Spar shop was next door, and a few tables were clustered on the dusty pavement directly outside, unremarkable and surrounded by weather-proof mulberry weave chairs.

Inside, Café 1900 presented a different world completely: dark wood, mirrors and marbled columns. It gave the impression that it had once been part of an old theatre or the reinvention of a former gentlemen's club. The café followed a gentle but deep curve through the heart of the four-storey building on Place de Bancs. Here customers had been mellowing into its quieter corners since the twenties.

The ex-pat ladies met here regularly on the last Tuesday of each month. They'd begun with just four of them around a single table, but now there might be as many as a dozen friends. And friends of friends. They still tucked themselves away at the back of the building, but now took up enough of the tables there that, for a couple of hours, the final few yards of the café felt exclusively their own.

A world within a world.

Today there were eleven of them, and the waiter knew them well enough to fetch pastries without being asked. Mary Osborne sat between Claire and Doreen, two of the three founder members of her ex-pat coffee club. She valued these meetings more than anyone would have guessed. But earlier this morning she'd seen a British newspaper, and now this simple ritual of coffee, croissants and talk about nothing felt even more precious.

If she'd never walked past that news stand . . . if yesterday's *Daily Express* had been tucked away further behind the *Guardian* . . . if she hadn't recognized Gerry's face on the front page. Any one of those, and she'd now be giving this morning her full attention, instead of wasting time imagining that the police might be waiting on her doorstep when she got home.

'Mary?' Doreen nudged her arm. 'Are you all right?'

That made Claire look too. 'Are you about to cry?'

Then suddenly the whole table seemed to be staring at her, ten pairs of eyes, all of them curious and concerned.

Mary swallowed, panicking at the thought of breaking down in front of them all, at the unmistakable tightening of her throat and tingling in her eyes. At the other end of the café, the daylight shone in from the street, promising open space and fresh air. She gripped the table, about to rise, but before she had a chance to consider any other thoughts of running, that beckoning rectangle of distant daylight vanished behind a closer and more solid shape.

The man was middle-aged and thick-necked, with scaly tortoise-like skin around the eyes. One part cholesterol, two parts jobsworth. On any other day she might have assumed he was a public health inspector or some type of bureaucrat, but today she'd only been looking out for the police.

'Mary Osborne?' All eyes had turned to him as he spoke; now the collective gazes swung back to her.

She nodded mutely. She'd been many things in her life, but she had never enjoyed being a liar. It was a small and pathetic gesture, but nodding instead of speaking seemed the honourable thing to do.

Chapter Twenty-six

GOODHEW HEARD THE car slow down as it approached. He turned in time to see Kincaide lowering his side window and swinging the vehicle into the kerb. 'You've pulled,' Kincaide smiled.

'What's up?'

Kincaide cocked his head towards the passenger side. 'Orders from on high.'

'Marks?'

'The man himself. He has a nice little job for us both.'

Kincaide didn't seem in any hurry to offer more information but drew away from the kerb again even before Goodhew could close his door. Something had galvanized Kincaide, and keeping Goodhew both in the dark and firmly in the supporting role probably added to that mood. Maybe that was an uncharitable assumption, but Goodhew doubted it.

'So, who are we seeing?'

'Jackson.' Kincaide kept his eyes on the road ahead and didn't elaborate.

'Why?'

'Even without his conviction, he'd had a close relationship with the Osborne family, so why wouldn't we?'

'No, no, I meant why us? Why not Marks himself?'

Kincaide shrugged. 'He can't be everywhere at once, I guess.'

'Guess not.'

Goodhew's thoughts drifted back to an occasion several months before Jackson's release, and to the single conversation he'd had with his DI. He recalled what Marks had said, word for word. *I then made a mistake. A serious one. And, as a result, a man who should have received a life sentence was jailed for only ten years.*

Goodhew had dug around and discovered that the knife used to kill Becca Osborne and stab Genevieve Barnes had been recovered and handed over to DI Marks. At some point between then and reaching the laboratory it had become cross-contaminated with other samples, and therefore all but dismissed in court.

The murder charge had been dropped and it had only been thanks to the testimony of Genevieve herself that any conviction had been secured.

Maybe Kincaide knew all this, but it was more likely that he didn't, and Kincaide's dubious attempts at camaraderie didn't motivate Goodhew enough for him to share the information. He reminded himself that this was precisely the same petty tactic that Kincaide had been using just a couple of minutes before, but Goodhew's stubbornness refused to disperse. And he knew it would take far more than a couple of days of goodwill from Kincaide, feigned or otherwise, before he'd thaw.

Kincaide drove back towards the town centre.

'Is Jackson at Parkside right now?' Goodhew asked.

'No, round the back, in City Road. He lives there.'

'Really?'

'So he says. We'll check out if that's true, then ask him how he pays for it.'

The houses in City Road and the surrounding streets were mostly narrow terraced properties. The roads and pavements round there were narrow too, congested by limited parking and awkward turning spaces. But the area nestled so close to the heart of the city that local prices had been pushed ever higher. It was hard to imagine many occupants that weren't either professional people, well-funded students, or those whose ownership dated back to at least the 1990s.

Goodhew was about to ask Kincaide for the house number when he spotted Jackson standing in the open doorway of a house about fifty yards further down the street. There was a single gap in the row of parked cars and Jackson approached it and waited until they had pulled alongside. Then he held out a postcard-sized square. Kincaide lowered the window and Jackson thrust it towards him.

'It's a parking permit, for visitors – in case you need it.'

Strictly speaking, they didn't, but Kincaide displayed it on the dashboard, and they both followed Jackson inside.

He was wearing jeans and a red shawl-necked jersey, both of them streaked with pale dust. He'd pushed the sleeves up above his elbows, revealing that his forearms were dappled with tiny paint spots. He led them through the front door and a hallway stacked with boxes, then up a steep flight of stairs on to an uncarpeted landing. A dank smell sank down to meet them between floors. There were just three rooms up here. They passed the doorway of a front bedroom, then the bathroom; both were bare apart from mould patches crawling up the external wall.

The third room was a smaller bedroom, and no more than eight foot square. But this one was newly decorated, and freshly furnished with a single bed, small chest of drawers and a plug-in radiator.

'You can sit.'

Goodhew did, but Kincaide hovered, splitting his attention between Jackson and the view from the window. Jackson remained standing too, and between them the little room became overcrowded.

Kincaide looked back up the hallway. 'Was this a squat, or what?'

Jackson shrugged. 'It was empty, then it got auctioned.' He pushed his hands deep into the front pockets of his jeans and scowled towards Goodhew as he replied. 'That's all I know.'

'And now it's a live-in job, right?'

'Yeah, plaster and redecorate it from top to bottom. I know some decent people in the business. I used to do maintenance for them and they've taken me on again. Low wages but rent free and, let's face it, I've been used to living in a small space.' Jackson made that sound like a joke, but his eyes held an angry glint.

Kincaide glanced around the room once more, then back at Jackson. 'So you've been here since your release?'

'Pretty much. Is that why you're here – to ask about my home life?'

'I'm sure you know it's not.'

Goodhew looked from one to the other. Each man wore the same knowing expression, each courting confrontation but pretending not to. He sighed. 'Why have you been hanging around Pound Hill, Mr Jackson?' He ploughed on before Jackson could deny it. 'Was it to see Jane Osborne, or just to stand and stare at the house itself? And if you were simply fascinated by the house why would you also have been in Newnham Road and Castle Street, like you were watching for Gerry Osborne?'

Jackson's expression remained impenetrable. Goodhew paused until the moment Jackson was about to speak. 'Or following Genevieve Barnes?' he added.

Jackson's gaze flashed in surprise. It was enough to prompt him to sit down next to Goodhew on the edge of the bed.

'Do you know what I enjoy about decorating?' he said.

'No.'

'The total absorption. Silence. Letting my thoughts wander wherever they choose. It's cathartic, when it works.' Jackson scraped at a knot of plaster embedded in the seam of his jeans, not satisfied until it had broken away. He cupped the gritty particles in his palm. Goodhew realized that there were no signs of dust in the room. Jackson's handiwork showed precision and, as he spoke, he revealed a depth of feeling that caught Goodhew by surprise.

Jackson ran his finger through the air, as if tracing the line where the ceiling met the top of the wall. 'I lose myself in the detail, then every so often I complete a section of work and step back and see the enormity of everything that still needs to be done. Then my mind wanders outside and I think of the enormity of what you people did to me.' He turned his head towards Kincaide, and then back again. '*He* knows. I remember him. He was in on it with the scum that sent me down.'

'What do you want from Jane Osborne and Genevieve Barnes?'

He again tilted his head towards Kincaide. 'Same thing I'd want from him. Someone knows I didn't stab either of those women. That paramedic woman sent me down, but someone put her up to it.'

'She just told the truth, Jackson,' Kincaide replied. There was no confrontational tone now, just firmness. 'There's been a development, and we've come to ask you a few questions.'

Jackson ignored him, addressing Goodhew instead. 'She'll tell me one day.'

'Jackson?'

'Yeah, I heard.' He swung his gaze towards Kincaide, and again Goodhew saw hardness in his eyes. But he smiled. 'You have the whole road blocked off, so I'd say the whole of Cambridge has heard. Now I suppose you've found something there and as I've set foot within a mile of the place, *voilà*, here you are.'

'We have uncovered a body.'

'And what? You'd like me to confess to something? I don't think so.'

'We'll be speaking to everyone who may have had access to that house, and who may be able to help us to identify the body or identify other visitors to the house or maybe pinpoint dates of building work. Given your relationship with both Mary and Becca Osborne . . .'

'No, not interested.' Jackson rose to his feet. 'You may as well leave.'

'They're very straightforward questions.'

'And my straightforward answer is, no, I'm not answering them.'

Goodhew stood too and followed Jackson out on to the landing.

Kincaide followed reluctantly, and carried on talking to the back of Jackson's head, listing his questions. 'You were a regular visitor,' he added finally.

'A regular visitor? That's your euphemism for what, exactly?' Jackson was downstairs at the front door by then. He opened it wide and pressed his back to the wall to make as much room as possible for them to pass.

'It wasn't a euphemism for anything.'

Jackson's expression filled with distaste as he shook his head. 'Just fuck off, will you?'

Kincaide stepped out on to the pavement but Goodhew didn't move. 'Aren't you even curious?'

'No, not at all.'

'It could be someone you know.'

'It could. But it won't be anyone I care about. She's dead.' He paused. 'Becca's dead,' he added, as though he'd needed to clarify.

'You haven't asked the sex of the body, how long it's been there. Nothing.'

'Because I don't care.'

Jimmy Barnes's words came back to Goodhew then: *What the fuck is the wrong expression?* Perhaps it was time to try to find out. He levelled his gaze at Jackson and nodded slowly. 'So,' he said, 'you *did* stab them.'

If Jackson could have stepped back a pace, he would have. Instead he pressed himself harder against the wall, his eyes widened momentarily and for a full second he seemed completely stunned. He took a breath. 'You'll need to explain that one.'

'If you hadn't killed Becca, you would be hoping a new body might exonerate you. What are the odds of two separate killers hitting one family? If there's only one killer, you're it.'

'Who says it was murder?'

'No one. But if you knew nothing about it, you'd hope that it was. You'd actually be praying for it, because, finally, there would be some glimmer of hope that that body in the Osborne house would somehow clear you of involvement in Becca's death.'

Jackson's lips pursed sourly. 'Yeah, right.'

'And if you *know* that body isn't going to clear you, it's because you put it there.'

'Fucking ridiculous. Maybe I'm not thinking about that body because that's just not the way my mind works.'

'I disagree. I think it's exactly how you think.' Out of the corner of his eye Goodhew could see Kincaide hovering restlessly. As long as Kincaide stayed out of it, Goodhew sensed Jackson was oblivious to anything apart from the two of them. 'Tell me something, did you love Becca?'

'What the . . .'

'Did you actually love Becca?'

'I was her boyfriend.'

'That's actually the answer to a different question.'

Jackson's expression darkened. 'You're pushing my buttons now, Detective.'

It occurred to Goodhew that Jackson and Gerry Osborne were similarly easy to rile – or perhaps he'd uncovered a new talent for being able to irritate people.

'That's not intentional,' Goodhew replied placidly. 'I just want to know.'

Jackson suddenly held up his hands. 'I suppose I thought I loved her at the time. We hadn't been together that long, but of course I had feelings for her.'

'And yet the only way you didn't stab Genevieve Barnes is if you ran away from the scene. That means you slipped out of the gate and cleared off when your girlfriend was critically injured.'

'For fuck's sake, you know this. It's in the case notes. D'you think I'm proud of it?'

'My point exactly. In a tight spot, who do you think about? Number one. So, yes, it *is* how your mind works. Your first thought on hearing about a body would have been *How will it affect me?*'

Jackson shook his head slowly as he glared at Goodhew. 'You don't have a fucking off switch, do you? Yeah, I thought about it. I hoped that body got put there while I was inside, because I assumed they'd try to pin *that* one on me as well. I don't buy the idea that anything's going to *exonerate* me. That's fantasy land. And what if I was proved innocent, how do I get seven years tagged back on to my life? No one else looks out for me in this life, so, yes, I cleared off when I knew Becca was getting help. I went out of that road and watched the police and ambulances arrive from a safe distance.'

'And never saw the killer follow you out?'

'I never did because he never came out.'

'Even though he dumped the knife on the way?'

'Says who? A bunch of people who wanted to prove I killed her. All of you know this stuff already. No.' He continued shaking his head, 'Just no.' He pressed his head back against the wall.

'OK. One question?'

Jackson stared up at the ceiling and bumped the back of his head two or three times against the flock-wallpapered wall. 'What?'

'Why do you think Jane knows something?'

'You work it out.'

Goodhew studied him for a few moments longer. He'd stopped the thudding on the wall, but his head and upper body continued to gently rock. 'Mr Jackson, I appreciate your time.'

Kincaide unlocked the car with the remote and said nothing until they were inside. 'Wasn't it obvious to you that he wasn't going to tell us anything?'

'Don't you think he did?'

'Screwed with your brain for twenty minutes. What do you know now that you didn't know earlier?'

'You were there too. You heard the same as me.'

'Yeah, a big fat obstructive stream of shit.'

Kincaide pulled away from the kerb with a few hundred too many engine revs and his irritation still buzzing in the air.

Goodhew turned his head towards his window and allowed himself the smallest of grins. *Welcome back, Kincaide.*

From the corner of his eye he saw Kincaide glance over. By the second junction he'd slowed and, when he spoke, his voice sounded thoughtful. 'Or did I miss something, Gary?'

Goodhew turned to look directly at his colleague. Kincaide was doing a reasonable impression of genuine interest, but Goodhew couldn't see anything beyond Kincaide trying too hard at being the new and sincere version of his former self.

Goodhew shrugged. 'No, I just heard the same as you,' he replied. Jackson's body language had said so much more than that, however. Jackson was isolated, defeated and angry and, in his mind at least, Jane Osborne held the answer. 'It's not just about what he said though, is it?'

'Meaning?'

Goodhew took a breath and tried to remember reasons why cooperation with Kincaide would be good for both of them. 'Nothing,' he lied.

Chapter Twenty-seven

'I THINK JANE and Becca Osborne were in touch with each other when Becca was murdered.' Goodhew had been heading towards Marks's office when he crossed paths with the DI himself crossing the first-floor landing. There had been no preamble, just the blurting of the latest idea to fill Goodhew's thoughts.

Marks barely broke stride. 'Come with me.'

He said nothing else until they'd reached his office and he'd closed the door behind them.

'Tell me.'

'Jackson thinks Jane Osborne knows something, or he wouldn't keep hanging round.'

'I've just spoken to Kincaide, who says Jackson was a waste of time.'

'Jackson wasn't intentionally forthcoming, no. But there's something he's holding back.'

'And you discussed this with Kincaide?'

'No, I thought about it just now on my way up the stairs.'

'And *that's* the DC Goodhew contribution to modern policing? Well done. Now sit.'

Goodhew started recounting the conversation with Jackson, but Marks was busy logging on to his computer, and after a couple of sentences Goodhew realized he was wasting his breath. 'Sir?'

'I'm waiting for an email. It's not here yet.' Marks rested his elbows in the arms of his chair, interlocked his hands, then surveyed Goodhew from behind steepled forefingers. The gesture made Goodhew feel as though Marks was trying to read his mind. 'Apply your brain to this. Mary Osborne moved to Limoges in 2007. She's sent postcards home but, apart from that, has avoided contact with her family. The French police have now found her, but she's not prepared to come back to the UK.'

'They've told her about Jane coming home?'

'Yes. But, from my experience at least, I'd say she's not the most maternal woman I've ever encountered.'

'Does she know she has a granddaughter?'

'I believe so. But the same point applies there too. If she's not the family-bonding type, then it might not be enough to bring her home.'

'So what's her reasoning?'

'She's happy to answer questions, but won't leave France. And we'd have to apply to the French courts for an extradition ruling if she continues to refuse.'

'That would slow things up.'

'And we can't even prove she's obstructing the case at the moment. So we need to demonstrate the legitimacy of our request, and until we can show a connection between Mary Osborne and the body in the basement, we're scuppered.'

Goodhew frowned, not sure what Marks expected of him.

'What's the main reason Mary Osborne would have for not coming back?'

It was rhetorical, but Goodhew answered in any case. 'Because she's scared either of being arrested or scared of someone here.'

'Exactly. And what's your best guess?'

So guessing was now counted as an official modern policing method? 'Apart from the body in the basement?'

'And apart from the obvious, like husband, lovers and so on . . .'

The *obvious* thoughts here were too obvious. Marks was clearly expecting something from Goodhew, and Goodhew had no idea what that might be. Marks reached over and clicked the 'refresh' button on his mailbox even though Goodhew knew it would automatically update as soon as anything new arrived.

'Have any results come back on the body in the basement, sir?' The phrase *'body in the basement'* now sounded as though it had concatenated into a single word.

'They're hoping for basics any time now.'

'Too soon for DNA?'

'Absolutely.'

Goodhew nodded slowly. 'Have you personally spoken to Mary Osborne?'

'Briefly.' Marks tore his attention away from his inbox.

'How did she sound?'

'Older. And weary.'

'Are you sure you'd recognize her voice after this long?'

'I'm sure I wouldn't, actually. I frequently phone in here and don't know which DC I'm speaking to, or phone home and find it takes me two sentences to work out whether it's my wife or daughter that's picked up. And that's without a seven-year gap. So what?'

'How do we know that the woman is really Mary Osborne?'

'Birth certificate, driver's licence, bank details. The French police have confirmed her identity.'

'But not someone who actually knows her?'

Marks suddenly looked pleased. 'They're emailing a photograph right now.' He swivelled the screen so they could both see it, and then they both sat and waited. It was a long ten minutes; neither of them spoke, and the only movement was from Marks, alternating between tapping the tips of his fingers together and strumming the edge of his desk. Finally they heard a dull *click* and, after a slight delay, a new email appeared at the top of the list. The bold-type title read *Mary Osborne*.

After one double-click on the attached file, the image itself appeared. The woman's hair was darker, straight and thick. Her face was thinner and her expression seemed flat and guileless. The age was approximately correct but, beyond that, she wasn't even close to resembling Mary Osborne.

'Well done, Gary. You've earned yourself a trip to Limoges.' Marks nodded at the screen and continued nodding as he turned back to Goodhew. 'Get your passport. We'll leave immediately.'

'Isn't that discovery enough to agree extradition?'

'Come on, Gary, since when do you feel happy to wait several days for answers?'

Chapter Twenty-eight

FLIGHTS FROM STANSTED to Limoges took a little over an hour and a half, but unfortunately they only flew three times per week and the next one wasn't for another two days. After some negotiation, the French police had agreed to escort the mystery woman to Paris, whilst Marks and Goodhew travelled by train from Cambridge to London, then from St Pancras International to Paris Gare du Nord. After a fifteen-minute taxi ride they had been delivered to a sweeping building that, at first glance, looked more like a former thirties department store than a police station. As they waited in the foyer, Goodhew spotted a plaque and discovered that it had been purpose-built in the nineties, in the same way that the charcoal-grey cube of Parkside station had been in the late sixties. But this one had less of the ugliness.

Now they sat in an interview room very similar to one of their own and waited for the arrival of the woman claiming to be Mary Osborne.

'I wonder who she really is,' pondered Goodhew.

Goodhew had built a picture of the physical Mary Osborne in his mind, mostly based on photos, but enhanced by the comments of others too. She stood at about five foot four, with an average frame and a big bust.

An ample bosom, as his grandfather would have said.

She enjoyed her figure too and, in all but the photos taken at Jackson's trial, she'd worn tight T-shirts or low-cut tops and jeans that grabbed her at every curve. In every photo her hair had been streaked at the front, and straightened: her take on Rachel from *Friends* perhaps, since the shots were several years old now. She'd often been snapped holding a drink out towards the camera, and most often grinning into the lens with a coquettish tilt to her head. Some people never quite grew up; and he didn't think that as a criticism. Personally he felt as though he'd somehow skipped being a teenager, and couldn't help feeling some fascination towards perpetual teenagers like Bryn and, maybe, Mary Osborne.

The woman was ushered into the room by a suited man who spoke a few sentences to her and nodded towards Marks and Goodhew, before he took a seat near the door and left them to sit on either side of a narrow table.

In the flesh she was even further from Goodhew's mental picture of Mary Osborne: several inches taller and with broader features. Unvarnished nails and sensible shoes, unremarkable clothes and a cautious look in her eyes.

Marks introduced them both and she murmured, 'Hello'.

'We're investigating the discovery of a body at the former home of Mary Osborne.'

'I saw it in the papers. I've never been there.'

'We need to ask you about your relationship with Mrs Osborne.' Marks shifted in his chair, settling down for the long haul. 'What's your full name and date of birth?'

'Are you going to try to get me back to England?'

'You're not in a position to negotiate with me.' Marks had his pen poised over a pad of paper, where it didn't waver. 'We know you've been living as Mary Osborne, and at the moment we have no other contact details for Mrs Osborne, so your cooperation is vital to us.'

'I don't know who you've found, but it's not her body.'

'Is that a question or a statement?'

'She's not in Cambridge.' She took a breath. 'OK, I said I'd talk to you, and I will. But I need to stay out of the papers – and stay here, if I can.'

'Your name?'

'Lesley Bough. Like the bough of a tree, and spelt the same, B-O-U-G-H.'

'Date of birth?'

'11 February 1964.'

'Where were you born, Lesley?'

'Stone, in Staffordshire.' She'd only answered a few simple questions so far, but her voice had grown in confidence already. 'But I lived in Cambridge for several years. We had a flat in Milton Road and I worked at the Milton Arms when I first moved down, so it was handy.'

'Who is "we"?'

'My husband and me. I was married then.'

'And you knew Mary Osborne?'

'From work, yes.'

Marks looked surprised at this, and cast a questioning expression in Goodhew's direction before turning his attention back to Lesley Bough. From the case notes, Goodhew couldn't remember Mary ever being employed, but something tugged at his memory anyway.

'And where did you and she work together?' Marks asked.

'We didn't work together.'

And as she said it, Goodhew remembered. Mary had once been the almost silent partner in a small recruitment agency. 'Kado Employment,' he interjected.

Lesley nodded. 'Except it's pronounced *cadeau*, as in the French for gift. It comes from the names Karen, Drew and the O from Osborne. Mary said she wanted to call it MKD Recruitment but gave in when she realized that KADO sounded so much better.' She smiled at the memory. 'She'd probably been running it for years by then, but still couldn't let go of the fact that her initial wasn't the one at the front. She was a funny woman.'

It was the first time Goodhew had detected anyone expressing any warmth towards Mary Osborne.

Marks didn't pause to consider that. 'When did you last have contact with Mary Osborne?'

'2007 – just before we left England.'

'What else do you know about the other partners, Karen and Drew?'

Lesley Bough shrugged. 'Nothing except that they were husband and wife. I don't even know their surname. Mary worked a couple of days each week, including Tuesdays. Tuesdays was my day at college so I'd go into the agency then, and chase up work. It was always Mary I saw, so that's how we got chatting.'

'And how would you describe your relationship with her? Purely business, or more as a friend?'

'As a friend, I think. I always felt she was drawn to anything transient. I'm the opposite and, because of her outlook, I always expected that we'd drift apart eventually. But planning to break off all contact with home and, therefore, with each other? It meant we parted on a good note for both of us, and I still think of her as my friend.' As she looked at them both in turn, her smile had faded and there was slight bewilderment in her expression. 'Even though she probably doesn't think much about me,' she conceded.

'Where is she now?'

'Spain. In theory.' She stared at the nib of Marks's pen as it flicked deftly across the page. 'Mary had more things to pull her back home than I did. I did wonder whether she'd stick it and, if she didn't, whether she'd say too much about me. I never thought I'd be the one giving the game away.'

Marks stopped writing before she stopped speaking, and hadn't finished rallying his thoughts when his phone began to vibrate inside his jacket pocket. 'Excuse me, I need to take this,' he said. He reached for the phone as he stood up. 'Goodhew will continue to ask you the necessary questions.'

Goodhew moved across to Marks's seat so that he could face Lesley Bough directly. He scanned down the page of notes that Marks had left, feeling sure there had been ambiguity in something she'd said. His finger found the point on the page. 'You said "before *we* left England". Do you mean you and Mary, or that you came here with someone else?'

'Before Mary and I both left England. We left at the same time but travelled separately. She flew and I took the train. First to Paris, then after a couple of weeks I moved on to Limoges.'

'OK, so from the beginning . . .'

Her laugh, soft and filled with regret, interrupted him. 'You just want to know the whole sorry mess, don't you? And I'm going to follow the flawed logic that it's easier to keep going than to turn back. Am I right?'

'Please tell me.'

She rested her elbows on the table and sank her head into her hands so that her eyes were covered and she now spoke from behind her ringless fingers. 'I didn't like Mary at first, I found her abrasive. She seemed pleased to see me each time I dropped in, though; perhaps she was bored. She liked to tell me about all the clothes and treatments and luxuries she had, and all the new things she planned to buy next. In fact, she talked more about the things she wanted before she got them than she ever did afterwards.'

'And these things were out of your price range?'

'I wasn't jealous, if that's what you're thinking. I was chasing every job I could because I *needed* the money. Worrying about it was my only obsession. But then here was someone who had it, but was no happier than I was. I wondered whether I should learn to be content with my life, and I also wondered about her and all the other things she had that brought her so little joy.'

She lifted her head and looked at Goodhew through splayed fingers. 'I know where you think I'm going with this. You're sitting there remembering *Fatal Attraction* and *Single White Female* right now. But I'm actually far too dull to boil bunnies.'

'So, what did you do?'

'I started asking her about herself and, although she had always been happy to boast about anything she thought I might admire, she was much more reticent when it came to personal details. It was fair enough; I've always been quite a private person myself. So I shared a few stories and soon she opened up a little. A lot, in the end. We both did. It was the beginnings of our odd friendship.'

'Not so odd. Plenty of people bond by learning about each other.'

'Rather premeditated on my part, though.'

'Does that really matter?'

She didn't bother to reply. 'We had some similarities: our unhappy marriages for one. And our ever decreasing options for another. I was trying to keep up with the course fees, while my husband was out running up debts faster than I could pay them. I told her I dreamt of slipping out during the night and leaving him with all the bills. She seemed to think I was joking, at that point.'

'But you weren't?'

She sighed and finally her hands fell away from her face. 'No. It wasn't a clear plan or anything, but once I'd voiced the idea, it didn't seem so stupid.'

'But she wasn't interested?'

'Not immediately, no. I'm sure you know as much about Mary as I do, but she was part way through her divorce when she found out that Greg . . . that her toy boy lover had taken up with one of her own daughters. I thought she'd brush it off, then one day she phoned me. She sounded scared and asked me whether I'd been serious about vanishing. When I met her, she had a bandage on one hand, then she lifted her T-shirt and showed me her ribs. She was a mass of bruises down one side. She'd been kicked, and her hand had been damaged as she tried to stop him.'

'Who?'

Lesley shook her head. 'She refused to say. She said it was obvious, now she'd seen it. Then she was adamant that she needed to use the money gained from the divorce and leave.' Lesley screwed up her nose. 'I suspected Greg had hit her – he had a wild streak, "He liked it rough" as she would say. She said she liked it too, at the time – said it increased the orgasm. Those were the kind of details I never wanted to know. And violence is still violence, in my mind.'

'So Greg was still around then?'

'Yes, we planned this before Becca's death.'

Goodhew shook his head and slumped back in his chair. 'That doesn't make sense.'

'We had almost everything in place, but Mary couldn't then leave in the middle of a murder trial. I thought she'd shelve the whole idea, but she phoned me soon after Greg's conviction. I was desperate by then, so I jumped at the chance.'

'Explain the plan.'

'We chatted about all sorts of different ideas, but what did either of us know about fake identities? Nothing. So we needed to come up with an idea that was as simple as possible. Both Mary Osborne and Lesley Bough are average English names, so we set up new bank accounts in each other's destination country, then just swapped our documentation. Only our passports were risky; we both ordered new ones. We used our own photos but chose hair, make-up and clothes that suited the other person.'

'So you left the country on Jane's passport?'

'Yes, with Jane's picture in it. It was one trip each, and once we were out of the country we planned to stay out.' She shrugged. 'It has worked so far and if anyone had found me, the plan was to say, "Sorry, must be a different Mary Osborne".'

'And why didn't you?'

'I saw the news stands. Gerry Osborne in the papers was one thing but when I realized Jane had turned up I thought . . . I don't know, actually. When it came to it, I couldn't pretend.'

'And the postcards?'

'We tried to guess how we'd feel one year, two years and further down the line. We wrote them one night and swapped cards so we could post each other's home at regular intervals. I posted Mary's to her old house. Is that how you found me?'

'It was the biggest lead.'

She looked a little rueful. 'I wondered if those cards were a step too far. They were my idea actually, so a bit of an own goal then.'

'Don't you miss home?'

'No. My husband's debts spiralled – way over fifty thousand pounds as far as I could tell. Then my mother died, leaving me just under twenty thousand pounds, and I realized that if I took that and ran I might just have a chance to make a new start. I can't go home, because some of those debts are in my name, and my husband's not . . .' she fished around for the word. 'He's not a decent man,' she concluded.

'That sounds like an understatement.'

'I just want the chance to stay clear. I'm now the happiest I've ever been, and I'd be pleased if you can tell that to Mary.'

Goodhew paused, and doodled a small cube on the corner of the page. 'Sure,' he said finally. 'Please excuse me.'

He'd run out of things to ask for the moment. Of course there were plenty more questions, but right now he was too distracted by Marks's phone call and his subsequent failure to return. From across the table, Lesley Bough watched him with the same open expression he'd noticed in the first photo he'd seen of her. The foreboding he now felt hadn't seemed to reach her side of the desk but, then again, she didn't know about Marks's phone. The same phone that Marks had taken with him because only the major incident team had its number. Or the message Marks had left which read: *phone this mobile if it's urgent.*

Chapter Twenty-nine

THEY'D ARRIVED BACK in the UK in the small hours, before travelling by taxi back up the M11 to Cambridge. Now they stood side by side in the morgue, staring down at the corpse. Neither he nor Marks spoke, but Goodhew guessed they were wondering pretty much the same thing: *Is it her?*

Some bodies were horrific, others were so far gone that it was almost impossible to believe they'd ever lived. This one fell somewhere between the two.

At first glance it was little more than a skeleton, badly damaged, depersonalized and sexless. The burial and staining from the damp earth had left it looking like it had come from a film set, or was an ancient relic: one of the exhibits lying in museum display cases, which school children ogle and want to replicate for Halloween.

But they were both focusing more closely now. Sykes, the pathologist, rested one gloved hand on the corpse's forehead. 'Adult female, by the way.' He held a pointer that resembled a broken aerial in the other hand, and rotated it over the centre and then the lower half of the skull.

'The body was packed into a small area, force being involved at that point, then the crushing from earth, hardcore and finally stone slabs would have caused even further damage.' He checked that they had both absorbed this comment before moving on. 'It would be easy to attribute that compression as the cause of this damage, but it isn't. The facial area received repeated heavy blows that caused collapse of the nasal and jaw areas. In two places' – he directed the pointer at the centre of the chin, then under the lower jaw – 'the blow was struck, with force, by a thin but hard edge.'

Sykes straightened and demonstrated what he meant by gripping an imaginary handle, as though he was holding a canoe paddle and stabbing it vertically. 'A spade would be my first suspect, pointing downwards the first time, with the victim lying on her back on the floor. Then, the second time, more at the angle you'd shovel coal.' He emphasized this point by changing the angle and repeating the action a couple more times.

'And, given enough force, the damage would be catastrophic,' Marks commented.

This struck Goodhew as a case of stating the obvious and, judging by the pathologist's own expression, Sykes probably agreed.

Sykes drew closer to the body again. 'There was no shortage of force here. It didn't kill her, though.'

A tremor of nausea rippled through Goodhew's gut. 'She was dead already?' he asked hopefully.

'Well spotted.'

'I haven't spotted anything. I was just being optimistic.' *That sounded wrong.* The nausea took another minute to drift away.

Marks frowned. 'What killed her, then?'

'That's straightforward enough.' Sykes pointed to the ribcage. 'See that?'

'Oh yes.' Goodhew saw it too: the bones scored by a blade that had penetrated between the sixth and seventh ribs on the victim's left side. 'How many times was she stabbed?'

'At least four. This one is the most obvious incision but then there are other marks – here, here and here. The attacker used a great deal of force and, because of the relatively close proximity of the wounds, either restrained her or continued to stab her when she was beyond the point of struggling. Judging by these marks, I think we're looking for a blade that's about four centimetres at its base, and likely to be a minimum of fifteen centimetres in length.'

Goodhew recalculated. 'An inch and a half by six, sir.'

'Imperial's easier to picture,' Marks explained.

One side of Sykes's mouth smiled. 'You've used that one before.'

Goodhew's attention had meanwhile moved back to the head. 'That damage wasn't an attempt to prevent identification, though, was it?'

'Working out people's motivations is hardly my field. This kind of damage could well have slowed identification, but if the body had been found quickly there's no reason to think we wouldn't have fingerprints. Even now there is still plenty of opportunity for at least a partial match with dental records, while the possibilities of DNA identification go almost without saying. So, no, there is nothing much here that will prevent us from identifying her. But the plan may have been to delay the identification, or make it difficult for anyone apart from us.'

'That would seem to imply that someone else was expected to discover the body.'

Sykes shrugged. 'As I say, the crime itself is your field, not mine.' Sykes double-tapped his pointer on the sternum. 'That's not all this corpse can tell us, though. Look at these.'

Both Marks and Goodhew leant in closer to the right-hand side of her chest.

'Broken ribs,' Marks observed. 'How long ago?'

'Three or four years before death. The breaks themselves occurred during the same incident, and at the same time she shows—'

Goodhew spoke up before Sykes could finish. 'That she had broken bones in one hand.'

'Very difficult to spot, but you are correct.'

Marks spoke next. 'And this injury is likely to be the result of the victim trying to defend herself?'

Sykes nodded. 'But during the earlier assault, not at the time of her murder.'

'Yes, yes, I realize that. And how long for DNA and dental identification?'

'DNA? Not this week. The dental won't be tonight, but possibly tomorrow. Who do you think she is?'

'Mary Osborne.'

'Rebecca Osborne's mother?' Sykes studied the body and exhaled slowly through his nostrils as he did so. 'It's more than possible, not just because of the location of the corpse either. You'd be surprised how often I see one family member in here, then another arriving later. Do you have any idea how often a sudden or violent death is followed by an accidental one a couple of years later?'

Goodhew's memory jumped back to several incidences where the bereaved had explained how a new death had been the second or third to strike their family in a short space of time. He felt surprised that he'd never actually made the same observation himself, but clearly Sykes had been right when he'd said his view of any case was different from theirs.

'Except, of course, neither was an accident,' Sykes continued, 'and we're looking at the same cause of death for both.'

'And the same killer?'

'Highly, highly probable. I conducted Rebecca Osborne's autopsy too, and the force of the attack and the determination to kill was simlar in both.' Sykes looked up brightly. 'And if that's the case, and if this is Mary Osborne, then Greg Jackson is in the clear.'

Goodhew's thoughts were already converging on Rebecca Osborne, and he suddenly became aware that he was staring at Sykes. He glanced at Marks in time to catch his boss's expression.

'We'll need to update the family,' Marks said. He began to fasten his jacket. 'Goodhew, are you ready?' He turned to thank Sykes who then followed them towards the exit.

'I'll send you the full report as soon as – and let you know if anything else turns up in the interim.' Sykes raised his gloved hand instead of offering it for them to shake. 'I don't think any of us were expecting this development when we ate breakfast this morning,' he added, as they left.

But Goodhew had noticed Marks's reaction, and he wasn't quite so sure.

MARKS SAID VERY little during their taxi ride from Addenbrooke's to Parkside.

'When will you be visiting the Osbornes?' Goodhew asked.

'Straight away, I think.'

'It's about three a.m.'

Marks turned on the courtesy light over his head and scrutinized his watch for several seconds. 'I hadn't realized. In the morning, then.' He turned the light out again. 'People don't think clearly in the small hours. Me included,' he added finally. He then leant back in his seat, with his head on the headrest. He closed his eyes.

Goodhew knew this was a sign to stop talking. 'How much will you tell them?' he asked.

Several seconds ticked by before Marks answered. He spoke softly, so that the driver couldn't hear. 'Two facts only: Mary Osborne's not in France, but she might be . . .' he paused to think through the words in case the driver could overhear, '. . . she might be with Sykes.'

'And what about Jackson?' Goodhew murmured.

Eyes still shut, Marks's head gave a tiny shake. 'Not now, Gary.'

And he said nothing more until they arrived back in East Road, where he asked the driver to drop them at the front door of Park-side station. 'No need to come inside, Gary. Leave it all until the morning.'

Chapter Thirty

NEVER TRUST ANYONE more than you trust yourself. Jane Osborne held this higher than any other personal belief. When her instincts shouted to her, she listened. Yes, she might be wrong, but at least it would be her own problem. If she let someone else take her down the wrong route, then her error was double.

All day she'd been feeling restless. Waiting for news from her mother. Or news of her mother? And, as time ticked on, the idea that news was being withheld grew and continued to multiply, until the room seemed to shrink.

She was in a B & B on Madingley Road, occupying a pleasant room in a pleasant house. She kept the TV permanently tuned into BBC1 and watched the local news updates, scanning the background of the footage taken from outside the house in Pound Hill and listening to reporters quoting the police. She tried to decode the subtext of every comment.

The police are not expected to make an announcement until tomorrow morning. Didn't that suggest there would be an announcement in the morning? Which meant they had information. Which meant she was being kept in the dark.

She phoned Parkside after that disclosure. They brushed her off. She asked for DC Goodhew but an incurious voice at the other end simply told her that he wasn't there.

She phoned her brother, and his wife picked up. Roz, sister-in-law and complete stranger, offered to go and fetch Dan.

Jane, also sister-in-law and complete stranger, just asked her if there'd been any news. There hadn't. She'd put down the phone and now she paced the room.

She opened the window. Nothing blew in. The air was dead quiet, dead calm.

Dead, dead, dead.

The photo above the bed showed cattle grazing on Newnham Common, and she knew she needed to get out in the fresh air. Needed to walk and think until someone found her and told her what the fuck was happening.

So, at a little after midnight, she left the B & B and started walking towards the city centre. She stuck to the right-hand-side footpath, away from the road but an equal distance from the fences too. She walked quickly and with purpose, not wanting to look vulnerable. But she didn't feel vulnerable either. She headed in the general direction of home. Instincts seemed to draw her that way. She glanced up Pound Hill as she passed. The street was quiet, and a police car parked near the house was the only sign of anything happening.

She wondered if the police had anyone inside the house right now, or whether they were just waiting and watching nearby – and what they expected to see. But instinct told her to keep walking.

And the further she walked, the more determined she became, not prepared to slow down on anyone's terms but her own.

Why are you so angry, Jane?

How many times had she been asked that question? And how many times had she rejected it, railed against the unreasonableness of it even being asked?

Now she'd asked it herself.

She lowered her head and walked on. She reached the next roundabout and deliberately took the less well-lit road. When had she ever come to harm from strangers? And if fate wanted to do that to her, well, bring it on. Her hands balled into fists and she felt her anger flash even brighter.

And she walked harder.

She imagined unleashing it all on anyone who tried touching her.

She turned down Queens Road, crossed to the other side and took the footpath that ran through the wide ribbon of grass separating the road itself and the Backs.

And she walked from one end to the other, through the trees, into the shadows and, where it was too dark to see the footpath, deliberately walking with one foot on the path and one on the grass. She listened for footsteps behind her and watched for movement ahead, but only ready to challenge anyone who dared intrude. Sweat had stuck her shirt to her back and her heart raced.

No one had the right to make her feel this way.

She stopped at the corner of Silver Street and looked behind her.

No one had the right and, so long as they thought they did, then she'd stay angry. Fucking angry. That was her prerogative and now was not the time to let that feeling go.

As GOODHEW CROSSED over Parker's Piece he heard the sound of bells ringing half past three. The four lights of Reality Checkpoint glowed in yellow fuzzy-focus at the intersection between the two diagonal footpaths that crossed the green. Goodhew left the path at the lamppost and cut across the grass to Park Terrace, knowing that he was almost directly in line with his own flat.

He didn't notice the figure sitting on the step by his front door until he was just about to cross the road. It was impossible to see who it was from there, but he recognized her as she stood up, and also realized that he hadn't imagined it could be anyone else.

'Jane? Why are you here?'

She descended two steps. 'I want to talk to you.'

He was right up to her before the small glow of his entrance light enabled him to properly see her. She had that same look of suspicion as she'd had the first day he'd met her. Funny, since she'd now come to him.

'How did you get my address?'

'Internet electoral-register search. There are only seven Good-hews in Cambridge, and only one G.'

Goodhew looked at the front door, then back at Jane. 'I can't ask you in. And we can't talk here.'

She frowned. 'Why can't you ask me in?'

'You're part of an active case.' He corrected himself. 'Even after it's over, I couldn't.'

'Once it's over, why would you, anyway?'

Goodhew had no doubt that Jane's own experience in antago-nizing other people with her questions far outdid his own. If she was looking to start a row with him, then any answer he now gave would be turned back on him. He paused, more to think rather than to avoid the question.

Jane mowed through the gap he created. 'Once it's over, I won't be here.'

'In Cambridge?'

'No, here on your doorstep. Just because I turn up and speak to a bloke doesn't mean . . .'

'Jane, stop,' Goodhew broke in. At least she stayed quiet long enough for him to draw a breath. 'Police-station coffee machine or the University Arms Hotel?'

Without replying she descended to the bottom of the steps, then turned towards the hotel. They were seated in the late bar within a couple of minutes. Goodhew centred his glass of Pepsi on a beer mat and watched her. She'd ordered orange juice and lemonade, which arrived in a Stella Artois glass. She now cradled it in both hands and made no attempt to drink it.

'Have you received any contact from the police since I last saw you?'

'That WPC with the dark hair, she dropped me off at the B and B. She didn't seem to know anything new.'

'OK, you went to some lengths to find me, so how do you think I can help?'

'Where did you go today?' Answering a question with a question. He didn't think she was being evasive, just single-mindedly pushing the conversation towards her own objective.

'I was working on something.'

'Connected with my mum?'

A giveaway hesitation, then: 'Yes, actually it was.'

'Did you speak to her?'

'Look, DI Marks is arranging to speak to your family in the morning.'

'Before he speaks to the press?'

'I wouldn't know anything about that.'

She stirred the ice with the tip of her little finger. 'You didn't speak to her, did you?' She glanced at him quickly, as though expecting to catch him off guard.

He really had no desire to play games – even less to lie to her.

'No,' he said quietly, 'we didn't.'

'And why was that?'

'She wasn't there after all. As far as we know, she isn't actually in France. We thought she was there, but we were mistaken.'

She nodded, biting her bottom lip as though she wanted to stop herself from saying anything too quickly. Finally she spoke and there was an unmistakable catch in her voice. 'So the body could be hers?'

Goodhew nodded slowly. 'It's a possibility.'

She mulled this over. 'A strong one?'

He knew how he ought to respond but, like Lesley Bough when it came to it, he couldn't pretend. He nodded again. 'I think so.'

She put her glass on the table in front of her, and Goodhew let several minutes pass before he continued.

'Jane, were you in contact with any of your family before Rebecca died?'

'She thought he loved her.'

'Becca thought Greg Jackson loved her?'

Jane nodded.

'And what did you think?'

'That he was the big finale in Mum and Dad's crap marriage. Becca was Dad's remaining daughter by then, so she must've known how he'd react. I wondered why Becca couldn't find a bloke of her own.'

'Did you ask her?'

'She said she had – found a bloke of her own, I mean. Jackson was halfway between Becca and Mum in age, and Becca decided that Mum had just used him – like he couldn't say no or something. She said Jackson and Mum's relationship was about no-strings sex. People see things how it suits them, I guess. The whole thing's fucking weird, but then . . .' She stopped mid-sentence. 'Maybe Becca was angry at Mum too, and just got her own back in a different way to me. Mum loves men, always has, and we grew up keeping her visitors secret from Dad. And we were pissed off with him because Dad was too obsessed with his "career" to notice.' Jane changed her mind about her drink and took several swigs.

'Jackson thinks you know something. He wants to talk to you.'

'Really? Jackson can fuck himself. All Jackson cares about is himself. He says he wants to know who killed Becca, but he's a liar. It's not about Becca for him; it's about the years of his life that have been "stolen". Mum's infatuation with him was the usual – fifty per cent sympathy, fifty per cent admiration. She still liked them talented but tormented. As far as I could work out, he's always blamed everyone except himself for every disappointment he's ever suffered.' She put her glass back down and edged forward in her chair. 'That's me done with sharing, so your turn now. If it's her, how did she die?'

'I don't . . .'

'You *do* know.' There was absolutely no question in her voice now. 'Don't take the piss. I know you know something.'

This time not telling the truth came easily. 'No, I don't,' he said firmly. 'But I do want to know why you didn't come forward when Becca was killed.'

'No way.' Her eyes grew suddenly dark. 'If you want me to talk, *you'll* have to talk to *me* first.'

'Look, Marks will speak to you in the morning.' She stood up, and Goodhew stood too. 'Jane, please sit down again. I think you can help us. And we will know more by tomorrow.'

'I don't care about hearing it tomorrow.' She spoke slowly, enunciating each word. 'I just want to know what you know *now*.'

'No.' He was firmer this time. 'When did you speak to Becca last?'

She shook her head and it looked as though there would be no room for negotiation, yet he continued to press her.

'Jane, what do you know about your sister's death?'

She set her jaw, shook her head, then moved away from him.

'Jane, why didn't you contact us when she died?'

Then, just as he thought she might, she turned and hurried towards the door. He followed her to the entrance, then watched as she bolted off down Regent Street.

Chapter Thirty-one

STAY ANGRY.

Jane took off from the University Arms Hotel and was in Castle Street in about ten minutes. From the front, her brother's house seemed to be in complete darkness. Jane soon discovered that the high rear gate was firmly bolted, but next door's gate wasn't even locked. She used their compost bin as a step to the top of the fence dividing the gardens, dropping from there on to Dan's flower bed. After a moment she realized that the only light in his house was a dim glow in a back bedroom, which soaked through pink butterfly curtains. Reba's room.

My niece.

The first-floor window next to Reba's had frosted glass.

Jane cupped her hands round her eyes and peered through the outhouse windows. Once she was sure her father wasn't sleeping inside, she clambered back the way she'd come, passing through next door's rear garden and back out on to Castle Street.

She stared at the front of the property and contemplated banging on the front door or shouting at the windows until Dan answered. Instead she phoned him, and watched till the ringing caused a bedside light to illuminate.

'Dan?' She realized that she'd whispered, as though she was the one that needed to remain quiet. 'Dan, it's Jane.'

'I know who it is.' He sounded irritated, 'Are you all right?'

'I'm fine, but I need to speak to Dad.'

'God, Jane, you pick your moments.'

'Is he here?'

'No, I think he's at his workshop. Are you sure you're OK?'

'I'm fine.' She saw the curtain move then and the sash window slid open a few inches.

'You said "here",' Dan explained. He leant out by a few inches. 'Why didn't you just knock? You can come in, you know.'

'Not now.' She shook her head. 'Mum wasn't in France.'

He paused. 'Where is she, then?'

'No idea. I want to ask Dad.'

'He would have already told me if he knew. Jane, why don't you leave it alone? Forget about her.'

'Dan, don't you think that' – she waved her hand in the direction of their childhood home – 'might be her?'

'She sent postcards. That's not her.'

'I still want to ask him.'

'He'll be here about ten. Why don't you wait here, watch some TV, and meet Reba when she wakes up?'

'Sorry, Dan, I can't. Not yet.'

'Suit yourself.' He always said that, usually with a half shrug and an apologetic smile compressed by his lips.

She turned away, even though she wished she didn't have to.

Stay angry.

Night had faded and feeble shafts of dawn sunlight were glancing from the rooftops. She cut her way through the back streets, and past the house in Pound Hill. The police car was still there and, once again, she found herself on the outside of her childhood home, with no right to go in.

She glared at it, but didn't slow. Then, after that, she glared at nothing beyond the next few yards of footpath ahead of each step she took. She focused like that until she stood at the door of her father's studio.

Then she hesitated, not sure what to say to him. She wished she could see him before she spoke, since his mood usually showed in his face.

Stay angry? Where was that anger now? She had let it be bullied into submission by just the assumption that he'd shout her down, or dismiss her as irrelevant or stupid. These were the very reactions from her dad that should have made her angrier; instead they'd crushed her for as many years as she could remember being close to him.

She stood outside his doorway now, just as she'd stood in that entrance all those years before, waiting for him to put down his tools and indulge her with that same attention he devoted to his work.

But usually he'd had something more important to do.

Surely all those years away from home must have given her some immunity from his rejection. She was twenty-five now, not eight or nine or ten or however old girls were when they craved their father's undivided attention. She shifted her weight from one foot to the other, and rubbed her hands to stimulate the circulation, even though the walk had left her flushed. And the moment she stopped scratching around for the courage to speak and the right words to say, then she suddenly found her voice. She heard herself shouting at his door.

'Dad, I need to talk to you.'

A couple of seconds passed and she heard movement. A couple more passed and he still hadn't spoken.

'Open the door.' She tried the handle, then banged her fist in the middle of the centre panel.

He spoke then, 'Jane!', followed by something indistinct. She heard a piece of furniture dragging across the floor, then the door was jerked open.

He wore a boiler suit with an unbuttoned plaid shirt hanging loose over the top of it. 'What the hell are you doing?'

'That's not *your* question, Dad. It should have been my question fifteen fucking years ago. And every year between. And right now I'm the only one of us two who has the right to ask it. So, what the hell are *you* doing?'

'Come inside.'

'What, so the neighbours won't hear? Look around, Dad. You're camping out in a shitty lock-up industrial unit. It's not a house, there are no neighbours – just you sleeping in your overalls, and pretending you're working.'

He scowled and began to close the door on her.

'No, oh no.' She lunged forward and forced herself inside. 'Your way it is, then.'

The temperature of the room was several degrees colder than outside. It smelt of mildew and solder, and was littered with the detritus of his latest 'work': a crouching and gnarled piece that filled up one wall. She circled her father so that she could turn her back on it.

'Mum's not in France,' she said.

'So what? Why do I need to know?'

'Think, Dad. Who else has just been brought up from your cellar?'

'No.' His usual expression was dismissiveness, but that was chased from his face in a moment. 'It can't be that,' he added, but he still didn't appear as stunned as she'd hoped.

He studied her expression, searching there for what she actually knew. She stared back, trying to work out what he thought she was thinking. Stalemate. She'd once read that the first to break eye contact was actually the stronger. Today it would be her. 'I need to know what happened, Dad.'

He blinked quickly and turned away. 'When?'

'All of it.' She watched the back of his head, noted that his hair had thinned and his shoulders had become more rounded. Age got everyone who didn't die first, but seeing it on her own dad . . . 'I'm not too scared to ask any more.'

He turned back to her again. 'I don't know what you want me to say.'

For the first time, she noticed the loose skin under his chin. It hid behind his beard and she also saw the lines and sunken flesh around his eyes. 'It's laughable, Dad,' she smiled sourly. 'All those years spent creating a legacy; did you think your sculptures were your own little slice of immortality? What a waste. You forgot to live the life you really had, didn't you?'

'Everyone has regrets, Jane.'

'What a cliché. Just look at this mess. You're turning into a sad old man living in a hovel. You've destroyed everything good in your life, and for what?' She pointed behind her. 'For the creation of shit like that and constantly chasing the approval of strangers.'

The words flew from her mouth. She'd finally released the demon, the whispered truth that he'd run as far as he could with his limited talent and been chasing a hollow dream. It was another secret that their mother had made them collude in and, in only seeing his work from Mary's viewpoint, they'd shared her mother's pity regarding their father's delusions. Even in the face of the adoration from the art world, Mary had known better.

Jane's words should have been provocation but, instead, his frown lines softened and his belligerence deserted him. 'Of course I wish things had worked out differently. What do you take me for?'

She eyed his sudden calmness with suspicion. 'Saying the right things is easy, Dad. People's words don't always match their actions, though, do they?'

He leant back against the wall, crossing his arms. 'You've come for something, Jane, and it's not to build bridges.'

'I was in Cambridge before Becca died, Dad,' she said quietly. 'She told me about her and Greg. She told me she'd spoken to you.'

'Yes, she did.'

'She told me everything she said to you.'

He said nothing.

'Prostitution, Dad. That's what she told you, isn't it?'

He turned his head away. 'She said she'd "done some bad stuff". She didn't say what it was, and I don't want to hear that ever repeated again. If there'd been any truth in it, or drugs or similar, then it would have come out during the trial. So I don't know why she said anything about it.'

'How can you twist things like that? She said it because it was true. She'd been into real trouble, Dad, and she was finding her way back out. She liked to think Greg loved her, but that wouldn't have lasted – and I'm sure she knew it. She wanted a fresh start, that's all.'

'She came to see me, asking me to accept him. To forgive him for his relationship with Mary. With my *wife* who, in her most vindictive moments, delighted in telling me how he pleased her in ways that I hadn't managed for years. Mary even boasted about the things they did.'

He paused for breath. 'Of course I rowed with Becca. And then she threw that off-the-rails story back in my face: how Greg Jackson had been the one who'd pulled her back from the edge. How I should be grateful. *Grateful.*'

Jane chose her next words carefully, and she spoke them quietly, conscious that she still sounded angry but hoping that she'd done enough now to encourage him to talk. 'You did a terrible thing, but I could picture what happened. I genuinely believed that the guilt would punish you more than any conviction would.'

There was a long pause before he spoke. 'What the hell do you think I did?'

'And I promised myself I'd never come back again. But things change, and now that I am here I want to know why you killed Mum too. Why you couldn't just let her get on with having a life without you.'

'Jane, no . . .' His hands fell to his sides and he stared into her face. She stared back steadily into his. Finally he gave a little moan. It came out more like a growl, followed by the words, 'You're wrong.' Then, with no warning, he lunged forward, grabbed her arm and heaved her towards the door, flinging it open then shoving her out into the yard. 'I never killed your sister,' he yelled.

She staggered back a few steps until she'd recovered her balance. Then stood squarely in front of him . . . until he slammed the door between them.

Chapter Thirty-two

SUE GULLY ADDED extra milk to her coffee. It was the first mug of the day, despite the fact that, for Goodhew, it was only brewed a couple of hours after what he'd decided to call the last one of the night before. Goodhew had left his coffee black; he hated black coffee but right now he also needed it.

'I don't understand why you don't get more sleep,' she remarked.

'It didn't work out like that.' He didn't bother telling her that he was now in the middle of a two-week spell where he could barely sleep at all. During a phase like that, trying and failing to sleep could be more disturbing than just staying awake.

'Make sure you don't attempt to drive.'

'Of course I won't. And anyway the sugar's medicinal,' he told her, as he stirred in an extra spoonful.

She seemed satisfied with that. 'Tell me what you did then,' she asked, seamlessly jumping the conversation back to two minutes before their coffees had been poured.

'I followed her. She went inside and I waited out of sight.'

'For how long?'

'I really don't know. There was shouting and I was trying to hear, but I couldn't catch much until the end. She thinks her father killed them both.'

'His own daughter? Anything's possible, but you'd think his wife Mary would have suspected it.'

'He was shouting at Jane and I wondered at one point whether I'd need to intervene. He did seem genuinely angry, but then I guess he would be, and especially if he'd actually done it.'

'Exactly.' Sue hesitated with the cup close to her lips. 'Did Jane seem scared of him?'

'No, she was too wired for that. When she left me at the University Arms, the streets were empty. I allowed her a head start so that she wouldn't spot me, but then I found I had to move very quickly to keep up.'

'On a mission, then?'

'Something like that. Determined to see him and not stopping to consider any danger to herself. She's been regularly walking round Cambridge by herself in the middle of the night, too.'

'You're right, that doesn't make her a personal-safety poster girl now, does it? So what did she do after she'd visited her father?'

'Nothing. Just went back to her B and B.'

'She's probably sound asleep right now, Gary.'

'I doubt it somehow. She's more likely to be staring up at the ceiling and wondering who killed her mother. It'll be a relief when these reports come back from Sykes and forensics.'

Sue stood and picked up her cup. 'Are you having more coffee?'

He shook his head. 'I'm going up.'

'The other one's on Marks's desk, by the way. I signed for it and took it up earlier this morning.'

'The other what?'

'Report from forensics. The one about the boat.'

He hurried to his feet, too. 'Did you just forget to tell me about it?' he grumbled.

'Sorry, Gary. It came in first thing, just as I arrived, so I offered to drop it on his desk. You and I were talking about Jane Osborne, so I didn't give it a second thought.' She seemed to sense the immediate shift in the atmosphere, and suddenly her mood darkened too.

'It's fine,' he conceded. 'I'll go up and read it now.'

'Actually, I'd rather you didn't. It was me who took it up there and it's addressed to Marks, not to you. I don't think you should now make me feel as though I've done something wrong, just because I didn't mention a report that's not even addressed to you.'

He looked genuinely surprised. 'I didn't mean to.'

'Why don't you leave it, for once?'

'Sue, I really didn't mean to upset you.'

She reddened, a habit of hers that had become less frequent but was still not unusual. 'I don't want to fall out with you, Gary, but when you go off on your own like this, it has the potential to screw things up for other people. I don't want to get in hot water because a report has been opened when it shouldn't have been. And I don't want to feel like I have to cover for you if something goes wrong when you're too tired to be at work.' Her redness deepened. 'And I don't want to see you screw up your career, either. Marks gives you more slack than he should, but his patience won't be endless, will it?'

'I'll wait for Marks,' he conceded. 'And I'm sorry.'

'It's fine.' She nodded, even though she knew it wasn't fine. And then they left the canteen before either of them could say anything else.

Chapter Thirty-three

THE FORENSICS REPORT had come by courier in an inch-thick reinforced and tamper-proof envelope. The address label was printed but Marks's name had been underlined in green marker pen. The same pen had written 'ADDRESSEE ONLY' above it. Three different parcel tracking bar codes were lined up beneath the franking.

All in all, it looked like one of the most stealable items Goodhew had ever clapped eyes on.

He prodded the centre of it, just to prove to himself that the contents were as thick as the envelope looked. Then stood in the doorway for the next ten minutes, waiting for Marks. He knew Gully had been right, but walking away without reading the report just wasn't an option.

Marks could walk through the door any second, but equally it might be hours. So the conundrum was simple: removing it from the office would be going too far, reading it at the desk would take too long. There would be a solution: he just needed to think of it.

Goodhew pulled Marks's phone number up on his mobile but didn't immediately press 'dial'. It then took a couple more minutes for him to come up with a useful game plan; Gully's words of warning had also come with the helpful comment: *Marks gives you more slack than he should.* Goodhew smiled and pressed 'dial'.

If Marks was speaking to anyone, he would usually let his voicemail pick up. If he now answered, Goodhew would need to improvise. It gave three rings, then he found himself being welcomed to the O$_2$ messaging service. He stepped back into the office and closed the door behind him.

'Hi, sir, I'm in your office because I've had a conversation with Jane Osborne that I want to make you aware of. I'm going to make a note of the basics and leave it on your desk . . . oh, and the forensics report is through . . . the one from Paul Marshall's boat.' He added a deliberate pause. 'I'm really sorry if this is the wrong call but, as I know a bit about this one, I'm going to check whether there's anything in the report that can't wait.'

He hoped he'd sounded tentative and sincere, worthy of a bollocking but not a terminal one. The envelope had a rip cord style opening and he pulled this before sitting himself in the ageing swivel chair and writing out his note to Marks. He scrawled quickly, using bullet points to cover the details of his meeting with Jane. He was on the last item when his mobile buzzed.

It was Marks. 'Are you still in my office, Gary?'

'Just finishing that note, sir.'

'And did you open the forensics report?'

'I undid the envelope, but I haven't read any of it. I decided to wait in the hope you'd ring.'

'You have some conscience at least, which amounts to a lucky escape for you, Gary. Leave it as it is. I will be back in twenty minutes or so. And, in future, don't.'

'Sorry.' He made a mental note not to apologize any further, or it would start sounding suspicious.

'Tell me more about this conversation you had with Jane Osborne.'

'She was pressing for news on her mother. There's a bit more to it than that, though.' Goodhew had already decided that he needed to tell Marks everything. 'Can I tell you when you get here?'

'You'll need to as, after that, I'm going straight out to meet them. The positive ID came back an hour ago. Mary Osborne, just as we thought.'

Goodhew had planned to leave the DI's room as soon as this call was over, but instead he rotated the chair 120 degrees to the left and stared across at one side of the University Arms Hotel. He tried to recall whether he'd said anything to Jane that might have raised her hopes regarding her mother. No, he didn't think so.

But for him the final confirmation of any victim's identity came with a jolt. Sometimes news of a death hit estranged relatives surprisingly hard. As someone who barely saw his own mother, he understood this – still picturing her almost ten years younger than her current age.

He spun the chair back as he heard someone enter the room. It was Kincaide.

'After the boss's job, Gary?'

Goodhew smiled. 'I don't think it would suit me.'

'You'd struggle with the politics.'

'And the staff.'

'Is he around?'

'Back in twenty minutes.'

'And you're just going to sit there?'

'He might be early.'

'He never is when he's busy, Gary.'

Goodhew swung the chair in the direction of the window again. 'I'll be able to see him pull in from here.'

'And scoot down to meet him like a happy spaniel? Anyway, I'll come back later,' Kincaide said, then added the word 'Sad' under his breath before leaving.

As soon as he'd gone, Goodhew checked his watch. He'd already easily lost the first five minutes of the twenty that Marks had inadvertently given him. But Kincaide was right: Marks often ran late.

Goodhew scooped up the envelope and slid it into his shirt, then moved three offices further down to a vacant meeting room. He locked the door and slid the contents of the envelope on to one of the tables, then, one page at a time, photographed everything using his phone.

And ten minutes later the file had been returned to Marks's desk.

Goodhew sat back in the chair and again looked out across Parker's Piece and the rooftops of Cambridge. He felt surprisingly alert for someone who'd managed to get so little sleep. Good old adrenalin.

He suddenly saw Marks reflected in the same window, and spun slowly toward him.

'Kincaide told me you were enjoying my office.'

'Enjoying the view, actually.'

Marks touched the envelope, lifted the open end and glanced at the ends of the very squarely collated set of printouts inside it. Goodhew was confident that they appeared untouched. Then Marks picked up the sheet of notes which Goodhew had written. 'You actually saw her?'

'She was outside my flat when we arrived back.'

'Talk me through it.'

Goodhew explained while Marks listened in silence. He added some notes of his own to Goodhew's bullet points. 'So you've had practically no sleep?'

'I feel fine.'

'Go home.' Marks glanced at his watch. 'Come back at four and we'll review it then.'

'I won't be able to sleep.'

'You sound like my daughter – but when she was still in infants' school.'

Goodhew sighed, defeated, then pointed at the envelope. 'Aren't you even going to open it?'

Marks picked it up. 'As soon as I've seen the Osborne family; their situation is more pressing this morning. Everything's in hand, Gary. Now just get some sleep.'

Chapter Thirty-four

STEPPING ON TO that boat now seemed like a month-old memory; meeting Carmel Marshall had slipped away even further. But when his phone finished its download, and the forensics reports appeared on his screen, it all came back fast enough.

Goodhew closed the curtains of his grandfather's former library and spread out on his own battered-looking sofa, newly relocated from the flat he occupied above. His jukebox and the laptop provided the only two pools of light in an otherwise gloomy room. The report included pictures which he'd refused to study as he'd copied the file, but now he zoomed in on the photo-of-a-photo images. Some were poorer quality than others, but they all dragged him back inside that stifling cabin.

The first eighteen shots were for orientation, layout of the boat and to provide a record of all the evidence in situ. Later shots had been marked with lines and arrows and other notation that would tally with details given in the body of the text. He flicked through the early photos, which all corresponded with his memory, although he dwelt a little longer on the twelfth, which showed the back of the cabin door. The shape of the woman's body and arms was less well defined than he had remembered. He skipped forward to the next shot, and then more quickly through the remaining ones.

The final, unmarked, photo had been taken at floor level from the doorway. Goodhew had moved on rapidly, and was halfway through the annotated shots, when he remembered the nausea he'd felt when he'd been at the same spot in the boat. He clicked back.

The nausea still threatened – or at least the memory of it.

The area had been brightly lit for the photographs, and items that had previously been obscured by shadows now stood out. The carpet tiles looked synthetic, trodden down in the middle of the central aisle but still bright, with a plasticky finish, further under the beds. Goodhew wiped his fingertips against his jeans as he remembered the dirt and clamminess of the floor. Except, under normal white light, it appeared fairly clean with none of the staining that the UV lamp had revealed. The dish he'd seen had been a stoneware dog bowl, with a discarded lead lying next to it. In the corner behind that was some crumpled fabric.

The cabin didn't look as rancid here as it had felt then, but the feeling of queasiness still hung close. Some unknown element of crouching low on that floor left him wanting to puke. He jumped to the notated copy of the photograph, and found 18-1 marked on the floor, 18-2 on the fabric and 18-3 on the dog bowl. He jumped forward again, this time to the notes that accompanied it.

The report had the title *Carpet and Floor-Level Evidence within Cabin*.

It ran for seventeen pages and the carpet, 18-1, described as *100 per cent polypropylene construction*, had given up enough information to fill fifteen of those pages. Thumbnail images had been inserted at various points, and most of these had a ruler shown on two of the four sides to demonstrate the size of each particular sample. The first appeared to be a semi-translucent carpet fibre; Goodhew read the accompanying paragraph to discover that it was a pubic hair. The report also listed head hair of several colours and lengths, further pubic hair samples, and a single eyelash. DNA sampling had been conducted on a cross-section of these, though it was far too soon to expect any results. Fingerprinting was always faster, and four distinct sets had been isolated, referred to as belonging to Persons A, B, C and D.

There were two broken fingernails, both fragments, and several bitten sections of nail. Also an earring mount and the broken tip of a kohl-eyeliner pencil. Traces of cocaine in multiple locations. No animal hair, but fibres from clothes and flakes of dirt brought in on people's shoes.

All that before the techs had even started on the invisible-to-the-naked-eye stuff. Why people ever committed crimes on a carpet was a mystery.

Goodhew paused to disconnect the landline, turned his phone to silent and increased the volume on the jukebox, since he didn't want any distraction from outside the room. He grabbed an apple and returned to the sofa.

The analysis of the stains took up the greatest number of pages, and they began with a diagram showing the shape and position of the marks involved. Although he would never have been able to draw from memory what he himself had seen under the UV light, Goodhew now recognized it immediately. He blinked slowly and a white hot version of the image glowed on the back of his eyelids.

There were tiny splatters with comet tails, dappled marks and smudges – like finger painting – and in the centre of the aisle, between the bed-settees and just before the end mattress, was the darkest of the marks he'd seen. It was longer than it was wide, almost oval apart from a small spur that had trickled at an acute angle. The overall shape reminded him of a child's mitten.

The report concluded that the blood had come from a nosebleed sustained by someone who was lying on, or very close to, the floor. A person who also had little or no ability to move freely. Mucus appeared in the stain and more in the splatters. The trajectory of those splatters had required the head to be close to the floor, largely immobile and freely bleeding out on to the carpet. Spray had hit the side of one of the mattresses, and the forensics examiner had concluded that it was most likely that this had been the result of blood running back into the throat, a subsequent choking sensation, followed by a panic reflex that raised the head and expelled blood and mucus with force.

The 'thumb' of the 'mitten' included saliva and, along with several other smaller marks, indicated that more blood had been spat from the mouth.

Each item and stain had been carefully numbered. Fingerprints had been taken from the bulkhead, from the bed frame, doors, windows, everywhere, and the same four people showed up repeatedly: A, B, C, D. No one else at all. Every print had been catalogued and cross-referenced in relation to all the other evidence, providing a list which included semen, sweat and saliva. And, here again, there would be more results to follow.

He turned to the next page: *18-2 Fabric Items.* These had been photographed separately and consisted of three pairs of knickers and a bra. All of them black. The images ran in a column down the right-hand side of the page, the explanations down the left. The bra was described as a *32D in a balconette style* and the knickers as *G-string type thongs. Size 8*. It had never occurred to Goodhew that a G-string was a type of thong and not merely another word for the same thing.

This was the kind of detail that Bryn would know – not that Goodhew would be asking him.

The bra and one pair of knickers had been worn, the others had no sign of either use or having been washed. All four items were a brand called *Ingénue Lingerie*.

The final page, describing photo 18, was entitled *18-3 Dog Bowl, Collar and Lead*.

It has not yet been possible to identify the source of any of these items and they are likely to be several years old.

It repeated the previous finding, but this time showed it in bold: *Canine DNA was not present in any of the tests conducted.*

The collar and lead are both leather, dark brown with chromed metal fittings, 41–51 cm/16–20 inches and intended to be suitable for a medium-sized dog. Human skin samples were recovered from both the collar and lead. Several partial fingerprints were also recovered.

The dog bowl is ceramic and measures 20 cm/8 inches in diameter, with a depth of 5 cm/2 inches and with the word 'DOG' embossed on the side. It has been used for containing cooked food, and saliva staining indicates that the food was eaten directly from the bowl. Human saliva was present from which DNA samples were recovered. The fingerprints on the bowl are clear matches and belong to Person A and Person B.

The words *Person B* had been circled with a line linking out to the handwritten memo *See notes for photo 12*.

Photo 12 was the back of the cabin door. He flicked through the report to the relevant page. The photo had been enhanced and highlighted with a clearer outline, showing the same shape just as Goodhew remembered it. He scanned down the page. *Suspended by meat hook, or similar.* He stared at the silhouette left by her sweat.

A heavy ring is mounted to the wall, tested to sustain a weight of 100 kg. A partial fingerprint, possibly caused by a person reaching up whilst bound, was found on this ring and it is a match for Person B.

Goodhew reread the end of the sentence: *a match for Person B.*

He tried calling her Victim B or Woman B, but neither was better.

All such terms sounded one step short of giving her a serial number, and he wasn't that desensitized that he could let himself refer to her like that. The whole business was too degrading without then referring to her in such a depersonalized way.

There were just a few lines of text before the end of the page, mostly referring to the chronology of the various findings. A's fingerprints had been found overlapping – or overlapped by – each of the others. The other three lay in just one date sequence: D, then C, then B.

It made them sound like multiple choice. And he hated it.

He averted his gaze from the screen. It was the wrong time to let any emotion take hold. He lay back on the settee for a few minutes, resting his head on the arm and staring up at the ceiling. Then he covered his eyes with the flat of his hand, breathed deeply, and let the music from the jukebox flood inside his head.

A haze of tiredness briefly descended, and even promised sleep, but waiting for it to arrive would be fruitless. At best he would manage a dream ridden hour. He sat up again, then pulled himself to his feet and drank a pint of tap water. He left the empty glass in the sink, then returned to his laptop. He moved the mouse to reactivate the screen. His brain felt clearer now, and his gaze jumped three-quarters of the way down the page to a subheading: *Identification through fingerprints*, then jumped from there straight to some words further down: *Two positive identifications have been made so far.*

The atmosphere in the room shifted again and he felt an unexpected unease as he clicked the mouse to turn the page. It was, once again, the moment for final confirmation of identities. He prepared himself to put a name to Person B; instead, two familiar names jumped out: *Person A, Paul Marshall. Person D, Carmel Marshall. Persons B and C remain unknown.*

He felt no surprise, the Paul Marshall ID had been almost certain. Carmel Marshall? He hadn't seen that coming, but now, with the certainty of hindsight, it seemed totally logical.

He shut down the laptop, crossed to the window and let the afternoon sunlight back into the room. He pressed his hands to the glass as he leant forward to look out over his private view of the city. Somewhere roughly south-east from him, beyond the Catholic church and over the Botanical Gardens, the Gogs rose out of the surrounding flatness. Paul Marshall had died over there, and Person B had become Daisy Tattoo.

He knew more now. And it would be enough to find her.

Chapter Thirty-five

GOODHEW GRABBED HIS phone and jacket and rushed off towards Parkside station. It was already 3 p.m., but Goodhew still had a whole hour. With the right questions and a little luck, an hour might be plenty.

He knew Marks would read the report soon, and revisiting Carmel Marshall would then be obligatory in any case, so just for now he pushed her from his thoughts and hurried up the stairs to find Sergeant Sheen.

Sheen was an information hoarder, the man with the tidbits that added flesh and perspective to the skeleton of the Cambridge street map. And all this without ever appearing to leave his desk.

Sheen peered out from behind his computer. 'Which murder brings you here today?'

'Pardon?'

'Mary Osborne or Paul Marshall?'

'Oh, I see. I'm looking for a . . .' that sentence was about to end badly. He started again. 'I'm trying to locate a woman who may have accepted payment for sex.'

Sheen beamed. 'You're looking for a prostitute? I never thought those words would come from your lips, Gary. I'm sure someone would . . . several in this building possibly . . .'

Goodhew held a dead-eyed expression as he waited for Sheen to finish.

'Well,' Sheen pulled a lever-arch file from the shelf behind his desk. 'Let's see if we can't put a smile on that face of yours.'

'Sheen, I'm in a hurry and I know this is a tricky one.'

'There are a few individuals here but most of the pages list escort sites, classified ads and so on. So much of it is online these days, that there will be plenty of sites we haven't spotted yet, I'm sure. Who are we looking for?'

'The girl on the Gogs.'

'With the daisy tattoo?'

Goodhew finally smiled. 'Where did you hear that?'

'Your mate Sue told me.' Sheen opened the file in the centre. 'Some of this stuff is old now, and keeping it up to date is like trying to count a pond full of fish.'

'The answer would be *one*.'

Sheen scowled at Goodhew. 'One what?'

'One pond. Never mind.'

'The fish, Gary. The fish.' He sighed. 'Tell me about her.'

'Late teens, early twenties maybe. IC1, probable native English speaker, blonde, slim.'

'Local?'

'I think so, or at least with a connection here. As far as I can work out, she came from Cambridge and was heading back when she was seen up on the Gogs.'

'Could she be a student? There's a lot of it amongst them at the moment. Pressure of increased tuition fees, apparently. Personally I'd rather skip the education.'

'Thanks – that's put some unpleasant images in my head.' Goodhew had skipped through the file but now closed it. 'Student prostitution, then?'

'Some sign up to contact sites, some advertise directly, though that's risky. It means they're out on their own then, without any protection or without the client having the impression that someone might know where they are, or who they're currently with. We've come across quite a few discreet agencies in town over the years: small-scale operations usually, but with some kind of access to the students.'

'Surely first-timers would be more likely to be introduced to it by someone they've met in person?'

'Careful you don't start making too many assumptions about her.'

'I don't think I am. Think of Marshall for a minute. If his game was to humiliate her, then he's not going to pick a girl who's already been systematically abused. Where would his thrill be then?'

Sheen shrugged. 'I dunno.'

'And, equally, where would be her incentive to stay quiet. This girl so far hasn't said a word.'

'There's plenty of prostitutes who wouldn't be prepared to speak to us.'

'Yes, but also plenty who would – or would at least make sure we got to hear about any mistreatment, right?'

Sheen nodded. 'Yes, word often makes its way back.'

'But regarding a student, pretty much all of them would want to keep it very quiet.' He knew he might be wrong there, but instinctively it felt right.

Sheen reached up for a different file. 'There are thirty thousand students in Cambridge. *At least* thirty thousand. This one's packed with every student adviser, official organization, and society I can find.' Sheen kept one hand on the file and with the other reached inside the top drawer of his desk. He pulled out an A4 sheet of printed card that had been folded in two as if to make a tent. He stood it on the desk. 'What d'you reckon?'

It was emblazoned with thick lettering: *No files to leave this area.*

'I know your rules already.'

'Well, stick to them. Sit here and go through it.'

Goodhew checked his watch: it was 3.45. So much for his ambitious hour. Still, fifteen minutes was fifteen minutes. 'I'll come back,' he told Sheen. 'I have to see Marks at four. Actually, it might be better tomorrow.'

Sheen tapped the sign. 'Don't forget what it says.'

Gary next grabbed a coffee, making a call as the kettle boiled. He was waiting outside Marks's office by 3.55, hoping their meeting would be quick, because he now had another appointment to keep at 5.30 p.m.

MARKS ARRIVED WITH his own mug of coffee and Goodhew followed him into his office. 'How are you feeling?'

The report on Paul Marshall's boat lay in its envelope, and was back in the prime spot on Marks's desk.

'Good, thanks.'

'You don't look any different to me. I've seen you like this in the past, Gary, and I assume it is only tiredness?' Obviously content that it was, he carried on talking without waiting for a reply. 'Is it that you can't sleep or because you avoid trying?'

'I'm just awake,' Goodhew replied, and didn't elaborate. In reality he would lie in bed thinking through all the things that called for his attention, and even when he fell asleep he dreamt about them until they pulled him into consciousness again.

'See a doctor if you need to.'

'I will, sir,' he lied.

'I'm serious. You don't seem to realize you're the kid that gets one-to-one time with me for the wrong reasons. I'm keeping you on track because I want you to run a great race, not end up as supermarket burger meat.'

Goodhew nodded silently. He'd long since decided that, when Marks began mixing metaphors, he was irritated over something. Often it was lack of resources or lack of progress, and today Good-hew could understand if it were both.

'I held a briefing this afternoon, most of it you're already aware of, but there are a couple of points you will have missed. The family have been officially informed of Mary Osborne's death. I visited them this morning.'

'How did they react?'

'Jane wasn't surprised. I assumed that might be because she'd spoken to you. What exactly had you told her?' Marks looked interested rather than annoyed.

'She asked me whether the body was her mother's. I didn't tell her that I thought it was, but I didn't build her hopes up either.'

'That's fine. Lack of tact with relatives has never been one of your shortcomings. I spoke to Gerry, Dan and Jane Osborne all at the same time. Dan's wife Roz was there, too, and I had the impression that it was the first time that she and Jane had ever met. More than anything, they seemed incredulous when I told them. Dan asked how long her body had been there, while Gerry kept asking us about the house.'

'What about it?'

'Whether we'd caused damage, whether its address really needed to be publicized, and so on. Quite bizarre questions from both of them, really.'

'Especially as the search has already been reported in the press. If anyone knows Cambridge, then they know where that house is.'

Marks nodded. 'Have you seen the news this afternoon? Mary Osborne's murder's now out in the public domain, complete with pictures of the property itself.' Marks opened a drawer in his desk and slid the latest edition of the *Cambridge News* across to Goodhew. 'I pushed those photos of the house out there just to see whether they'd generate some kind of reaction that Gerry or Dan Osborne had hoped to avoid.'

'And?'

'Nothing yet.'

Sometimes the incident room would be taking calls within minutes of the first announcement, but there seemed little correlation between the volume of calls and the number of truly helpful ones; one productive call could turn everything around.

'But we'll see,' Marks added. 'Jane asked when she'd be allowed to move back. I noticed Gerry Osborne open his mouth to answer, then he realized she was asking me from the point of view of the investigation. None of them objected, just seemed surprised she'd want to return there. In fact, she's back there now.'

'Although I'm used to being alone in a house, I'd find that creepy.'

'But there was no reason to stop her either. The second point you missed from this afternoon's briefing is the announcement that the investigation into Rebecca Osborne's murder will now be reopened. It'll be days before we have much back from forensics, so until we have conclusive evidence that the two Osborne murders aren't connected, we have to assume that they are.'

'There's no way Jackson could have killed Mary. That means he'll be in the clear.' The tension rising in Marks's expression was unmistakable, though it subsided almost at once.

'Unless he wasn't working alone,' Marks suggested, though he didn't look convinced. 'I now want your opinion on something. What impression do you have regarding how Jane felt about her sister?'

Goodhew thought carefully before he spoke. 'She clearly had some bond with her or she wouldn't have come back here, and when you told her about Becca's death, you said her grief seemed real. She clearly has issues with the rest of the family, and perhaps that's why she left in the first place.'

'Since you told me that Jane was actually in Cambridge when Becca was killed, I've spent the entire day mulling that over. If she cared about Becca, you'd think she'd want to help.'

'She wouldn't tell me anything.'

'Of course. She says she can't remember. She's coming in tomorrow to make a statement, then we'll go over it with her until there's some progress. At the moment she flatly denies even remembering where she was when she first heard about Becca's death. I don't believe that for a second.'

Neither did Goodhew.

'I thought perhaps you might have picked up on something?'

'No, I can't even work out whether she's angry as a form of defence or just naturally aggressive.'

Without further comment Marks moved on to the next topic. He picked up the envelope that still lay in front of him and reached inside it, sliding the sheaf of pages half out before he spoke. 'The business of waiting round for DNA analysis delays everything. It's frustrating in the Mary Osborne case, and just as irritating in this one. I've read it, by the way, and I've decided to keep you over on this investigation, more specifically following up evidence contained in here.'

Goodhew shuffled forward in his chair. 'OK if I look?'

Marks finished sliding them out and handed them to Goodhew, who scanned carefully the first few lines, then flicked through the batch of photographs. 'I'll read it right now, if you'd like me to.'

'By tomorrow will be fine. I'll be going to visit Carmel Marshall shortly.'

'Really?' Goodhew had wanted to do the same as soon as he'd finished looking for the girl from the Gogs.

'Her fingerprints were found on the boat.'

'And Paul Marshall's?'

'Yes.'

Goodhew packed the report back into its envelope. He'd gone too far to come clean and admit he'd already read it, but playing dumb would be foolhardy. Insulting to Marks, in fact, and that wasn't something he was prepared to do. 'Can I take it?'

'Back to your desk. Not out of the building.'

'Sure.'

'I'll speak with you again sometime after I've met with Carmel Marshall.'

'I don't mind coming along, if that helps.'

Marks shook his head. 'You'll see why when you read it, but I need to take a female officer with me. Three of us going in mob-handed isn't what's needed here. But thanks.'

Goodhew checked his watch as he returned to his desk: 5.20. Just ten minutes to spare. He opened out the report, but only for show. He next dialled the number, still remembering the pattern of digits from earlier. It rang for close to two whole minutes before anyone answered. He then introduced himself and explained what he wanted. She agreed to wait until he arrived. By 5.24 he was heading out through Parkside's front entrance.

FOR A LITTLE while now, the area of Cambridge that was home to the greatest concentration of independent shops had been called the Boutique Quarter. Maybe if someone explained the logic of the term, then Goodhew might have thought it made more sense. But, as it was, every time he heard it, it bugged him. Firstly, plenty of Cambridge streets brimmed with shops offering quirky, artisan and specialist items, and they weren't all located in the 'Boutique Quarter' by a long shot. Secondly, apart from hearing the odd mention of the 'Art Quarter', he didn't know if there were any others. With all Cambridge had to offer, the idea that the Boutique Quarter and the Art Quarter were the only two to deserve this extra recognition seemed a little pretentious.

But Tizzi's in All Saints Passage wasn't at all pretentious, just a small family-run shop, selling clothes that had, in the main, come from local designers. The owner/manageress/sales assistant was called Val. She had a great smile that offset her overly severe eyebrows and tightly pulled ponytail.

'So you've come about the underwear? The Ingénue Lingerie?'

'I believe you're the only stockists of that line locally?'

'It sells here, online and in Covent Garden.'

'I take it it's expensive, then?'

'Not compared to what some women will pay. Having said that, Ingénue would not sell for any more; it's found its price point. So which items are we talking about?'

Goodhew used his phone to show her the pictures: one of the knickers, one of the bra.

'*Astonish* – that's the name of that range.' She looked back and forth between the two shots. 'Yes, the thong and the balcony bra. They've both sold well.'

Oh good.

'I will have all the sales records, so I'd know when the items were sold but not who to, unless they paid by credit card, of course. You do know the sizes, I assume?'

'Size 8 and 32D.'

'That's a good start.'

'In what way?' he asked, because he actually wasn't sure whether she was being sarcastic.

'We would have had either four or six of those bras in stock. Do you know when it was purchased?'

'Before 28 July, but I don't know how much before.'

'Yes, this is making sense.' She spoke partly to him, partly to herself, and then pulled a diary out from beside the till. She also tried drawing her sharp eyebrows into a frown, though the muscles barely moved. On 1 June she'd written a list of bras and sizes which included the *Astonish* in a 32D. 'I rarely reorder,' she explained, 'but several models had sold better than their matching knickers. I queried whether more were available, and they weren't, but I'm sure it was selling the last 32D that would have prompted me to check.' She part-frowned into the book. 'No, perhaps it was the 34D.'

Goodhew waited.

Val chewed her lip and gazed up towards a corner of the ceiling. 'Something's ringing a bell,' she pondered. 'Any idea who ended up with them?' She looked at Goodhew. 'Or can't you say?'

'I don't know. The description is of a young woman, late teens, maybe, or early twenties. A tattoo of daisies across her foot?'

She brushed that comment away. 'It feels like most of them that age have tattoos. Unless they covered her face, I wouldn't have noticed.'

'One witness described her as *kind of Scandinavian . . .*'

The memory clicked into place and Val's eyes widened. 'Long blonde hair. I do remember her now. She came in with a hundred pounds in vouchers. Oh, yes, that's right. She looked at only this range of underwear, but spent quite a while choosing. My daughter was working with me that day, and neither of us had seen her before.'

'Did you speak to her?'

'Briefly, and she was English, not Scandinavian at all.' She clicked her fingers several times. 'Hang on, there was something else. My daughter might remember.' She whipped an iPhone from her pocket and assaulted it with some rapid double-thumb texting. He couldn't read whatever she'd written, but joined her in staring at it and willing it to flash up a reply. The incoming message made the sound of a repeated plinking of a piano key. She tutted, then tapped a message back, spelling *I-n-g-é-n-u-e* under her breath. When it plinked the next time she read it swiftly, then passed the phone across to Goodhew. 'The *woman said she'd been hand-painting on silk as part of her degree.*'

'An art degree?'

'Fashion or textiles, I would think. I do actually remember having a conversation with someone who was asking if we'd consider selling anything like that here on their behalf, but I would have said no. It wouldn't work in here. I don't know anything else, so I hope I've been some help?'

'Definitely. And, one more thing, you wouldn't know who originally purchased those vouchers, I suppose?'

'No. We're a small business so our vouchers are printed like cheques in a book, and numbered. There won't be many for a hundred pounds. I'd be able to go through the accounts, find out which vouchers have been used and let you know when they were sold, but nothing more.'

He passed her a card printed with his landline number. 'That would be very helpful. Just let us know when you've found them, and an officer will come back for the details. If that isn't me, just repeat everything you've said.'

Chapter Thirty-Six

THE FACT THAT it was now 6.15, with everybody dispersing for the evening, was the precise reason Goodhew resented the idea of having been sent home to rest right in the middle of the day. Of course he hadn't slept, but if he'd followed Marks's instructions to the letter, then he'd be even further behind. If, on the other hand, he'd been able to read the report an hour sooner, he might have made it to the Cambridge School of Art before the staff had left for the evening.

He crossed back through town, past Parkside, and had made it halfway down the wide university steps before realizing the irrelevance of his train of thought.

It wasn't even term time.

He stopped in his tracks and sat down on a dry but dusty step. He couldn't even be bothered to swear. His frustration lasted moments, until he realized how much more he now knew than even one hour earlier. And there were always methods to summon staff back to any teaching establishment, term-time or not. If he was going to swear he ought to direct it at himself, because maybe he had really been too tired to see the obvious.

He glanced along East Road, in the direction of Parker's Piece, thinking he ought to head back that way, go straight home and go to bed. Or put the jukebox on repeat and lie on the settee to see whether sleep really might catch up on him by accident. But he associated every bout of insomnia with lying endlessly awake up there so, for all he loved his flat, going back there now didn't appeal. He stood, turned his back on it and set off the other way. He decided on coffee instead, and turned down Norfolk Street and into the CB2 café. Only one table was free, a corner seat away from the window, then he ordered a macchiato and a cappuccino, both at the same time, rushing the first then savouring the second.

Over the next half cup he spent the time studying the café's clientele. Some were students, plenty weren't. Work by local artists hung on the walls, and flyers advertised acoustic music nights and poetry readings. He wandered over to the counter and found even more events advertised, most aimed at the student population. He held up one flyer to the man behind the counter. 'Do you know of any regular fashion events?'

'Like what?'

'I'm guessing there's somewhere in Cambridge where would-be fashion designers meet?' *Would-be fashion designers?* He cringed at his own use of words.

'Not here, but if you go up the steps there, right to the back, you'll see a table of eight. Ask for Olley . . . or if there's someone wearing a maroon beanie, that's him. He's a bit like a student what's-on guide.'

Goodhew found Olley immediately, the beanie gave him away. There were only two men at the crowded table in any case and, as Goodhew headed over, the other one grabbed a couple of empty glasses before offering to buy the next round. As his first words were, 'Oi, Olley,' that pretty much clinched it – beanie or no beanie.

Olley had a D-shaped grin, blue eyes and a fringe of lightened hair protruding from under his hat. Judging by the attention he received from the girls seated at the table, Olley was comfortable with his role as the lead man in the ensemble.

Goodhew introduced himself and the curiosity of the group settled them into silence.

'I'm trying to locate a female student who'd be studying for a degree in fashion, or in fact any course which includes painting textiles. I was hoping there might be a venue or a society or something. If it was poetry, I'd look here.'

Olley looked from Goodhew to the assembled girls. A couple of them shrugged and all but one of them stared back blankly. The girl sitting closest to Goodhew leant forward on her elbow, the fingers of her supporting hand entangled in strands of long dark hair. In a barely-there Spanish accent, she announced, 'I know what you mean. I expect she's a student over there.' At which she pointed in the direction of Anglia Ruskin University. 'The Cambridge School of Art is in there.'

'I know, but it's not term time, and it's urgent that I find her.'

'I don't know anywhere else to suggest, but all of us here are students there, except for Olley. What's her name? Or do you have a photo . . . or a description?'

Olley smiled in mock apology. 'Though apparently I'm now just an *ex*-student, I might even recognize her too.' He nudged the girl who had spoken playfully. 'You never know.'

She nudged him sharply in response, and was still smiling when she looked up again at Goodhew. 'Tell us about her, then. One of us *proper* students might know.'

'I don't have an actual name, but she is slim with long, straight blonde hair. And probably with a tattoo of flowers running across one foot and curving around her ankle.'

'Benz knows about tats.' She leant over to the only red-headed girl in the group. 'Who's got a daisy tat across her foot?'

Benz shook her head. 'I don't know that one.'

'I've seen it.' All eyes turned to back Olley. 'It's a daisy chain, isn't it?'

Goodhew nodded. 'I think so. Do you know who she is?'

'Not exactly, but she must be coming into her third year by now. I first noticed her at some fresher events that would have been during the start of the academic year before last – like two years ago next month. She was drunk and apparently she'd drawn the daisy chain on with an ordinary pen.'

'Where was this?'

'Revolution, maybe, or the Fez. Probably the Fez because I hardly missed it back then. Next time I noticed her was at Lola Lo, and the daisies had been henna-ed on by then. She said she was trying them out before making them permanent. I didn't come across her anywhere after that, so I never saw them properly inked.'

'And this is nearly two years ago.'

The Spanish girl leant towards Goodhew. 'He remembers women so well, even when he pretends not to.' She arched an eyebrow. 'You can trust him for what you're after.'

'She had a bloke's name,' Olley added thoughtfully.

'Like Dave?' Benz shouted out, then laughed rather too loudly.

'No, Andie. She's called Andie.'

'Fuck, yes.' Benz suddenly sobered. 'I know who you mean now. I've seen that tattoo as well. Andie Seagrove, that's her. I used to see her on Facebook.' Several of the others nodded then. 'But I haven't seen her for months.' And they nodded at that as well.

Chapter Thirty-seven

EVERYTHING HAD CHANGED. But it was going to be OK, Andie understood now. As of this morning she was grateful to be alive – and not just ordinary living, breathing alive, either.

She'd draped a towel over the full-length mirror from day one, and still wasn't ready to take it back down. But this morning she'd been finally ready to fully open the curtains and let the sunlight flood into the room without shrinking from what else she might see.

Dust particles had tumbled through the air. Chocolate brown and cream leaf print warmed walls that had seemed monochrome for as long as she could remember. The room had gone from being barely satisfactory to the only place she'd been prepared to be. But she'd also realized that it couldn't stay that way. And the hours she'd spent allowing herself to daydream of a fictitious life with safe outcomes had gradually evolved into visions of what her own life still had the chance to be.

Perhaps there would come a day when she saw that deep regrets were as life-affirming as hard-won accomplishments. Unlikely.

But she'd have to push herself to bring about such accomplishments if she wanted to test that theory, so today she must set about purging her life of all the evidence of her own stupidity.

It was early evening now, and the bedroom was close to empty, while the area next to the front door was piled with bags destined for one of the charity shops in Burleigh Street.

During the last two trips between her room and the hallway, she finally developed the feeling that she'd done enough. The front door itself was solid, apart from a fan of glass near the top, a spyhole in the middle and a letterbox at the foot. The view through the spyhole showed an empty street beyond, but it made the outside world look distorted and distant. The idea of stepping out into St Matthew's Street still overwhelmed her, but tomorrow she would have to try.

She pulled away from the door then and, without letting herself think about it for too long, opened it. The air outside was warm and smelt of a neighbour's barbecue: sausages and onions. She sucked in several deep breaths, and then leant on the doorframe for another few minutes, watching the traffic passing the end of the road.

When she was finally ready, she returned to her room. The wardrobe doors hung open and the only items of clothing that remained were the ones that she'd brought with her when she'd first come to uni, and the ones she'd brought from home since.

She felt satisfied with the room's new and sparse appearance and, in spite of her tiredness, pushed herself on until she had cleaned down every surface and vacuumed into every inaccessible corner. Then she showered, and for the first time in weeks she washed her skin without breaking down.

Instead the shuddering began as she dried herself. Her hands started to shake as she pulled her pyjamas over damp skin, fighting with the legs as they clung to her thighs. She put on a sweatshirt over the top, then bundled herself on to her bed, folding the duvet around her body and then up round her ears. Knowing the room was actually warm didn't help her stop shivering; the coldness ran to her core.

She reached out from her cocoon and flicked through channels on the television until she found the right level of bland. Snooker today. She didn't even know the rules. The placid green rectangle of baize, hushed audience and the tapping of cue and balls played out meaninglessly. Bit by bit the warmth returned and the panic died away.

Andie closed her eyes, still listening to the comforting rhythm of the frames being played. Those sounds eventually drifted into the background as she visualized tomorrow's trip to Burleigh Street, mentally walking herself along the route and promising herself that she could do it. A week ago that idea would have felt hopeless, but possibilities were gradually appearing, and budding gently where four weeks earlier everything has been razed.

She lost herself in these thoughts, drifting between them for a while, until she jolted back into the moment. As the interruption came loud and hard, she reorientated herself, then realized – someone was knocking at her door.

Chapter Thirty-eight

CARMEL MARSHALL WASN'T impressed.

She hadn't even been impressed when Gully had rung to inform her that Marks himself planned to visit. Gully had explained that she'd be accompanying him, as it was 'protocol for a female officer to be present in certain situations'. Carmel Marshall's mood had darkened further.

'If there's someone else you'd like to have with you, that's fine, Mrs Marshall.'

'Like a friend you mean?'

'Or a colleague.' As she'd said it, Gully remembered that Carmel didn't work. 'Or relative,' she had added.

'But you're coming with the policeman because of the sensitive nature of the conversation we'll be having?'

'There are some questions he'll be asking . . .'

'I get it and, no, I don't want someone else there. I'm not at all impressed that you think you can just turn up and demand to see me just like that.' She'd snapped out the words, then the receiver had rattled angrily back on to its rest.

And when she'd opened the front door to them she'd made it clear again. Even if she'd opened the door smiling, and claiming to be keen to help, Gully doubted she'd have warmed to her. Carmel Marshall looked like the kind of woman who didn't pick 'n' mix her own outfits, but shopped by purchasing the mannequin's whole look. Attractive but unimaginative.

They'd followed Mrs Marshall into the sitting room, where she pointed them towards the settee. She positioned herself on the armchair furthest away before reciting another couple of reasons why they'd failed to impress her. 'If you are going to call me at no notice and just expect me to make myself available to you, then I'm not really being given the chance to get my head straight, am I?'

Marks had switched immediately to his diplomatic but firm tone. 'Any investigation of this kind is protracted and, by nature, will involve elements that we can't plan for, or inform you of, ahead of time. I'm sorry but these are questions I am forced to ask.'

'I don't have anything to say.'

Marks spent several more minutes going over the situation, and barely seemed to notice Carmel Marshall's complaints bouncing back at him. He'd probably see her tetchiness as a natural reaction to the stress she was under. Of course, he'd be right to at least give her the benefit of that doubt. Gully reminded herself that she was there to support, not judge. She stood up, produced her best attempt at a serene expression and offered to make hot drinks.

'I don't want you in my kitchen,' Carmel snapped.

'I'm only looking for a way we can break the ice here. Would you prefer to make some tea? I can keep you company while you do.'

Carmel remained stony-faced, and Marks then cut in.

'There are two of us here for a reason, but part of our training is to understand that you may find it hard to begin to talk to me with a third person in the room. And PC Gully is trying to give the dialogue a chance to get rolling.'

Carmel leant back in her seat, folded her arms and glared. 'Make your drinks, then.'

Gully disappeared into the kitchen, filled the kettle and hoped it would be slow to boil. *Unlike me*, she thought, reflecting that her own suggestion of coming out here while Carmel made drinks had filled her with dread.

The colour scheme in the kitchen and adjoining dining area had come from the same 'natural' palette as she'd already seen in the hall and living room. It looked to her like several shades of cardboard.

What was her problem with this woman? So what if the furnishings and décor in this room had been bought with the same mindset as her clothes. Gully would not have been surprised to open a 'kitchen and dining' page in last year's *Next Directory* and discover that this room had been an item A – P replication of their show model. She guessed that her inability to imagine herself in any kind of home-making role might be at the core of this feeling. It wasn't therefore a reason to disrespect the woman.

But equally, what was Carmel's problem with them?

Gully still had no answer by the time the kettle had finished boiling, and she now substituted those two questions for a single, simpler one.

What would Goodhew say?

She poured water into the mugs and took her time mashing the tea bags while she tried to think of the answer.

In the end she sent him a text: *'What are you doing?'*

'Walking.'

'Got a minute?'

'Two minutes for you!'

'She's got my back up. I need a strategy?'

'You never did like the liars, even when they're OK people.'

'What does that mean,' she muttered to herself. '????' she texted.

The phone vibrated silently and he then spoke without pre-amble. 'The house, marriage, car, clothes, topped-up tan, regular pedicures and a couple of weeks to somewhere sunny each year. Somehow they're irritating you, right?'

'Yes, but why should they? It's none of my business.'

'Well, it's just a façade. Obvious to you, me and Marks, but that's what's got your back up. And the fact she's a liar, even if only to herself. It's only your cut-the-crap instinct butting in.'

'Carmel will have to face up to the reality of the situation?'

'Exactly. But in the meantime she's clinging on to a lifestyle that, to be frank, vaguely repulses you. You wish she would just snap out of it, so we can make some decent progress with the case.' Goodhew paused, and Gully said nothing. 'Am I right?'

He was spot on, but he wasn't going to hear that from her. 'So I should give her a break?' she concluded.

She finished the call and, not for the first time since arriving at Parkside, pondered why she was of any benefit to Marks at all. She was supposed to provide support, an open mind and comfort whenever required. She didn't understand how he didn't recognize her cynical streak. Almost any other female officer in the building would have been a better choice.

She carried the three mugs back through and delivered the drinks.

They both wore the same expressions as when she'd left. 'I didn't even ask how you like it, but this is white, no sugar,' she said to Carmel.

'That's fine.'

Gully manoeuvred a second armchair round so that she could sit closer to her, as Marks continued. 'I've already explained the search of the boat to Mrs Marshall, and touched on some of the evidence found there. Now that Sue's returned, I'll carry on.'

Carmel's chest rose visibly as she drew a deep breath. She now held it as she waited for the body blow.

'Are you aware of the purpose for which your husband used that boat?'

She seemed frozen suddenly, and even her mouth barely moved. 'No.' She drew a small top-up of air into her lungs.

'But you have been a visitor to the boat?'

Her face twitched from side to side, in something less than a shake of the head.

'We have discovered evidence that you were present on your husband's cabin cruiser on at least one occasion.'

'No.' Finally her lungs deflated, and she stopped trying to suppress her words. 'No, you're wrong.'

Marks stroked the bridge of his nose as he perused the notes. 'The thing is, Mrs Marshall, we have recovered some of your blood from the scene. It came from a nosebleed – one which required medical attention.'

Carmel pressed her right hand against her cheek, the third and fourth fingers pressing against one side of her nose. Her left hand held the mug, and for the first time Gully noticed there was an indent around her third finger where a wedding ring had once been.

'We believe that at least two other women were subjected to serious sexual assault on that same boat. It you refuse to help us, you may be charged as an accessory to those crimes.'

The gravity of the threat startled Gully; her attention darted from Carmel to Marks and back again. He had returned to reading through his notes, apparently unconcerned by the desperate thoughts his words had unleashed.

Carmel fumbled with the mug, and Gully reached out and caught it before it fell. 'It's OK,' she assured her. 'We can sort this out.'

'There's nothing to sort,' the woman began, but there was no conviction in her voice and her words dried.

Over the years Gully had heard plenty of sayings regarding the philosophy of life. One sprang to mind now and she paraphrased it in her head: Carmel hadn't ever steered the plough that cut the furrow of her own existence.

'Carmel?' Gully spoke softly so the words seemed just between the two of them. 'You may have put it out of your mind, but we know most of what happened. Tell us the rest, because there are at least two other women out there needing help.'

'They're prostitutes,' Carmel muttered.

'Do you know what he did to them?'

Carmel bit her lip, silently shaking her head.

'But you knew about them?'

A further shake, then a nod. Gully could see that Carmel's breathing was becoming uneven.

'You must have thought . . .'

'Just sex. That's all it was.'

'And that was OK with you?'

She shook her head and swallowed hard before she replied. 'Of course it wasn't OK. And I didn't actually know, I just guessed.'

'How often?'

'I don't know. We still did it ourselves, whenever he wanted it. But I don't see why . . .' Her voice trembled, poised between shouting and crying. 'I don't know why he needed to.'

'Could he have wanted something else?'

Carmel pressed her face into her hands, then finally she nodded. 'All right, I'll tell you.'

MARKS HAD LEFT Gully to lead the interview, and he now sat at the edge of their field of vision.

'Paul and I had a good sex life.' Carmel concentrated as she thought back. 'Well, I thought we did, but there are always little signs, I suppose. I thought I was open-minded, and initially it didn't bother me that he'd always be pushing things further.'

'Can you give an example?'

'Yes, many. Funny things at first, like dares that gave us a thrill. Just games. One day I met him in town, naked apart from my shoes and my coat, and he took me for lunch in this posh restaurant at Grantchester. Several times the waiter offered to hang my coat in the cloakroom. "Let him take your coat," he kept telling me. It was embarrassing but funny, and we went outside afterwards and had sex down by the river. We all do it, right, when we're first with someone?'

Er, no. Somehow Gully managed not to blush. 'Go on.'

'Every time he persuaded me to do something new, I felt kind of excited and humiliated at the same time. I got myself sucked into his way of thinking: *how did I know I wouldn't like it unless I tried it?* And he was hard to say no to.'

She paused and shot a wary glance at Marks.

'I know what you're both thinking. And, you're right, I could have walked away.'

'That wasn't what we were thinking at all,' Marks answered, 'but we do have specialist counsellors available if you become uncomfortable speaking to us.'

She turned her head sharply to focus hard on Gully, who used this opportunity to speak. 'Did you lose track of your friends, too?'

Carmel's mouth curled into a bitter smile. 'Actually, I did. At first he made me feel superior to them, and I believed him. So I hung around less with them and relied more on his company. I was a supply teacher at a primary school, but I'd started helping out with the jobsheets and sending out invoices for him, too. I didn't seem to have time for anything outside work except him. I've been thinking about it a lot since he died, and I don't know whether I should really complain, considering I have all this.' She made a point of scanning the room slowly, as if admiring the mushroom-toned walls. 'Some things are very hard to walk away from.'

Gully hoped that the woman's sweeping 'all this' statement had included the couple's two daughters. 'You were telling me about the early part of your relationship with your husband,' she said, steering Carmel back to her account. 'You'd describe it as intense, then?'

'Sex was important to him and while I was with him I tried to make myself into the ultimate "hot girlfriend". I dressed up for sex and watched porn with him, we drank too much, did coke and roofies.' Carmel's unabashed openness about their relationship suddenly faltered; there was no obvious break in the words but the tone of her voice changed. She now sounded distant. 'But quietly I was wondering when we'd reach the limit of whatever he wanted to try out. So I asked him, and he laughed and just said, "You love me, don't you? And I love you?" I said yes of course. And he said, "And we're having fun, aren't we?' and I wasn't going to say no. You don't tell a bloke you're in love with that you're not having fun, without expecting it to be over. Right?'

Wrong. 'So what happened?'

'He asked me to marry him.'

It wasn't an answer Gully could have anticipated.

'Of course I was thrilled, thinking finally he was going to calm down. I wanted the big wedding, to invite the friends I hadn't seen for months, all the family too, and make it something really special. But he was keen to push ahead with it and, in the end, we booked a time at the Cambridge Register Office for the end of that month. And then he had this boat . . .'

The speed of Carmel's speech had accelerated through the last few sentences, but stopped abruptly at the word *boat*. She reached for the mug of tea; it had to be cold by now, but she gulped down several mouthfuls very quickly.

Marks waited for a few seconds longer than it took for her to drain the mug, then he prompted her, 'You mean the boat at Point Clear?'

She nodded as she placed her mug back on the table. 'I'd never actually been there. I imagined . . . well, certainly not that. It was in the run-up to the wedding and he said the weekend away would do us good.' Her voice faded momentarily, but then came back firmly. 'The thing was, sometimes when we had sex he was great, other times he'd get this dead look in his eyes, like I wasn't even there or something. On the way to the boat he was flirting, told me how he'd been fantasizing, that it was to be a surprise.

He said something like, *You're always up for playing with me, aren't you, Car?* And I just laughed like I was flirting too. But that was when I noticed the dead look on his face. I don't remember much else then until the morning. I woke up naked on the floor of that squalid little boat. It was cold and damp and I could barely move.'

'You'd been drugged?'

'He claimed I'd chosen to take them. It's possible I might have done. But it wasn't just the drugs that stopped me moving, because I was shackled, ankles and wrists. He had me on a lead, too, calling me his dog.' She tapped her temples. 'I couldn't reason with him, he was a different person. My head started clearing and then I started hurting for real. I had bite marks on my breasts, back and shoulders. Not love bites, but teeth marks. He'd actually broken my skin.'

Gully's gaze automatically dropped to Carmel's body; if any mark still remained, it was hidden by her clothing.

'He gagged me and made me stay on the floor like that, only pulling me up on to the bed when he wanted to have sex with me.'

'You could have pressed charges,' Gully argued. 'Or at least called off the wedding.'

Carmel glared. 'No, I couldn't. I told myself it was a one-off.'

Oh, for fuck's sake, when was it ever? Gully felt a wave of anger, but it wasn't at Carmel, just at the situation. Carmel had been subjected to the three steps that Gully associated with classic domestic bullying and abuse: isolation, manipulation and control.

'Actually, because of that I had to wear a different dress for the wedding, one that covered my shoulders. He laughed about it in his speech, pointing out that most of my mates had never seen me ever wearing so many clothes. Most of my "mates" weren't even there, by then. Just a bunch of his own friends and their wives laughing at me. I had a fake smile on my face the whole day. I can't even look at the wedding photos without remembering how small I felt.' Carmel strummed her fingers on her knee, trying to find her next sentence. 'Overall it was a good marriage, though. He gave me everything I needed, but we didn't have the same tastes in sex.'

Gully had once heard that if a frog was dropped into too hot water it would jump straight back out; but drop it into cold and heat it gradually, and it would stay there until it boiled to death. Carmel had been in that water for years.

'How often did he make you do things you didn't want to?'

'He didn't make me. I let him.'

'With coercion?'

'I'd known what he liked before I married him. So he said we should find a compromise.'

'Which was?'

' "Special weekends", once in a while.'

'On the boat?'

She nodded. 'No limits – whatever he wanted. He didn't care if I was off my head on coke or something, as long as I'd gone through the pretence of asking him to take me there, and thanking him at the end.'

Gully wiped her hand across her brow, screwing her eyes shut, then reopened them while controlling the urge to visibly recoil. 'How often did this happen?'

'Probably twice each year. I skipped a couple of times when each of the kids was due to be born. He didn't want sex at all when I was pregnant, and I was worried that he'd go off with someone else. But he didn't.'

That was lucky, then. Gully shifted in her seat. 'You mentioned prostitutes – is that when you think he started seeing them?'

Carmel raised her eyebrows, pulling an expression that made it look as though this was the first time she'd ever considered the idea. Clearly it wasn't. 'That was definitely the first time I thought he wasn't getting enough at home. He said I had an issue with jealousy. He caught me going through his phone, but I never found anything.'

Gully had no doubt that would have come with some form of punishment. 'Was that why he broke your nose?'

'No, the nose was later – spring last year, I think.'

Marks glanced at his notes and nodded. 'It was March.'

Gully had never doubted that he'd been listening to every word, but she could tell that his voice had now distracted the other woman. 'Carmel? What triggered it?'

'Paul had been stressed over work, and I knew it had been longer than usual since we'd been to the boat. It always went better if I asked him first. I had the feeling that it was time I asked him again, and the thought of him getting angry was making me uptight. So I suggested it, but when we got there, I realized that he'd changed things: different bedding and carpet, and he'd repainted all the woodwork.'

Gully could feel her own frown deepening and forced her face back into neutral. 'And this caused a fight?'

'The cabin had always been deliberately squalid – not at all like this.' She indicated that she meant the house in general. 'He liked the boat that way: dirty. I didn't even know he'd been to visit it, but he'd clearly been down there cleaning it up. It was obvious to me that he had taken someone else there and had needed to clean it up. So I got angry. Suddenly I didn't want to go through with the sex either and, when I refused, he knocked me to the floor, tied me down and did it anyway. The punch in the face came straight after he'd finished.

'Because you'd been reluctant?'

'Because I hadn't thanked him. It wouldn't stop bleeding. That's when he drove me to the hospital.'

'And was that the last time you went to the boat?'

'Yes, it was. And it was the only time he was ever violent towards me, too.'

'Apart from the sex?'

Carmel tilted her head enquiringly and stared ahead for a few moments, before blinking Gully's comment away. 'He said he was sorry he'd hit me, and then told me he'd got rid of the boat. He'd always been a great dad but, after that, he spent even more time with our children. And finally we felt like a normal family. Until my jealousy messed it up.'

'Really?'

'I couldn't believe he'd had such a turnaround. I should have left well alone, but I was suspicious. First, I realized he was hiding money from me, then later I found he had a second mobile and, whenever I could, I checked it. He was texting women to find out what services they offered. Eventually there was one being contacted more than the rest. Someone called Andie.' Carmel took a deep breath. 'A student prostitute.' She said those three words in a tone that implied she was disgusted with him. 'And for the first time I wondered if I still loved him.'

Gully had once seen a Jackson Pollock exhibition at the Tate. She'd been unexpectedly drawn to it, even though she couldn't understand how art that must have made sense to the artist, could be so totally incomprehensible to her. Carmel Marshall was having a similar effect on her now.

'I really didn't know about him using the boat until that other detective came, but then it all added up about the missing money, as five grand sounds about right.'

'For carte blanche? For permission to rape?'

'No, five grand for fifty hours.'

'What else did you know about this "Andie" before then?'

'Her?' The marriage-wrecking-whore tone was back in her voice. 'I kept my eye on the texts between them. He'd arranged to pick her up outside the Man on the Moon, so I hid in the deli across the road. He dropped her home afterwards and I followed her.' A small but triumphant smile touched her lips. 'I know where she lives.'

The relief that spread through Gully was palpable. Carmel hadn't closed down at the last.

Marks had offered to make some more tea, but Carmel had gone into the kitchen instead. 'I need to phone Parkside,' he said to Gully, 'and get back there now, too. Stay and take a full statement. I'm going to send a rape counsellor over here to assess her. We'll take it from there.' He touched her arm. 'Well done, Sue. You'd better go and join her. Stay close just in case.'

Gully pushed open the kitchen door to find Carmel sitting on the floor, leaning back on the sink unit. She wasn't crying, but Gully guessed it was too soon for that. She finished making their drinks, then sat down next to Carmel and passed her the mug of tea. The sound of Marks leaving the house reached them as she did so.

Carmel sipped her drink. 'I'm starting to see how fucked up it all is.'

Neither of them spoke for a while after that, then Carmel made her full statement, patiently re-explaining everything she'd told Gully and Marks the first time round.

Gully guessed she'd always find it hard to warm to the sort of woman that needed the eye of an in-house corporate designer to match her curtains with the correct side table, but on this occasion she'd just about managed it.

Chapter Thirty-nine

THE ROADS BEHIND the Crown Court in East Road formed the area of Petersfield Ward. The streets had once been packed with like-for-like Victorian terraces, but most of these had eventually been replaced in waves of redevelopment, with splashes of Edwardian, inter- and post-war commercial and residential buildings now lining the streets. St Matthew's Street ran through the heart of it all, and Andie Seagrove lived in the only remaining terrace at the Norfolk Street end.

Goodhew knocked on her front door, then immediately stepped closer, listening for any activity inside the house and half expecting to encounter another individual only prepared to grant a reluctant conversation through the letterbox. Instead the voice came from somewhere to one side of him: 'Are you from the police?'

She'd opened a small front-room window that was level with the upper part of the front door. She must have been standing on the window ledge inside. He caught sight of a tuft of blonde hair.

He held up his ID.

'Can you pass it to me?'

He slipped it through. 'OK,' she said, but didn't pass it back. 'You can't come in.' She sounded neither timid nor aggressive, just matter-of-fact.

'OK, but we do need to talk to you.'

'About what?'

'I'm not going to explain it out in the street.'

'Say it so I understand then.'

'Andie, I know about the boat.'

She didn't reply straight away.

'It's important we talk.'

'We are talking, aren't we?'

'Yes, we are, but talking through a window isn't standard procedure.' Despite everything a small smile crossed his lips. 'Or you can phone Parkside station and check on me.'

'And I suppose I can use your phone for that?'

He called up the number for DI Marks, then held the phone up to her. 'That's my DI. Press "call" and he'll confirm my identity.'

She didn't take hold of it, though. 'What are the options here?' she asked.

'Either talk to me or another officer here, or to me or another officer at the police station.' For the first time he thought seriously about the protocol of their situation. Now he'd located her, he ought to inform Marks before anything else. 'It would have been better if I'd contacted you first and offered you support from a female officer. And I must contact my DI and let him know. But I just found your address and came straight round. Is there anyone else in the house with you?'

'No, the others went home for the summer.'

'Look, Andie, I'm glad we've located you, but I'm now going to call for another officer.'

'Don't bother, I'll come out. Give me five.'

She actually took less than two, and Goodhew heard her at the door as he was in the middle of phoning Parkside.

PC Kelly Wilkes picked up. 'Can you get a message to Marks?' he had begun. 'Let him know I'm with an Andie Seagrove . . . Hang on, Kelly.'

Andie just then opened the door, without the chain, and stood a few inches back from the threshold. Perhaps she always looked pale, but her blonde hair and magnolia skin tone made her look more faded than he'd imagined from the CCTV snap.

Andie first passed him back his ID. A sweatshirt covered her wrists but he could still see the yellowing of old bruising that discoloured her skin down to the base of her thumb. 'Are you coming outside, then?' he asked her.

'You can't come in, remember, so I'll come to Parkside with you.'

He nodded to himself, but spoke into the handset. 'I'll be in shortly. Miss Seagrove will be with me.' He hung up. 'We'll be walking, but it's not far.'

'I'm glad to walk.'

'You've been pretty elusive.'

'I haven't left the house since.'

'Since' could be used on its own when there was only one moment that mattered. He guessed she'd use 'before' in the same way too. Still, he had to ask. 'Since the boat, you mean? Really?'

'Groceries delivered, appointments missed or cancelled, and an unanswered front door – till you showed up.'

'You must have spoken to someone?'

'To my parents.'

'Do they suspect anything?'

'No, I don't think so. Maybe they think I've been a little anti-social, I don't know. Apart from that, all my friends have gone home. I sent a couple of emails just so they wouldn't send out a search party. As if.' She managed a smile. 'I've spoken to myself a lot, and to the TV once or twice too. But I turned a bit of a corner this morning, so made myself promise that I'd go out tomorrow. Then you turned up . . . which felt like good timing.'

'You seem very calm about it.'

'No, I'm a pragmatist, and once I've decided on something, I do it. I haven't decided on much yet, but I have worked out that there are so many things I still want to do in this life. And it's best if I tackle the mess I'm in first.'

They were already walking slowly but, as they turned on to East Road, Goodhew noticed she slowed again.

'You're in pain? Can I help?'

'No. And it's better than it was. It's just like I said, this is the furthest I've walked since. I know he's dead, by the way.'

'So why didn't you come forward?'

'I didn't know he had kids until I saw it in the paper. He was dead, I didn't . . . don't know anything about his death and, from a personal point of view, what was I going to gain at that point?'

'Before that, then – after he dumped you out on the Gogs, you could have made a complaint.'

'And I'll give you all the reasons why not when we get there.' Her voice had an in-pain edge to it. 'So change the subject.'

'Tell me about your degree.'

'I'm nearly done. My last year is coming up.'

'Then what?'

'No idea. Find a job, if I can. One day I want to create designs for fabrics – not the clothes but the fabrics themselves. I've painted some of my design ideas on to ready-made clothes, and I've even sold one or two. So I think that's what I'm going to do.' Reaching the traffic lights on the last corner before the station, they waited for the little green man to instruct them to cross. Andie was silent throughout but when they reached the other side she spoke again. 'What we do now is who we are, isn't it?'

'Is it? That doesn't sound right.'

'Ever heard that theory that, unless you're living under some kind of duress, you are living the life you actually want?'

'No, I don't believe that.'

'No? Me neither, actually, but I thought I was heading in the right direction with my degree, and instead I wake up to find I'm a prostitute. I can't undo it now.'

'But are you finished with it?'

'Totally.'

'That's a start, isn't it?' They'd reached the station by now, and he caught her quiet reply as they stepped inside.

'Promoted to ex-prostitute,' she said drily. 'Wow, aren't I clever.'

ANDIE HADN'T BEEN wrong when she'd called herself a pragmatist. She'd recognized the need for making a frank statement, and was now answering every question without hesitation. Goodhew hoped she's be able to stick to this pattern as the interview progressed. Sometimes her hands shook, other times fear welled in her eyes, but she never hesitated throughout.

He'd asked her at the beginning whether she'd prefer to be interviewed by a woman, or just have one present in the room.

'Last thing I want is another woman in the room judging me.'

'No one's going to judge.'

'OK, well, I don't want to say what I need to say, in front of another woman. You're recording it, right?'

'Yes.'

'I'll talk to you and the recorder then. I can manage that.'

'OK.'

Andie wore no make-up, and without it looked younger than she actually was. In fact, she could have passed for fifteen or sixteen. Her eyes were the same shade of green as Goodhew's, and it was there that he detected the strength that would carry her through this ordeal.

'I don't know anything about Paul Marshall's murder,' she declared firmly.

'Just forget the murder investigation at this point. All I'm interested in is what happened to you. Let's start with how did you meet him?'

'I was advertising on a members-only website. It's supposed to be safer that way. The other men were all fine.'

'I'm sorry, Andie, but I'll need to make sure this recording is as unambiguous as possible. So try to be specific and I'll ask if I need anything clarified. In this instance, please explain that advertisement.' He kept eye contact with her, nodding encouragement.

She gave a little nod in return. 'I'd advertised on a message board used by people offering escort services in return for payment. Prostitution, then. The message board appears on a website called *Student Services*. I'd started doing so in the Easter break, after I'd run out of money. I'd had a few one-night stands and I hadn't regretted them. I liked sex, I suppose, and it had never been a big deal for me, inhibition-wise. I didn't think there'd be much more to it than that.

'And, yes, the first couple of times are scary, but then, after that, it became straightforward. I adjusted my normal to include three of four sessions with men each week.'

I adjusted my normal. He'd remember that one. It was a phrase that covered the slide into crime made by so many people he'd interviewed.

'How many clients did you have?'

'A few one-offs, nine or ten regulars.'

'We'll need details.'

'I thought you might. Paul was my favourite. Some guys didn't even look at me, just bent me over and got on with it, stuffed sixty quid in my hand and said *Cheers, love* or something similar. Paul chatted with me. We had a laugh.'

'Did you know he was married?'

'Most of them are. And, from my point of view, I thought they were safer than a sex-obsessed loner or a bloke that's bitter about the women who've rejected him. But, yeah, I knew he was married and, no, I didn't feel bad about that.'

It wasn't for Goodhew to ask why not. In any case that would have smacked of judgement, when it actually would have smacked of curiosity. She answered anyway.

'I didn't feel guilty because I wasn't the one who'd promised to be faithful. But, then, I don't think too much of the whole idea of men and marriage.'

'How did you meet him?'

'Paul? He texted me initially. Said he wasn't sure whether he should. All tentative at first, like he'd never paid for it in the past. Of course, I later found out that was just part of the game. The whole thing was a game with him – and I didn't see it coming.' She picked up her cup, realized it was empty and put it down on the table.

Goodhew checked his watch. 'Fresh drinks will be here in a few minutes.'

'The first time was in his van. He apologized, said he hoped I wasn't upset because it had seemed a bit sordid, then promised something better if I'd agree to meet him again.

'There's a motel out on the A505, where he booked us in the second time. Paid me extra because of the travelling time. It became at least once a week after that.'

'Across what sort of period?'

'Maybe a couple of months, but I'd have to check the texts. I trusted him, though.' An uncontrolled twitch of nerves made the ring finger of her right hand tremor. When it didn't stop after a few seconds, she folded the other hand protectively around it. 'We gradually started to spend longer together. He talked about his wife, said he wouldn't leave her, though. He was very upfront about that, but I'd crossed a line by then and started feeling like she was the competition. Whatever she gave him, I wanted to show him I could do it better.'

The drinks arrived then, and they paused for a couple of minutes. Goodhew made an attempt at small talk but Andie stopped him. 'I'm trying really hard to be brutally honest, and that means stepping outside myself and seeing everything for what it is. Stop being nice to me, right now.'

'Sorry.'

She looked exasperated. 'OK, ready?'

He pressed 'record'. 'Ready.'

'Paul was still paying me, but it had started to feel like a relationship. He admitted that he found it hard to think of me with other men, but knew he had no right to object, and somehow that conversation skewed into one about belonging. Initially I just thought he meant it in the emotional way, but he steered the conversation round until we were talking about sexual belonging. He asked me if I read any novels like that.' She paused, remembering Goodhew's advice about being specific. 'I mean the kind of books they call mummy porn. The girls at college call it fuck fiction. He said his wife read them but wouldn't try anything. I think his exact words were "She can't give herself to anyone totally". And what did I then say? "I *can*."' She tipped her head back and released a long, slow breath. '*So* stupid, so, *so* stupid,' she muttered. Tears rose in her eyes, till it looked impossible that they wouldn't tumble on to her cheeks. But, somehow, she managed to make them recede.

Goodhew said nothing and just let her compose herself.

After a minute she sat up straight again, then leant closer to him with her elbows on the table. 'Once I'd promised that I'd give him the sex that his wife wouldn't, then the dynamic between us shifted. There's no point in second guessing which elements of that weekend I initiated and which Paul had set me up for. I don't know the answers, myself, though I'm sure that I was out of my depth there all along.'

'Were you expecting to be taken to the boat?'

'No, I don't really know what I expected. I suppose I imagined a blindfold, and ribbons tying me to the bedpost. More fantasy than reality, a kind of kinky-themed normal, if that makes sense.

'The next time I saw him, he brought up the subject of money. He said the whole thing needed to be organized properly, and he'd worked out that he should give me five thousand pounds. I was stunned. He asked me if that would be enough to make me stop seeing other men. And, stupidly, I assumed that amount of money was more about his feelings for me than how I'd be expected to earn it.' She stared into the middle distance: somewhere through the wall, across Cambridge and into the past. 'At the outset I'd told myself that the escort work was only a short-term fix, and that Paul was presenting me with the quick way out of it. I remember also wondering why I didn't feel happier. I guess that was because it was his decision, not mine, and that made me uncomfortable in a way I couldn't put my finger on. I should have trusted my own instincts.'

She paused to stare at the digital voice-recorder. It would have been obvious for either of them to then mention a cliché or two about hindsight or life experience, but instead they silently watched the timer speeding forwards, counting out time in hundredths of seconds.

As it hit the next full minute, she spoke again, reverting to her most matter-of-fact tone. 'Paul said we should do it properly, so I signed a contract agreeing to be completely at his disposal from that Friday evening till Sunday evening. He gave me the cash, and I paid it into my account at the bank before we left.'

'Where did you think you were going?'

'To his boat, of course. He had told me about it being moored on the river. I imagined it would be plush . . . you saw his car, right? It was only that one time in his van that I saw him around anything that was even slightly rough – and that van was used for work. Oh shit, scratch that last bit, because I'm making it sound like the boat was the problem. Anyway, I got into the car and he asked if I was ready.

'I had this second of doubt. "It's a game, isn't it?" I asked him.

'He said it was a game that would only work if I played along. He told me to bend forward so my head was close to my knees. I don't know why he did that . . . but I didn't really understand anything much after that. I just know it wasn't about sex. It was all about hate and anger, and for some reason it was my job to pay the price.' Without warning she pulled her sweatshirt off and dropped it on the floor. Underneath she wore a vest top and no bra. She held out her arms. 'Most of it has gone now.' The artificial light blanched her skin, leaving just the darkest veins of the marbled bruising visible at first. As Goodhew's eyes adjusted, he began to pick out yellows, greys and khakis, too. She then turned to show him her back; the bruising to the lower ribcage and on the very top of her neck looked to be at a similar point of recovery. The entire area between her neck and waist was rife with freckled and scored patches of fresh skin.

'It was a safe bet I wouldn't go to the police,' she continued. 'How many students want their mums or dads to know they'd gone to uni and become prostitutes? And I had agreed in writing, too. I should have guessed earlier that he never cared. That five grand had seemed too much – and you get what you're paid for, I guess. So maybe this is what a five-grand weekend looks like.'

She crossed her arms over her chest and stared at Goodhew. 'Is that enough of the sex stuff, or do you want it in full detail?'

'No. With Paul Marshall now dead, there are no assault charges we can bring against him, and I'm not sure what kind of statements will be needed from you at this point. Full statements will definitely be needed, though.' He said it as if it was a question.

'I understand,' she replied.

He frowned then and looked down at the notes in front of him. 'When did he stop assaulting you?'

Her gaze remained steady. 'About five minutes before he told me to get out of the car.'

'Have you had any medical attention, Andie?'

'Aspirin and Sailor Jerry.'

'We need a doctor to examine you. But *you* need that too.'

'Sure, whatever.' She gave a shrug but he sensed that any trepidation was also mixed with relief.

'Where exactly did he drop you?'

'Somewhere on the Gogs. Plenty of cars drove straight past me. One foot was so swollen, I couldn't even keep my shoe on, so I was up there barefoot and all these drivers saw me. I got offered a lift in the end but, fuck it, you'd never think that so many people would just drive on by. That driver took me all the way to East Road, so I suppose I was luckier than I might have been.'

'When did you hear about Paul Marshall's death?'

'Pretty much about the same time as everyone else, except I saw the picture of his burnt-out car in the *Cambridge News*, and its location too. That was before they'd released his name, but I already guessed who it might be. Part of me hoped it was, anyway.'

'And the other part of you?'

She raised an eyebrow. 'I don't want to become someone who wishes other people dead, no matter what they do.'

Goodhew nodded to himself; he understood that outlook. 'Paul Marshall was tortured. We don't know why, but the two most likely reasons would be either to extract information or exact revenge. All along I've felt you somehow hold the key. It can't be a coincidence that he was tortured right at the spot where you were dumped.'

'No one knows what happened. Not the details.'

'But someone knows something.'

'I cancelled seeing the other men on my list. I apologized and suggested they went back on to the website and booked with someone else.' She smiled at what she'd just said. 'Customer service is a better career than servicing customers. That could be my slogan.' She looked embarrassed, at once. 'Sorry, that wasn't very funny.'

'Morgue humour. It's a good sign.'

'Really?'

'Absolutely. Check it out. So tell me exactly what you said, and to whom.'

'Nothing, actually. I just told my clients I was leaving the area, and so was finishing. I even cancelled my account on the website. I don't know if someone complained, because the website emailed me back and asked my reason. I just told them I was giving up.'

'Not moving away?'

'No. I didn't want the landlord assuming that I was going to leave. There are so many other students looking for rooms this close to town.'

Goodhew scanned down through his notes, even though he already knew the answer wasn't there. 'What does your landlord have to do with the escort service?'

'It's through him that I found out about it.'

'That doesn't answer my question.'

'I couldn't bring blokes back to a houseful of other students and, like I said before, most of the men were married. They won't all be ready to pay for a room, on top of paying the escort – especially if they're paranoid about the CCTV cameras that are always fitted in those places. Andrew usually has an unoccupied house to spare somewhere, so he lets the girls use its rooms.'

'For a fee?'

'Yes, of course.'

'Who pays?'

'If I wanted use of the room, I paid. I booked through the website. I took a premium listing for the day I wanted a room, and then they would send back the details of whichever one I could use.'

'But who is *they?*' A note of frustration slipped into his voice, and he immediately regretted it. 'Who is your landlord and who runs this website, Andie?'

'His name's Andrew Dalton. *He* could be behind the website too, for all I know. He has an office above one of the takeaways in Milton Road. I'm sorry, but I didn't realize it was important information.'

'Andie, I really appreciate how frank you've been. And brave.'

'It's my first better day since. That's all. I know you don't switch off trauma. I'm just having a pause before the rest of it hits me. And I need to do everything I can to get back on track before then. Now, if it's OK, I think I'd like to phone my mum.'

PC KELLY WILKES then swapped places with Goodhew. 'Andie would like to phone her family now,' he explained. 'She'll need a doctor too.'

'Don't worry, Gary. The doctor's on the way and I'll keep a close eye on her meanwhile.' He was glad Kelly would be taking care of Andie; she would never be the judgemental type of woman that Andie most feared. 'Go see Marks,' Kelly whispered. 'He's through there.' She nodded her head towards the room adjacent to the interview room. Goodhew knew then that Marks had been observing the interview.

Goodhew pushed the door open gently. 'Sir?'

'Carmel Marshall gave us Andie's first name and approximate address, but I came back here to find I didn't need to discover the rest. Here you were already. Nice interview, Gary.'

'Thanks.'

'She's a strong witness, and it's such a pity Marshall's too deceased to be charged.' It was clearly meant as a quip, but it was obvious that the last thing on Marks's mind was smiling. 'Sit down. There's a problem.'

On the table in front of him Marks had written 'Andrew Dalton' in the centre of his notepad, with the *Andrew* above the *Dalton*. The letters were uniform and sharply drawn, as though the name had been written very slowly.

'It makes perfect sense,' he continued, 'because some students will always get out of their depth. And, once they start struggling, plenty will go on paying for their phones and everything else to do with their social life, before they pay their rent and bills. A sharp landlord will be in a good position to exploit that.' Marks retraced the letters A and D with his pen. 'Young's gone to check, just in case it's a coincidence.'

'What?'

'How are you with coincidence, Gary?'

'Uncomfortable.'

'OK, so would it be a coincidence that there are two separate business premises in Milton Road run by two different Andrew Daltons?'

'Yes, but maybe not so huge if they're, say, father and son, or if it's a common name for that part of town.'

'What if I said they were both businesses renting property to students, and both located over food outlets?' Marks tilted his head slightly and looked hard at Goodhew.

'Then I'd be surprised if they weren't connected. I'd guess that either it's the same business or two businesses owned by the same Andrew Dalton.'

'I am similarly skeptical, Gary. Therefore I think DC Young will come back at any moment to tell us that it's just one man and one address.'

Goodhew studied Marks as he tried to rewind the last few sentences. He then shook his head. 'Sir, I feel like I've missed the first five minutes of *Wallander* and now I can't catch up. I don't have a clue how another Andrew Dalton has come into the picture.'

Marks tutted. 'Go and find Young, then maybe we'll know where this is going.'

Goodhew pulled open the door and stepped out into the corridor. He'd only taken a few steps before Young himself came into view at the far end.

'What did you find?' Goodhew asked.

'He's the same man: one Andrew Dalton, one address, two business names.' He carried a folded sheet of paper. 'Here's the detail.'

Behind him the door reopened. 'Let's have it, then, Gary,' Marks said, before Goodhew even had a chance to unfold the paper. They returned to the room and their seats but, to Goodhew's surprise, checking out the sheet of paper wasn't Marks's priority. He didn't say anything further until he had his pen poised over the name written on the notepad.

'Remember Lesley Bough?' the DI began.

'Of course.'

'Remember how she met Mary Osborne?'

'Sure. Through the employment agency Mary ran.' Goodhew stopped and his mouth formed a silent 'O'. 'The same place where Mary Osborne met Greg Jackson.'

'Yes, Lesley was almost correct in her explanation of the agency's name. Mary ran it with her friend Karen.' Marks wrote down 'Karen' above Andrew Dalton's name, and 'Mary Osborne' beneath it, emphasizing with his pen the K of Karen and the O of Osborne.

'Paul Marshall's murder and Mary Osborne's are linked?' It was Goodhew's rhetorical question, but Marks unfolded the paper for confirmation,

'Just the two businesses: A.D. Property and KADO Employment. In addition there's the escort agency, which isn't listed here. I'm therefore guessing that *Student Services* is probably unregistered. I'll make sure it's passed on to Revenue and Customs, too.'

Marks had jumped further down the line, thinking of ways to shut down *Student Services* and wield an axe blow against the Daltons that would be hefty enough to prevent them from restarting that enterprise under another name.

But seeing the name KADO appear on the page had sent Goodhew's thoughts in a different direction. The coincidence wasn't just that two murders were linked by one business, when that business served the relatively small city of Cambridge. Paths crossed here, and re-crossed – physically as well as metaphorically.

When he'd been a kid, looking down from his grandfather's library, he'd come to the conclusion that everybody in Cambridge must have crossed Parker's Piece at least once. It wasn't improbable that occasionally, two approaching people would recognize one another. This case was like that, up to a point, except there weren't only two people involved here and the coincidence of the timings seemed to count for everything.

He hated coincidence. He now considered the odds.

Could it be just a coincidence that Jimmy Barnes, Genevieve's husband, had asked to meet Goodhew so soon after Marshall's murder? Or a coincidence that Jane's arrest had been just a day before that? Or that Andie was linked to Mary Osborne by one route, and to Marshall by another?

Goodhew often drew spider diagrams to help him think. He'd start them at the centre and work outwards, but he had no idea where the centre of this one lay. Facts now floated aimlessly, no longer anchored together in the way he'd imagined.

He closed his eyes and tried to draw links between the various strands. It was impossible to picture it all without drawing it. He opened them to find that Marks had finished speaking, and Goodhew had no idea what he'd just said.

'Is it just one big case?' Goodhew wondered.

'I don't know. I need to think it through.' Marks rose to his feet. 'Tie up the paperwork with Andie Seagrove. I've already called for the on-call doctor, then make sure she's seen by everyone who needs to see her. She mentioned her mother, but does she have any other family?'

'Yes, definitely *both* parents.'

'Good. She'll be needing plenty of support. After that, go home and get some sleep. But, if you happen to lie awake, then tell me if something strikes you.'

Chapter Forty

MICHAEL KINCAIDE SAT at his desk, lists of figures and copies of bank statements lying in front of him. Chasing figures bored the crap out of him but he also knew that, if he concentrated, he was pretty good at spotting funds where they shouldn't be. Today they looked as meaningless as wingdings or hieroglyphics.

He rested his elbows on the table and then his chin on one cupped palm, as he tried to figure out the exact moment the week had turned sour. Before then he'd been filled with so much anticipation that he hadn't imagined anything could totally dampen it. Even the first mention of the Becca Osborne case barely bothered him. He doubted that any officer could make it through his career without taking a risk or two, and there was no reason to think that, in his own case, it should catch up with him when it never had yet.

Even Jane Osborne's appearance hadn't bothered him; she knew nothing, after all. At some point, though, the idea that his career might unravel had started to grow in his mind. And by the

time they'd visited Jackson, it had grown enough to be as distract-
ing as having another person in the room.

He'd stood on the pavement outside Jackson's house and realized that being at the heart of this investigation had to be the safest
place to be. Now he slapped his hand down on the paperwork and
told himself to concentrate.

He went to fetch some coffee, then came back with a new focus
on the figures. *Follow the money.* Just like it seemed to be the law of
politics, it was often also the law of crime. Some of the banks hadn't
provided all the financial details that were required, so he decided to
ease himself back into the right mindset by chasing the missing ones.

Those banks frustrated the hell out of him, but he pulled the
receiver from the handset and tapped out the first number. As his
call was placed into a lengthy sequence of automated options and
call queuing, he checked off the information so far received.

In fairness the bank had already provided the necessary details
of Gerry and Mary Osborne's joint accounts up to the time of their
divorce, and the bank accounts she'd subsequently transferred her
money to. He could see there the proceeds from Gerry buying out
her half of the house, and that money subsequently sitting in her
current account. Then the balance gradually fell as she'd begun to
withdraw it in modest parcels of cash, right up until the day she
was supposed to have departed the UK.

What he now wanted was quick results on the long-winded
process of tracking down any new accounts that she might have
opened since, either in her own name, or as Lesley Bough, or
under another name entirely.

After twenty minutes of rising frustration he felt as though he
was hitting nothing but a succession of dead-ends. Surely a *murder*
investigation ought to have enough significance to outrank the

Data Protection Act. All he'd had so far were junior administrators who'd been trained to ram those three words into one and use them to bat his requests back at him.

DataProtectionAct.

Followed up by: *Sorry, I do understand, but you'll have to put it in writing.*

'If you can't help me, then put me through to your manager.'

The current call was being fielded by an insipid-voiced woman who was dumb and undoubtedly blonde.

'I haven't asked for personal information,' he repeated with forced patience. 'I've asked for advice on how to speed up the information request you've already received from us.'

'I'm sorry, sir, as I just explained, my role is to speak to existing customers only.' *No one really sounded that pleasant.* 'And unfortunately you don't currently have an account with us. Would you like me to put you through to our new business section, sir?'

Unbelievable.

He should have negotiated with their staff until he'd been handed up the food chain to someone actually able to help. Instead he'd jabbed the 'end' button and was silently thinking of the most satisfying and expletive-ridden response he might have used. He picked up a sheaf of the statements, planning to go through them to decide which bank to tackle next.

A voice from the doorway took him by surprise.

'Something wrong, Michael?' It was Marks.

'No, of course not.' Kincaide recovered quickly. 'I've been chasing up the banks that haven't come back to us yet.'

Marks seemed happy enough with that, so Kincaide guessed he'd still been alone in the room when he had actually told the phone to piss off.

Marks settled into Goodhew's chair. 'Do you remember Andrew Dalton?'

The skin on the back of Kincaide's neck began to tingle immediately. He frowned at the bank statements still in his hand, then slowly looked up at Marks while continuing to frown. He shook his head, then hesitated as if some little snippet of recall had just come back to him. 'The first Osborne case?'

'Yes, a partner in KADO Employment along with Mary Osborne.'

'With his wife . . . I remember now. Why do you ask?' For no particular reason, Kincaide proceeded to separate a few of the statements, carefully avoiding eye contact with Marks.

'Andrew and Karen Dalton are landlords for one of the women assaulted on Marshall's boat. I'm talking about the woman from the Gogs.'

'Uh-huh.' Kincaide placed the entire sheaf down now. Better that than drop them.

'They appear to be running a student prostitution website. That's how Marshall first met her.'

As hard as he tried, Kincaide couldn't manage to break eye contact this time. Luckily Marks did as he moved towards the door. 'Let's get down there now. We can't discount the possibility that the Osborne and Marshall cases are linked now.'

Kincaide hesitated, feeling as though he needed to say something. 'They can't be,' he muttered, and felt his gut lurch.

'Come on.' Marks jerked his head towards the corridor. 'I know you're a bigger fan of coincidence than me, but even you're not going to buy this one. They're being brought in right now so I have about ten minutes to explain.'

They headed for the interview room almost in tandem, Kincaide staying close enough to his DI's shoulder for Marks to know he was being listened to, but at an angle too awkward for Marks to easily make eye contact.

Kincaide's mind was racing.

The DI continued briefing him on all the leads that had driven the path to Karen and Andrew Dalton, but Kincaide's thoughts revolved around snatches of conversation and phone calls, and the recurring sick feeling that kept clawing at the pit of his stomach. These thoughts repeated themselves until he'd all but blocked Marks out.

He'd been inexperienced, he assured himself. *He'd panicked*.

He'd found a business card and made a call. No big deal.

And it had gone on from there. And it had become beyond his control.

All these excuses meant nothing, though, all that mattered was that he'd made wrong decisions, allowing himself to be pushed into small but precarious steps that had jeopardized his own career and given Jackson a seven-year sentence instead of life.

These thoughts continued looping round his head until he saw the Daltons being ushered into interview room 1. They'd arrived sooner than he expected, and Marks was through the door after them before Kincaide had had any chance to stall.

They were both in their forties now, though Andrew Dalton may have been a year or two younger than his wife. He was below average height but solid with the kind of physicality that belonged with full-contact sport or full-contact street brawls. Dalton was shaven bald, with just the shadow of stubble across two-thirds of his skull. Bald undoubtedly suited him. Kincaide could remember him well, but he remembered his wife better.

Karen Dalton was brunette, about two inches taller then her husband, with polished skin and whitened teeth. Everything about her hinted at efficiency and high standards. It wasn't the first time Kincaide had wondered how these two had ever got it together. They might look mismatched, but Kincaide had also experienced their fierce loyalty.

Kincaide nodded to each of them, while his superior remained stony-faced. But, then, no one else smiled either. Marks directed them all to sit around the table, two on each side, strictly police versus public. He then laid out the parameters of the conversation. Both of them continued watching Marks. Andrew Dalton sat further back, with his elbows resting on his knees, hands clasped and his face tilting slightly upwards. Karen Dalton seemed to listen intently, but twice her head turned away from Marks as she gazed dispassionately at Kincaide.

'Do you both admit to knowing Andie Seagrove?'

Karen Dalton answered, her tone languid, 'As a tenant, Inspector, nothing more. She seems pleasant enough.'

Andrew Dalton nodded, said nothing.

'We have evidence that you own and run a website named *Student Services*.'

She smiled easily. 'That's my baby, isn't it, Drew?'

Another nod.

No hint of a smile from Marks, of course. 'It's a site promoting and encouraging prostitution in Cambridge,' he remarked coldly.

'That was never my intention. As you know KADO is an employment agency, which we started up to supply catering and housekeeping staff. Most of the jobs are unskilled and minimum-wage, and most of the workers who fill them are students.' She ran her hand across her lap, smoothing out the fabric of her skirt. 'Some of those students are attractive, sociable people with more to offer.'

Andrew picked up the next sentence virtually seamlessly. 'Some of the students asked us to set it up. Escort work can have a seedy reputation but plenty of men are visiting from abroad and just don't want to dine alone.'

Karen ran her tongue across perfectly even teeth. 'In fact, if you look at the website, you will see the advice "*We categorically discourage students using this site to give out personal contact information and suggest that all initial meetings occur in a public place.*" As you can hear, I've quoted it so many times I know it by heart.'

Kincaide knew the score: if the interviewee turned on the theatrics, so could Marks. The Daltons seemed very sure of themselves. Marks had listened and grown very still. A trickle of sweat ran down Kincaide's spine.

Only Marks's eyes moved, switching slowly between Karen and Drew Dalton. 'Are you under the impression that there is an unwritten understanding between escort agencies and the police?' he asked softly. 'The escort agencies always trot out this urban myth about happily married and respectable businessmen who can't stand facing an empty seat at dinner. Do you really think the police will say "Our apologies. As you were"?' He paused for a second. 'No one hires out a bedroom for a couple of hours so that a student and a "respectable businessman" can eat dinner there.'

Andrew glanced at his wife. 'I think he means the study rooms,' he told her.

She smiled again. 'I know *Student Services* is used by men who like the company of students, and vice versa, but we don't police it. Everyone pays a monthly fee.'

The dialogue passed back to Andrew. 'And if a student needs to study, we'll rent them a room. If they decide to meet up with someone there, that's their choice.'

And finally back to Karen. She tilted her head slightly and studied Kincaide for a moment. She only slid her attention back to Marks as she began speaking. 'You know what, I rarely visit the site, but I'd be disappointed to know that supposedly decent people are abusing their positions.'

Kincaide's thoughts fell back seven years again. In the same situation, he'd behave differently now. No one would ever gain that kind of hold over him again. Even now, Karen Dalton was certain that she had leverage over him. And, in truth, perhaps she did.

Marks had been asking more questions, but Kincaide only tuned in at the end as he realized he himself was now being spoken to: '. . . find out whether Clark has that list ready, would you?'

Kincaide hoped Clark would be at the furthest end of the building, with at least two shots of coffee therefore possible between being given the list and passing it back to Marks. Depressingly, DC Clark was standing outside, leaning with one shoulder against the wall. He held out a single page.

'Is that it?' Kincaide asked.

Clark looked surprised. 'They're managing twenty-two properties, and they own four of them. That's plenty for most of us, Mike.'

'I meant, is that the only list he's after?'

'Oh yeah, far as I know.'

Kincaide ran his eyes down it. One address jumped out at him. It was the first time he'd felt like smiling since before Marks had hauled him down here. He pulled a pen from his pocket and marked it, writing his note in carefully formed letters so there would be no chance that Marks wouldn't be able to decipher it.

He sat back down alongside his boss, and passed the sheet of paper across. From the corner of his eyes he saw the boss's hand give the page an involuntary squeeze, and Marks sit a little taller in his chair.

'You have a property in City Road?'

'It's being renovated,' the man said.

'It's empty,' she added.

'Apart from Greg Jackson?' Marks suggested.

'Yes, well, I was about to say that,' Drew replied.

Karen still smiled, but her posture had turned rigid and Kincaide suspected she was gritting her teeth behind those compressed lips. Marks had struck a nerve.

Marks picked up the phone, deliberately making the call in front of the Daltons, and watching them carefully throughout. 'Young? Last thing for tonight, arrange for Jackson to come in for questioning. Pull him in a.s.a.p. and we'll talk to him first thing.'

And after that, the pair avoided answering any further questions. The rest were rebuffed with persistent responses of 'Don't know' and 'No comment'.

'Were you aware that Paul Marshall met a woman through your website?'

'No comment.'

'Were you an acquaintance of Mr Marshall?'

'No comment.'

'Do you know any reason for his murder?'

'No comment.'

In the end they were bailed, but stopped from visiting their offices until a thorough search had been completed. Over three hours had passed by then, during which time the Daltons' confidence barely seemed to falter.

Kincaide then showed them to the exit. He held open the front door and stood outside, leaving just enough space for them to go through one at a time. They would not be making an easy target of him that way. Neither was Karen Dalton the only one who could smile on demand. Kincaide's smile was discreet and cold. 'Don't try anything,' he warned her.

'Come on,' Drew Dalton murmured as he passed, 'don't we all want the same thing?'

'To be left alone.' She answered for her husband, accompanying her words with another meaningful stare at Kincaide. Then she slid an arm through her husband's as they walked away from the police station.

Marks had gone back to his office, and Kincaide took a slow walk up the stairs, trying to rerun the sections of the conversation when he'd felt most at risk. Marks didn't even look up when Kincaide arrived; that had to be a good sign. They finished up shortly afterwards, Marks debating the case, Kincaide quietly concurring with each subsequent thought put forward. Finally they headed towards the exit, side by side this time. Kincaide was just desperate to reach home and think things through.

'So have you told anyone else, on the quiet?' Marks asked suddenly.

The question threw him, and Kincaide scratched around for an answer, feeling like he had 'caught-out' written all over his face. 'Told anyone what?' he muttered anxiously.

Marks fished in his pocket for his keys. 'Your promotion, of course, Michael.'

'Oh, I see. I'm sorry, I was still busy thinking about the case. Well, there have been a couple of cracks about me seeming unusually upbeat. People know I did the exam months ago, and I'm surprised no one guessed, but they didn't. And I haven't told anyone – no one at all.'

'Except Jan?'

'Not even Jan'. He was sure his wife would have merely found a way to sour it. So he had thought he'd enjoy it while he could, and let her know once his own excitement had abated. Now he had to tread carefully, because he felt overshadowed by the thought that it could all unravel. He couldn't bear to tell her, then have it totally thrown back in his face if he was knocked back down to DC – or something worse.

'I'll announce it at the next appropriate meeting,' Marks said.

'Thank you, sir.'

'And, talking of genuine coincidence, Becca Osborne's murder was one of the first you worked as a DC, wasn't it? Has it occurred to you that this will be just about your last case as DC? And, if it goes on long enough, one of your first as DS. Funny thing, eh?'

An hour later and Kincaide was still considering those words. *Your last case as DC.* That could go either way. He really, really needed it to go *his* way.

Chapter Forty-one

GOODHEW WAS AT home and in his grandfather's former library. The end wall had been re-emulsioned back to its original white. It had needed four coats, with evidence of the marker pen he'd previously used to write on the wall leeching back through, each time he went over it. Of course there was a special product for 'preparing walls stained by marker pen' which he discovered only after coat three. He'd had no more plans to draw on the walls again, feeling that he'd be able to accomplish just as much by writing on sheets of flip-chart paper and then spreading them out on the floor.

Those sheets lay there now, but it didn't seem the same. No matter where he stood, some pages assumed far more prominence than others. He climbed on a chair but he couldn't recreate the same perspective as viewing the wall from the other end of the room.

His phone rang, and Bryn's mobile number flashed up on the screen.

'What's the deal with standing on the chair, then?'

Goodhew turned to find himself looking down on a roof and driver's side view of Bryn's turquoise and white Zodiac. 'Are you spying on me, or what?'

'No, I'm keeping my eyes open in case I ever catch you at home.'

'Same thing. What if I'm deliberately avoiding you?'

'No chance.' Bryn locked up the car and crossed over. 'Put that phone down and let me in, then.'

When Goodhew opened the front door, he found Bryn dressed in what looked like a Second World War flying jacket. 'My dad used to have one of those,' he remarked.

'I love it. It means I'll be able to drive in winter with the windows open.'

'It's August at the moment.'

'Yes, I'm roasting, but I wanted you to see it before I took it off.' He turned round. An air-brushed picture of Ava Gardner in a leopard swimsuit stretched across his back.

'OK, it's impressive. Is that instead of the tattoo?'

Bryn followed Goodhew up towards the former library. 'No, I didn't use the calendar hula girl. Instead, I went for one of the vintage pictures you have. And as the tattoo's vintage, I thought the jacket should be too.'

'You really had it done?' Goodhew had no idea which picture Bryn was referring to, but he had no doubt he'd be seeing the inked-on copy at any second.

'It's incredible, and it took Fabio four hours. I'll show you in a minute. It took Maya just as long to do the jacket.'

'Maya? This is the one with the graveyard tattoo?'

'Yeah, Maya,' he grinned. 'I am so out of my depth . . . Oh, well.' He noticed all the papers lying on the floor. 'What's this?'

Goodhew steered him towards the settee. 'You can't look. It's all confidential.' He gathered the sheets and sat down next to Bryn. 'It's like one of those impossible pictures where the staircase goes upwards at every turn.'

'They don't work in real life, only on paper.'

'I do know that, thanks, Bryn.'

'No, I mean the illusion works because it's flat. You can stare at it for ages and it's impossible to see which bit is the trick. But if you could touch it, you'd know straight away.'

'That's deep.'

'You think?'

'Either that or you were stating the obvious. I'm actually too tired right now to know. Are you going to show me this tattoo, then?'

'When you offer me a drink.'

'I'll go and get something in a minute,' Gary promised, but neither of them moved. They both stared at the blank wall in front of them. Gary's eyelids began to droop. Bryn gave his arm a light nudge, 'D'you want me to leave you to it?'

Goodhew didn't open his eyes, but shook his head. 'Can you wake me in an hour?'

Bryn checked his watch. 'OK, and then I'll get the car home.'

HOWEVER ELUSIVE GOODHEW found sleep, there were moments when it also knocked him sideways and gave him little choice but to succumb. The impossible staircase had done it. The one he imagined ran along each side of a square parapet. He shut his eyes and ascended at each corner.

Then, in his sleep, he'd got down on his hands and knees, closed his eyes and felt the risers, making sure each one climbed to meet the tread above. He counted back and thought he'd completed seven right-angled turns without rejoining the start. Then, when he'd proved the illusion one way, he traced the steps back down.

Goodhew opened his eyes, now awake enough to think.

Maybe some theorist who could think beyond his own abilities would say differently, but the only way it made sense to him was for the stairs to follow a long square spiral. The illusion was the appearance of the stairs ever returning to the same point. How could they?

You can't go back.

The words arose from deep in his memory. He thought maybe his father had said them when his mother had left. Goodhew ran his fingers through his hair, untidying it further, and pushed away thoughts of anything but waking up.

He checked his watch and realized that he'd been asleep now for four hours.

Bryn slouched at a crazy angle across the settee, quietly snoring. Goodhew climbed to his feet and wandered upstairs to the kitchen in his flat. He made two mugs of coffee and watched the element in the toaster glowing as the bread turned brown. He gave a start when the slices popped out, realizing he wasn't entirely sure where his thoughts had just taken him – but he'd been somewhere.

He put Bryn's coffee and toast on the side table at his end of the sofa, but then decided against waking him. Instead he stood in front of the blank wall, pen poised, waiting for the first words to come. For no real reason he reached out and wrote 'LESLEY BOUGH' in fat black marker-pen strokes. Then he drew. He drew names, arrows, circles, dates and places – anything that reached the pen. Sometimes his hands moved almost without conscious direction. He included everything he could remember writing down on the sheets of flip-chart paper, but now, on the solid wall space, they found their proper place.

Partway through, he stopped and drank Bryn's cold coffee. From across the room he could now detect the first signs of order. It didn't look at all like a staircase – no risers or treads. There was information missing, but in his mind's eye its shape was forming. There were two strands in there, twisting and inseparable, like a double helix of facts.

He returned to the wall, finally checking against the flip-chart sheets to ensure nothing had been missed out, and satisfied that now he'd found one solid place to start.

He checked his watch: it was almost 6 a.m. and he remembered Bryn's Zodiac outside. He checked it from the window, relieved to see that the car, although damp from morning dew, remained in one piece. He wouldn't want to be the one to tell his friend if anything bad had happened to it. He looked back at Bryn whose hanging-out-the-window arm was draped over one side of the settee, lying at an unnatural angle, so that the very bottom of his new tattoo protruded from the shirtsleeve. Goodhew leant closer and tilted one arm over so that he could see the full image. His brow puckered at first, then his eyes widened and gradually his expression changed. Bryn had been right: as tattoos went, it was stunning.

He grinned to himself, then grabbed a clean sheet of paper and wrote Bryn a note, leaving it under the sleeping man's car keys. He then slipped out of the front door and headed across to Park-side, phoning Bryn as he went.

BRYN'S MOBILE BUZZED in his jeans pocket and, when he finally woke enough to retrieve it, he discovered one arm too numb to even move. The display announced 'Gary'.

'What's happening?'

'I overslept.'

'What time is it?'

'Just after six. Your car's fine. Help yourself to breakfast. Can we catch up for a proper drink in a few days?'

'Sure, Gary. I'm knackered, can I crash here a bit longer?'

'No worries. Great tattoo, by the way.'

'Thanks.'

'Got to go, but there's a note by your keys. See you later.'

BRYN DOZED AGAIN, then made his own toast and coffee before he remembered the note. He slid it out from under the keys, even though they weren't actually obscuring the words. 'Have a look at the leather-bound photo album. It's in the bookcase where you found the hula girl.'

He located it immediately, about three inches thick with a sand-coloured cover and a palm tree painted on the spine. The first page showed a beach and a pink hotel behind it. Then Gary's grandparents' wedding . . . Then the honeymoon . . . Then . . . oh, fuck.

I've got a tattoo of Gary's grandmother.

Chapter Forty-two

WHEN GOODHEW HAD left home, the air had been fresher than on previous mornings, and the short path between his front steps and the pavement glistened. Bryn's Zodiac wasn't the only car that sparkled in the pale sunshine and, between them, they cast a row of dank shadows on to the tarmac. Autumn wouldn't be long now, and he didn't feel ready for it.

But, even as he crossed the very centre of Parker's Piece, he noticed that the sheen of dew on the grass had begun to dry. The day would be at a perfect temperature by ten but unbearable by eleven, and he didn't want that either. No doubt there'd come a point in winter when he'd be wishing for this moment to return, but right now he felt unusually discontented. Unsettled even.

After phoning Bryn, he tried to contact Jane Osborne three times, and felt rising irritation when she failed to pick up. Arriving at the station, he went straight to his desk, throwing his jacket across one end of it and dropping into his chair before powering up his PC. His home screen appeared just as Gully entered the room.

'You've just stormed straight past me, Gary. What's up?'

Goodhew held up his hands in a don't-panic gesture. 'I'm sorry. Maybe I was distracted. I've tried phoning Jane Osborne three times this morning: the first two times it rang out, then the third time it went straight to voicemail. She's avoiding me.'

'Maybe you woke her up and she finally switched it off.'

'She would have seen my number.'

'You called her when, six a.m.? If that was me, I'd have gone for the off switch without even opening my eyes.'

Perhaps Gully had a point. 'I'll give her half an hour and try again.' He then continued, speaking to himself as much as to Gully. 'I need her to get hold of her ex-boyfriend, in any case. And I need to email Marks.'

'He's been in already.'

'Really?'

'He wanted Jackson in for questioning last night, but he wasn't home. There's still no sign of him this morning and, because it's Jackson, Marks is getting agitated.'

Goodhew reached for the spare chair and rolled it towards her. 'Why does he want to question Jackson now?'

She pushed the chair back to him. 'It's not that complicated . . . just strange. It turns out he works for Karen and Andrew Dalton.' Her eyes narrowed. 'Why are you smiling?'

He opened up the gallery on his phone, then passed it to Gully. 'I photographed my wall, look.'

'I can't believe you wrote over it again, Gary.' She picked on the centre of the shot and enlarged it. 'Is this what you were about to email Marks?'

'Yes, but now I'll print it instead, and add a line connecting Jackson to the Daltons.'

'It looks like a mess of spaghetti to me.' She offered the phone back to him but, instead of taking it, he pointed to the screen.

'Look, two main strands here: the Osborne family and Marshall's murder, running on a timeline. The lines crossing them are the connections, and somewhere back here . . .'

'. . . Is the mystery single starting point. Yes, I get that.' Gully looked unimpressed. 'I'm not thick, Gary, but I still don't understand what that proves.'

'Unless all these links are just coincidence – which is highly unlikely – there has to be a logical way of fitting them together. So therefore they're in a sequence apart from merely chronological, and they've triggered each other.'

'Cause and effect, then?'

'Exactly. Now, recent events include Andie being spotted up on the Gogs, Marshall being murdered, Jackson following Genevieve Barnes, and Jane being brought back from Leeds. I've tried different scenarios to connect them, but nothing that triggers Jane coming back to Cambridge.'

Gully shrugged. 'She was arrested, therefore the timing is a coincidence.'

'I don't think so. She'd left her boyfriend and she was arrested at one of the major stations used for trains going south. I think she was coming home, anyway. She either lied when she said that no one knew she was there, or something she learnt gave her a reason to come back. There's only one event on this wall that is timed right.'

'Marshall's murder?'

'Yep – and it made the national news. She found out he was dead and that's what made her decide to come home.'

'So Marshall's murder was significant to her?'

'Precisely. She knew him. I'm waiting now for a call back from her ex-boyfriend, then I'll visit her.'

GOODHEW LEFT PARKSIDE fifteen minutes later, knowing that if he walked quickly he'd reach Pound Hill in fifteen more. On a congested day, without sirens, it took longer than that to drive through East Road alone. Across much of town the traffic was at a crawling pace; all it had taken was the combination of a minor collision at the top of Lensfield Road and a water-main repairs in Trumpington Street for the backed-up traffic and gridlocked junctions to ensue. From open car windows, drivers cast dirty glances at pedestrians who dared to outpace them.

No one would have known from his expression alone, but Goodhew's mood matched theirs. The two things he thought he hated most in life were spite and lies. Jane Osborne had lied to him, and his disappointment was illogical and surprisingly intense.

When he arrived at Pound Hill, she opened the front door just a few inches. Jane wore jeans and a baggy sweater that looked as though they'd been doubling as pyjamas. She gripped the blue-painted edge of the door and demanded, 'What?' White-knuckled, red-eyed, and clearly in a similar sleep-deprived state as Goodhew himself.

He pushed on through to the hallway, before turning on her. 'You knew who Paul Marshall was, didn't you?'

She shook her head in denial, but he could see he was right.

'You've been a liar in the past, Jane – a compulsive liar – and now you're lying again. I can see it on your face.' He stepped away from her, to lean up against the balusters. 'How many times have you been back in Cambridge, and watching your family without them knowing?'

Indecision was written on her face. 'I haven't.'

He'd known from the start that Jane was a survivor and survivors made the best liars, but it also took more than just lies to make someone a bad person. *I'm taking this too personally.* No one could be expected to suddenly stop lying after ten years of living that way. Telling the truth had to come one answer at a time, until it became the natural instinct. He softened his tone to sound less confrontational then. 'Forget the past for one minute, Jane. I need to be able to believe what you tell me now.'

'You'll think whatever you want to think,' she said stubbornly.

'Jane, listen to me. In the last few weeks, Jackson started following Genevieve, also Marshall dies, and you come back to town. All three are somehow related, and you are possibly the only person who knew that fact before us. I need to know what it was that pulled you back home, Jane.'

'I didn't come home. I was arrested, remember?'

'Yes, but at a railway station. Where were you planning on travelling from there? I think – arrest or not – you were coming back here to Cambridge.'

'It was just a thought, not a plan.'

'Come on, Jane, there's more to it than that. You'd left home, remember. I've spoken to your boyfriend, Ady.'

He saw her eyes glint with a flash of anger, but she said nothing.

'Ady remembers clearly. He tells me *he* showed *you* the burnt-out Evora on the internet. It came up on a news channel, and you seemed very uptight after that. A few days later you'd cleared off, and what appeared in your search history? Cambridge, Cambridge, Cambridge.'

She stepped back until propped against the wall, mirroring his stance. She shoved her hands deep into the pockets of her jeans, staring down at the floor as she thought. He watched her expression, half expecting to see the trademark scowl, or that she would simply turn away.

In the end, 'I've had enough' was all she said. She looked across at him. 'I don't *always* lie and, even when I do, it's not always planned. I say the first thing that deflects attention so that I can just carry on with life in the way that suits me.'

'Just tell me as much as you can,' he prompted quietly.

'Can we sit?' They went through to the kitchen. She'd had a furniture upgrade since his last visit, involving two plastic storage boxes. She upended them now so they could sit facing each other, their knees almost touching.

'All three of us kids used to lie awake at night listening to them shouting at each other.' She cast her eyes up towards the ceiling, as if Dan and Becca were still upstairs somewhere, then looked back at Goodhew. 'It was endless. But you cope . . . we coped. Dan stayed outdoors as much as possible, Becca tried to please both of them, and I just got more and more defiant. Especially with Mum.' She seemed puzzled for a second. 'My anger with Dad . . . all his energies seemed to be split between his sculpting and fighting with Mum.' Emotion snagged in her throat, and she took a breath. 'She didn't hit us or anything, but we still needed protecting from her. He was an adult; he should have realized.' She looked as though those last words had come as a complete revelation.

'Didn't you know you felt that way at the time?'

She shook her head. 'No, I didn't.' Her voice trembled and she made a *wait* gesture, taking several more breaths before she'd composed herself again. 'I couldn't stand the idea of Dan and Becca talking about moving out, when I was still stuck there. All I felt was anger – at all of them.

'I think it was around then that Becca started sleeping around. Not like changing boyfriends all the time; it was more blatant than that. She was lashing out too, I suppose, and I saw the pain that it caused Dad. Then, one day, I had a massive fight with him, and he accused me of casting a shadow over the house. He said, "*At least Mary and Becca are happy with the kind of lives they lead.*" See, I can still quote him on that. His view of the pair of them seemed to be his view of women in general, but worse. And in his eyes I deserved even less respect than they did. It still hurts now, but back then it was enough for me to leave home and never come back.'

'But you did?'

'I think it took me about a year to calm down. Then I found Becca online, it was Friends Reunited – or MySpace back then – and every couple of months we'd meet up in Peterborough or York.'

'Because they were easy stations to reach from both Cambridge and Leeds?'

'That's right. Becca told me about the prostitution. She didn't call it that . . . though I did. She called it "escort work".'

'Do you know if it was arranged through an agency or website?'

'Yeah, Mum's business partner ran it . . .'

'*Student Services?*'

'Yes. Karen Dalton's another one who thinks money is god. Becca herself had adopted Mum's logic that you should get whatever you can from a man. She said that a bloke would shaft you anyway, so he may as well cover the expenses. That was a version of one of my mother's lines.'

'Charming.'

'See, it's surprising I'm not more fucked up.' She raised a small smile.

'And Paul Marshall?' he asked, and her smile vanished again.

'He was one of them. In fact, he's the one she'd used as an example of how it wasn't just sordid sex with undesirable men. Everything she'd told me about her feelings for Paul Marshall, apart of course from the money changing hands, could have applied to a normal relationship. Until the very last time.'

He interrupted her before she could say more. 'He had a pattern, you know. She wasn't the only one he attacked.'

'Well, then, you know he must have been a clever man. I witnessed the change in her. He said he wanted her to think of him every time she ever thought about sex again. And the only other "man" she had after that was Greg Jackson.'

'Your mother's ex.'

'Yes, well, Becca had tried to tell Mum what Marshall had done to her, but Mum shut her down. I don't know whether she didn't really believe her, but I think she just didn't have the capacity to want to know. I'm sure Becca was paying her back by stealing Jackson away. And, unlike me, Becca didn't shut the door on the woman either. They were toxic together, constantly baiting each other.'

Goodhew wasn't sure who exactly she meant. 'Becca and Jackson?'

'No, Becca and Mum. Becca rang me a couple of hours before she died, saying she and Mum had had another bust-up. She used to carry a bunch of cards with the website for *Student Services*, and the slogan *See you in detention* underneath. After Marshall, she'd thrown them all away, but Mum had found one remaining and pressed it into her hand, telling her that was all she was good for.

'It wasn't their normal scrap. Becca said to me, "You have no idea how cruel she is." I asked her to explain, of course, because the idea of our mum being several steps more cruel than I already knew seemed . . .' she fished for the right word '. . . unlikely.'

'What did your sister then say?'

'She just said she was about to tell Dad everything, including that she planned to marry Jackson. It seemed like it was all just to spite Mum, and I thought Becca was crazy. Only Mum could goad Dad like that and get away with it. Becca said we should meet again so I could hear "*the whole fucking saga*" in person.'

'But of course she never got a chance?'

'No.' Jane leant back against the wall, looking pensive.

'Is that why you thought your dad killed her?'

She pressed her lips together, managing a small smile. 'You don't miss much. It was my first thought. My *only* thought.'

'What about Jackson?'

'The court came to its conclusion and I came to mine. It didn't mean I was correct, though. I followed it in the paper and I genuinely wanted it to be him, rather than a miscarriage of justice. I hoped the evidence would be conclusive, and then I'd know that my dad was innocent.'

'The evidence wasn't enough, though, was it?'

'No. But I didn't feel any pity for Jackson either and, to my shame, I suppose I didn't think I'd care even if he'd gone down for life. Maybe Jackson did actually kill her. But I was just sure Dad had done it and, through a perverse sense of loyalty, I kept that belief to myself. I just vowed that I'd never come home. I simply hoped that Dad would realize he'd been the cause of losing two daughters, and that it would make him suffer enough.'

'And now?'

Her voice grew quieter, as though there might be others within earshot. 'I never thought he'd touch Mum, but as soon as I heard it was her body they'd found,' she shook her head, 'I was just as sure as I had been regarding Becca.'

'And what about Marshall's death?'

'Did Dad even know Paul Marshall? I have no idea. But when Ady showed me the photo of that car, Marshall's name just jumped out at me. It's not a rare name but I kept checking, and as the details were released, they all matched.'

'So why come back here?'

'I hadn't decided that I would, but I felt very unsettled. Despite everything I still wondered about Mum and Dad and Dan. I didn't actually *want* to come back, but at the same time I couldn't leave the idea alone. So maybe I would have actually travelled down. And maybe the arrest was fortuitous.'

'And cheaper than the train?'

'I'm not that devious.' She smiled.

He shifted his weight slightly: the plastic crate was less than comfortable. 'How do you manage here?'

'It's OK. I'll sort out a couple of rooms and get by.'

'And your dad's OK with that?'

'I think he'll let me stay for a while. He's hoping to build some bridges, I reckon.'

'And you?'

'I'm not the type to stick by Dad if he's killed them.' She shook her head. 'But if he hasn't? No, I still don't think so. Anyway, he still has Dan's family. Dad should be thankful for that.'

'Don't you want family, Jane?'

'Dan's invited me to meet Reba. I don't think of myself as being very child-friendly but I'm looking forward to it. Have you met her?'

'Yes, briefly. I didn't have a police dog or a uniform, so apparently she thought I was really boring.'

'That's funny,' she laughed. It was an unguarded moment and she continued to look amused by it as she carried on talking. 'I never imagined Dan with kids. I always thought he'd be single, with an apartment full of gadgets and the social life to go with it. He was one with the get-rich-quick plans, but instead of that he's now settled. I saw his wife, too, and she's really pretty.' Goodhew saw her lean slightly to her right, to take a sneaky peek at her reflection in the side of a saucepan. She promptly tidied her hair, stroked across her eyelids with the tips of her fingers, then blinked as if to freshen her eyes.

It seemed such a normal thing to do – good to see, he thought – but then he spoke again and ruined the moment. 'Who else knew about Marshall's assault on Becca?'

She barely reacted. 'Mum, Jackson and me – that's all I know of. I was thrilled when I saw what had happened to him.'

'Really?'

'He totally deserved it.'

'Hang on, Jane, you weren't worried? What if your dad *had* found out what Marshall had done to Becca?'

'Dad didn't kill Marshall. He wouldn't have planned it like that. He would have just gone and done it. In fact, who would hate anyone enough to do that and yet still spend all that time planning it?'

He opened his mouth to reply that he didn't know, but instead he now saw that the answer was very clear. He jumped to his feet and she stood up, too. 'I'm sorry,' he muttered, 'I have to go.'

She followed him to the front door. 'Did I say something important? Is it something about my dad?'

'No,' he reached for the door catch but delayed a moment to reassure her, too. 'It's not about your dad – he's a line of inquiry, that's all. I'll come back and take a statement from you as soon as I can. And if you think of anything else . . .' He closed his small notebook and was in the process of slipping it in his pocket.

'Yeah, yeah, I have your card,' she said. She paused. 'What is it?'

He closed his eyes and played back the call between Genevieve Barnes and the emergency services. *A card on the ground.*

'That card your mother gave Becca? You said it was just before she died?' He nodded, encouraging her to acknowledge that she knew what he meant.

'What about it?'

'Can you describe it, Jane?'

'I still have one.' She shot out of the room and returned with a small leather wallet. She opened it so that the notes section gaped and slipped her finger and thumb inside, retrieving a grubby business card. The lettering was in red and fuchsia and, sure enough, the words *Student Services* jumped out at him.

'You travelled to Cambridge with little more than you stood up in, so why would you keep a card like that?'

She handed it to him.

'Turn it over. Becca wrote on the back. It was a joke; she said everyone should have a business card, so she made that one for me on the back of one of hers. I kept it because it's the only thing I have left with her handwriting on it.'

He flipped it over, and smiled when he read what it said: *Jane Osborne – Smaller but smarter.*

Chapter Forty-three

MR AND MRS Jackson lived just out of town in a street called The Pightle, at an address that Sheen had pulled from his memory without the need to double-check. 'Pightle's a marvellous word to use in Scrabble; it means a small place,' he'd explained.

And when Goodhew arrived, he'd found himself standing outside a bungalow that looked no bigger than a double garage. A modest home by any standards. The garden was also small, almost half of it devoted to flower beds filled with a display of well-behaved annuals. Impatiens and begonia spilled from hanging baskets on either side of the door, with no sign of a dead-head amongst them. The interior of the house reminded him of a holiday chalet, an effect helped by the row of three miniature blue-and-white beach huts on the windowsill. Goodhew suspected these were toothbrush holders.

Mr Jackson was asleep in the only armchair when Goodhew arrived. Mrs Jackson finished making tea while her husband still dozed.

'He's been prescribed painkillers for his back, and they're knocking him sideways.' She spoke slowly and every word seemed carefully considered. 'A policeman contacted us earlier and, as we told him, we haven't seen Gregory all this week.'

'When did you see him last?' Goodhew sat down at one end of a small two-seater sofa. She sat next to him, both of them facing her husband. Goodhew then took a sip of his tea: it tasted oddly bleachy, as though the water had been standing in the kettle too long.

'A couple of weeks ago now. We met him on the day he was released from prison, and he's been home twice since then.' He noticed the way she seemed careful with every detail. 'Have you spoken to his parole officer?'

'A colleague has, who passed back the message that you had some concerns, nothing else.'

'We've noticed signs,' she confessed.

'But specifically?'

'We visited Greg a couple of times each year while he was in prison. We would have been happy to go more often, but that seemed to be enough for him.' She sipped her tea but her eyes never left Goodhew. 'It's inevitable that he would change in that time, but he became so . . . disconnected. I thought he was struggling, mentally and, even more after his release, he was always obsessing about his conviction. So we contacted his parole officer because we wanted to make sure he received the support he needed.'

'What kind of support?'

'Someone to talk to . . . maybe a doctor.'

That was just the sort of vague concern that would have been duly noted and filed. The comment *I think he might need to talk to someone* was never going to stay on any parole officer's radar when nearly everyone else on his caseload would have benefited from counselling. The parole office probably received these kind of messages all the time, and there were never the resources available to follow up any but the most worrying.

'It was the prison sentence that did it, of course,' she continued. 'I'm not saying it was wrong, but in all honesty we were never sure whether he was guilty or not.'

Without opening his eyes, her husband suddenly spoke up. 'Of course, he always had it in him. We'd seen him lose his temper in the past.'

'Not against women, though,' she said.

'How would we know, Joan?' He sighed deeply and manhandled the arms of the chair until he had pulled himself into a sitting position. 'He's been an adult for over twenty years, love, and when you say he became disconnected, you mean from us. He was already troubled, and we don't know whether he was better or worse with other people than with us, do we?'

'No, I don't suppose we do,' she replied.

Her husband turned to speak to Goodhew, instead. 'We have two sons and they've had the same upbringing, but with two different outcomes. Two different personalities, almost from birth. A seed can fall on fertile ground and still grow towards the thistles, Detective.'

'Just say what you mean,' she muttered.

He gave Goodhew the sharpest of looks. 'You know exactly what I mean, don't you?'

'I do,' he nodded, and considered the little he knew about Greg Jackson. 'And these thistles you refer to aren't people, are they?'

'No.'

'Thoughts, maybe, or perhaps something more?'

'I'd call them core values. Things that seem right to him that don't add up for Joan and me. We saw his qualities, too: he was a handsome lad, bright – probably even brighter than his brother – and so creative.'

Joan cut in: 'He's a skilled carpenter, you know.'

'But bitter because he never made it as an architect. Even when they were kids, if you gave them a pound each, his brother would be thrilled, but Greg would wonder why he hadn't been given more. He always finds the world against him. And, sadly, the blame is never his. We still hope he'll find his turning point.'

'See the light, perhaps,' she added. 'People find it at their darkest moments.'

Goodhew guessed these two weren't so much the type of couple who finish one another's sentences as the type to have discussed the subject matter so frequently that they had settled into a comforting rhythm of familiar words and platitudes.

'Where do you think he is now?'

'We have no idea,' Mr Jackson replied, 'but he isn't the type to do anything stupid.'

'To himself, you mean?' Goodhew's tone made the question sound unintentionally loaded, and Jackson stiffened. Any moment now, they would realize that his visit here hadn't been primarily motivated by any concern for their son. He glanced from one to the other, deciding they were honest people even if they were lying to themselves about their son. 'OK, we do have one cause for alarm.' He said it as though he was reluctantly sharing a confidence, when in truth he was only stalling for time.

Joan looked anxiously at her husband to check if he'd appreciated the sudden gravity of this moment. He had, so she turned back to Goodhew, who found himself pinned by the stares of both parents. The timing seemed good, so he saw his opening and jumped at it.

He turned a little more towards Joan. 'We think your son is armed, ready to attack the person he believes put him in prison.'

Her hands lay in her lap, her fingers clasping each other a little tighter. In Goodhew's peripheral vision, nothing else moved.

'Who?' she breathed.

He took his gamble. 'He made threats before he disappeared, involving torture, gardening wire and pliers.'

From the corner of his eye, Goodhew saw Mr Jackson grip the arm of the chair again, a sudden snatch for support. Goodhew turned sharply in his seat. 'Tell me, Mr Jackson. You say he isn't the type to do anything stupid, but is he also the type to let old scores go unsettled?'

'No. At the end of seven years, you're meant to cancel any debts.' If it was a quote, it was one that Goodhew failed to recognize. 'That had no effect on him, though,' Jackson's father added. 'As you can tell, my son and I don't share the same outlook.'

'We're looking at the possibility of carefully planned revenge. Disablement, torture, possibly death.'

To Goodhew's left, Joan drew a sharp breath.

'Do you think your son capable of planning that way?' he asked.

'No,' she replied, but any further words were immediately drowned out by her husband's.

'He might not follow it through, Detective, but he would have considered and refined that plan in minutest detail. In his eyes, at least, without the shedding of blood there is no forgiveness. I have some idea of the life he lives within his own mind; and I realize he fantasizes about revenge. I hoped he wouldn't follow it through.'

'And if he does . . . please help us find him.' Goodhew's eyes met Mr Jackson's and he held his gaze firmly. 'It could save your son – or someone else.'

Jackson hesitated and Goodhew waited for him to connect these latest words with the description of Paul Marshall's murder that already existed in the public domain. But Mr Jackson's thoughts were clearly following a different path, as his head turned towards the window.

Chapter Forty-four

GOODHEW WAITED WITH Mr and Mrs Jackson until two uni-
formed officers came to relieve him. He didn't recognize either
of them, but passed on the relevant details and slipped away as
quickly as possible, glad to break free of the pained silence that
had overtaken Greg Jackson's parents.

Marks had been the first person Goodhew had rung, updat-
ing him on the conversations with both Jane Osborne and the
elder Jacksons. By the time he returned to Parkside, part of him
expected to find Marks's office empty but, as Goodhew turned
aside from East Road, he glanced up and spotted his boss standing, sentinel like, at the window.

The corridors were deserted and, between the front desk and
reaching Marks's office, Goodhew encountered no one. 'Mr Jackson senior believes that it's from the same roll,' he said, as he
passed the evidence bag across the desk. Marks straightened the
clear pouch so that it sat squarely in front of him. The three-inch
strip of wire that had looked so nondescript on the garage floor
now held the potential to turn their investigation around.

Through the plastic, Marks poked one end with his finger. 'Forensics are already sending someone up to collect it. In theory they may be able to determine whether it came from the same roll of wire, or else spot if the same wire cutters were used on the wire that tied Marshall to that tree. How confident are you, Gary?'

Goodhew pulled up the spare chair and sat himself directly opposite Marks. They both eyed the evidence bag. 'Jane Osborne asked me why anyone would plan so vigorously to kill someone else – why not just do it. She was right to point that out. Greg Jackson had seven years of festering in which to plan how to inflict sufficient pain to get his full revenge.'

'But Paul Marshall was the wrong man.'

'Jackson obviously didn't think so when he grabbed him. Marshall was a sadistic rapist, who had already attacked Becca, so when Jackson heard about the attack on Andie . . .'

'Yes, it's easy to see how he jumped to the wrong conclusion.'

'Or he assumed Marshall knew the truth.'

'But none of this is evidence, Gary.'

'I went to Jackson's parents in the hope that I'd be able to nudge something free. I gave them a few details regarding the attack on Marshall, but speaking as though it hadn't yet happened.'

Marks rotated the evidence bag through ninety degrees. 'And this is what fell out?'

'Pretty much. There's still no sign of him?'

'Not yet. We have as many people as we can on it. The next option will be a public appeal.'

'What can I do to help find him?'

Marks shook his head. 'Forget Jackson for now, and just show me Becca Osborne's card.'

Goodhew slipped the fuchsia and red business card from his wallet.

Marks held it at arm's length to focus, a habit he'd only developed in recent months. 'So she thinks Becca may have been carrying one similar to this the day she died?'

'I'm going to show Genevieve Barnes, just in case she recognizes it. I phoned her on the way back. She has a lunch break at midday, so I'm meeting her then.'

Marks handed the card back to him, 'OK, then.' He reached across to the end of his desk and, for the first time, Goodhew saw a familiar pile of papers. 'I had these brought down from Kincaide's desk; I wanted to check the progress on these bank records. Michael's currently at Andrew and Karen Dalton's house and office, where they're taking photos and packing up any potential evidence. But I want it done by this afternoon, as we can't keep the Daltons out forever. In fact, I have officers in every direction, so it's unusual for you to be the only one sitting still.'

He slid the papers towards Goodhew. 'Have you looked at these at all?'

'I had a glance at some of the most recent, but I didn't want to interfere with any work Michael had already done.'

'Or it was a bit dull-looking, perhaps?'

Goodhew screwed up his nose. 'There was a bit of that, too.' He noticed several envelopes under the pile that he didn't think he'd seen before. 'Are those replies from the banks?'

'A few have come in but so far they're all a dead loss. We haven't found one bank that can identify any potential accounts that may have been used by either Mary Osborne or used to hide her money.'

'But there's still whatever the older bank statements can tell us. How far back can we go with what's there?'

'Pretty much as far as you like.'

'How about around the time of Becca's death?'

'And before.' Marks pushed the pile towards him. 'There you go.' He checked his watch. 'You have a couple of hours still before noon.'

The bank statements ran into hundreds of pages. Goodhew had already scanned the last six months but without anything piquing his interest. It was 10.15 now, so he didn't have two hours; closer to one by the time he drove to Addenbrooke's.

The whole pile looked daunting; he loved figures and logic, but hated dealing with money. Or was he looking at it the wrong way? He carried the collection of pages back to his desk, then placed his palm firmly on the top of the stack, and slid the pile around until the documents were fanned across the entire width of the desk. Spending patterns wouldn't help.

He walked to the water cooler, then back again, and stood with his back to the window, staring at the desktop.

Patterns. What *did* he know?

A new wave of tiredness hit him, but he wasn't about to stop and consider how little sleep he'd actually had. Neither was he prepared to sit and blindly look through several hundred sheets of paper. He smiled wearily. *Blindly look:* that didn't sound right. He took a deep breath, turned to the window and pressed his forehead against the glass.

He stared down at Parker's Piece. It was really nothing but a rectangle of grass, but sometimes, like now, its timelessness anchored him.

There were many days, like today, when a steady trickle of pedestrians and cyclists crisscrossed its open space, but little else happened there. But go back far enough and there were sketches of 15,000 people sitting down to celebrate Queen Victoria's coronation in that same space. And, of course, YouTube footage of the music festivals that rattled his flat's windows for one weekend in July each year.

All of those things created patterns: patterns of activity and congestion – and, most of all, patterns of spending. And the same thing would apply in reverse. He turned back and the pile looked just as daunting, except now he would look at it in the light of what he did already know. He knew the date when Becca had died, the dates of the trial, and the dates of every other key event that could be considered to belong to the Osborne family.

He dropped into his chair, then began investigating from a year before Becca's murder, and made notes of each occurrence of one single item: *Money in.* Mary had paid herself a regular wage. He made a note to apply for the requisition of the KADO Employment bank accounts, although he was confident that Marks would already have that in hand. The other amounts, low in value and appearing only sporadically, were sales of Gerry's sculptures. Sponsorship from an arts foundation came in one lump sum; it and a few very modest speaker fees had been paid via bank transfer, and were clearly described.

He'd gone just one month past the date of Becca's murder when the taxi arrived to take him to Addenbrooke's. He carried a section of the pages along with him and, by the time he was dropped at the front entrance of the hospital, he had formulated the beginnings of a list. He'd drawn three columns: 'event', 'amount' and 'description'. On most lines the date and amount only were noted, but every few lines the corresponding chronological milestone was logged, too. So far he'd marked three: Becca's death, Jackson's arrest, Jackson's trial.

He closed the notebook, slipped it into his pocket and headed through the long hospital corridors to Costa Coffee, where he found a vacant table.

GOODHEW RECOGNIZED GENEVIEVE Barnes from images that had appeared in the newspapers during Jackson's trial. She seemed to have aged by more years than had actually passed from then until now. Her complexion had an outdoorsy ruddiness but it wasn't a healthy enough glow to mask the haggard look of worry that accompanied her.

'Hi,' she said, as she shook his hand. Her manner was refreshingly straightforward. 'You're the officer who met with my husband.'

'He told you, then.'

'We've had a struggle undoubtedly, so the least we could do was be honest with one another.' She had a very direct gaze and didn't seem aware that she was scrutinizing him as intently as she appeared to be. 'Have you discovered something?'

'There is an ongoing investigation and once that concludes, we will contact you.'

'That's not all, I hope.' Her eyes flickered continually and she seemed to read his expression as closely as she must have read Jackson's. He therefore thought he would know immediately if the business card meant anything to her. 'I mean that's not the only reason you're here. You said you had something to show me?'

He took his wallet and held it, partly opened, as he spoke. 'I have a card here. It is similar to one that Rebecca Osborne was given on the day of her death.' He took it from its pocket and placed it in her hand, all in one move. 'Please tell me if you recognize it.'

Her fingers jolted as if a shock of electricity had run through them. She nodded slowly a couple of times. 'Yes,' she whispered, then continued staring down at it for a few seconds more, with her head bowed. Emotion had flushed her cheeks an even deeper red.

'Do you understand what this means?' She shut her eyes. 'I could never have properly described this card but, now that I've seen it, I *know* this is what I saw. This is the answer to seven years . . .' The words caught in her throat, and silently she began to cry. The tears slipped from her tightly closed eyes, some falling on to her lap, the others on to the grey tabletop. 'Seven years of feeling doubted . . . of doubting myself.' Goodhew grabbed a couple of serviettes from the counter behind him, took Becca's card from her and pressed the tissues into her hand instead.

She looked up for a moment, her face crumpled with anguish, and he cursed the stupidity of arranging to meet her in such a public place. 'I'm sorry. Maybe we should go somewhere quieter.'

She shook her head. 'No, it's fine,' she murmured, and she didn't seem to care that she'd been sobbing openly. She clutched the ball of damp tissue in her fist. 'I've remembered something. A man's foot. He stepped closer to my face as I fell forward. Then he went the other way, back into the house. It was never Jackson. He didn't do it.'

Chapter Forty-five

GOODHEW HELD BECCA'S card in one hand, turning it over as he explained it to Marks. He had almost phoned the DI from the taxi on his way back, but decided to wait as he wanted to see his expression. Now he was in front of his boss's desk, and looking straight at him, but was none the wiser. Marks was at his most inscrutable.

'Sir?'

'So the evidence *was* tampered with?'

'Yes, someone took the card.' Goodhew had said virtually the same thing a few minutes earlier, but now he guessed that Marks had moved on to thinking about the knife that had killed Becca and stabbed Genevieve Barnes. Or, more specifically, whether that had also been interfered with.

But it took another couple of minutes still before Marks was ready to voice his thoughts. 'That knife *was* deliberately mislabelled for forensics,' he said finally, 'and, because of that, we couldn't prove the chain of evidence. It was therefore disallowed.' He was speaking almost to himself, but with total certainty.

'Who would have done that – and why?'

Marks seemed to consider this carefully, but in the end his expression flickered till his gaze fell squarely on Goodhew. 'I don't know. Perhaps I made a mistake, because I was distracted.' He double-blinked. 'Forget the knife for now,' he urged, seeming oblivious to the fact that he was the only one who had mentioned it.

Goodhew pushed the bank statements back across the desk towards his superior. 'One thing jumps out, sir,' he said, and tapped at a few notes he'd written in summary across the front page. 'Gerry Osborne received some arts funding and some critical recognition but, until the publicity surrounding Becca's death, he had never earned a penny. He sold some small pieces, it's true, but never enough to cover his costs. As a result, the accounts steadily dwindled.'

Marks read the summary but then flicked through to the detail and cross-checked several minor points. He stopped when he was satisfied. 'Go on, then.'

'If you check the months after Becca's death hit the headlines, after the press had jumped all over it with that whole *tortured artist* angle, it was only then that the sales and exhibitions start to come in.'

'Unless he's just under-reported income for the benefit of his accounts?'

'I don't think so. The amount he charged for individual pieces rose sharply, while before then he wouldn't have made a living even if he'd sold all of them.'

'I remember. We looked into the family finances during Becca Osborne's murder inquiry, and there had been family money inherited from Gerry's parents.'

Goodhew nodded. 'But it had shrunk considerably, till a year later, it was down to virtually nothing. He employed his son Dan as the sales started to come in. But by the time he bought back the house from Mary, he was left struggling again.'

'Sheen always pointed out that Gerry Osborne smashing that work of his, *Singular Fascination*, could be just a publicity stunt. I've never agreed, mind you, but maybe it did give his profile a boost just at the right moment.' Marks picked up his phone and tapped a four-digit extension number. 'Tom? Would you pop down with anything you have on Gerry Osborne's sculptures – I mean exhibitions, sales and the like. Pull out everything you can, but we're especially interested in anything that relates to actual sales of his work.'

He put the phone down. 'What do you think of his sculptures?'

'I don't know what any of it is, or what anyone would do with it.' Goodhew shrugged. 'That probably means it's good in someone else's eyes.'

'Apparently it is. And no one could have foreseen the effect of Becca's death on his sales. I doubt it's any more sinister than a sad case of any publicity being good publicity, and Dan Osborne being there with the foresight to seize hold of the moment. You could give the audit department a call, see what they think.'

'What audit department?' He already knew what audit department, so his actual question should have been *Why have I been wasting my time going through financial statements, when you have a trained auditor already doing so?*

'Fresh eyes and brains that know the people *behind* the figure work,' Marks said, reading Goodhew's thoughts with ease. 'If I'd asked you to do anything apart from looking at financial information, then you'd have been more than happy to go poking your nose in where it doesn't belong.'

A sharp rap on the office door interrupted them. It was Sheen in the unfamiliar surroundings of any office other than his own. 'Here you go,' he began. 'Copies, so you can keep them. I put this note on top. They used the same gallery every time, so I thought you might want to have their details handy.'

Marks glanced at the Post-it note, before passing it over to Goodhew.

Goodhew nodded. 'I'll follow it up,' he said and headed for the door, relieved to be setting his mind on something fresh.

Chapter Forty-six

THERE WERE FIVE art galleries in King's Parade, with The Sidgwick Gallery standing in the heart of them. The heat was now bouncing off the pavements and, by the time Goodhew had walked there from Parkside, he could feel the fabric of his shirt sticking to his back. His annoyance had cooled. He wasn't an auditor or an accountant, but that wasn't the mindset Marks had expected either he or Kincaide to use. By the time he pushed open the gallery door, he'd promised himself that he would apologize.

One of Gerry Osborne's works occupied the most prominent position. It was unmistakably his, but less violently angled than any of the other pieces Goodhew had seen. Instead this one curled upwards and drew the focus of his gaze towards the ceiling.

He headed towards the counter and waited for an assistant to waft into the room. In his experience, wafting staff were a sure sign that he was out of his cultural depth. But the man who eventually came through didn't float in silently, or seem at all offended by Goodhew's wilted appearance. He was small-statured, in his forties, ponytailed hair and wearing one earring.

Goodhew introduced himself, enquiring, 'Do you work here?'

'Yes.' He shook Goodhew's hand. 'I'm Carter, officially the artist in residence.'

'Painter?'

'That's right. The idea is that visitors can see the art while still in progress. It stimulates interest in the artist's work. Apparently.'

'Not in your case?'

'Turns out I can't stand them all looking over my shoulder, so I work out the back there until someone comes into the gallery. But even so, as an artist, it's the least isolated working experience I've ever had.'

'Is the manager available?'

'That's me, apart from Saturdays. I know the shop intimately, so try me.'

Goodhew pointed to the sculpture. 'What do you know about that piece?'

'The latest – and Gerry's best one, I think. It's less fractured, more harmonious and so saleable.'

'Who would be a customer for something like this?'

'It depends. We do have occasions where a visitor will fall for a piece and purchase it spontaneously. Or perhaps return several times first . . . although those are often the ones that don't go through with it at the last minute. We have a customer base scattered all over the world, often those who have visited us once in person and then continue to view the work via our website and online catalogues. We don't usually get to see where our items are finally displayed.'

'And Gerry Osborne has such a following, I take it?'

'Absolutely. And I know he's also received commissions for several high-concept commercial projects. Experienced collectors will understand how that strengthens an artist's portfolio, and ultimately makes their investment more secure.'

Goodhew fought to stop his eyes glazing over. He glanced at the other exhibits. 'Is this the only one he has with you at the moment?'

'Probably until his next show.'

'Will you normally contact his customers to invite them to attend an event like that?'

'We contact all names on our mailing list for every such event. And these days we provide a virtual tour of every exhibition for those living further afield. Sales of Gerry's work rarely come via that route, though. In fact, I don't even know the names of the main collectors of his art.'

Goodhew frowned. 'You mean they're anonymous? Surely you must know who takes delivery?'

Carter shook his head. 'The bulk of Gerry Osborne's sales come from his own contacts. The actual sale is made through this gallery, but his son Dan deals with the dispatch.' Carter must have spotted the look of query on Goodhew's face, and he continued. 'That's not so unusual. Some artists prefer to sell through a third party, while collectors may feel that purchase through a reputable studio adds kudos.'

Goodhew frowned. 'So they choose to insert an extra link into the sales chain? Isn't that just what everyone else in business is trying to avoid?'

'Artists, eh?' A small smile touched the man's lips. Carter then touched Goodhew's arm, directing him back towards the sales desk. 'This is just my personal opinion, but I sometimes think he buys the pieces himself.'

'Why?'

'Look at this.' He guided Goodhew to the doorway leading into the back room, where there were as many as twenty paintings hanging on the walls. 'These are mine and the best of them will appear in my next show. Also the best of them will hopefully sell. I can't afford to carry on if they don't, and I can't ever have them back if they do. The pieces in which I feel greatest pride are, sadly, the ones I may never get to see again. Damien Hirst repurchased much of his output.'

'Gerry Osborne's hardly in that league?'

'No, no, that's very true.' Carter suddenly seemed crestfallen, as though he'd instantly lost faith in his theory. 'The only money Gerry has comes from his sales, therefore he wouldn't be able to afford to – any more than I would.'

'So what made you suggest it?'

Carter gazed across at his current canvas, a view of the spiral stairs at Great St Mary's. Solid steps, crisp brickwork, and all of it bathed in sunshine. 'Probably because I dream of buying my own work back all the time,' he replied.

'So you assume the same thing about other artists, too?'

'Actually, no.' Carter's expression brightened a little. 'Maybe it isn't quite so far-fetched, then.'

'Then why suspect it of Osborne?'

Carter didn't seem to give any real thought to that question. Instead he just shrugged, and replied, 'I really have no idea.'

Goodhew doubted that Carter and Gerry Osborne approached art with the same mindset in any way at all. Goodhew's impression of Gerry was a man who loathed most things most of the time, and would therefore be happy to see his pieces go.

No, Carter's logic wouldn't apply easily to Gerry.

And yet.

And yet.

Goodhew went back to the new sculpture, labelled: *Rejoice, by Gerry Osborne* and Carter followed him into the shop.

'Were you here the night he smashed that other one?' Goodhew asked.

'*Singular Fascination?* Yes, people were circulating the main room, and I noticed Gerry standing there, looking distracted. He was just staring at it but his eyes looked glazed. The next moment, he attacked it. It was as if he was possessed, trying to haul it through here and away from the guests. He apologized to the Gallery the next day, and said it was no longer for sale.'

'So he kept it?' Goodhew asked, even though he thought he already knew the answer.

Carter straightened up and brightened again. 'No, he thought we still had it, but Dan had picked it up weeks before and stored it somewhere else, so his dad couldn't get hold of it.' He frowned suddenly. '*That's* why.' He stepped through into the back room again and picked up the phone. He paused, poised to dial a number. 'This is all legitimate, isn't it?' he asked.

'It really is.' Goodhew nodded. 'I can put you in touch with my DI if you'd like confirmation?'

'Suspicion is too draining, I try to avoid it.' Carter shook his head. 'That way of thinking wouldn't work in your job, I suppose.' Carter turned away slightly, his attention now focused on the phone call. Goodhew could just pick out the miniature sound of ringing at the other end, then the compressed sound of a man's voice. But, beyond the first 'Hello', it was impossible to hear what he said.

'Bill? Where's that storage yard you drop off at?' Carter listened for a few seconds. 'No, it's for art, so I need the same one that Dan and Gerry Osborne use.' More listening. 'Yes, I know you've told me before. I've just forgotten . . . don't worry, the address is fine . . . Thanks, smashing.'

Carter scribbled on the top sheet of a jotter block, then passed it to Goodhew. '*Yellow Box Secure Storage.*'

'Phone him back.'

'Why?'

'Ask him what's in it.'

'I've just pretended I wanted to rent one.'

'Well, unpretend then . . . or give me the number.'

Carter pressed redial on the handset, passed it to Goodhew, then grabbed it back and waved Goodhew away. 'He won't know you,' he hissed. 'Bill, me again. How much fits into it?'

Carter listened as the other man spoke, then replied. 'Yes, I need space for a whole collection.' More listening. 'Yes, yes, I see.'

Carter finished the call and looked at Goodhew. 'Wow, if Bill picked something up here, it went into that store. Gerry and Dan have bought nearly every piece.'

'Both of them?'

Carter smoothed the hair running into his ponytail and considered the police officer's question. 'I wouldn't actually know. But, out of the two of them, only Gerry loves the art and only Dan deals with the money.'

'Therefore Dan must be the one to know. He would have arranged for the collection and settled the bill with this gallery.'

'But why would he want to keep a lot of pieces he doesn't even like?'

Goodhew now felt sceptical; he had previously assumed that Dan worked for Gerry simply because of the enthusiasm that came through whenever he discussed his father's art. He said, 'I thought he was a fan.'

'It isn't love of the art that fuels Dan's enthusiasm. I see Lucian Freud written all over Gerry.'

'Meaning?'

'Dan seeks his father's approval, but Gerry's a man too enamoured with his own art to give his children what they need. That talent for sculpture is Gerry's golden child.'

Wafting or no wafting, Goodhew was out of his cultural depth now. Carter finished speaking and looked expectantly at Goodhew. It felt as though he anticipated the minimum of enthusiastic agreement, and even possibly a round of applause.

Goodhew shook Carter's hand. 'Thank you so much.' He left the gallery and hurried back to Parkside, reaching for his radio and mobile the moment he stepped outside.

Chapter Forty-seven

THERE HAD BEEN calm since Goodhew left. Jane had photographed the business card with the camera on her own mobile phone before she let him borrow it. She hoped Goodhew would bring it back, but he hadn't promised to. She understood, and figured she'd lost worse.

As he'd left her house, a wall of summer heat had pushed its way through the front door. Maybe it was only cold and dark within this particular mausoleum. She opened the back door and ventured on to the grass, heading to the sunny patch in the centre. She let the sun warm her right through but went back inside before her jumper left her uncomfortably hot.

As she showered, she found her thoughts constantly settling on her niece Reba. Or, at least, on the thought of a niece. Jane didn't know if she was in any way maternal, and she had always found the idea of children completely alien. But, even so, the thought of meeting Reba was calling loudly to her.

She checked the time and found it was almost 12.30.

She hesitated, phone in hand; her invitation to meet Reba was set for tomorrow, and she didn't want to start off badly. But a new feeling of urgency had sprung up and she didn't want to wait.

She called their number. It was Dan's wife Roz who answered.

'Hi, it's Jane . . . um, Dan's sister. I was just wondering whether I could drop by. I mean in a minute or two.'

'Dan's not here. He's off with his dad. Sorry, *your* dad, obviously.' Roz paused awkwardly. 'Reba's excited about meeting you.' In the background, the child overheard heard her name and asked her mum who was on the phone. 'Dad's sister Jane.'

'My new aunty Jane?'

'That's right, my love. Sorry.'

That *Sorry* sounded as though it had been aimed into the receiver, so Jane assumed it was for her. 'It's OK. I was just wondering whether I could pop round right now. Just to say hello. To break the ice with Reba before we sit down for tea tomorrow?'

Roz gave a little 'Oh' of surprise, then spoke to Reba next. 'Jane says she can come by and say Hi now.' Reba's response was a gleeful *Yes*. 'That would be lovely. How soon?'

'Ten minutes?'

Jane changed into her only remaining clean clothes – black combat trousers and a grey vest – and hurried off to Dan's house. Another ten minutes after that, she was sitting, mug in hand, watching her little niece cut and shape a plasticine flower. 'My granddad makes great big sculptures, but not flowers. Do you know my granddad?'

Roz was in the room, but not hovering over her child the way Jane had seen some mothers do. Not sure how much she was allowed to say, Jane looked questioningly at Roz, who nodded.

'Your granddad is my daddy.'

'And he's my daddy's daddy. Is that why you're my aunty?'

Jane smiled. 'That's right.'

The house phone rang just then. Roz checked the display, smiled and picked up the cordless handset from the table. 'Hi . . . She's here right now.'

Roz's grip on the phone visibly tightened, and Jane pretended to take closer interest in Reba's bloom. 'What sort of flower is this, then?'

'A pink sunflower.'

Roz moved towards the hall. 'Reba was excited.' She lowered her voice but the urgent whisper carried more clearly still. 'Dan, listen, how did I know it would be such a big deal?'

Reba glanced up at Jane. 'My dad says you're trying to steal the house but you won't get it.'

'Your granddad's house?'

'Uh-huh. Granddad doesn't use it.' She found herself smiling encouragement at Reba. The little girl didn't smile back; her tone was now too earnest for that. 'Daddy says one day we'll own the whole world, and the people we don't like will get eaten alive.'

'Wow, eaten alive!'

'Don't worry, Jane, I'll tell Daddy that I like you.'

From the corner of her eye she saw Roz returning.

'Well, Reba, I like you too. And you have a lovely house here, much better than that old one I'm staying in.'

Roz put the handset back on its stand. 'That was Dan.' Roz looked uncomfortable.

'I guess it's not a good time?'

'I'm sorry . . . something to do with your dad, I guess. If you're still OK for tea tomorrow, though . . .'

'Sure,' Jane replied. Roz was clearly making an excuse, though she doubted it was connected with her father, and she wondered why Dan had a problem with her being here at a time when he wasn't.

Reba stared up at them both with a frown. 'Mummy, I was asking Jane about Daddy's other house. Is it haunted?'

Roz seemed too distracted to pay full attention to what her daughter had just said. 'There aren't any ghosts here, darling,' she replied. 'I'm sorry, Jane,' she said, and her embarrassment seemed genuine enough.

Jane clambered to her feet, winking at Reba. 'The best ghosts are in *Scooby Doo*, you know. Will I see you tomorrow?'

Reba grinned. 'Unless the monster gets you first.'

Chapter Forty-eight

KADO EMPLOYMENT OCCUPIED both floors. Inside the building was an internal staircase joining the two levels, but the fire door at each end had been locked by the police, in order to keep their search of each storey as separate as possible. In fact, downstairs had been handed back to the Daltons late the same morning. Officially they could now reopen and continue trading until the almost inevitable fallout from Marshall's death brought down the shutters for the last time. But as they hadn't been left with a single PC, telephone, diary or timetable, opening the front doors was clearly pointless and the shop front had remained locked and unlit.

Upstairs had been handed back in the last half hour, and the Daltons' subsequent comings and goings had been only via the external rear door, which stood at the top of a rusted-metal fire escape. Kincaide already knew this and had parked at the furthest point away where he still had a clear view of the backs of the Milton Road shops. He would know when anyone left the premises.

Karen and Andrew had arrived in separate vehicles and it therefore seemed logical to Kincaide that one might leave before the other. He'd kept his distance and waited. He didn't care which of them he got to speak to, as long as it was just one of them.

Now Andrew Dalton was leaving. Kincaide watched him slip out into the traffic without any backward glance towards his wife or the business, his attention focused only ahead. Kincaide pulled out of his parking space and into the rear alley, leaving his car blocking in her Lexus.

The door at the top of the fire escape was still ajar, and he hoped he could make it up there before she spotted him and had the chance to slam it in his face.

In fact, she didn't notice him at all, and he stood in the door-way for a long minute, watching as she crouched to collect some fallen items of unused stationery.

'We didn't leave you much stuff, did we?'

He could sense that he'd startled her, but she calmly rose to her feet and crossed towards him without any sign of nervousness. 'What do you want?'

'You and Drew are in the middle of it now. It's not like last time, and it's not going away. Don't think of trying to black-mail me.'

She'd halted just a couple of feet in front of him, pursing her lips. 'We'll do what's necessary to minimise damage.' She blinked, slow and reptilian, with her lids sliding shut, then pausing a moment before snapping open again.

'You don't have the hold on me that you may think you do.'

'You used our girls, Michael, so—'

'Stop there.' He took a step closer. 'I'm going to be specific here. Yes, I slept with two women who both happened to advertise on your site. I was a new DC who made a small mistake, which you and Drew then used against me.'

'You phoned us, remember?'

'Yes, to warn you.'

'Right, and to make sure your name disappeared from our records. What we did was mutually beneficial.'

'And now it's not. So don't even try to implicate me. When you wanted that evidence destroyed, I thought I'd helped Jackson avoid a life sentence.' Was she even listening? He raised his voice. 'I thought he was guilty, but did you know all along that he wasn't the killer?'

'Of course not. That card would have pointed straight at us. We thought we were being set up.'

'So who killed her?'

'How should we know? But it wasn't us, and we weren't going down for it either.' She smiled, and it was an expression that said *So that's settled now.*

She reminded him of his wife just then.

'You arrogant fucking bitch.' He moved closer and grabbed her arm as she tried to step away from him. 'I'm not altering or destroying anything more for you.'

'How are you in a better position to negotiate than before?' She smirked. 'You still have a career, and it's still there to be ruined.'

'You have had –' he shoved her away with both hands – 'all you –' *shove* – 'will have –' *shove* – 'from me.' With each push she stepped back, but her expression remained defiant. The next time his hand reached out it wasn't to push her. Instead he snatched a handful of her hair and pulled her towards him.

He held her close with her face only inches from his own. 'Are you one of those women who doesn't know when enough is enough?' He jerked at the hair closest to her scalp, shaking her and pushing his face right into hers. 'You and Andrew have fucked it up. Between the police and the tax office, you are losing everything – and you will not take me down with you.'

'Andrew will kill you,' she hissed.

'No, Karen. I am never going to risk what I have. And the second I think you are a threat, I will tell Jackson what you did. He went down to save your skin, not mine. He'll make you *both* pay.'

He gave her one last push and turned away. She stumbled back against one of the tables. Its feet squealed in protest but she stopped herself from falling. He didn't look back, though, and the door slammed in his wake.

The din they had created was more than enough to cover the muted sound of the internal door to the staircase being unlocked from the other side. And Karen Dalton was facing in the wrong direction to notice the handle begin to move.

Chapter Forty-nine

AFTER JANE HAD let herself back into the house, her hands trembled as she held the kettle under the tap, making ripples spread across the surface of the water that filled it. Then she watched it boil and practised her breathing: in through the nose and gently out through the mouth.

The steam from the spout rose first in lazy ribbons, then started to thicken. It skimmed the wall, the dampness feeding the mould that blackened the grout between the tiles, with condensation forming beads of wet on the painted wall further along. And it was when it passed over the glass front of the crockery cupboard that she saw his reflection. He was watching her from the hallway.

'Hello, Dan.' She turned slowly. 'When did you get here?'

'I came as soon as I discovered you had been to my house. I invited you tomorrow, not today.'

The kettle clicked itself off. 'Tea?'

'No. Actually, I think you should come away from the kettle, Jane. Out of the kitchen is probably best.' He indicated for her to move towards the front of the house. His tone sounded calm, reasonable even, but from that she knew that she should do what she was told.

Despite an absence of ten years, she could still read him well. She remembered following after him through school, where he'd been popular and sporty and ambitious. He looked like the kid who had it all sorted. She'd trailed behind, unremarkable and inept.

At school he'd seemed a stranger; at home he'd been her brother – the perfect public image didn't exist there. She thought she'd known his flaws, and empathized with the disgust he felt towards their parents.

Now her heart began thumping.

Of the three of them, she'd usually been the angry one. The exception came only in the moments when Dan's temper flared. Logic would leave, reasoning with him became impossible, and always the safest route had been to stay clear. Jane had been careful to watch out for the warning signs: Dan brooding, introspective, and festering over some perceived slight.

She could feel that same energy coming from him now. Like he was about to pounce.

Despite its probable futility, she needed to say something to him. But her head was empty of words. A silent vacuum. He stopped just short of the front door and turned to look at her. 'I came to talk to you. I actually *want* to talk to you.'

Despite that comment, he said nothing else at first.

She heard herself speak. 'Do you have a plan, Dan?' It had been an old phrase of hers, and she hoped its familiarity would strike some kind of note.

There wasn't even the glimmer of recognition. 'Shhh, I need to think,' he told her.

'I thought you wanted to talk?'

She noticed him move only a fraction of a second before his fist connected with her abdomen. It then felt as though she folded in on herself, and the floor rose to meet her. He'd never hit her before. Ever. But she had no doubt now he wanted her dead.

Had this version of her brother always been the one fighting for supremacy? Had the infrequent rages been his true face after all? She tried to think but she realized how much she must have forgotten, too. Her whole life spent in this house seemed to be fading.

She gasped for air and gradually her lungs refilled. She looked up at him and watched her brother's expressions run through a gamut of tiny changes. She wondered whether she'd become just a shadow in his memory, too. His head tilted to one side and he stared deep into the corner of the hall. His lips were parted and sometimes twitched with ghosts of the words running through his thoughts. An almost imperceptible tremor came at the end. In his mind he'd thought it through, reached the end, and said no.

Do you have a plan, Dan?

His eyes flickered, refocused elsewhere and his brain ran the cycle again.

Do you have a plan, Dan?

'Tell me when I can speak.'

'I'm still thinking.'

Stubborn Dan; she remembered that now. His terms. At his speed. Well, her last minutes alive would not be spent like that.

'Campbell will be watching, and he'll see us if we go out. He'll already know you're here now.'

'Shut. Up. No one saw me, Jane. No one saw me.' His weight shifted from foot to foot. 'Now be quiet.'

She ignored him. 'Why kill Becca? That's what I want to know.' He kicked out then, but she managed to move aside just enough to protect her ribs with one arm. It still hurt. 'Becca loved you,' she persisted.

'Becca was our mother all over again.'

'No, Dan, she wasn't. You're kidding yourself. Becca was warm and generous and sad. Becca was *sad*. Just tell me why you killed her.'

She thought he'd kick her again then, but he refocused. 'You have put that well. Yes, she was all of those, wasn't she? And most of the time she hated Mum too.' He glanced up the staircase. 'It's falling apart,' he said, but she was sure he didn't just mean the house. His demeanour had settled into an artificial calm. 'Mum was going to disappear, just start over and leave the rest of us fucked. I'd already told her I needed help with money, but she turned on me. I wanted to kill her at that moment, and the feeling never went away.

'She told me I had no right to anything.'

He continued to stare up at the vaulted ceiling above the staircase. 'This house belongs to this family – not her family but Dad's. And we have spent every fucking day in her shadow. It wasn't her moment any more. I had every right.'

'To kill her?'

'Every right to be free from her. Every right to stop her taking any more.'

'What about Becca, Dan?'

'I planned to kill Mum on the night she left. I was the only one who knew what she had planned until one day she drank too much, and screamed it all at Becca. And Becca ran crying to me. I needed no one else to know.'

'And two people can only keep a secret properly when one of them is dead?'

'In the original quote there were three, and two had to die.' Without warning he stopped speaking then. 'Come upstairs, Jane.'

She didn't move.

'It's not about money, Jane. It's about the life they gave me compared to the one I ought to have. Now move.'

She looked at him and saw only darkness.

And, at that moment, her mobile began to ring.

Chapter Fifty

GOODHEW DIALLED JANE Osborne's number the moment he stepped back out on to the pavement. It switched to voicemail. 'Ring me at once, Jane. Or get over to Parkside. It's urgent.'

He pulled up Marks's number, then changed his mind. Instead he sent Jane a follow-up text. *I'm coming to your house right now.*'

He was now about the same distance from Parkside as from Pound Hill, but in opposite directions. He grabbed his radio then started running towards Parkside, darting between cyclists and pedestrians.

He shouted for a car to go to Pound Hill, then he felt his mobile buzz and saw a text box sent from Jane's number flash on to the screen: *'Going to see Dad at his studio.'* 'Scratch that,' he told the dispatcher and redirected the car to the studio in Newnham Road, though he didn't even know the number.

'Patch me through to PC Gully.'

'Where are you, Sue?'

'Parkside, just got in.'

'Find Marks. It's urgent.' People were turning as he passed them in the street.

'Where are you?'

'Regent Street,' he shouted. 'I'm on my way there now. Find all the Osbornes, and bring them in. Then get down to the back car park. We need to go.'

He cut off the call and ran out into the road, sprinting along the central white line and only heading back across to the pavement when he saw a clear run to Parker's Piece.

Five hundred yards ahead of him, a marked car pulled out from the side of Parkside, turned on its lights and sirens, then jumped the lights to race up East Road. He could still hear it in the distance as he pushed open the front door, then rushed straight through and out to the car park at the back.

Marks was waiting there with DC Young and PCs Gully and Wilkes. Goodhew stopped in front of them, breathing hard. 'Dan Osborne killed them.'

For a long moment no one moved. Evidence? Justification? The odds that Goodhew was totally and utterly wrong? All these were questions for which Marks had every right to demand answers.

Goodhew was grabbing another lungful of air to explain further, but Marks spoke first, barking instructions. 'Sue, Kelly, get to Pound Hill. Young, to Castle Street. Everyone's out after Jackson. There's no one else, dammit . . . Gary, come with me. I'm driving.'

The vehicles poured from the car park, turning right along East Road, just as the previous car had done. 'That first marked car was heading for Newnham Road, too.'

'I guessed. Who was it?'

'PC Jarvis. Get an update from him. He should be there about now.'

Marks wove the car through the other vehicles, jumping a 100-yard queue by cutting through oncoming traffic. They ran the next set of lights just as the radio operator spoke again. 'It's PC Jarvis. He's advised that there's just one male occupant at the address. State of intoxication.'

'ID?' Goodhew demanded.

'Gerry Osborne.'

'OK, we'll take Pound Hill. Advise PCs Gully and Wilkes they are not now required on this one.'

'Ouch, they won't thank you for that,' Marks commented. He had just made the left into Newnham Road, where he swung the car in a wide arc across the road, doubling back up Queen's Road.

'He's dangerous.'

'Spill, Gary.'

'It's that thing Kincaide often says: *Follow the money.* Becca's death gave Gerry Osborne's work sudden prominence, so prices went up, and Dan grabbed the opportunity to start working for his dad. He juggled the money around and managed to keep himself out of trouble. When he killed his mother he made sure he got his hands on her share of the money in cash. He's essentially been laundering that money through the gallery, buying pieces at high prices, pretending that they've been bought by a private buyer, then putting the money into Gerry's account.'

'Minus the gallery's commission.'

'But that's fine, because Gerry's pieces then garnered a reputation for having great sales potential. That translates into artificially higher prices commanded at the next exhibition. It is all the publicity and receipts from the gallery that make it look above board. But that's just the paper trail. Just look at Mary's body – even post-mortem he carried on inflicting damage on her.'

'That's frenzy, not control?'

'But it was carefully planned. It's only during the killing itself that his emotions overwhelmed him.'

'We'll need more than that to charge him.'

'But not to bring him in.'

Marks killed the siren before they turned into Pound Hill, then swung into the road itself. He took the turn at the bottom of the hill and noticed the lone figure of Campbell standing outside his flat. He was facing the Osborne house, but turned his head to look over his shoulder at them.

Goodhew jumped from the car.

'Is she there?' he shouted.

Campbell nodded, then his head seemed to swivel in slow motion as he followed Goodhew's dash towards the house.

Marks ran, too, towards the front door.

From inside Goodhew heard the sound of splintering wood. Marks banged on the door. Goodhew grabbed a broken fence post and ran round to one side of the house.

Neither of them heard the dispatcher asking for the nearest available car to attend suspicious activity reported at an address in Milton Road. Neither of them, therefore, heard PCs Gully and Wilkes respond.

GREG JACKSON HAD spent the night in the open. The night hadn't been so cold and part of him knew that this might be one of his last chances at freedom. Drew had rung him late. 'They'll be pulling you in. Nothing to worry about. It's OK to tell them about *Student Services;* they already know.'

But it wasn't all right. Not at all.

Drew and Karen had been his only support since prison, but he hadn't told them everything. Didn't tell them that once each week he had been visited by one of their girls: Andie. Blonde, hopeful and a little melancholy. Not so different from Becca, in some ways.

Andie had become the measure of one week to the next. It wasn't love. But it was a little bit of hope.

It had worked for both of them, until the week she didn't come. She'd sent a message: 'Sorry, I've given up.' He'd never been to her shared house, but knew where she lived. She wouldn't open the door, but one evening he spied her through a chink in the curtains, and he knew what *I've given up* might have meant.

Paul Marshall. Depraved Paul Marshall.

There had been a time with Mary when they'd played rough. Merely *played* rough.

But he'd already seen what Marshall had done to Becca. And now he'd seen it done to Andie. Where did cruelty like that end?

Jackson had slept on that thought, and he began to wonder whether that wasn't all. What if Marshall had come back and actually killed Becca? What if Marshall was the reason for Jackson's own seven years in jail? Marshall had to *know* what they'd all suffered.

Jackson shared none of these things with Drew, however. Instead he'd just explained that going to the police now wouldn't be an option. Drew and Karen were in a mess of their own, but Drew seemed to understand what Jackson needed too.

'I'll leave the spare shop key. Once the police have finished searching the building and it's empty, go in and you can stay upstairs. As soon as I can, I'll drive you somewhere out of town.'

But Jackson had arrived too soon. Karen was still in the building, and a car he didn't recognize was parked close to hers. He suspected the police at once. He waited out of sight for a minute, then decided to let himself into the downstairs shop. Partly to hide, but partly to slip up the internal stairs and find out who exactly was there.

Getting into the shop was fine, opening the internal door took longer, and in the end he found a screwdriver and encouraged it. He heard the voices the second he stepped on to the bottom step of the stairs. By the time he'd crept to the top, he understood exactly what every word meant.

Did you know all along that he wasn't the killer?

With Marshall he'd wanted to hear the truth, to decide at that moment whether he had the will to kill him. But it hadn't reached that point before the wire had severed Marshall's neck. In fact, Jackson still couldn't decide whether Marshall's death had punished him sufficiently or let him off. With Karen Dalton there was now no such debate.

She had to die.

GULLY AND WILKES pulled up on the pavement outside KADO Employment. It had been closed only for a few hours, yet the signs of a failed business were already evident. Lights off. Post lying on the mat.

'No sign of forced entry at the front of the property,' Gully reported back.

Kelly cupped her hands to the glass. 'The internal door's been forced, Sue, like the witness thought.'

'We're checking the rear now.'

A Lexus was still parked near the bottom of the fire escape.

Wilkes ran the PNC check. 'Belongs to Karen Dalton.'

Gully checked the ground-floor back door. Also secure.

Kelly meanwhile had already mounted the fire escape. She still hovered near the bottom, waiting for Gully to join her. Together they began climbing it.

'We shouldn't be doing it this way,' Sue whispered.

'And lose them when they shoot out through the front of the shop?'

'That's why we need backup.'

Kelly now stood close to the top.

'Can you hear anything?' Gully asked.

She made her decision then. If it was Greg Jackson in there, he was potentially dangerous. She radioed for support, then looked at Kelly. *Wait for me*, she mouthed. Halfway up, Kelly raised a finger. 'I can hear him now, he's shouting.'

'At her?'

'I guess.'

Gully reached the top, too, then stood back from the door and shouted, 'This is the police. Please open the door.'

The words had barely left her mouth when the door flew open wide, and Greg Jackson came tanking out.

GOODHEW RAISED THE fence post to smash his way in through a window at the side of the house. He scrambled into the room beyond, pulling his way past the shards of glass still in the frame. He was aware of his clothes snagging, but didn't slow down.

Dan's voice was clear. 'Let it go, Jane,' he was shouting.

Three strides across the room and Goodhew was in the hallway, where wooden debris littered the carpet. Above him the run of balusters had collapsed, and Jane hung clinging to a newel post as Dan struggled to prise her away.

'Stop!' Goodhew yelled. 'Let her go, Dan.'

Dan Osborne had heard, but his only response was a volley of swift punches to her head. She let go, then. There was no time to reach her. As the post slipped from her grasp, Dan kicked her in the legs, and Goodhew saw her fall.

He lunged forward, clumsily snatching for her.

He collapsed under her weight, then was stunned by the collision with the floor as they both crashed on to it. Jane landed awkwardly and he heard the unmistakable sound of a snapping bone.

He groaned, trying to move, but he was still pinned under her. 'Jane?' She lay very still.

On the floor above them a sash window slid up, and from outside he heard DC Young shouting, 'The building is surrounded. Open the door now.'

Then from another direction he heard more shouting, a crash, a scuffle. Silence.

Goodhew again tried to move his arm. 'Shhh, Gary, keep still,' Jane whispered. 'They've caught him. You mustn't move. Just in case.'

'In case what?'

'Spinal damage.'

'You think you've hurt your back?'

'No, *your* back. I had a better landing than I might have. I'm just trying to stop you moving.'

'Clever.'

'Smaller but smarter, you know. They're coming in to get us.'

'Just so you know, your card's still in my pocket.'

'Cheers.'

JANE HURT. EVERYTHING hurt: physical, emotional, everything. And she felt it totally. She started to cry but the tears felt good. Really good.

JACKSON'S LAST FEW seconds of freedom were a blur. He hit the external door hard, bursting out on to the metal platform at the top of the fire escape – and cannoning directly into two female officers. One stumbled; the other crashed aside through the corroded handrail.

But his path was clear. He headed further down the steps, half running, half tumbling. He had made it as far as the end of the parking space before he spotted the figure of a man.

Kincaide had returned.

Jackson's legs became leaden, moving slowly as Kincaide dashed from his car. The detective's body hit his, felling him before he'd even finished turning to run the other way.

Jackson's resistance was now minimal. He was spent.

He heard himself howling like an animal. 'You did this to me, you bastard. You and her.' He tried to point towards Karen, but his hands were already hauled behind him as the cuffs were snapped into place. Kincaide read him his rights, then stuffed him into the back of his car.

Kincaide then began speaking on the radio, while Jackson looked back out at what he'd just done.

The PC knelt beside her fallen colleague, and the sirens grew closer.

'Tell her what you did, Kincaide,' Jackson shouted. But his words were lost behind the glass. There was no chance she would hear him now.

IT TOOK A while to manoeuvre Goodhew on to the spinal-injury board. They'd immobilized his head and neck, so for a while his only view had been up at the newel post leaning over the edge of the landing above him. He realized all the paramedic's efforts would be wasted if it now fell down and killed him.

Gas and air was great. The paramedic was great, too – a big Geordie guy named Ian who'd promised to report on Marks's every move, only on the condition that Goodhew kept his head totally still.

'What's he doing now?' Gary asked.

'Same thing.'

'Pacing?'

'Aye, talking on his phone and pacing.'

'Find out, will you?'

'I can't leave you on your own. Whatever's keeping him out there must be major, though, or I'm guessing he'd already be in here.'

'If it was that big, he'd have gone.'

'No, he's injured, too.'

'How?'

'Your fella went for him. He's one of those guys they couldn't pin down without a fight. We're ready to load you up now. Your boss is going in the ambulance alongside you, buddy. We patched him up but he insisted on staying with you.'

Ian saw Goodhew wince, and offered him the gas and air again.

'No, I want to talk to my DI.'

They moved him into the ambulance first, where he had to ask Marks to come closer. Marks leant over till his face filled the centre of Goodhew's field of vision. His superior's colour had drained to grey.

'Who died, sir?'

'Karen Dalton. They've just recovered her body. Jackson strangled her.'

'There's someone else, too. I can see it on your face.'

Marks didn't answer immediately. The engine note changed, and Ian intervened. 'I'll need you to strap yourself in now, sir. We're about to move.' Marks retreated from view, and he still didn't reply.

Goodhew stared up at the over-lit ceiling. 'Sir, how will it help me to hear about it tomorrow or the next day?'

'Gully and Wilkes attended a suspect incident. It turned out to be Jackson.'

Goodhew felt his world tilt.

'She fell, Gary.' Marks took a deep breath.

Goodhew closed his eyes and waited for the next words to hit.

'Kelly fell from a fire escape. It broke her neck, so excuse us if we're now taking every precaution with yours.'

Goodhew had stopped listening at the words. *She fell, Gary.* He didn't speak until he was sure he could manage to control his voice. 'How's Sue?'

'Shocked – but she'll be OK.'

Goodhew asked Ian for more gas and air then, and used it to push his thoughts back to a safer distance.

Good night, Kelly, he whispered as the drugs took hold.

Epilogue

Two WEEKS EARLIER, some lorries had pulled on to Parker's Piece and, over the next few days, the winter ice rink began taking shape. So autumn had gone and Christmas approached.

Three months had slipped past him. He corrected the thought. He'd actually turned away from all but a few people for those three months. He'd watched the large marquees being erected over those several days, passing close by them as he walked twice daily between his flat and Parkside swimming pool.

Then this morning he'd stood at his flat window and watched the first of the skaters trying out the ice. He'd phoned his grandmother. 'Would you like coffee at the ice rink?'

She arrived within twenty minutes and didn't want coffee at all; apparently, for her, only hot chocolate or alcohol went well with winter sports. She wore a blue Fair Isle jumper covered in white dots and snowflakes. Goodhew wore a thick black jacket, and stuck with coffee. If anyone was judging by outward appearances alone, it might be hard to see how they were related.

'Have you decided anything yet?' she asked.

'I think so.' He pulled an envelope from his pocket and placed it on the table in front of him.

'That's not the same as *knowing* so.' She arched one eyebrow. 'Be careful, Gary.'

'Do you think I'll regret it, then?'

As she turned her face to the window, he did the same, and they both looked across at Parkside station. He wondered if she saw the same thing. 'You were just starting secondary school when you said, "I'm going to be a detective one day." '

'I remember.'

'Do you know why you said that?'

'No.' He expected her to tell him more, but she said nothing and in the end it was he who spoke. 'I remember feeling like it was the only thing I'd ever wanted to be.'

'And it has remained the only thing, until now. So you need to be sure.'

He nodded but reached for the envelope. He'd spent hours on the letter, constructing the sentences with carefully chosen words. Saying enough but never too much. Then, in the end, deleting all but the bare facts.

He told himself that he wouldn't have spent so long over something that wasn't the letter he *needed* to write. 'I have to see Marks next.'

She just nodded, but hugged him tighter than usual before he left. And, as he crossed towards the police station, he felt sure she continued to watch him, and he gripped the envelope tighter still.

As he pushed open the front door, he clearly remembered the last time. The heat of that day then, and the way he'd wished it to end. He could see that the foyer hadn't changed, but he'd been away long enough to properly notice its tired appearance now: the scuffed walls and dog-eared notices, the clock that ran five minutes slow and the ceiling tiles that looked yellowed even without cigarette smoke to stain them.

Sergeant Norris glanced up from the front desk, smiled, then turned away. Norris wouldn't be the only one who wouldn't know what to say but, luckily, he saw no one else between then and his meeting with Marks.

The door stood open and he saw Marks had positioned a second chair, facing him, at the end of his desk, but without the desk standing directly between them. 'Come in, Gary. Shut the door.'

Marks had been a constant at his bedside for the first twenty-four hours after the operation. He'd insisted on being present as the doctors had explained how close Goodhew had come to paralysis. He'd returned during the following weeks, too, keeping Goodhew up to date with developments at work.

Most were forensics related to Greg Jackson or Dan Osborne. First, the fact that the tying wire recovered from Jackson's parents' house proved to be a match for the wire that had bound Paul Marshall. Then proof, a few days later, that Mary Osborne had fought hard, two loose hairs having been snagged in a detached fingernail that had survived burial. DNA identified them as Dan Osborne's.

Goodhew appreciated these visits though he was sure that some of the details had failed to penetrate his painkiller-addled thoughts. Eventually he realized that Marks needed to talk, whether or not Goodhew actually listened.

Despite that weird familiarity that had persisted until his eventual discharge from hospital, a strange formality now hung in the air. Goodhew could feel it, but didn't know whether he'd triggered it himself or whether he sensed it coming from Marks. He held on to the envelope, making sure that his hand obscured the address-ee's name until he was ready.

He'd arranged this appointment but could tell that Marks needed to speak first. His boss's gaze fell on the envelope, then, as though he'd already guessed its contents, he looked back up at Goodhew. 'I've resigned,' he said. 'Retired, actually.'

'You shouldn't.'

'It's done.' His superior's forearm rested on the desk; now he flattened his hand and spread the palm out on to the surface. His fingertips stroked a few inches of the surface, as though this was to be the last time; as though he was leaving right now. 'I've agreed to stay for six months. It's longer than I wanted.'

Goodhew looked away, didn't speak.

'My judgement became compromised, Gary.'

Goodhew now understood what Marks had really been saying throughout those hospital visits. *I'm sorry . . . I made mistakes . . . I can't take them back.* Goodhew shook his head. 'I understand why you think so, sir, but I disagree.'

'Prison made Jackson a killer.'

'And how is that your mistake? Someone else tampered with the evidence.'

'Marshall died. Karen Dalton died.'

Goodhew was glad that Kelly's name wasn't mentioned in the same breath.

Marks waited a few seconds, then spoke as though it was a fresh conversation. 'None of us could have predicted Kelly's death, Gary.'

Goodhew added a '*but*' to the end of that sentence, and he was sure Marks had done the same. He didn't comment, however;

just handed over his envelope. Marks opened it and read silently, at one point giving a small nod. 'There's a right time for you to resign, Gary. It's certainly not now.'

'And I could say the same.' Goodhew drew a breath, as now wasn't the moment to leave things unsaid. 'There's nothing that has happened that's altered the respect I have for you, sir.'

The DI's expression softened for a moment. 'Gary, I didn't even know you were familiar with the word.' His smile faded. 'This is the right choice for me – for the right reasons.'

'But there are more reasons why you shouldn't.'

'No, Gary, there are more reasons why *you* shouldn't. One day there will be a right moment, but it's not now. Not under a cloud. There's more for you yet, Gary.' Instead of handing back the letter, he tucked it into the top drawer of his desk. 'You're not due back yet, so pass your medical first. We'll discuss it then. OK?'

Goodhew nodded. 'OK, then,' he agreed.

'One more thing?'

'Sir?'

'See Gully before you leave the building.'

'Don't worry, I was going to anyway.'

GULLY WAS SITTING alone in the room. He glanced at Kelly's desk, which had a new-occupant look of order. It clearly belonged to someone else now. Sue spoke without turning around. 'Please tell me you asked Marks why the hell he's promoted Kincaide.'

'DS Kincaide doesn't sound good to you?'

'Right up there with *Smoking's medicinal* and *Don't worry, it's not loaded.*' She spun her chair round slowly. 'You know, I would never have forgiven you if you hadn't stopped by to see me.'

'Marks told me I had to,' he teased.

'And you always do what he tells you, eh? You know he's leaving?' She didn't wait for an answer. 'Are you going to sit down or what, Gary?'

'We could go out for coffee?'

She glanced towards the window, then shook her head. 'No, there's too much Christmas out there.'

'Not in the mood?'

She screwed up her nose. 'Not really.'

He pulled Kelly's old chair over closer to her. 'So, what's the latest?'

'Specifically? Do you mean Jane Osborne?'

'I wondered.'

'She's staying on in Cambridge. Decorating that house.'

'Really? I thought they'd sell it, demolish it even.'

'No, she said she'd not letting *"some fucking house"* get the better of her.'

'She's mellowed then?'

'As if.'

'And Andie?'

Sue sagged back in her chair and stared up at the ceiling for several seconds before she sat up straight again, fighting her annoyance at him. 'She's OK but, you know what, I don't even want to tell you that much.' She leant forward and squeezed his arm. 'You can't keep doing this, Gary. When it's over, it's over.'

He understood. And knew she was correct.

He didn't have the words to explain why he couldn't totally let go of some of the cases he worked on. Perhaps because he didn't know the answer himself. He stared down at her hand gripping his arm.

'I miss her,' she whispered. 'And I can't say that to anyone else. I know why you might want to leave, Gary. But please come back.'

The Soundtrack for
A Cry in the Night

A picture may paint a thousand words but the power of music is equally potent. These are the songs I played and used as inspiration as I wrote *A Cry in the Night*. I have spent many hours with this playlist now and these songs will, to me at least, always be the soundtrack to this book. I hope you enjoy them.

'Atlantis' – The Shadows
'Black Cat's Bone' – Hot Boogie Chillun
'Breakaway' – The Detroit Cobras
'Come With Me' – Jacen Bruce
'F***ing Sweet' – Hot Boogie Chillun
'Go Home' – Eliza Doolittle
'I Heard Those Voices Again' – Big Boy Bloater
'Insanely Happy' – Big Boy Bloater
'King of Love' – Dave Edmunds
'Little Star' – The Elegants
'Queen of Hearts' – Dave Edmunds
'So High' – Eliza Doolittle

About the Author

ALISON BRUCE is the author of five Gary Goodhew novels, all published by Witness. Alison lives in Cambridgeshire with her husband Jacen and their two children.

www.alisonbruce.com

Discover great authors, exclusive offers, and more at hc.com.